THEOPHILOS

Michael D. O'Brien

Theophilos

A Novel

IGNATIUS PRESS   SAN FRANCISCO

Cover art: *Freedom*, by Michael O'Brien

Cover design by Riz Boncan Marsella

© 2010 Ignatius Press, San Francisco
All rights reserved
ISBN 978-1-58617-368-5
Library of Congress Control Number 2009350085
Printed in the United States of America ∞

It seemed good to me also, having followed all things closely for some time past, to write an orderly account for you, most excellent Theophilus, so that you may know the truth concerning the things of which you have been informed.

Visum est et mihi, adsecuto a principio omnia, diligenter ex ordine tibi scribere, optime Theophile, ut cognoscas eorum verborum, de quibus eruditus es, firmitatem.

Ἔδοξε κἀμοὶ παρηκολουθηκότι ἄνωθεν πᾶσιν ἀκριβῶς καθεξῆς σοι γράψαι, κράτιστε θεόφιλε, ἵνα ἐπιγνῷς περὶ ὧν κατηχήθης λόγων τὴν ἀσφάλειαν.

CONTENTS

A Letter   9

Journals   17

Examinations   169

Morphaeon   369

A Letter   441

A LETTER

Anthesterion—Dies Solis XV Kal. Aprilis DCCCXVII anno
Urbis conditae

Gortyna, Crete

Theophilos to Loukas,
My greetings.

The letter you sent me from Caesarea arrived last night, on a
ship that came from Rhodes. A crewman brought it up to the
city directly, for it seems you paid the captain well. His ship
remains in the harbor at Fair Havens for a week or more,
awaiting good winds that will take it back to Rhodes and from
there along the coastal islands to Samos, then to its home port
Paphos on Cyprus, and finally to Caesarea. Your letter is now
two months in transit since its writing, and it may be that this
reply will take as long to reach you. Longer, if you have departed
the city and it must follow your trail through your chain of
friends in Asia Minor. I will ensure that it is first delivered to
the house of Diodorus in the Street of the Silversmiths. Perhaps you are still there.

Three days ago I left the city and went by donkey cart across
the mountains to the north side of the island, desiring a change
of air and feeling quite disgusted by the city's torporous intrigues.
The winter was harsh this year. Snow lingers in the passes.
The journey was uneventful, however, and I descended into
the coastal warmth without mishap from weather or brigands.

Though I have friends and acquaintances in the villas of
Limenas, I avoided it altogether and made my way unaccom-
panied to that place which, for us, is so sacred in memory:
yes, the little promontory that you and I climbed when you
were a boy, the spot on the cliff overlooking the sea near Iraklion. There I picked up small white stones and wondered, as

I often have, if you had touched this one or that one, which you surely must have done on the day we worked side by side to clear the small space of its rubble. Our tiny theater remains undisturbed among the jagged rocks; the sea is still our audience, the sighing waves our chorus.

Do you remember what we discussed there together that first day? The plays of Aeschylus and Euripides. How old were you then, my nephew-son? I think you were about eleven years, for you had only recently arrived from Thessalonike, to live with us in your time of grief.

Your cousins, Theodosia and Mila, had remained behind at home with their mother, and so we were alone. You looked a long time over the waters toward your homeland, after first asking me, "Uncle, in which direction lies Thessalonike?" When I pointed to the northwest, you turned and stared at it, with no tears, no trembling. Such stillness in a boy, I thought. Even then, at such a young age, you were ever one to keep all evidence of emotion within yourself. Or so I assumed. Has he no feelings? I wondered. Or has he enclosed it all within? Is he too soon a man, and has he untimely learned through his loss and exile that men must put their sorrows in second place lest they cease to act?

Unlike women, who feel much and deeply, gazing inward to the family to nurture the young and tend the food that sustains us all, our fate is to look beyond the hearth fires to different fires that threaten on the horizon. Ours is to protect and preserve by gazing outward, by standing at the ready always, and thus we must not be crippled by our fears. None of this did I say as I considered what sort of boy my sister's son really was, for I had not known you since your infancy.

Then you turned to me and asked in a thoughtful tone:

"Uncle, have you seen the play *Agamemnon*?"

"Of course," I replied. "Many times have I seen that dark tale performed. And read it too. Have you?"

"Yes", you said. "It is dark, yet there is much in it to tell us how to live."

In that play there is far more that tells us how not to live. I did not give voice to this, but in my heart there was a foreboding, since one so young should not ponder the truths that may be learned from such a tragedy.

I recall examining your very sober face with some concern. What were you thinking? What were you seeing as you gazed at the infinite sea? It seemed most strange to me at the time, for it is proper to the realm of boys to seize upon the finite and to meditate little, if at all. At first I wondered if you were trying to express—in words that were rather too advanced for you—that life is dangerous and that one must fight in order to survive, and yet even in the fighting there is futility, for death claims us all in the end.

Then you whispered the lines, "Zeus, who guided mortals to be wise, has established his fixed law—wisdom comes through suffering."

"Ah, the chant of the old men of Mycenae", I said, "as they await the return of the king from the war."

"Yes", you nodded like a sage. "They are in great fear."

"Well-grounded were their fears, though they knew not all the perils that would come."

I made other literary observations, which you acknowledged with a smile, though you said no more.

As I mentioned, three days ago I returned to the promontory. Overturning the little white stones, I was surprised to find one on which you had scratched your name. What year did you write that? Were you still a child, or had you become a man? Was it merely a boyish whim that prompted you to leave a token of your presence there? Or was it a pang of extreme homesickness? Or perhaps you wrote it immediately before your departure, in a moment of mild nostalgia? I brought it home with me, and it now sits on the window sill of my surgery in Gortyna—a daily reminder of you.

Why did I risk the arduous climb to the promontory at my age, with my poor legs, you may ask? I returned to it because it was where you and I first spoke of serious matters, and also it was a place where even at this late hour of my life I might learn a new silence, gazing across the Aegean to where you are now, and perhaps see you with the eyes of the soul.

During the years you lived with us, you called it the "seeing place". Often as a youth and young man did you return there to ponder life's joys and woes, but always you preferred to go alone. Whenever you were missing for days, and longer when you were older, I knew where you had gone and so reassured your dear aunt who was born a worrier of the worst sort, and we left you to your search. Now I wonder, Loukas, why throughout all those years you lived with us were you always searching the horizon? What did you hope to see? An unexpected ship bearing a missing king?

This large manuscript you send me with your letter is itself a letter, since you have addressed it to me. Yet it seems to me a chronicle, a historian's document, as if you have been brought by the fates among that minor people, the Jews, that endlessly troubled race, neither by interest nor natural attraction, being drawn to them for reasons I cannot fathom. Do not misunderstand me. I read your account carefully and with an open mind. Even so, I recognized certain passages in the text where your excitement inflamed your training in science and rhetoric and when your love of poetics overwhelmed your reason. You had taken care, my beloved son—and here I smile to you across the waters—you had taken care to revise and correct the undercurrents of your passion for your subject, but nevertheless I recognized the spirit that impelled it. I know your mind. I know your heart as well. So while I remain cautious about the veracity of the events you recount, I do not doubt that you think them true. If what you have written happened as described, though mediated to you through the accounts of second and third parties, it will overturn the world.

My dear Loukas, I do not believe it will overturn the world. It is a story created by a fierce yet powerless people in order to hold hope on high. Such is all myth. Such are the myths that gave courage and insight to our ancestors. I pray to the gods—whatever they may be, persons or principles, we do not know—that you will be aided from on high as you continue your journey, that you will employ your great mind to discern rightly between the illusions of men beguiled by mystics and magicians, and the clear sight of genuine philosophy. Was not this obscure wandering teacher an *eikon* of their nation and a symbol of their religion? It seems he has been rejected in both ways by his own people, and then crucified by the Romans. Now he is alive, you say. Are there not many such myths in the world, with most, if not all, originating in the imagination, in the metaphysical fever swamps of Asia?

Death, man's enemy, finds us all. None escape from its embrace. Yet few can face it honestly and without fear. Your new myth is for consolation, and there is nothing wrong in this. But I entreat you never to take it for material reality, for along that path you will meet either madness or despair.

I am
your Theophilos.

JOURNALS

Gortyna
Anthesterion—Martius

Today I packaged my letter to Loukas in oiled cloth and sealed the wax with my symbol ring, the staff of Aesclepios. The captain sent his servant to me, as we had arranged he would do if the winds changed and he intended a swift departure. The courier was a Cypriot, in his forties by the look of him, with an accent as crude as his unwashed feet, roughly clad and roughly weathered by a sea life. When I gave him some coins for himself, he bowed, promising to convey the letter safely into the hands of the captain for delivery to Caesarea.

His eyes swiftly scanned the name inscribed on the package. This was interesting—who would have guessed that such a man could read!

"Do you know the Loukas to whom the letter is addressed?" I asked.

Caught in the act, he stammered, then replied that he did not know the man personally, had never met him, but that his reputation was good among both "the great and the small" along the coastal regions from Chios in the north and as far south as the great harbor at Caesarea.

"My son is a quiet man", I said, wondering if I were being flattered for the sake of an extra coin. "How is it that one who never draws attention to himself is so well known?"

"Your son draws no attention to himself," he replied gruffly, "yet praise may be heaped upon one who does not desire it."

"Heaped?" I smiled.

"He travels much", the man said cryptically.

"And always returns to Caesarea?"

He shrugged. "So I hear. It may be that he only passes through the city. Back and forth he goes among many people, many places, it is said. Your son is a physician—a good one—which crosses the barriers between men of station, high and low."

I looked more carefully at the fellow, for this could not have come from a thoughtless person.

"He is kind even to slaves", the courier added. Too late, I noticed the scars on his forehead, just below the hairline, which he had brushed forward in order to hide the marks—a typical clumsy attempt to remove the blue letters tattooed there by a former owner. Usually, slaves are tattooed only if they are caught for thievery or flight.

"You are a freedman?" I asked.

His face flushed; then he recovered and lifted his chin in imitation of confident self-pride, nodding once. Was he lying to me?

I said no more about this but requested that if perchance he should meet my son, he commend himself to him and pass on my greetings with a handclasp. As I extended my hand he did not at first understand, but then he took it, lowering his eyes, and firmly shook it. "I will give him your hand", he murmured, and was gone.

This, then, was the Hermes whom I hope will bear my cautionaries to Loukas. More likely it will be the captain himself who delivers it, for he prides himself upon his reliability and his loyalty to me, and his life-debt, as far as men in these times can be reliable or loyal. I once excised a tumor from his spine, a horrible, necrotic thing. He screamed throughout the operation, wept and cursed, and when it was done and I had sewn him up like a burlap bag, and he had consumed a great quantity of wine, he declared that I was a god. He knows I am not a god. The only living god to be seen by human eyes, as all men in the world know, is a fat man in Rome who has terrible vices and writes even more terrible verse: Bacchus, ruling from the throne of Jupiter. Translated into my own psychological *kosmos*—loathsome Dionysos, ruling from the throne of Zeus.

There is much that disturbs me in Loukas' chronicle, much that agitates my spirit disproportionately. Why has he associated himself with these people, who are to be found, I hear, even on Crete? I will discuss the matter, as circumspectly as possible, with Gaius. He will know more about the situation to the east, for he has friends in the province of Syria. Judaea is always a boiling pot. Crete is a pool of tranquillity by comparison, long domesticated by our imperial liberators. While the island remains in culture Greek, with the passing of time it seems to become more and more Roman. This is a thing of mixed fortunes, good and ill. In the mountains and villages the Cretan people remain tough and resentful, as they always have been and doubtless always will be. But there will be no revolt here.

These descendents of Minos graze their flocks and tend their garden plots among the ruins of their old cities. It is said that the ancients who lived here spoke a strange tongue—some say Phoenician, some say Greek, still others say it was entirely different. Regardless, nothing stirs the embers of resentment like constant reminders of lost glory. I should say stolen glory, because, to tell the truth, it was not entirely theirs in the first place, for the Cretans are mixed in blood with the waves of Greek colonizers, of whom I am a very late one. Indeed, I have my own lost glories, the true myth of my grandfather's birth in Athens. My grandfather was a slave, a learned man, a philosopher and household teacher of spoiled gymnasium-age children of the rich Romans who occupied the city after Sulla's conquest. His manumission in old age sprouted a new shoot of the laurel, for he migrated to Crete where in advanced years he sired my father, Ariston by name, who became a physician, studying in Alexandria for a time before returning to the island. He in turn taught me. And thus I taught the art to Loukas. Such are the fates in these complex times. I do not resent the thralldom in my past, but neither must I forget it. All men are slaves, each in his own way.

Gaius was the military commander under the governor during those years when I was a young physician. I once saved him from death during the year of the plague. The bond between us began then, though it lapsed during his years in other provinces. Now he has returned from his service in Spain and Nearer Gaul, an ex-proconsul of reputation, yet in essence an old retired fellow like me, content to oversee his vineyards and to ship his amphorae to Italy and beyond. Thus, I am his friend again. He can consult me about his gout and his soul. This unusual Roman is an honest man, who practices the virtues and honors his gods under Latin names though he admits that his gods are Greek in origin. He is humble in this and other ways, within the limitations of his society and his offices, and that is why he is better than most. The new historians who are writing so many books these days will make no more than a passing mention of him, if he is noticed at all. Power, war, colossal deceits, and tragedy make history, for in these lie drama. The sensible administration of law does not make for drama, and Gaius is a most sensible, undramatic man.

We enjoy many excellent conversations, though we try to avoid difficult topics like politics. He is fascinated by the Stoics; indeed, he is something of a natural Stoic in his temperament and convictions. In his confidential remarks he will sometimes muse on the days of the Republic, gone these past hundred years since the death of Cicero and the rise of the Caesars. He laments the loss. A seditious viewpoint, but more significant is the fact that he says it in the presence of a Greek, however close we may be and though I am now a Roman citizen. This is the measure of his character.

He asks about Loukas from time to time, using the Latin *Lucanus*, but I think he inquires only as a courtesy, for I doubt he remembers the small boy in a *chiton*, who was ever mute in his presence. He has obtained for me a great gift, about which I will write to Loukas later in the year, when I have heard from him again and have certainty regarding his location.

Paeonia tells me I should not put certain topics to manuscript, not even in my private journals. They are dangerous, she argues, for who knows what eyes may one day read the words of my tame little seditions and bring us to ruin? Clearly, she has a point. After all, her eyes have read them without my knowing it.

She is calling me to bed, and so I must end this here.

*

[Journal entry, March 25, A.D. 64]

Gortyna
Anthesterion—Martius

Today, by chance, while rummaging in my library, I came upon the five-leaf tablet case over which I spent many an hour in my youth. The wax sheets were dry and brittle, the topmost crumbling into fragments at the touch, and it prompted a little musing on the transitory nature of time, for I read there a few symbols of the shorthand script I had tried to master as a youth—the system developed by Cicero's servant, Tiro. If the truth be told, I never mastered it—too many thousands of symbols. Perhaps it was Loukas' stylus that last inscribed these marks. Yes, it must have been, for beside each symbol was the proper word in Greek, but the script was a boy's, inelegant, laborious.

As one grows older, memories take their place in a crowd of dramas, jostling for position; at its worst the mind may confuse another man's memories for its own. For a moment I was

Loukas in his youth, and without warning a wave of sorrow swept over me. Not that Paeonia and I hadn't done our best for him. Indeed, he called us mother and father from his twelfth birth feast until his day of departure, a span of sixteen years. Now it has been nine years since we last saw him face-to-face, and we must be content with his letters. Nevertheless, he continues to search. Perhaps he does not know what he is seeking—though it is plain enough to me.

I flipped the case page and a well-preserved sheet of wax appeared, brittle but still whole, and upon it was inscribed the symbol for *beginning*. Beside it was the word in Greek, and beside that was the letter alpha. Below it, the symbol for *ending*, and beside it the word in Greek, followed by an omega. Curious. I wonder what he was thinking.

A mood of concern for him grew steadily throughout the morning, caused not only by his absence—physical absence being the mild foretaste of death—but by the chronicle he sent me. It continues to disturb, not because I think it factually true, but because Loukas thinks it is true. What, then, is the state of his mind, and what follies might he commit among that unhappy people at such a period of history as ours? Nine years have passed since he left us, and while time may pour balm upon the wound of separation, and the skin close over the unhealed abscess, it easily tears open again.

At once, I decided to seek out both consolation and information.

First, a long walk through the city to Mila's house. I found her in the garden draping wet laundry over her currant bushes to dry. She smiled and kissed me—the first consolation—for it had been a few days since we had seen each other, and the last time we spoke together she had been insolent, scolding me for my scolding her for scolding her husband for scolding her for refusing to allow little Helena a third mouthful of honey cakes. A grandfather has rights, I had argued indignantly. She had misunderstood my attempt at humor, grew hot in the face, and declared in a strident voice that a mother has rights, and that it is mothers who must deal with the results of another's indulgence. What she said was true, of course, but where feelings of love are concerned, truth too often dissolves. Now, all is mended without any surgery on the heart.

"I am sorry, Papa, for my rudeness to you."

"I am sorry, Mila, for putting my clumsy hands into your affairs."

"These big hands", she smiled, taking them both in her own, "have saved many lives. But you do not understand women."

"This is true", I murmured sagely in a chastened voice. "This is very true."

Which made her laugh outright. Suddenly, Philippia, age five, dropped out of a tree onto my shoulders, nearly collapsing me to the ground. I caught her and we did not fall. Chubby Helena ran into the garden at that point, and then we all embraced. It was one of those rare and beautiful moments when we see what family is for—what life is for. Consolation was complete. I ate lunch with them, and Cleon joined us when he arrived home from school. He brought news— actually gossip—a rumor that there have been fires in the city of Rome, though how extensive is not yet known. He had heard it from a Roman, the father of one of his students, and was uncertain of its veracity because the man is a tax official in the procurator's office, and tax men are notoriously loose with facts—so said Cleon the Just.

"Roman tax men, generally, are not liars", I corrected him.

He disagreed amiably. "Father, if you knew them as I know them, you would not say that!"

"Oh, tell me why you think it, then."

"Because corruption is part of their government, the hidden part, yet as universal and permanent as their more visible monuments."

"Yet the law punishes it severely."

"Yes, and condones it secretly, for they all practice it."

"Not all. Besides, it's the same with us."

I meant by this that within man's nature are fractures between principles and practices; right and wrong are at war within us, regardless of race. But my earnest son-in-law mistook my meaning and did not permit me to explain my point.

"No, no, never were we like this!" he declared. "Recall what Solon of Athens said: 'Society is well governed when its people obey the magistrates, and the magistrates obey the law.'"

I countered: "Recall also that he said, 'Men keep agreements when it is to the advantage of neither to break them.'"

So ensued a delectable sparring match that was, in its own way, consoling. Thoroughly fed and stimulated, I bade them good day and set off on the remainder of my walk through the city.

Beyond the temple of Pythian Apollo, I entered a public garden to cool myself under the trees, and there I happened upon a pack of boys stripping the pear trees. No possible enjoyment could have come from eating such unripe fruit, so their pleasure was entirely in the art of theft.

At this end of the city the three-story apartment buildings give way to modest villas. I went down a side street toward the Lethaios and stood on its grassy banks for a time, listening to the soft burble of its slender passage. After that, a pleasant stroll along a connecting lane brought me to the high walls enclosing Gaius' residence, the Villa Varus. A slave unlocked the front gate and let me into the foreyard, without seeking permission from his master. This was new behavior, and I presumed it meant not only that Gaius was home but that he had given instructions for my prompt admission. Am I one of the family now, or did my friend have particular need of me at this moment? He had not summoned me; how, then, had he anticipated my arrival?

In the interior garden, sumptuous decorative plants are in bloom or first fruition, and very colorful they are in contrast to the high hills visible above the walls, the coarse scrub woods on the upper slopes that are already brown from baking under the spring sun. The slave led me past the *tablinum*, where Gaius still does whatever commerce he is involved in, and through a double door into the atrium. There I found him reclining on a couch beside the little pool, with one foot stretched out on a cushion and the other, his bad one, up to the ankle in rainwater that had collected beneath the open skylight. His interest in Stoicism is a patchwork affair, for he loves his luxuries.

There has been scant rain so far this year—perhaps on other days the water is piped in from the Lethaios. The pool is his one possession that I covet, for the room is distinctly cooler than other parts of the house. I must discuss with Paeonia the possibility of renovating our own house. It would be expensive, tearing open the roof, rebuilding it, and excavating beneath the floor to make the pool. Would she like these foreign innovations? Enough. I will think about it another time.

Gaius raised an arm in greeting. "I knew you would come", he grinned.

"Why so?" I stood over him with a physician's examining frown. "Are you in pain?"

"No more than usual. Sit down, if you will, and have some wine with me."

I took a chair facing him, and because the household servants immediately left the room, closing the doors behind them, I assumed that for some reason he desired that we drink together without other ears listening to our conversation. He let me fill our cups from a jug. We sipped the wine and were pleasantly distracted for some minutes watching one of his grandchildren, a boy of two years, crawling about the floor pushing a little wooden horse and chariot, whinnying through his lips.

"I carved that for him", said Gaius proudly, as if this crude toy were of more importance than the bronze memorial mask, the official emblem of his proconsulate, pegged to the wall beside the family shrine. It would not be out of character for Gaius to value the toy more than the mask. By such apparently insignificant details does one come, with time, to see the interior of a man.

Gaius is no master of Greek vocabulary, and he knows only the vulgar *koine* dialect. We usually speak together in Latin, other than on those occasions when he is possessed by a whim to think himself a universal man. I am sometimes too harsh about human motivations. It may be that he strains to speak my language merely from generosity. But it is a relief for me when he reverts to Latin. And today it was to be Latin!

Gaius shook his head. "How does rumor speed so swiftly through this city? The trireme from Ostia docked only last night, and now all Gortyna knows."

"It seems I am the last in Gortyna to know what you mean", I said. "For I do not yet know anything about a ship or what it might contain."

He took the hint, and our habit of humorous banter was launched.

"Come, come, Theophilos. It contained news from Rome, man!"

"Ah, Rome. Is all well with the emperor?"

"I have no doubt that he is very well, thanks to the gods, among whom he is a fellow in good standing."

"But that is nothing new", I demurred.

"That is not the news. The city, or a great part of it, has burned."

"Rome, burned?" I exclaimed, pretending astonishment, though I felt only surprise that Cleon's rumor was now confirmed.

"The Palatine has suffered little damage—the capital buildings, the forum and temples, and the better kind of *domus* on the hills are untouched. But nearly half the city is in ruins, mainly large portions of the plebeian and freedmen wards. Many have died; many are without shelter."

"A disaster", I sympathized, shaking my head.

"Yes, a disaster. But not an unexpected one—those crowded tenement blocks, more than ten thousand *insulae* with hundreds crammed into each wasp cell—just waiting for an errant spark."

Gaius knows Rome from temple top to floor of the lowest police cell. He was not only born and raised there, he became its *Praefectus Urbi* for a time, after he left Crete. A powerful position, but he once confided to me how much he hated what the city had become. "A sewer—brilliantly designed in the beginning—now maintained with enormous outlay of skillful organization, a million people crammed together, sprawling and ever growing—the census cannot keep abreast of it—mankind's worst and best bobbing along in a wash of sewage." Doubtless he was an efficient municipal governor, but he did not stay long on that seat, a year or two, and was moved from there to the provinces, where he was happier and continued to rise in authority at a safe distance from the Palatine.

Since there was not much more I could say about the fire, I merely looked grieved, and actually felt it. The world, the world, an unceasing chorus of suffering.

"It puts me in mind of Crassus", said Gaius in a musing tone, after a judicious draining of his cup.

Which Crassus? I wondered to myself. Is he referring to some new politician? Seeing the inquiry in my eyes, my friend explained: "Don't you remember the wealthiest man in Rome during the final days of the Republic, the rival of Pompey, funder of Julius Caesar?"

"Oh, that Crassus."

"Yes, that Crassus. And he *became* the wealthiest man in Rome when he was chief of its fire department. A very good head for purchasing inflammable real estate, that fellow."

I sipped my wine, glanced at the pool.

"Fire", he went on, staring up at the bright blue rectangle visible through the skylight, "is political."

"An extreme idea", I muttered, meaning that I wished he would not pursue this line of thought. He was welcome to take risks with his own life—not with mine.

"We live in an age of extremes", he continued. "There has never been a time so full of wonders as our own nor one so brutal."

A delicate moment—what wonders and what brutalities did he mean? Those made by his own people perhaps? Or not? As I tossed this around behind the expressionless mask of my face, he watched me closely, smiling to himself.

"Well done, Theophilos", he said in a low voice. "But have some more wine, and let us speak as men equally free under the sun."

"We always speak as such", I retorted.

"No, we do not, my friend. We do not, but that is more an accident of birth than of the gods' gifts, which have been distributed fairly between us."

"Though the gifts differ in kind."

"Yet overlap in part. Can we not speak together in that forum where our minds are one? Do you trust me?"

I do not tell lies easily. I lowered my eyes.

"You say everything with that look", he went on. "Even so, I trust *you*."

30

I smiled appreciatively but did not speak, for I did not know where he was leading me.

"I believe in the Roman peace", he said. "I believe in what it has brought to the world because on the frontiers I observed, throughout forty years in soldier's gear and consular linen, what happens when we do not rule. Man is brutal by nature—all men in all places. I have seen horrors that even a surgeon could not bear to hear of, let alone see with his eyes."

He paused. I nodded for him to continue.

"Do you think it has made me cruel and unfeeling? Yes, of course you do, for you remember Sulla's conquest of Greece and you remember that a hundred years ago Caecilius Metellus conquered Crete and destroyed her cities, including Knossos, leaving only Gortyna intact, prostrate and in total submission. How can you not think of this and draw your conclusions?"

Interestingly, he used our word *Krete* instead of the Latin *Creta*.

"War is ever brutal", I contributed with a tone of neutrality.

He eyed me soberly, and the silence stretched long between us. We sipped our wine.

He said: "Here is a thought for your educated mind to consider: Civilized brutality has as its purpose the steady reduction of all that is brutal in men, by imposing efficient organization on human activities with the rule of law as guardian. Is this not preferable to myriad barbarian brutalities that flourish in the name of freedom for a time? Like untended vineyards, they produce waste upon waste and ever-smaller yields of fruit, and in the end no wine."

He withdrew his foot from the pool, reached for the jug, and refilled my cup.

"There is truth in what you say", I admitted. "I tremble to think what the world would have become if Hannibal had been victor."

"That son of Dido would have spread slaughter upon slaughter. The Carthaginians would have sacrificed whole peoples on the altars where they sacrificed their own children."

"A civilized race", I said, pointedly.

He smiled, enjoying my irony—and the point, I think.

He stood and hobbled over to his library, a wall of shelves with compartments shaped like cells in a beehive. A very pretty piece of furniture. I must now, privately, correct myself—I covet two of his possessions. I am appalled at myself!

He returned to the couch, sat down with a groan, and handed me three rolls of *volumina*, bound by a red ribbon.

This past year he has made loans to me of his recent acquisitions in Latin—Strabo's fascinating geographies, Livy on the Punic Wars, Ovid's *Metamorphoses*, and this new Spanish writer Seneca, who retells our myth of Medea quite ably. Also some Horace, though I own the latter's books in truncated versions. Reading Horace never fails to move me.

I thought at first, therefore, that he was offering me something new. But it turned out that he was returning one of my loans to him.

"I have finished reading the final part of your Plato book. His dream republic could never become reality."

"I agree with you," I said, "but I am curious to know how you arrived at the conclusion."

"It is very clear that he minimizes the brutality in human nature."

"His book intends to deal with it wisely, does it not?"

"Intends, and fails. He sees his own great soul too much in others."

"He understands our nature very well. Have you not read the dialogues?"

"The *Symposium* only." Gaius grimaced and waved his hand around. "What a complex hash he makes of love. Why, any

32

simpleton knows what love is and needs no symposium to explain it for him. But the *Republic* is a different matter. He says many true things and made me laugh at his wit too."

I unrolled a scroll and found a line familiar to me.

"Such as this?" I asked, and read aloud: "'Democracy is undone by the same vice that rules oligarchy. But because democracy has embraced anarchy, the damage is more general and far worse, and its subjugation more complete. . . . The truth is, excess in one direction tends to provoke excess in the contrary direction.'"

"Yes, yes, I liked that part. Very astute."

"He goes on to say that an excess of liberty—in the state or in an individual—seems destined to end up in slavery. The most savage form of slavery results from pushing freedom to the extreme."

Gaius nodded emphatically. "I agree with that."

"So, how can you say that he is a dreamer and minimizes the faults in human nature?"

Gaius furrowed his brow. "I did not say he was *all* wrong—he just hoped for too much. Really, Theophilos, you should read Cicero. He is as intelligent as your sage but sensible and practical too."

"But I *have* read your Cicero. Or I should say that I have read parts of his works, for there are rather a lot of them."

"One page of his oratory or letters defending a real republic is worth ten of Plato's dream republics."

"The proportion, in fact, is quite the reverse", I murmured, irritated by his shallowness. "You may have noticed that your real republic no longer exists."

He did not take offense at my tone. We sensed an argument looming, one that has its roots in soil deeper than philosophy. These are the differing configurations of the psyche that opposing civilizations create in the minds of ordinary men such as

Gaius and me. We grew silent together, not uncomfortable, but even so, at that moment I think we were both musing on the same thing—the hidden dynamics of history and fortune. His earlier point about civilizations reducing brutality returned to me, and I wondered what the world would have been like if our Greek city-states had ever collected their wits sufficiently to cease tearing each other to pieces and endlessly killing their best sons in useless fratricidal wars. The Delian League and the war against Troy notwithstanding, Greek experiments with unity are always temporary. It need not have been that way. The world itself might have become the *polis*, and Plato's dreams might have become reality. Then, perhaps, a philosopher-king would have arisen for all mankind, and Neronian Bacchus would not now sit on the throne of Jupiter, burning his children for sport or profit.

The problem is insoluble. And I value my friendship with Gaius enough to know that whenever we bump into the walls between us, though we walk toward each other in goodwill, it is better to shift course, seeking a window or door in the wall.

He was the first to move, and only later did I understand— just now as I write—that it was a conciliatory gesture.

He stood and hobbled to a cabinet beneath the garden window. From it he took something and brought it to me, walking carefully so as not to drop it—a pot. When he put it into my lap, I was surprised by its lightness, its fragility—very thin clay. And the extraordinary form, nearly a perfect sphere! One wonders how the delicate handles by the lip could have supported the pot when full. Wine, oil, fish sauce—yes, the latter, I think.

"A vessel of exceptional beauty and of great age", I said, overcome with emotion. "Could it be from the time of Minos?"

"It may be as old as that."

"Where did you get it?"

"It is a gift from the governor. His men discovered a tomb in the ruins of Knossos while hunting for king's gold." He laughed. "They found this and other pots, but no gold."

"I disagree, Gaius, for this is indeed gold."

"It is no more than clay and paint, yet I suppose it has some value as a memory of . . ."

"Of a civilization?"

The shape invited the hands to turn it, caress it, its perfection restful, inducing meditation.

He took it from me and held it in his own hands. The decorative design painted in the glaze was startling both in beauty and originality. I have never seen anything like it. The entire surface was embraced by a black octopus that stares forthrightly at the person who holds the pot. Both the shape and the decoration were produced by a master artist. How old is this marvel? And what genius created it?

Gaius blew a breath into the tubular neck, making a sound like the lowest note on a flute. Then he turned the pot slowly around, showing the eight tentacles that clamped the entire object in its embrace. Around and around again came the eyes, looking at me, and there it finally stopped.

"Some say the earth is a sphere, Theophilos. Do you think it is a sphere?"

"Yes, I believe it is, as did Aristotle and others."

"Most believe it to be flat."

"That is what our eyes tell us, but how often the eye deceives."

"True", he nodded, and resumed revolving the sphere.

A strange moment, this—very strange, considering that Gaius is more at ease building bridges and administering laws from a codex, or writing his book on vineyard care. He is strongly averse to flights of fancy. Yet now he continued to stand before me, his face exceedingly grave, even reflective, revolving the pot.

He met my eyes and held them for a few moments, then returned the pot to its cupboard.

More wine was offered, but I declined. I admonished him severely, as I have so many times, to eat unspiced foods and to stop drinking if he wishes to be free of gout. He promised he would change, and I know he will break his promise within the hour. And he knows that I know. With handclasps, we parted.

*

[Journal entry, June 8, A.D. 64]

Gortyna
Thargelion—Iunius

A long lapse between my notes. I have been ill for a month, having caught, or been captured by, the new disease that comes by ships out of Africa. It does not kill many, mostly the elderly, the poorly fed, and weaker slaves. Still, I feel exhausted, and it is difficult to think more than mundane thoughts. Instead, one drifts on feelings, memories, dreams. Paeonia is sweet when I am low like this. There are wives who kick their husbands when they are down, thinking such behavior goads their men back into robust health, returning their eyes to fires on the horizon. For drunkard or idler husbands this may work well enough, but it is a bad policy in general.

I love her, have always loved her. The love of youth's beauty ages like wine into companionable love for the other's being, a presence like no other. I think I am this for her, as she is this for me, though she would not have words for it—in any event, not words like mine. Plato often refers to this mystery in our nature. There is a line somewhere in the *Republic* about the tyranny of love. All men know what it is to live under this tyrant, he says.

I have ordered more paper but from a different dealer, the new shop in the street behind the praetorium. Several varieties are available there: traditional papyrus in its nine degrees of quality. For this volume of journals I chose *hieratica*, a quality two steps below the best. I purchased a single sheet of substance that resembles papyrus yet is constructed in an entirely different manner. There is no weave. The dealer told me that he imported it from Gaul but that he will not bring any more to the island since this is clearly an experimental material and is unlikely to last—linen fibers dissolved in the liquid of ash, then dried without pattern in thick sheets with glue and pressed to thinness. Interesting, but a fad—and all fads die out quickly. Because I have ever been intrigued by curiosities, I also purchased, at uncomfortable expense, a sheet of an invention that comes from somewhere far beyond Persia, from a land where men have eyes unlike all others in the world, not cyclopean but almost as strange, the dealer told me. Those people make a cloth that is woven from finest threads, which grow on trees, and the sheet is also made from the threads. It rustles like papyrus but is more malleable, soft, amazingly thin, translucent. I found filaments of fern and flattened parts of insects accidentally imprisoned in it—very pretty—and could not resist it.

I brought it home, not sure what I would do with it. Trying to get my mind moving again, I penned a quotation from Aristotle across the sheet, the last letter of the word *metaphor* alighting on a miniature mosquito wing. It made me laugh, though I do not understand why I laughed. Does the mind make connections, see relationships, which logical thought does not immediately apprehend? It must be. I will think more about this—that is, when I am able properly to think again.

For now, memories and dreams.

Earlier this morning Paeonia awoke from a troubling dream. She wept but could not explain why she was weeping and had already forgotten what the dream was about. She was quickly comforted, however, for I said all the right things. She patted me affectionately and shook off the last wisps of sadness, rose and dressed, then energetically launched herself into the household tasks as the sun rose. I heard her scolding our kitchen servant Calliope, whom Paeonia privately calls Cassandra whenever they are angry at each other. Today she loudly called her Cassandra to her face. I heard it from our bedroom though the kitchen is at the other end of the house. Such screeching. Why do we keep that old woman? Well, because she is a widow and childless and needs her wages and has no one other than us. I do not know the cause of the quarrel, but I know for a fact that they will be kissing each other's cheeks by lunchtime. I do not understand women.

Later, my good wife entered the surgery as I sewed up a rip in the foot of one of Cleon's students. The lad suffered the needle bravely, went white as I pulled the threads, drawing his severed flesh together, his lips blue with compression. But no tears, no sounds.

"Poor child", said Paeonia when the boy was carried away home by his family servant. "Poor child." Then she burst into sobs. She has seen far worse than this, countless times over, so why did it cause such tears?

"What is wrong?" I insisted.

"The dream", she whispered. "It told me that something terrible is going to happen."

"Do you know what it is?"

"No, I can't remember it."

"Ooo-ooo", I soothed, trying to put my arms around her. She pushed me away and said, "Death is coming! Death! I know it, I feel it all around, and it will strike our family."

Nothing I said would console her.

So, what is a man to do in such situations? I went for a walk.

My feet took me unsteadily out through the city gate into the foothills. As I progressed, my strength increased. It felt good to be active again, to feel the sun on my face. Man grows rightly under a friendly sun, just like grapes. There had been a strong rain the day before, and now the bright blue sky conspired with the wet earth to make fruitfulness. The field workers were singing; the drivers of carts coming out of the mountain pass from the port on the north side of the island gave me pleasant nods. They know my face, since I am the healer, which is my public *eikon*. Even a line of ten soldiers displayed a passing courtesy, one of them dipping a crested helmet to me. How hot those caps must be, how burdensome to carry so much heavy leather and weaponry with one's skull boiling inside a metal pot.

It was hot enough for me though I wore only my sandals and a short white *chiton*, more suitable for a boy than a gray-head, a leather belt, my wide straw hat, and a stout staff of plane tree wood as my walking stick. Doubtless, I looked like the god Aesclepios himself. I also brought along my bag, in case of emergencies, the one that Loukas made for me from the hide of the *kree-kree* deer. No weight to speak of really but good to have on the jaunt, for the symbol of healing burned on its front flap is a badge of identity that more than once in my life has brought me through unexpected peril. The bag contained a few instruments, needle, thread, a glass vial of pine spirit for cleansing wounds, and a vial of rose water for cooling the burning effects of the pine.

As it turned out, I did not need it, but it did me the good service of bringing its maker to mind. There has been no reply to my last letter. The Cypriot or his captain surely must have delivered it by now. I am too anxious, an old man driven by habits of paternity, which the son in the fullness of his manhood no longer needs. I remain here as a sign and presence, a

39

refuge to which he can return if he should need it. That is my role, yet I so often forget it and slip back into the emotions of young fatherhood.

Stopping by a brook tumbling down from the mountains, I bent and drank from it, then sat on a stone to rest my limbs for a while. Perhaps it was fatigue that caused an unwelcome thought—I wondered suddenly if he writes to me from simple duty, a respect that would be consistent with his highly principled character. Then I rebuked myself for this unhealthy doubt, for it is false. He has written from places as widely spaced as Illyricum north of Macedonia, and Arabia south of Judaea, from Corinth in the west and Antioch in the east. He never expresses need, always describes vividly the interesting sites he encounters, and mentions those people he meets and has come to know. He has many friends, Greeks and Jews and even a Roman with whom he travels, a teacher from Tarsus in Cilicia. Plenty of good men to keep an eye on him.

Looking up from the tumbling waters, I saw numerous birds nearby that had come down to drink. Then I remembered that once, in his fifteenth or sixteenth year, we had stopped at this exact spot to drink from the stream. There had been birds aplenty that day too.

It was at a time when he had begun to read extensively from my library and had been snagged by the satirists. Like many an intelligent boy, he was passing through a period of self-discovery, trying on this or that mask—occasionally tragic, more often comic. It kept our heads spinning for a few years, straining ourselves to understand his moods. But on that sunny morning, he was acting the persona of the witty skeptic. It did not suit him at all, but one must let the young experiment. They will soon discard what is not consistent with their souls.

"All of mankind is here today!" he hooted.

"What?" I said.

"The birds", he grinned, pointing to the various species flittering or flying about.

"In what way are they like mankind?" I asked. "Ah, I see your thought. You mean to say that all creatures obey the laws of their nature. We all drink and eat and sleep, the great and the small alike."

"Not exactly, Uncle." That summer he had ceased addressing me as father—a brief interlude that was caused, I suspect, by the natural stages of growth, the need to separate, to be distinct, to find his own unique form. It did not last long, a few months, and then it was back to father and mother for us.

"What then, *nephew*?"

He pointed to a griffon vulture soaring above us. "That is the emperor Claudius", he said.

"Oh, is it? Well, please do not make your little jokes outside the door of our home, if you don't mind."

"Don't worry, I won't. And look, over there, see the Roman legionaries?"

He pointed to three red-footed falcons plunging from a cliff, seizing rabbits in a field of wild grain.

Chuckling to myself, I let him go on—encouraged it, actually.

"And who are they?" I asked, pointing to a flock of chukar, tawny partridge with yellow throats and black-striped wings, scurrying furtively in the bushes.

"Those are the Cretans."

"And those?" I nodded to a gawky wagtail, a bold but fretful bird that is ever busy, busy, busy ferreting in the grass, tossing its head and flicking its long tail provocatively.

His face reddened with the effort to keep his laughs from exploding.

"That is my aunt, your wife."

We both gave vent to our mirth.

When we had calmed ourselves, I said, "And where in all that crowd of humanity do you see me? Am I there too?"

"Yes", he smiled, his eyes dancing with mischief.

"Come on, you mockingbird, tell me—which one am I?" He shook his head and wouldn't answer.

"All right, keep your secret, but I know which one you think I am."

He raised his eyebrows, tilted his head, and grinned broadly.

"I'm that flycatcher, am I not?" I said, pointing to a dull little grayish bird picking insects from crevices in the rock not three paces away. It had to be me because this species, like a cohort of tiny doctors, scours the island of pests.

"No," he said with a pensive smile, "that is not you."

With a glance and a swift gesture he pointed to a rock upstream, and then I saw the bird perching on it—a species that is rarely seen this far inland, the small but noble king-fisher, which we sometimes call the *halcyon*. Under the full rays of the sun, its colors were aflame—emerald wings and crowned head, orange belly, and the flash of blue lightning down its back.

I had not seen it sitting there, which is inexplicable, considering its brilliance. But Loukas had noticed it all along.

"That is you", he said quietly, and looked away toward the mountains.

Reduced to silence, unable to speak at all, I pondered this awhile. Then at last I stood, clapped him on the shoulder, and said, "Come, let us return to the city now, lest we anger a certain wagtail."

And so we did.

Was it a day or a week or a month later that he appeared in the open doorway of the surgery late one afternoon? Totally engrossed in an Egyptian manuscript that I had recently obtained through a dealer in Alexandria, I was trying to distinguish between the Egyptians' ancient technical medical procedures and their magical practices.

"Uncle", he said quietly.

I looked up, somewhat irritated by the interruption.

"What is it, Loukas?"

"May I speak with you?"

I sighed, put away the manuscript, and sat back in my chair.

He stepped into the room and said, "If I were to change my hair, what would you think?"

He had always worn his hair long, braided into a single cord and wrapped around his temples, bound by a leather headband.

"What change would you make?" I asked, as if gathering data for an informed diagnosis.

"If I were to cut my hair short, as you wear it, and as all Romans wear it, would I lose my Greekness?"

"Greekness? That word means many things, depending on the time of history one speaks about."

All Greeks wear short hair, and have for centuries, long before the Roman invasion. Loukas, however, in imitation of his father, Timo, and a few philosophers, had pined for the older culture of Greece.

"You *are* Greek", I said to underline the point. "If you were to cut your hair short, you would lose a certain appearance of Greekness only."

"Yet I am uncertain of a thing. Does not truth demand of us that our interior and our exterior be as one?"

"Yes, in a man's essence, his character, his actions, and his words."

"But what of the things the eye sees? Surely they are part of him?"

"Some are essentials, some are accidentals. Some can be abandoned without concern, while others are abandoned only at the price of losing the true self."

"What are those?"

"The truthfulness in your face, for one."

"And hair?"

"It is a tradition, but neither truth nor falsehood are braided in it. Socrates, it is said, was bald."

"But you love our ancient ways. Why, then, do you shave your face and wear your hair short?"

"I am proud of our history and our ancestors, for their thought and their arts were greater than any others known to man. Yet there is no principle or moral contained in the shortness or longness of hair. As for me, in all truth, Loukas, I find it less hot, and if you decide to shave your chin and lip, and keep your skull open to the wind, you too will feel refreshed, even on the hottest days."

He smiled.

"Moreover, you would not waste so much of my olive oil on that horse's mane. We need not discuss the parasites that are sometimes found within it."

He laughed and said, "Will you cut it?"

"If you wish. Do you mean now, at this present moment?"

"Yes", he nodded soberly.

We agreed to meet in the garden, and I went to the bath chamber to find my barber's blades and honing stone.

We did the deed beside the statue of Aesclepios the Healer, me standing at the god's feet and Loukas seated before me on the marble bench, his back to me and the god.

Slowly, with what seemed reluctance, he untied the headband, uncoiled the thick black braid wound about his temples, and let it fall like a rope down his spine.

"You are sure?" I asked.

He nodded once, but said nothing.

And so I cut first into the rope at the level of his shoulders. It took no more than a minute, yet it felt as if a lengthy ritual were being enacted. When the braid was fully severed, he jerked forward involuntarily, as if a weight had been taken from him, which indeed it had. I coiled it carefully and laid it on the *plinthos* of the god's shrine. That done, I set to work on the rest of the boy's head. Because his hair had, as far as I know, never been cut until now, the job was laborious. To hack it all off would have been easier, but he would then have looked like a street waif or slave boy, cared for by none. Besides, he is proud, perhaps even a little vain, as is common with youths.

So I cut and cut—hair by hair, one might say—and throughout most of this long operation, he said not a word.

At one point, my dear daughters happened to enter the garden, and when they saw what was going on, they gasped and ran to us, their faces stricken: Theodosia, a year younger than Loukas, and Mila, three years younger, both of them hopelessly in love with their cousin.

"What are you doing?" cried the elder, in anguish. "Stop it! Stop it!" cried the younger, not knowing whether to sob or to fly into her customary rage.

"Why have you done this to Loukas?" and "This is madness, madness, Father!" were followed by other such protests and recriminations. The boy observed these voluminous outpourings from under his lowered brows.

"Sit still, Loukas, or I will nick your ear", I said in the unprovokable tone of a barber.

Fresh tears erupted from the maidens, who now began to jump about with desperate helplessness. I paused and raised the knife toward them and declared that they were next—off with all hair in the household! They screamed and ran to find their mother, the only force in their world capable of defeating their father.

So, with sighs from both the boy and me, the cutting resumed.

"Uncle," he murmured, "have you ever read the story of Aeneas by Vergilius?"

"Many times. Would you like to borrow my book?"

"I have already borrowed it. I was sure you would not mind."

"You know you have my permission. And how do you like it?"

"It seems to me that this is a Roman poet who tries to speak of his homeland as Homer spoke of ours."

"You have good eyes. Yes, it's true."

"Do you think he is striving to be a rival to Homer, to set on high the Romans over our people?"

"It may be, or equally may not be. There is such greatness and deep feeling in his verse, and understanding too, that I think this is not poetic theft but an open homage to Homer. We cannot fault him for telling the tale of his own people, as our poet did for us."

"Even so, Aeneas is not a Roman, nor from any tribes that lived in Italy. Aeneas is Greek."

"Trojan, to be precise."

"Yes, but a man of the Greek-like peoples."

"True, and Vergil makes this plain enough. How far into the tale are you?"

"I have finished reading it. But it seems incomplete."

"In what sense? The story is roundly concluded. It is the founding of Rome."

"Well, there are gaps, unfinished lines."

"Yes, he was still working on it when he died. Did you spot the irony in it?"

"Irony? What sort of irony?"

"It is my opinion that he speaks about imperial Rome through an antique setting. He had patronage from Augustus, you realize, but also much trouble. Consider his reference to the two gates, the gate of horn and the gate of ivory."

46

"Ah, yes, the gate of dreams that come true, and the gate of deceiving dreams. It is a good warning about dreams."

"It is more than a reflection on man's imaginings in sleep. It is about our imaginings while awake."

"What do you mean?"

"I think he is saying—in the only way he could say it, without having his head cut off—that the dream of noble Rome, the forgiving and just Rome, is an illusion. The practical reality, the gate of horn, is Rome's true nature. That is, the sword is always thrust into those whom she conquers."

"But Rome does not always do that."

"There are swords and there are swords. There is swift death and lingering death."

"It seems to me that our people have not died from its sword. Well, not so many of us. Not like other nations."

"We are something of an exception. They admire our civilized achievements and our courage of old. I believe that Vergilius desires to reinforce the Italian connection to Greece in order to strengthen the bond between our cultures and thus to further the cause of democracy."

"I did not see that in the book."

"Read it again. I think you will sense between the lines that there is a republican beneath his song of arms and the man, the blood and heroism of his poetic war."

Loukas said nothing, and pressed his chin lower onto his chest as I trimmed about his ears.

"What do you like best in the story?" I asked.

He did not reply, and at first it seemed he was giving himself ample time to consider the question. Then, as I moved beside him to crop the final wisps that stood up on the crown of his head, I noticed that his eyes were wet. I did not press for an answer.

"There is a scene that I love most of all", he said in a low voice, almost a whisper. "It is when Troy is burning and Aeneas flees. Everything he possessed is lost. Countless people have been slain, among them many whom Aeneas has loved. He escapes carrying his aged father on his back—and with his little son clinging to his hand."

I put away my instruments in their case.

He stood and said, "Thank you, Father."

And never again did he call me uncle.

*

[Journal entry, July 18, A.D. 64]

Gortyna
Skirophorion—Iulius

At last! It came in the evening, just as the ferocious heat of the day was easing a little, the western sky turning red over the Plain of Phaestos. I was reading by lamplight in the garden— filling my head and ruining my eyes, says Paeonia—when the courier banged on the door. All ears in the household were suddenly deaf, so I answered it myself.

The package did not come in the hand of the Cypriots but instead from a trade ship out of Ephesus bound for Cyrene—a straight course, direct from Asia to Africa with Crete exactly in the middle. The captain harbored for a night at Fair Havens and arranged for a dock runner to bring the letter up to the city.

Loukas wrote it only three weeks ago. He asks if I have received his longer letter describing the life of *Christos* in Judaea. This informs me that my response has not yet reached him, and now I see why. He has been traveling far and wide but no longer with the man from Tarsus, a Jew who is also a Roman citizen. This Paul, Loukas explains, has been in prison and is still, in some way that I do not understand, a prisoner. Yet he is free to travel? To travel in chains?

This morning I reread it, again and again. The letter is frustrating for its lack of details, but it was written in haste, for he had heard about the ship bound for Crete only hours before it sailed. He sends us his love, naming every member of the family and asking me to impart a kiss to each. He intends to return to Judaea by the end of summer to meet with other *apostoloi* and to gather from them more accounts, whatever they can recall of the life of their Christos.

I pray to the gods that this consuming interest is a passion for history and not an enslaving devotion. I suspect it may be both. However, he is too intelligent to fail to recognize the mind's—I should say the imagination's—vulnerability to the symbolism and mythic tales of cults. The world is awash in such feverish religions. In time, that excellent mind of his will return him to proportion and clarity.

These concluding passages stand out as significant:

I embrace you, my Theophilos, and earnestly pray for you and Mother and everyone at home, that you will be well and continue to remember me, as I remember you, for no passing day lacks its moment when I recall your endless goodness and patience with me. I am in this city for only a short while longer. It is a place of great beauty and great darkness. Ten years ago, Paul's teaching caused riots here; there were many conversions to the new faith, but evil lashed back mightily. The community of believers is not very great in number, yet it grows and grows. After the riots, he came rarely to Ephesus, for there are many fields in the world needing harvesters, and he ensured that good teachers remained here to raise up what he had planted.

I reside beyond the walls, up in the hills, in a humble house where once lived Miryam the mother of *Christos* and those who accompanied her, for Jerusalem has often been in turmoil over the brethren, with periods of persecution against those who openly follow Iesous. It was never safe for her in that city nor in Galilee, which was her home, for the Zealots are stronger there and Roman reaction to them made the region perilous at that time and ever since. She was willing to risk death, did not fear it, but the *apostoloi* had instructed her to come to Ephesus. She obeyed them because she was a truly humble woman. Her obedience was most astonishing when you consider that without her the *Kyrios* could not have come into this world.

During the year after I left Crete, when I was living in Antioch, I first met Titos, who knows our island well. It was he who brought me to Ephesus, and there I remained as a guest for two months in Miryam's house. I was with her when she died. The ones named *apostoloi* had for the most part returned to be with her in her final hours of life. The house was full, and numerous tents had been raised in the yard. The hearts of all were sorely grieved, yet the small rooms of the dwelling were filled with an inexplicable light. How can I explain this light to you, Theophilos? There is nothing like it that we have known until now.

When she died, the *apostoloi* and other companions carried her body to a tomb in the hills. Later the tomb was opened, and we found that her body was no longer within. You will doubt me about this, and I know you will seek natural explanations for it. From across the great distance between us, it is impossible to dispel your inevitable doubts, but I will tell you more details about this when we next meet.

You will perhaps wonder what sort of woman she was. She was elderly, gray of hair, yet young in spirit.

For those with eyes to see, her countenance was marked by the sufferings she had endured, though she was not sorrowful. She was rather childlike—serene, yet wise too. No ill word, no accusation against her son's tormentors, had ever crossed her lips, so said all. She comforted the grieving and sick, welcomed Jews and also Gentiles of any race, made meals for us. She was like a queen in a way, yet she chose to live as if she were a serving girl. She was never one to draw attention to herself, but in prayer she was foremost among us, because all who lived here reverenced her as their mother. When there were gatherings for a memorial feast, she recited the songs of the Jewish king David. She sang her own soul-words as well. It was a stirring thing to hear. It is difficult to describe—there was no one like her.

I asked her for an account of her son's life, especially his earliest years, and have written a little of what she told me, as you know from the letter I sent you in the spring. There was much more to learn that we did not discuss in detail, especially about the long years between his childhood and his public life. But there are others who knew him in Nazareth when he was unknown. I am revising my manuscript now and hope to send you a copy of the expanded account when it has been completed. With every journey, every encounter, I learn more and more about him—the anointed One—and truly it is astounding. Were I to speak of it without witnesses, none would believe me. But there are many witnesses still living, and signs of confirmation from the heavens as well, which I have seen. I will tell you more about this when I next meet you face-to-face—oh, I pray it is soon, for I am full of these wonders and desire very much to share them with you and Mother, that you too might know the joy offered to mankind.

> I am your son
> Loukas.

And below his name, this line, which puzzles me:

The Mother prays for you.

The Mother, the word capitalized. Has he exalted her in his mind to the status of a goddess? It is often the way with these mystery cults—for example, Diana of the Ephesians, Artemis the many-breasted Mother of Asia, a hideous abomination of womanhood, some artist's folly or the inspiration of a deranged priesthood. Infatuation with symbolic meaning outweighing reason, the discarding of harmonious forms, the ignorance of genuine beauty. These mystery cults so often begin with the invocation of fertility and abundance and end in frenzy, with doctrine and drunken lust entwined like caduceus snakes. And what staff could ever kill such snakes!

Yet—he speaks of her, this Miryam, this new mother, as a humble woman.

*

Later in the day, Theodosia arrived from Phoenix with her three little monkeys, my grandchildren. Oh, what a clatter and tumult ensued when they burst in, for we were not expecting them. After countless kisses, copious tears from feminine eyes, and sweets handed out to the children, the two boys ran to the trees in the garden and climbed upward into the branches to plunder my pears. "Icarus and Icarus, come down!" I commanded them, but they only giggled and shouted, "We must fly, Daedalus our grandfather!"

Thea, who is now walking, scampered to the fountain and jumped into the basin, splashing about, ignoring her mother's insincere reproaches. We all desired to do likewise, for the sun is scorching the earth again today.

I have missed them, their guileless embraces, the smear of honey and poppy seed on my cheek, the insatiable demands for stories. I will tell them stories tonight, when they have cooled their brows and quieted a little—if the latter is possible. Theodosia will be with us for a week, salving her loneliness for Leandros, who has gone to Achaia for a month to trade with lumber merchants. There is exceptionally fine cedar to be had at a good price, she says, and the rich of Gortyna are now calling it "wood of the gods" because of its warm color and its scent. Spoiled as always, the wealthiest families are bored with furniture made from African black-wood or our native cedar, and of course our plane wood is good only for their toilet seats.

A day of laughter, much happiness under our roof. The women are conspiring about something in the kitchen at the moment, and Calliope must be involved in it too because so far there have been no quarrels. Mila, Cleon, and their children will come for supper. It will be a fine and noisy evening.

So, with the children playing and the women busy about their secrets, what am I to do?

I will take a walk.

*

[Journal entry, July 20, A.D. 64]

Gortyna
Skirophorion—Iulius

A moment of peace. All the women have gone to the marketplace with the children, along with our hired gardener,

53

Tranquilatus. That little old mountain man knows how to wield a stick. They will be safe from cutpurses and street rowdies. His wages do not deplete my income overmuch, and he has good motivation. In terms of coinage, a slave of his age and health would be cheaper. But I have never owned slaves, though I could afford to purchase one or two. I dislike the custom because of my family history and because, on principle, I cannot agree that a slave is merely an animal with speech. Profit should never derive from falsehood. Moreover, human nature is such that one may draw a man forward with wages or drive him forward with the lash—and of the two approaches, the weight of evidence supports the side of enticement and reward.

I must record what happened on the walk that I made two days ago:

I went out into the street, locking the gate behind me, and set off with a vague notion of making my way to the banks of the Lethaios, where there is sometimes a breeze and always a spot to sit and soak one's feet. A favorite place of mine is an outcropping of stone at the back wall of the shrine of Hero, a shelter into which no more than two or three people can squeeze at a time. There are few devotees these days, and the building is falling into ruin. Theodosia often came here before she was married because of Hero and Leander.

The heat of the day had driven off the streets all sane people other than slaves, and even few of them were about. I found myself alone. The water ran by me as always, each drop never before seen, never to be repeated, the mountains and the clouds endlessly creating their children who are ever running away to the sea. Heracleitus said that all things flow, nothing stands still. The universe is like a river. No one steps into the same river twice.

There is a pattern emerging in my life. I have just noticed it. Often when I am sitting by water or walking near it, Loukas comes to mind. Is there a missing thought-connection? Does the image inform where reason fails? Yes, it might be: The mountains and clouds pour forth their life into their children and never see them again?

The water is so low at this time of year that the river's bed stones are visible and the music of the passing flow is louder than in any other season. The sound soothed soul and body and made me drowsy, as if I were under the spells of Morpheus, the dream maker. I leaned back against the wall of the temple with my bare feet in the water, trying not to fall asleep, batting away a bee or fly from time to time. And without warning, another memory returned. No, two memories, but I will speak of them in reverse order, and the god Kronos will not fault me for it.

The first is about the day I cut Loukas' hair. When the deed was finished, he stood and thanked me with a somber bow of the head, called me father for the first time in months, and retreated to his bedroom. Then an unexpected emergency called me to the surgery, and I forgot about the coil of hair we had left on the *plinthos* of Aesclepios. When I returned to the garden, it was gone. If I gave it any thought at all, I must have presumed that the boy had retrieved it.

Man's tendency to lose his memory is a worrisome thing. One sees it frequently in the very old. They can recall large numbers of details of past events but cannot tell you what they did yesterday. I am not quite that far gone, but I do feel some anxiety that a decline may be under way. Paeonia tells me that I fret over nothing, that people of all ages forget the most obvious things, and besides, my mind is so crammed with a thousand concerns, in addition to all that medical knowledge, and a host of friends to whom I write, that it is a wonder I can keep track of anything. I defended myself ably, said that I am not in the least fretful but am merely observing a patient—myself—as a physician should.

Now, back to the memory:

On an evening about three months after the shearing, a middle-aged man was brought to the house on a litter carried by four friends. Four rather drunken friends, I should mention. The stricken one was also drunk, screaming and cursing incoherently and apparently in great pain. He had fallen from an upper window during a carouse at the house of prostitutes in the disreputable Subura district, which, regrettably, begins only a few streets away from us. He hit pavement and had been raving like this for the past hour. At first glance there appeared to be nothing physically wrong with him, only a bloody nose that had now stopped seeping. I led them all into the surgery for a closer examination and called Loukas to assist. His knowledge of medicine was limited at that time, but his arms were strong, and it seemed likely that if any restraining of the patient were to be needed, the lad would do the job better than a company of wine bibbers.

I removed the outer clothing of the man—Balbus by name— and still could see nothing wrong. The four others interfered, babbling advice, warnings, threatening me, smoking the air with their curses, and all the while, the screaming of Balbus continued—until I lost my patience and drove them out with the aid of Tranquilatus and his stick.

I examined all the bones, toe to cranium—nothing wrong. The man thrashed about wildly, polluting the atmosphere too, and thus the examination was quite a challenging task. Loukas ineptly tried to hold the legs down by the ankles, and then a fist would swing and strike me or the boy. Loukas would then leap up and restrain the arms, only to provoke louder screams and a thrashing of legs. Oh, misery! What a pathetic creature is man! By love or by pain we are so easily reduced to the level of a beast!

Then I spotted it. So layered in fat was this Balbus that I had failed to notice the strange angle of his shoulder. It was dislocated and perhaps had suffered a minor fracture within. Loukas held the man's chest in the vice of his arms, and I manipulated the joint and popped it into place. With a terrible scream, Balbus lost consciousness and fell into blessed silence.

Loukas and I exhaled and straightened ourselves, looking down at the great porcine body, wondering if it would erupt again.

Really, if I had not taken the Hippocratic oath, I would never accept to treat people such as this. They depress my spirits and fill me with disgust. Why do they live this way? Judging from the full purse at his belt, the bright red sandals, and the gold ring on his finger, this was no poor man reduced by desperation to ignorant behavior. It made me angry, and in the heat of the emotion I said a thing I later regretted:

"This shameless ape does not deserve our services", I growled.

Loukas looked at me blankly, and just then the patient began to groan, his eyelids fluttering. With the man no longer thrashing or screaming, whatever limited mind dwelled within that skull was slowly returning.

Loukas knelt beside the pallet and took the hand of Balbus in one of his own. He put the palm of his other on the man's forehead. To my amazement, he stroked it gently. I cannot exaggerate the physical and moral repulsiveness of this Balbus, for though I have thrust my hands into many a piece of flesh that no others would touch, he filled me with loathing.

I stood behind Loukas, watching the recovery. There is much I could write about the minutiae, but that is standard medical knowledge. What remains in my memory is the look Loukas gave to the man as he awoke, and the answering look—first surprise, then disbelief, followed by tears of gratitude or shame, I know not which.

As I stood gazing down at this son of mine, whom I had thought I understood so well, I realized I hardly knew him at all. In the depths of his soul were reservoirs I had not known were there. One might call it his capacity for pity or for empathy, but it was more than that. And what it was, I still do not know.

Irrelevantly, I noticed that his hair had grown again, no longer a cap of black curls, but a short mane creeping down the back of his neck above the shoulders. Perhaps because I could not at that moment bear my own confused feelings regarding the luckless Balbus, I made an inane comment.

"You need another cropping", I said. "Whatever did you do with your horse's mane?"

"I burned it", he murmured, keeping his eyes on the weeping Balbus.

This surprised me, for though I had never asked about it before, I had assumed he must have given it to one of his cousins, who would have cherished it as a keepsake.

"Ah, a sacrifice to Aesclepios."

"No, I burned it in the field of the dead."

Stunned, I said no more, for the field of the dead is the place beyond the city gate where the unclaimed bodies of executed criminals, dead slaves, aborted children, and other castoffs are thrown. It is not a field; it is a pit. Though a fire is usually burning there to reduce the risk of pestilence, its stench sometimes invades the city when the wind blows from that direction. It is a place most people will not go near.

Aeneas, I thought to myself. Aeneas was in his mind when he burned the symbol of his past.

*

[Journal entry, July 21, A.D. 64]

Gortyna
Skirophorion—Iulius

I meant to write about two memories yesterday but could not go any farther than the first. Today, the second. With my apologies to Kronos, I now step back a pace to a time before Loukas sacrificed his mane.

He was, I think, in his fifteenth year—growing quickly, a voracious eater and an equally voracious devourer of the ancient books in my library, with some side interest in Latin writers. Each morning before first light, he would rise and go off to meet some fellows from his school, a half dozen of them who had made a pact with each other to become great athletes and one day run in an Olympics. And if it should turn out that they could not go to Olympos, they intended to establish a Cretan Olympics. Neither of these dreams later materialized, but they served them well enough at the time. The young Cleon was then a leader of the older youths and a fine runner in his own right; Loukas was at first a tagalong, but so swift and persevering did he prove that they let him join their company. Each morning they ran once around the old city walls, a distance of about fifty stadia, which is no small run. Then they galloped to their homes for quick breakfasts before a day of studies and chores.

Needless to say, Loukas did not suffer from sleeplessness, for he dropped onto his pallet early each evening and was lost to this world until the first cock's crow.

In the middle of the night I heard in my half sleep a faint cry from one of the other bedrooms. Paeonia's mother-instinct was strong, and I felt her bolt upright beside me, listening. There was no second cry, and so we assumed it was nothing, perhaps one of the girls dreaming or a sound from beyond the compound walls. Paeonia lay down again and fell back to sleep. I got up and went to the window, parted the insect curtain, and checked the stars. The Pleiades had moved a good way across the sky, though dawn was still far off. I closed the curtain and returned to bed.

Shortly after, a lamp flame appeared in our doorway and stopped there. It was Loukas, standing motionless as if carved from marble, girded about his middle with a white sheet. I had never before seen him so inanimate, for whenever his body is not active, his mind remains busy, and this he is never able to hide. Something had happened, something of great import. By the feeble light, I could see that his face was stricken.

I spoke his name, and it broke the spell.

"You are awake?" he whispered.

"We are awake", said Paeonia. "Why are you roaming around the house at this hour?"

He entered the room and slowly sat down on the end of our bed. My good wife leaned forward, put out her hand to him, and shook his arm gently. "Tell us. What troubles you?"

"A dream", he said, and for the first time looked away from the flame and into our eyes.

"Tell us about your dream," I said, "for speaking a fear dispels the night shades."

"It was not fearful", he whispered. Then I saw that he was not stricken but rather had been seized by a kind of awe.

We waited for him to go on. He sighed and seemed to come to himself a little, though he was still gripped by whatever he had seen in sleep.

"It was beautiful, but I do not understand it. I am in it still. I can feel it now, a feeling of wonder, like warm oil."

"There was oil in your dream?" I prompted.

"Not like a substance. It was something different—something new. I am a man—many years older than I am now. I am myself but I no longer look like myself as I am now, here in Gortyna. The room is not in Crete; it is in another land. I know this but I do not know how I know it.

"I am standing in a room with thirty or forty people facing me. They are seated on the floor or on benches. I am speaking in fine Attic. Even so, in my dream I know that most people in the room understand me though they are of different races.

"They are listening to me speak of a matter—I do not remember what it is, now that I am awake. I remember only that I am speaking well. The people are listening attentively. But I am dissatisfied with myself, for what I tell them is true but insufficient. Something is lacking. It is not a lack of knowledge or skill in rhetoric. It is a thing missing within me, and yet it is a thing missing in all men. I do not understand this.

"Suddenly, above me in the air there appears a very beautiful bird—a species I have never seen before, and maybe it does not exist in this world. Its color is not a reflection of the sun but glows from within—bright blue. It is smaller than a sparrow. It hovers above my head, and then it descends, growing and growing in size as it nears me, and when it perches on my shoulder it has become very great, though very gentle. It speaks into my ear, but I do not know its language. It keeps speaking, and its language becomes singing that enters into my heart, and then it flows through my heart and out again through my mouth. I cannot tell you what it is really like. It pours like warm oil, like water, like light, but it is my own voice speaking words. As I begin speaking in this new way, all those in the room hear it not only with their minds but with their hearts. It is so beautiful. It is nearly unbearable, this beauty, and I wake up."

[Journal entry, July 22, A.D. 64]

Gortyna
Skirophorion—Iulius

Yesterday I forgot to write down what we said to him after he told us about his dream. It is perhaps worth recording, for these many years later I still think our counsel was true.

"The muses, or a man's genius, sometimes speak through dreams", said Paeonia. "They are showing you a thing in symbols. You will not experience it like that in your life. You will not see a blue bird growing in front of your eyes, and it surely will not speak words to you."

Loukas said nothing, so I took my turn:

"It is an assurance for you. It tells you that despite your losses, you will continue to grow. It promises that you will become an instructor of others and that your teaching will not be an empty playing with words, as is the case with the Sophists. Your words will be from the great light of Athens and will change men's lives for the better."

Though he had then lived with us only four years, I had already come to respect his intelligence—though not always his wisdom, for he was a boy as other boys are and often lacked common sense. Even so, I had begun to believe he would one day be a notable rhetorician or philosopher.

In answer, he merely stood, bowed to us both, and bid us good night. I lay sleepless for a time, chewing on many questions, until the hour when "rose-fingered dawn" began to pale the sky. I heard him rustling about in his room, and then the squeaking of the gate door told me that he was off for his daily run.

*

Gortyna
Boedromion—October

I was born in this city, have lived my entire life here, with the
exception of the four years of study, two in Alexandria and
two in Thessalonike. I love Gortyna with my heart and soul.
My senses are fond of it as well: the good food; the mild seasons; the river; the wildlife and woody hills; the distant peaks
of the White Mountains; the bountiful orchards, groves, and
vineyards; and the southern sea, only half a day's donkey ride
away.

The rainy season has begun. This morning I went walking
in the cool air, desiring on a whim to see places around the
city that were dear to me when I was a youth. It may be that
the journal entry I made about the runners has brought to
mind the long-forgotten fact that I once regularly walked the
entire circuit of Gortyna. I was never a runner, being ever
susceptible to infections of the bronchioles, and I once nearly
died of a deeper infection in the lungs. My father insisted that
I must walk briskly every day if I desired to survive long enough
to become a physician. Lung disease is the biggest killer in the
world. Then and now, I have watched it sweep away the lives
of the weak and the robust. The latter class of victim is fewer
in number, and thus nature underscores its lesson.

The circuit path around the city cuts through new olive
groves and copses of older date palms. Here in the south we
are blessed with a climate that is more like North Africa than
Macedonia. I have rarely been chilled in my homeland yet
suffered constantly from the cold when I lived in Thessalonike. Both lands are beautiful, but Greece is like a passionate,
temperamental wife who blows hot and cold, while Crete is
like a loving, even-tempered wife. My Paeonia came to mind

as a perfect mixture of Greece and Crete—I stopped to laugh at my own wit and startled a goat boy stealing fruit from a tree. Our national culture, this kind of theft. He ran quickly away. Did he fear I would capture him and turn him over to the Romans? Or did he instinctively fear the sight of an old man dancing through random animal droppings and laughing to himself? Prudent boy! An eruption of affectionate wit in one man can appear as contempt to another, and for others it can appear as madness—and it may well be.

Why am I going on about this? I think it is because a long time ago I was that very boy. How swiftly my life has passed, though not uneventfully.

I hated living in Athens. The monuments to its lost glories were largely intact, and it was sweet pleasure to walk in the streets where Socrates walked, to imagine him turning a corner and coming toward me with a group of lads just like me, cracking open our facile presumptions and provoking us to real thought. But the city was also big and dirty and cruel. Perhaps it was always such, and idealization had washed it clean, repainting it as an *eikon* brightly colored and radiating its virtues. My father sent me there because he believed he had no more to teach me from the store of his own knowledge and because he disdained to turn me over to any plodding barbers of Crete and the large number of medical charlatans plying their trade among them. The medical school at Alexandria had enriched what I learned from him, especially my readings in the great library of that city, and the books I had purchased there—copies of the *Hippocratic Collection* and *Prognostics*; a work by Herophilus on anatomy; Erasistratus' intriguing text on pneumatology; Aristotle's biological treatises and his writings on entelechy. Each had expanded my knowledge of the body and articulated questions regarding the soul. Was it inherent in man's nature, or did it derive from an exterior source? I have yet to resolve this problem satisfactorily for myself. I came to love Aristotle's thought, but in some fields I felt that Erasistratus was superior. I emphasize that this was my feeling and sense rather than a certainty. In summation, Alexandria taught me that a man might spend a lifetime in its library and schools, merely skimming the surface of the knowledge they contained.

My father had studied there too, and he understood my situation. He had convinced himself that in Athens I would be guided to a mentor who would take me farther, who would give me extensive firsthand experience and instruction without overemphasis on philosophy, which, while important and even useful at times, tended to overwhelm my mind and push subjects like trephination and bonesetting to the side. Early on, he realized that philosophy would ever be my seducer—as it was his. And so he sent me off into the world, with hopes and trepidations and a little sack of hard-won coins to sustain me until a time when I might find a teacher.

Let me make a very long story a bit shorter by saying that plodders and quacks abound even on the heights of the most exalted cities of man. Moreover, no genuine master would take me on, for all such men were choking in crowds of disciples, and who was I, after all, but a shy provincial with no name to speak of except that of a former slave? I had no family and no connections. The coins dwindled quickly, though I used them with care.

I discovered all around me every form of corruption and learned that degrading activities were considered normal, even natural. Money was everything, and pride too, preferably combined. I was shocked most by the revelation that the ancient custom of exposing newborn infants continued. I saved a few of them, but I was so young I could not adopt them—I could hardly feed myself at the time. The best I could do was to strain every nerve seeking good parents for them, driving off the scavengers from the prostitution houses who would have raised these children for a trade more terrible than innocent death.

It was my grandfather's city, but he had been a slave in it, and enslavement by Romans was merely a variation of our timeless Greek custom of enslaving those we had captured from other peoples and from among our own. We spoke one thing with our golden mouths and did another. And thus what I had loved from afar, with my mind, became repugnant to me. A new stage of maturity began, a more sober weighing of the goods and evils that are to be found everywhere. Yet even now the sadness lingers: Athens, Athens, what might you have become?

"O, thou, our Athens! Violet-crowned, brilliant, most enviable of cities!" wrote Aristophanes. As I look back, the epithet seems more irony than descriptive praise.

I have always appeared to be too young. When I was a full twenty-five years, I appeared to be a stripling of eighteen. Skipping over half a century of time, I am still a man masked by deceptive appearance, through no fault of my own. My face was babyish as a boy, boyish as a man, and when I reached that stage when I began to desire a bench by the doorpost where I might nod in the sunshine and recount my stories to other elderly gentlemen, I was considered to be one in his prime. I do not complain of this, for it has its benefits—my grandfather sired my father at an advanced age, and I am quite capable of the same. I mention the illusion of appearance only to explain why, after three inglorious months in glorious Athens, I went to Thessalonike. It was like this:

One day I succeeded in attracting the attention of a well-known physician, a man of great reputation and I think unquestionable honesty. In desperation, I confronted him in the agora at the foot of the Acropolis as he walked by with a train of students. I blocked his passage by jumping squarely in front of him and blurted out my predicament. He listened with a cautious air as I listed my qualifications, but when I begged him to take me as an apprentice, he politely but firmly declined. To his merit, however, he looked me up and down, shook his head, and then as if a muse had whispered in his ears, he told me about a colleague of his in Thessalonike, a physician of skill and wisdom who had lost his eyesight. The man was impoverished, he said, and could use someone to be his hands, as long as I did not expect much payment.

"He is not blind Tiresias", the great physician quipped, prompting laughter from his disciples. "His name is Xanthippos son of Cimon."

I think he gave me this information as much to get rid of me as to help his old friend. And so I left Athens and went north on foot and by sea and came in time to my next and greatest teacher, who taught me much about the body and the soul of man. Of that stage in my life, I will write another time. I need only say that as I departed from the violet-crowned brilliant city, I did not look back, not once.

Now all these years later, I wonder what Aristophanes would have written about Gortyna.

"O, thou, our Gortyna, dust-crowned, sleepy and dull, most ordinary of cities!"

Yes, I feel sure that he would have turned a candid yet kindly eye upon us. Though human nature in all its manifestations is little better here than elsewhere, our extremes are milder, like our temperate climate.

With these meditations in mind, I passed through the olive grove and followed the winding path that led around to the northern suburbs, where cruder houses are scattered among the foothills, and the soil is poor. There was no wind, and for that reason I came upon the field of the dead before I knew it. I had not visited the site in years, because it was always Loukas or Tranquilatus who carried away the offal from surgery and discarded it here. There was no fire in the pit today. The stench was terrible. I did not look.

Swerving away, I cut across a swath of scrub brush that would bring me back to the path farther along. I could breathe again; the air was scented by the wild herbs crushed beneath my sandals—the intoxicating sage and sweet lavender. I stopped to pick a handful of the plant commonly called *origanon*, which I and my father called *Hermes-grass*, for its oils have healing qualities.

I shrugged off the thought of the pit, sad as it was, for no place in this world is free of death, and turned my thoughts instead to the beauty all around me. I regained the path and proceeded for some minutes in a more wholesome frame of mind. The trees are thicker than they were forty years ago when I was accustomed to walk there daily. Now the path winds among numerous copses of dwarf pine, into which oak and carob have been woven. There are many more myrtles, along with mastic and chaste-berry, occasionally an ebony, and several delightful strawberry trees.

The path dipped into a gully and rose again, rounded an outcropping of stone, and brought me to a small hill overlooking the east gate of the city. I stopped abruptly, for crosses were standing there, twenty paces away. Bodies hung on them.

How many crucifixions have I witnessed in my lifetime? A dozen perhaps. I could have seen many more if I had wanted to, but the cruelty of that form of execution revolts me, and almost as much do I detest the mentality of the audiences who inevitably cluster about to watch the entertainment. I know that Gortyna has a few crucifixions every year, though in times of civic instability there can be a host of them at once. But such incidents are rare, and the last is far back in my memory.

Now only the worst criminals are executed this way. It is not uncommon to see people in the streets with one hand missing, their stumps bearing mute witness to their punishment for petty theft. One seldom sees a cross on the hills.

Crucifixion is a dreadful way to die, for in such total agony a criminal must experience his pain as perpetual, each minute like a year in hell. Before my eyes hung eight men in hell. They were naked, their skin burned by the sun, covered in wounds, their mouths gaping, lips cracked, tongues hanging out. All fluids or matter that could escape such bodies had already been poured out, and what blood remained within them cruelly prolonged the slow ticking of their hearts. Were they conscious, I do not know, though low groans came from one or two. In the shadow of a rock lay a single Roman soldier, left to stand guard, stretched out asleep beside his spear, his metal helmet sitting by his feet. There were no onlookers or grieving family.

The feet of the dying were nailed to the posts near the ground, and I could have poured a little water into each mouth had I remembered to bring my waterskin along. I might have put pain-deadening oils onto their wounds, had I any with me, but a full amphora of oil would not have covered their bodies, such was their condition. I had nothing to give them.

So motionless was this scene, so stark yet so unreal did it appear to me, that it seemed a piece of tragic theater, like the darkest scenes in *Agamemnon* or *Antigone*. I am ashamed to write this because it sounds like a man using the worst experiences of others for a literary meditation. It is not. It merely happened to cross my mind as I stared at the living dead. We experience emotional *katharsis* when we view tragedy performed on a stage. We are struck dumb when we see it in real life. Here were eight lives. Two white-headed fellows of advanced years, three of middle age, and three youths of sturdy frame and once-fair countenance. The cutting off of life so young strikes harder—the old have lived. But what were their crimes?

Try as I might, I could not turn my internal disposition to my customary one—the detachment from emotion that I experience whenever I am faced by the shock of degraded human flesh and the degraded manhood that often accompanies it. A physician must see much, and do much, that would revolt others, but always it is for restoring the patient to health. *Do no harm!* we say.

Regardless of the gravity of these men's crimes, I could not bring myself to see this kind of execution as just punishment. I have never considered it to be so. Cut their heads off, if you will, or thrust a sword into their hearts. But not this! As I strode away, heading down directly toward the city gate, another horror struck me: I realized that this merciless torture had become so routine, so banal, that even the executioner sleeps through it. It is the boring, ordinary business of Rome.

*

[Journal entry, January 4, A.D. 65]

Gortyna
Poseideion—Ianuarius

Two messages today, the first unwelcome, the second very welcome.

Gaius sent me a letter delivered by his slave to our door. He inquires after my health and that of my wife and family. He then unveils his real purpose for making contact. He wants to know if he has offended me. This is because I have not bothered to visit him these past months. The speculations he makes as to the cause of my distance are laborious, so I will not record them here. Let me say only that he wonders if it was our discussion about the octopus pot or the things he said about Plato. When I read this, I laughed bitterly. All I could see at that moment were eight bodies on crosses.

I have not written in this journal since then. I do not know why. There is something depressed in my spirit. The second letter cured this swiftly, but of that I will write farther along.

I returned to the hill of crucifixion some hours later, bringing wine mixed with oils of myrrh and clove, which deaden pain. Again, no mourners or curiosity seekers were present. The guard was not there. In fact, no one was there, except crows and vultures tearing bits from the bodies. They were all dead. I bowed my head and thanked the gods that it was finished. In the face of death, which exercises godlike powers over us, we swiftly return to half-belief, or hope, in more benevolent gods.

I returned a week later to make sure—rather, to reassure myself—that the corpses had been removed and had been buried or burned. But no scrap of dignity had been allowed them. The bodies were still on the crosses, left by the Romans as a warning to potential criminals. The flesh was desiccated and dark brown, like dried smoked meat, strips torn from them by raptors, the faces sunken, eyes missing, ants and other insects swarming. The smell made me vomit. Here, I thought, when my stomach was more than empty, *here* is civic policy made manifest. *Here*, the underbelly of *pax* and *iustitia*!

I will say no more about it.

About two hours after Gaius' inquiry, another letter came. It was from my Loukas! Though a brief note, it is a relief to have news of him. He has returned to Caesarea, where he found our letters waiting for him. He promises to write soon, a reply worthy of his beloved parents and sisters, he says, and hopes to include with it the further volumes of his growing manuscript. He is in good health and good company.

I can write no more today.

*

[Journal entry, January 7, A.D. 65]

Gortyna
Poseideion—Ianuarius

Two days passed, and I had not the heart to reply to Gaius' note nor to wander over to see him at home. The impasse was resolved by a second message, which turned out to be an invitation.

> *Salve!*
>
> I wish to consult with my physician, if I still have one. I wish to speak with my friend, if he yet considers me such. The fault, I feel certain, whatever it may be, is mine. Do me kindness, Theophilos, and come to see me. Will you eat with me at midday?
>
> Gaius

And so, with reluctance, I went.

I found him in his garden pruning a fruit tree with a small curved knife. Barefoot and wearing only a rough *tunica*, he could have been mistaken for a slave, if it were not for the confident authority engraved in every line of his face. He is in his sixties like me, though his hair is still black and mine is now silvered. When he welcomed me heartily, I could not retain more than a sliver of my aversion to the Roman ethos of the place and the man. I also reminded myself silently that of the several Romans I have known in my life, this one least embodies their worst characteristics. I noted that he had lost a good deal of weight about the belly.

"How are your feet?" I asked.

"No pain now", he smiled. "I obeyed your instructions and am glad of it."

"Good", I nodded, and waited for more.

"Won't you share a meal with me? I had it prepared in case you came."

"Well, here I am, so let us eat."

He clapped me on the shoulder and led the way into the atrium. There, couches had been arranged beside the pool. We sat down and reclined. Two slaves brought salvers of small meats to awaken the appetite and placed them beside us on hexagonal rosewood tables. Another untied my sandals and put them neatly by my feet. Into two small cups Gaius poured wine half-diluted with water, which is their custom. Often enough he has told me that only barbarians drink unmitigated wine. Needless to say, we Greeks thin our wine with water too, depending on the occasion, but never to the extent that Romans do. As for myself, unmitigated is exactly how I prefer it, the richer and stronger the better. But he is the host and I am the guest.

There followed a courteous three-course meal, plain and simple, as befits a retired soldier who cultivates the more manly ways of the lost republican era.

We ate but said little.

Today the doors remained open—a signal—we would not discuss matters that other ears would bear away into the insatiable gossip markets of the streets.

"A long absence between our dialogues", he said with an inquiring smile.

"I have been ill", I explained.

"You have recovered fully, I hope."

I nodded in affirmation. In my mind's eye I saw the decaying meat of human bodies. I nearly smelled them but put the image away from me.

"I am glad", said Gaius. "I hope, as well, that you know how highly I value our friendship."

"Thank you", I answered mildly and with a wan smile. "Yes, we are able to discuss many subjects of mutual interest."

"You have grown formal during your illness."

"Merely fatigued. It has been a slow recovery."

"I hear that you stride around the city walls at great speed."

"It builds up the strength."

"I should do more of it myself." He patted his belly. "I have been retraining this old war-horse, but all it wants to do is graze in pastures."

"Do not listen to its groans of complaint. Be the commander."

He grinned at this and said: "Now I am assured there is no serious rift between us."

"There is none personal."

"Is there one impersonal?"

I said nothing.

"You mask your soul's expression", he said sadly. "I see it in your eyes. If it is not a personal offense, what is it?"

"I saw the crucifixion of the eight last autumn."

"The eight?" he said, frowning, as if struggling to understand. "There have been crucifixions this year, I am told, but none have I seen firsthand. Criminals, no doubt."

"It must be."

"It has blown upon the embers of your mistrust."

"Not mistrust in you, Gaius. Weariness over the condition of the world. And this island is my world."

"It is now my world also. It is my home. But why did it strike you so hard? Crucifixion is nothing new; you have seen it before, I am sure. Did you know any of the criminals?"

I shook my head. His eyes continued to observe me, not probing, but I think trying to understand what I felt. I was in no mood to explain, because, among other reasons, no good would have come from it. No words of mine would change policies and laws.

It seemed the right moment to change the subject. "How did you hear I stride about the hills?" I asked.

He shrugged. "The traffic in gossip is unceasing. My wife told me. She heard it from the governor's wife."

"Really", I laughed involuntarily. "The governor's wife?"

"They are bosom friends."

"How very fortunate for you."

He gave me the cold look this comment deserved. He refilled our cups.

"You will never trust me."

"Why do you desire my trust? What useful purpose is it to you?"

"No practical use, Theophilos. But a man grows old and ponders the truths of life, if he is wise. And though I am not wise, I wish to ponder them regardless of my faults, which are many."

This, at last, was a glimmer of the Gaius I had first been drawn to. He is a proud man, mistaking, as do all his race, the outer postures of arrogance for confident resolve. But there is more to him. Early on, indeed from the time when I brought him back from the mouth of death all those years ago, I knew he was without hubris. I should say, rather, that he was one of those least infected by it. A man with little hubris in his blood is capable of much good that evades the mighty and the clever.

So, I decided to risk a new step: "How do you get along with the governor?" I asked.

Without hesitation, but only after getting up and closing all the room's doors, he said:

"I get along very well with the governor. We are most cordial with each other. He has been careful to host the necessary and symbolic number of banquets at which the illustrious Gaius Publius Varus is among the guests of honor. We do business also. Only last week I was in his office to argue a reduction of the export tax on my wine. I asked him if he is enjoying his stay in Crete. He replied emphatically that he enjoyed it greatly and that he had just received a letter from the emperor commending him for the reduction of crime on the island."

Gaius paused and looked upward at the skylight above the pool. Without breaking his gaze, he said:

"Hundreds of years ago, one of your own poets wrote that 'Cretans have ever been liars, bestial, and lazy drunkards.'"

"Ah, you have read Epimenides."

"Er, no. The governor has that line inscribed on a slate hanging on the wall behind his desk."

"In Latin?"

"In both languages. I presume he wishes all suppliants to get the point."

"Doubtless it helps reduce crime."

"Indeed", Gaius said in an arch tone. He paused a moment, returned his gaze to my face, and went on:

"He knows that my father was a senator, my grandfather a consul, and my uncle a general and that for hundreds of years our house produced such men. He too has the masks of his ancestors in his home, blackened by age, but not blackened in name—at least not by any *unusually* vile crime we know of. He and I are from the dwindling ranks of the old great families. His wife and my wife are both from families of the *equites* class and are compatible in this way. Neither of them has ever ridden a horse, nor have their fathers, the knights, ever ridden one properly. But a fortune of a million sesterces guarantees a position in society that is in some ways better than inherited rank. Less honor but more power. The governor's wife hates it here—she is passionately lonely for Rome's stimulations and for her equestrian and patrician friends, the *splendidi*. My wife is a temporary substitute. They both understand completely this arrangement. They both know that the women of Rome rule the world. And of course they have much to discuss about the management of the difficult, highly placed political men to whom they are married."

I smiled appreciatively.

"But in truth," he went on, "we are not at ease in each other's company for other reasons. He suspects, rightly, that I do not respect the way in which he came to his seat of power—an uncle of senatorial rank, who doted on him as a boy, moves among the innermost circle on the Palatine, an *amicus Caesaris*. I have known numerous men like the governor all my life, among the officer class of the army, in the law *basilicae* and in the *curia*. The core of their souls, and their spines, is made of a soft yellow metal called ambition."

"Were you never ambitious?"

"Only on fields of battle—battles against barbarians, I hasten to add. This man desires more than the high seat in Crete. He sees it as a stepping-stone to higher and higher posts. He has already risen a level above his capabilities, yet he wants more. And he knows that I see through him. That is why he becomes nervous in my company and blusters overmuch."

"Are you nervous in his company?"

"Yes, though I hide it well. Such men, you understand, would slit your throat for a wider stripe of purple on their togas."

He stared at the floor for a few moments, sighed, and said, "Seneca is dead."

"The Spanish Seneca, the writer?"

"Yes. He was obliged by Nero to take his own life. Thus concludes his praiseworthy effort to mentor a shining emperor-philosopher. Hopefully, Plato in his heaven will take note of the incident."

"Plato would have predicted it."

"Would he have? Perhaps. In any event, all men of intelligence and culture now understand the nature of this beast-god who calls himself a poet."

"I see it is true what you say—that you trust me."

"I put my life into your hands. But then, it was in your hands thirty years ago and I came to no harm. Besides, I know you keep your own counsel."

"Physicians would not long survive if they did not guard their tongues."

"And physicians' wives?"

"Prudent physicians guard their wives from temptation, since gossip is gold coinage. But my Paeonia, though I keep her from knowledge of the weaknesses of my patients, is not a gossip. Only I and our cook suffer from her tongue."

"You are a blessed man."

"Yes, I am."

"And that, my dear Theophilos, is why I am grateful to the gods for a Greek friend."

Despite myself, I was moved.

We sipped from our cups. After a suitable silence, he looked up and said: "What use am I to you?"

"No use. Friendship, while it may be useful, is not built on usefulness."

"I agree, but is there nothing I can do for you?"

"You have already promised me a generous favor."

"Ah, yes. Are you still resolved to accept it?"

"I am, if Loukas delays his return another year."

"You worry about your son's fate a great deal, I think, in the manner of good fathers. But what can you do about it? He has chosen his life, and he is a man."

"Did he choose? This, really, is what worries me—did he choose?"

*

[Journal entry, January 8, A.D. 65]

Gortyna
Poseideion—Ianuarius

My journal entry was interrupted yesterday by screams—someone bellowing for help through the look-hole at the front gate. Another crisis, which devoured my time in the surgery until dusk when I found myself too weary and too eye-strained to write by lamplight. I went to bed, my arms around Paeonia for half the night, something we have done less of during the past several years. She awoke before dawn with a cry and subsequent tears. She said she had dreamed of something terrible that approaches. It will strike our family, she is sure. She has had this kind of dream a number of times, and nothing terrible happened. The surgery the day before had been full of the truly terrible. My life is a chain of terribles. Trying to cheer her, I laughed and teased and forced her to tell me her dream.

"You ran into a burning house", she sobbed. "I begged you and begged you not to do it, but you wouldn't listen to me. You went into the fire to save children who were burning inside."

"Did I bring them out?"

"I don't know. I woke up."

"Nightly do all souls dream. The little theaters in our minds enact plays, and most of them are not written by a genius."

"At times the gods speak through dreams."

"Seldom."

"They come to warn us when we will not heed a danger. When a man will not listen to his wife."

"I am at this moment listening to my wife."

"But will you heed?"

"What is there to heed, Paeonia? Listen to the calm, listen to the night birds and the wind. Peace is on the city."

"Peace is fragile. At any moment it may be broken without warning."

"You fear too much."

"You fear too little."

I held her closely.

*

No patients came to the surgery this morning. I was caught dozing in my chair by Tranquilatus, who woke me to present a sprig of almond from the garden, the first sign that spring is approaching. It is too early in the season for it to blossom, but the bud has popped from the aromatic bark.

"Wondrous is this morning", he said. "You should go out and see it." He explained no more and went away.

Later, Calliope, surly of face but for once not caustic in tongue, brought me a cup of hot wine without being asked.

"To keep away the chill, Master. Do not go out today, for evil is abroad this morning. An ill portent fell on the city last night—snow, though it is now melting. All Crete is covered by it."

A fall of snow! An extraordinary occurrence! I have seen it three other times in my life and never found it to be the harbinger of evil.

An unusual night—ice and fire. Now, a day for my warmest wool *chiton*, girded at the waist to reach my ankles and over it the thicker wool *himation* with a hood. Thus bundled, I went for a walk. The air was cold, though the sun was busily heating the dampness off the ground, making wisps of fog. It was very pleasant to be out in it, aesthetically, as if one walked among immortal souls on the Isles of the Blessed. However, my ankles and feet were soon chilled and prompted me to envy the ways of Persians and northern barbarians who wear the ungodly uncomfortable trousers on their legs and soft wool tubes inside sandals and boots. I returned home to sit close by the burning coals in my brazier and to complete my account of yesterday's meeting with Gaius. It was significant and needs recording.

I asked him what he knew about the followers of the Judaean teacher *Christos*. He gave me a simple sketch of the man's life, which by all accounts ended badly. He was but one of the many reformers and rebels thrown up by that people. I did not let on that I already knew the story, did not mention Loukas' chronicle. It was interesting to note the variations in Gaius' account compared to my son's. Loukas is gathering knowledge firsthand, Gaius merely recounted the events as they are now circulating in the world, mutating as they pass from person to person, from one psychological *kosmos* to another, with all the prejudice and embellishment this implies. Though more than thirty years have passed since they occurred, the basic events seemed to match. However, the personality of the Christos portrayed in the two accounts is markedly different. There is interpretation at work—which is inevitable. I mistrust both versions, since Gaius is too far from the subject and Loukas too close to it.

"Are there followers of this cult on Crete?" I asked.

"Oh yes, quite a few, and growing in number I would guess. The offer of victory over death is a potent drug. The unlettered and poor leap for it hungrily."

"So, you have met some of them."

"Yes. They are quiet people, generally. Quite harmless, I think." His face flashed irritably for a moment. "Nero has found it convenient to blame the great fire on them."

"Is there any truth in the matter?"

"No, none. It is not their way. The ones I have met would shun violence in any form. It is ridiculous to think of them burning down half the imperial city."

"Some say they are a branch of the Jewish rebels called Zealots who are always agitating, ever inciting Judaea to revolt."

"The Zealots are another Jewish faction. These Christos Jews are of a different sort altogether—in fact, it is something new among them. I spoke with one of their leaders here on Crete shortly after I returned, a man from Antioch named Titus or Titos. Strangely, he is not a Jew. He told me that people of many races now believe in the message of the one they call 'anointed'—a Greek term or a Jewish term, I am not sure which."

"*Christos* is the Greek for 'anointed', that is certain. The concept among the Jews, however, is particular to them. In their minds it means that a man is set apart for a special purpose by their deity, who is singular. According to their religion, there are no other gods. For a millennium they have awaited the coming of a high anointed one—whose mission is like no other."

"And that is the man executed under the procurator Pilatus! It puzzles me that anyone still believes in him."

"Apparently his teachings are of some value. As you know, I am much attached to the teachings of Socrates and Aristotle."

"Wasn't your Aristotle the pedagogue for Alexander the Great?"

"Yes. Evidence of the value of education, right there."

"Or the failure of education, one might argue. Were his conquests due to the blood of a Macedonian warrior-king in him or the seed of reason planted in his mind?"

"An excellent question, Gaius. We must dialogue more about it someday. But tell me, is it illegal to be a follower of Christos?"

"Not at all—at least not on the law books. You should know that Romans tolerate just about any kind of religion, as long as it is traditional and has its interesting devotions. We absorb everything. But new religions are regarded with suspicion, and this one looks more like extreme *superstitio* than *pietas*. The *imperium* probably considers them, perhaps only remotely, a potential threat."

A line I had written to Loukas came to mind. *It will overturn the world.*

Gaius continued: "I would wager that Tiberius and Caligula crucified a few of Christos' followers, but that was just part of the general madness. Nero is different. He loathes them and has been putting some to death for 'reasons of state'. As for blaming the fire on them, hardly anyone in Rome believes they are responsible for it. It is human nature to blame, and often to blame falsely, yet I doubt that any but the most ignorant have accepted the emperor's lie. The rest know who threw the torch."

I glanced quickly at the doors. Gaius observed me and smiled to himself.

"One of my house slaves goes to their meetings in the city. He is better for it, I would say, so I see no argument against the cult. The man Titus came to me to ask permission, since my policy was to refuse the slaves leave to roam beyond my walls after dark. And that is how I met him."

Gaius laughed abruptly. "He invited me to visit their community, a house where they gather for prayers, near the south gate. I thanked him but declined the offer. Then he said that learned Greeks throughout the world have joined them and tactfully mentioned that more than one senator in Rome has attended the talks of their teachers, and that some of the patrician class have become believers in their *Kyrios*. This was surprising news but failed to convince me that I should be involved in any way other than tolerance."

"Was he a fanatic or mystic of some kind?"

"He did not strike me as such. There was nothing suspicious about him; he seemed to be a dedicated yet reasonable man, and if his religion is superstitious it does not appear to be the extreme kind. In any event, I leave well enough alone. Let them do what they do. Three slaves from my vineyards, and my accountant, are involved with them now, and are in better humor and give better service because of it. As I said, it is harmless, and perhaps consoles them, for their lives are hard."

"I would like to meet this Titus or Titos."

"I hear he has gone. For several years he came and went and came again, organizing their communities throughout the island, appointing their elders. But his work is completed, and where he is now I do not know."

Gaius yawned. It was time for his daily nap. It was time for my nap also.

We bid each other good day, and I made my way homeward through crowded streets, the whole populace, it seemed, coming out from their winter shelters to bask beneath the cloudless sky. There was no indication that the mildness of this late afternoon would change overnight to portentous snow and dreams of fire.

Paeonia and Calliope made a good supper. Lentils and onions, steamed shredded cabbage—which is my favorite, the best vegetable in the world—black olives in vinegar, and a dish of boiled octopus.

*

[Journal entry, January 9, A.D. 65]

Gortyna
Poseideion—Ianuarius

Today I felt drawn to reread the account Loukas sent me last spring.

I reread the opening lines:

84

Many have undertaken to compile a narrative of the events that have been fulfilled within our midst ...

What does this mean? Does he see a fulfillment happening in his presence? If so, what kind of fulfillment?

... precisely as those events were transmitted to us by the original eyewitnesses and ministers of the word.

Who are these "eyewitnesses"? How clear are their eyes? How intelligent are their minds? What are their motives? What do they hope to gain by it?

I have decided to set it in writing for you, my dear Theophilos, so that you may come to understand how reliable is their testimony, and would desire to learn more of it.

The chronicle again provoked in me a deep disturbance, an unease that grew into nameless dread. I looked at the story from several angles. If the events described are literally true, they are the most important thing that has ever happened in the world. If they are not true, then they are an apotheosis of delusion—one, moreover, that has taken my son from me. It may lure him to an early death as well, if he does not break its spell.

I sense the void ahead of me, the precipice over which all men must fall into nonbeing. Our songs, our poetry, our laughter, our myths, and our petty debates with death are our attempts to ignore the very pit of nothingness that is our end.

But suppose it happened as described, the events related more or less precisely, yet the interpretation of it has gone badly askew? This third possibility presents more problems than the first two. Confusion spreads from the split between the original acts and the ensuing theories that are spun from them.

Where was I when all of this apparently happened? Their Christos died about thirty years ago. That would place me in Gortyna, a young physician working night and day to build my practice, newly married and the father of two little girls. It would place Loukas in his parents' home in Thessalonike, playing his childhood games or splashing about in the shallows of the river Axios. Both of us going about our small affairs while all around us the *kosmos* reeled in astonishment!

It is abundantly evident that the *kosmos* is not staggering in amazement over this Christos. The world continues its relentless course along the track of time, just as it always has. Nothing has changed. If anything, human affairs have grown worse.

The chronicle is delusion. I fear it more than ever.

*

[Journal entry, May 22, A.D. 65]

Iraklion
Thargelion—Maius

Can it be so many months since I found myself with a free day in which to take up my journal again? There have been plenty of opportunities, but I have been restless and distracted, disinclined to record my ponderous musings since there is too much self-examination in me as it is. A patient who is always pestering his physician, discussing every potential ailment and imaginary ache, soon finds himself with little time to live, and thus he loses the state of health that is maintained by the proper balance of action and meditation.

I am writing in my room at an inn near Iraklion. It is a new establishment, and the owner must be wealthy, for he has taken care to enclose the windows in glass. The house stands close by the sea, and there are winds. In summer this is nature's balm, in winter its scourge. Now spring has arrived, the winds are fair, the turquoise sea heaving but not turbulent. The rhythm of surf meeting land soothes but does not dominate the mind. Gazing down the rocks to the shore, I see the first swimmers of the season, diving for sponges and shellfish.

Earlier today I climbed again to the theater Loukas and I made on the promontory when he was a boy and first came to us. I was last there a year ago, but so familiar is it to me, so full of memories this small space, that it seemed I had not been away for more than a moment. It is a circular flat *discus* a tall man's length in diameter, surrounded by a waist-high wall of white stones. Around one half of the arc, we had positioned larger flat stones as audience benches. Today I sat on one and remembered the times we had recited passages from tragedies and comedies. He was often alone here, more and more as he grew older.

Thessalonike is in my thoughts. The pains of my two-year apprenticeship are long faded now, and only the major scenes return. These are primarily about personal tragedies and comedies. But they are also about the figures who played portentous roles in my formation. The mind recalls such people vaguely at first; then the inner eye focuses and we see them looming large in our old age, though they were considered minor when we knew them. It is interesting how we recall events that teach us by hindsight though we gave them little thought at the time they occurred. Of course, it is because we did not understand their meaning. But how generous of the gods to allow us our life seasons, a time to act and a time to meditate. There are periods when we do both, but the meditation is weakest when we are young, for then we are gathering experience as the harvester gathers grain. The grain is later ground and baked into bread. And if it is good bread, we eat.

I see Xanthippos seated on a tree stump in the dooryard of his hut, a little old man no taller than Tranquilatus, rocking backward and forward, staring upward into the air above him, two moons in his eyes, issuing forth a stream of instructions that I nervously, with some error, obeyed. We lost few patients. I with my hands and he with his mind saved more hopeless cases than any other surgeon I have met in my long life.

"You must accept, Theophilos, that in trying to save life— always to save life—you will find yourself, at times, death's instrument."

I was too easily cast down by failure in those years, and he sometimes heard me weeping on my pallet in the dark of the night. "Ooo-ooo, so young", he sang like a grandfather to a sickly child whenever I succumbed to the mood of grief or more dangerous discouragement. At such moments I would hear him crooning his *ooo-ooo* from his bedroom, connected to mine by an open doorway, separated only by a hanging cloth. I hear it now, and it makes me smile. I hated my weakness then, my propensity to tears, my too-much feeling. Little by little, he taught me that it was not weakness, after all, that afflicted me, but the apprenticeship of love.

"To love mankind merely in the abstract", he once said, "is one face of a single coin, and on its other side is hatred of mankind in the abstract. To love *in truth* is to serve the suffering person before you, and to do what you can to assist him."

Another day he said: "You must serve the ill or wounded patient—even the most vile in form or character—as if he were a visiting god. Which, indeed, he is."

Yes, he was as much a philosopher as he was a *technites* of human flesh. Indeed, he showed me that man is not a mechanism but a mysterious being in whom *soma* and *psyche* are one. The soul, he said, is eternal. When the body falls back into the earth, the soul rises.

"But Elysion is under the earth", I protested. "Surely the soul goes to that happy land below! Or else, if it travels to the Isles of the Blessed, it yet holds to the world. In neither case does it rise above."

"It rises. The shape of the *kosmos* is not as we think; above and below have different meanings than we apprehend, for we are misled by appearances, bound by the invisible hand that pulls our feet onto the ground, as the plum and the olive invariably fall from the branch. Only with effort do we lift our feet, and never for long do we succeed."

"But that confirms *my* thought more than it does yours", I said.

This made him laugh hilariously—a rare but delightful occurrence—making him topple from his perch. With some irony I picked his little body off the ground and placed him upright onto the tree stump.

His philosophy was greatly put to the test by witches. His aversion to them seemed to me very akin to hatred.

Thessaly has ever been the home of sorcery, and Medea does not fail to produce her offspring, generation after generation. We even felt their presence in Macedonia. I remember one who came to Xanthippos, suffering from a massive infection of his arm, with black-blood in the veins, a condition aggravated by the filthy amulets hanging on his body. The hideous man had tried to treat the infection with poultices composed of wicked things, but none of this magic had succeeded in making him well. His health and his reputation were gravely at risk, and thus, secretly, he sought a genuine physician for help. My mentor was courteous enough and did not try to humiliate him. It was plain to me, however, that he despised the witch and reduced his service to the basic physical necessities, completely masking his expression. Of course, I was to be his hands. That part I will skip over quickly—needless to say I hated the procedure, and the witch himself. This was no god. This was an extremely cunning, subtle, and dangerous mad dog—our natural enemy.

I washed the entire arm with ashes and oil, then with water. The process needed repeating several times until a clean human arm appeared beneath the filth. Then, obeying Xanthippos, I cut open the black veins and drained them. Heating the entire arm with boiled oil cooled to a proper temperature opened the veins still further, until only red blood flowed. This was followed by more cleansing. This procedure was one my father had not taught me. Moreover, the next step was new to me as well. A vial of pine spirits was heated to the burning point and poured in a thin trickle into all the incisions, which caused screams and incomprehensible incantations to erupt from our patient. Then I washed the entire mess with rose water and packed it with healing herbal unguents. Finally, I wrapped the arm with a linen bandage, which in turn I smeared with oils that ward off ill vapors.

Done, disgusted, my face doubtless full of revulsion, I sat back on my heels. The witch scrambled to his feet, leered, and warned us that if any word of our meeting was spoken to others, he would curse us. He took the trouble to toss a coin at our feet, bared his hind end in insult, and stomped out the door and away into the woods.

"He will recover", said Xanthippos in a mild tone, after a merciful breeze had cleared the air.

"Unfortunately", I muttered.

And, for once, my mentor did not rebuke me.

I recount this unpleasant experience because of what occurred some years later. But more about that farther along.

During the latter half of my second year at Thessalonike, my parents died in the pneumonic plague that had struck Crete. It was like a demon, that plague—sudden soaring of the body temperature, blood in the sputum, death within three or four days. Unlike the ordinary lung sickness that fills up the lungs with fluid and can kill with equal finality, this plague acted swiftly and was highly contagious. Its causes were unknown. One could easily have believed it was a punishment from the gods, were it not for the fact that it invariably touched a land first at its seaports, which indicated that it was borne about the world on ships. From the ports it always spread inland, sometimes burning itself out before it destroyed everything in its path. But wherever it went, it killed many, some old and some young, some weak and some strong, usually leaving survivors to tell the tale. In the spring of that year my sister arrived by ship unexpectedly, and she brought with her the dreadful news. She was alone in the world, save for me.

I loved my sister as the apple of my eye. She was the child of my parents' old age, eight years younger than I. Her name was Theantheia, and one of my granddaughters is named for her. The name was a play on words, for my father loved both flowers and God. He was devoted to the writings of Plato and believed, for reasons that are unclear to me even now, in a single God, a good Creator. He told me when I was a boy that the original intention of this God was benevolent, yet the world had been damaged by a dark archon of the heavens, one of the *angeloi* who had gone bad and in malicious spite had come down to break or befoul God's work of art. I found this incomprehensible, since it seemed to me illogical that evil could proceed from its creating Good. When I voiced this objection to him, my father said:

"Logic does not *contain* the universe. Rather, the universe contains logic, for logic is merely an instrument of man's thought, and man too is a creature, limited by his nature and contained within the universe."

Unconvinced, I kept silence.

"Moreover, Theophilos, we are within an epic tale, as great or greater than the myths of the gods. The story has not yet come to its climax and its completion, and what those will be we cannot guess."

Thus, the origin of his children's names.

Thea was very distraught when she arrived, full of grief and haunted by fears. Our house in Gortyna was locked up and guarded by a neighbor, but nothing remained for her there save the bones of our parents and a multitude of sorrows. She wanted me to sell the place, if any would buy, and for us to begin a new life together in Macedonia. I was undecided. I missed the island greatly, its warmth and color—above all its *homeness*. We agreed that the decision could wait until I completed my apprenticeship under Xanthippos.

I moved my sleeping pallet into the old man's room at his invitation, and Thea took mine. Henceforth, we two men enjoyed a time of better food and much better humors, for the lack of a woman's presence in our midst had been a lamentable gap. For her part, my sister came to love the old fellow as a father. He was as wise in the ways of the heart as he was in the ways of medicine, and she needed him sorely to salve the ache of the missing. Throughout my whole life no better man have I known. Close to forty years have passed, and still I miss him. I loved my mother and my father as the givers of my life, as the ones who loved me well and trained me in the way I should go, but it seems to me now that we love most in this world the person who has been the highest good for us. If I could check my tears, I would write about him at length.

A few months after Thea's arrival, Timocrates, a son of Heron of Thessalonike, entered our lives. At the time, our patients were the poor of the region, since Xanthippos' reputation, which had once been great, had long been eclipsed by his blindness. It was only now slowly recovering with my aid. But the recovery was at an early stage, comprised of a scattering of lesser merchants who had begun to consult him about minor ailments.

Our first sight of Timo was the morning he simply appeared in the open doorway, knocked once on the post with a humble dip of the head, and took a step back into the dust of the yard, waiting politely for an invitation to enter. He was a man near my age, tall and broad-shouldered, holding himself in dignity but without haughtiness. He was bronze-haired and bearded, the hair braided into a thick cord and wrapped about his temples in the ancient style—as if he had just stepped off the *Argo*. He was dressed somewhat formally in a fine linen *chiton* and wool belt, the garment hitched high for brisk walking. About his shoulders hung the folds of a dark blue *himation*, and on his large feet were sandals made of clumsy leather straps that I later learned he had cut and woven by his own hand. He seemed an odd, if admirable, sort. Xanthippos called him in.

I cannot remember what he wanted—probably some advice for his father. Xanthippos listened carefully to his voice, as he always did with newcomers, making his assessment of whatever character might lie behind the words and tones. Coming to some obscure conclusion, he asked the visitor to lunch, and throughout the years they knew each other, his good opinion of the man never changed. I do not know how he was able to assess so rightly, for voices can deceive as elegantly as visible demeanor. Clearly, this Timo was decent enough and probably possessed some excellent qualities, but this was a conclusion that demanded no effort. I refer instead to something deeper about character and temperament that is not immediately apprehensible to most men. Though Xanthippos *may* have been wrong about people at times, I never saw it.

I must now leap across much that could be told and read with interest, if only by my natural descendants. Timo was struck dumb by his first sight of Thea, lowering his eyes and whispering his thanks when she served him a plate of beans. In similar fashion, she lowered her eyes and cast not a glance at him for the remainder of his stay. Needless to say, his visits to our house steadily increased in number, and he must have stretched his mind to the breaking point to find justifications for them. I do not recall when or how they bridged their mutual silence. It was blind Xanthippos who first saw where it would go, and he told me well in advance. He knew, even before the young couple knew, that they had been pinned together for life by the spear of the divine. Such love is sought after by all, and known by the few, to whom it is given from above and can never be seized by human will.

I lingered in Thessalonike for a few months after their marriage—long enough to see Thea safe in a home of her own, a small house on the hills above the port, cherished by a man who, if not wealthy, was comfortably employed by his own father in the small shipping business owned by the family. Timo was a hard worker, honest in all practice and true in all speech, also a maker of semiuseful things such as better sandals, ingenious water clocks, and atonal musical instruments that were test pieces for his later inventions. Lettered, he owned books—not many but well selected. He liked riddles and fables that conveyed a point, and he would tell them in his slow, thoughtful way, if asked, though never did he press his thoughts on others. Surprisingly diffident, this mighty fellow was one who would have stood firm at Thermopylae had it occurred in our times. Timo had become our friend, and had I remained with them, as they pleaded with me to do, he would have been the brother I did not have, for my parents lost five children at birth and through sickness, leaving only my sister and me. I had ever missed what others so thought-lessly enjoy. And now I would sorely miss them both.

I embarked on a ship bound for Crete only when Thea's belly had begun to swell with the baby who would become Loukas.

*

[Journal entry, May 26, A.D. 65]

Gortyna
Thargelion—Maius

I am home from Iraklion, physically refreshed, invigorated as well by memories, in my melancholy fashion. The humors of the psyche have always intrigued me. Much depends on the body's health but equally as much on the training of the thought's attention, like a river course that must be contained and directed by strong embankments, lest floods break out and the river spread a mile wide and an inch deep. Or worse, drain away entirely into stagnant swamps, losing its true self. The melancholic temperament is most disposed to this, though it should be kept in mind that there is happy melancholia and miserable melancholia. For the most part, mine is happy. Yet today I feel it slip away into pools of grief.

I have never before written about it, and now I think the time has come to do so. Catharsis is often pleasurable in the-ater and can be useful for the bowels, yet it is an unreliable medicine. However, let me operate a little on myself.

More than a year ago, I wrote to Loukas that I had seen him in his infancy. This is not strictly accurate. I meant that I had seen him at the origins of his life, as he grew within his mother's womb. I was in Crete when he was born, and my only mental picture of him until his eleventh year was com-posed of details sent to me in letters from his parents. His personality, his physical appearance, his small triumphs and woes were conveyed through other eyes, with much left to the imagination.

Even so, from the beginning I felt I knew him. I saw him in infancy, in the sense that he was surely present and alive behind the screen; I did not see his hidden face, yet that face was surely there and I loved it. There are some who believe that a child is not a human being until he passes through the body-gates into the light and becomes visible. There are others who consider him disposable until he can speak. As for myself, I hold with neither of these ridiculous opinions, since it would be as well to say that a man does not exist as long as he is inside his house and cannot be seen, then suddenly exists when he puts his head outside his door and says good day to you.

No, no, the world is sick, and its fevers derive from a swamp in the mind. The one who despises a hidden face is blind to his own face, or if he does see his own, he fails to value it. All killers kill their true selves before their bodily deaths, and take others down with them before the end. Hippocrates knew this.

Eleven years after moving back to Crete, word had reached me by various means that the buboes plague had struck here and there in Attica and Euboea and then over the course of a year had begun to appear northward in the smaller ports of Thessaly. It was creeping up the coast past Olympos and would soon be rounding the Thermaic Gulf and heading toward Thessalonike. That much I patched together, but I allayed my fears by telling myself that it had traveled slowly, which meant that it was borne from one place to another either by human carriers on foot or by the small boats that ply short stretches of coastline along the gulf. It might bypass Thessalonike altogether or burn itself out before reaching the city.

Then a Heron ship ported at Iraklion. The moment it dropped anchor, a crewman came ashore and ran from there across the island, stopping neither for food nor water, nor the threat of brigands in the pass. He outran all obstacles and by midday reached me in my surgery—my father's surgery it once had been. Panting as if his chest would burst open, he lay himself down on the floor while I read the letter he had brought. It was from Thea. The plague had reached the city; all physicians had fled, save for Xanthippos, who had had the sickness and recovered but was very weak and could do nothing. Timo was down, but there were signs of rallying. Others in the household had been struck, including three of their children, and on the morning of her writing she had felt the onslaught of shivering, then sudden heat and soreness in her body. She begged me to come in haste. Her father-in-law's ship would bring me to her.

I dropped everything and gathered what medical baggage I thought might be of help, and within the hour, after a tearful embrace with Paeonia and Theodosia, and a kiss to sleeping Mila, I set off with the runner back across the island. Because I was capable of no more than a trot and needed frequent stops to catch my breath, it took us eight hours to reach Iraklion. Arriving there, we quickly boarded. The captain up-anchored and set the sails and pointed the bow to the north.

The letter was dated two weeks before; the winds that brought the Heron ship to Crete had been the best. Now we were forced to tack this way and that as we made our way with torturous slowness through the Mirtoan Sea toward the Aegean. The voyage took more than four weeks.

As the ship eased toward the wharfs of Thessalonike, I scanned the city with my eyes, noting that during my eleven-year absence it had grown, with its waterside borders spreading and several new villas on the upper slopes. Few people were about, and these moved with burdened posture or with stealth. Columns of smoke rose from a dozen large fires burning in various sections of the lower town. When we landed, the captain and crew scattered into the city, for it was their home port and their families resided here. I made straightway up the hill to the house of Timo and Thea.

Hoping for good news to greet me, I rounded the corner of a block of houses and spied the white walls and red roof just ahead in the large yard of olive trees. Then I quickened my steps, for smoke was rising above the compound walls, and the front gate had been torn open and lay broken in the dust of the roadway. Through the gate I ran in haste and came to a full stop, for there before me was a spectacle that chilled me to the bone. The house was in flames, and by its open door stood several figures, among them one whom I at first only vaguely recognized. Stood? No, he danced! An old man leaping about, screaming and chanting, jangling amulets and making lewd gestures, along with three women doing the same. Then I recognized him. It was the witch whom Xanthippos and I had cured twelve years past. He screeched as he whirled in circles, this spawn of Medea, brandishing his two quite healthy arms in paroxysms of hateful glee.

I will not record here what the demon said. Let it be understood that he was calling down curses upon all the "brood of Herons" and upon his old enemy "the thief Xanthippos", who were burning within, the alive and the dead, upon their funeral pyre—he screamed the news exultantly.

I would have struck him with my staff, had I not instantly leaped toward the flames in the doorway, for I could not tell if any might still be alive within, and I intended to pull them out. But a hand grabbed the back of my cloak and hurled me down the doorsteps to the ground. When I tried to scramble to my feet, I was held fast by the butt of a wooden staff planted in the center of my chest. A man bent over me—not one of the witches but one of the onlookers.

"There are none alive in those flames", he said. "All were dead of the sickness before the witch torched the house."

"All?" I cried, covering my face.

"All", he replied without feeling, for it was no concern to him.

And so I knelt in the dust and watched the flames devour the house and the ones I loved. I felt as if the world were ending. I could not move. I could not think. In time, the witches ceased their frenzy, gathered what they had looted from the house, and went away. The onlookers too gathered up their loot and departed, leaving me alone.

I lay in the grass of the yard that night, intending to retrieve the bones of the family when the fire was out. At dawn there were no flames left, only a heap of embers within the walls of an oven. There was nothing I could do until it cooled.

I returned to the waterfront and found that the ship I had arrived in was now gone. From there I next went to the House of Heron office by the waterfront, hoping to locate anyone from Timo's family to whom I might convey the bad news. I found the street door ripped off, the shuttered windows broken, and everything inside the building in disarray, parchment and shattered money boxes scattered about. In a back room I came upon a bed on which lay a man clenching a sword by his side. He had been stricken by the plague but had not died, yet he was weak. He raised the weapon to fend me off but could not sustain it, and it clattered to the floor.

"I must find Heron's kin", I explained. "Are you one of them?"

"A servant", he croaked. "Heron's kin are dead. There may be one still left—a son who lives on the hill with his wife and children."

"Timo?"

"Yes, him. Heron may be with them."

"They have all perished", I said, barely controlling my voice. He closed his eyes and turned his head to the wall.

I shook his shoulder. "Surely not all the Herons succumbed. Is there no one left?"

"Only Xanthippos, their friend."

"He died in Timo's house."

The man turned again to face me, puzzled. "But he is here. I heard his voice calling me a moment before you entered."

I found my old mentor in a back room, lying on a pallet, staring wide-eyed at nothing. I knelt by him and took his hand.

"Theophilos", he breathed, recognizing me by my touch. He was very weak, but not destroyed.

"Yes, it is me, my little father. I will look after you now. Fear nothing."

"I fear nothing, my son. But what of Thea and Timo? Why have they not come? I was the first to be brought here; the others were to follow later in the day, for the family was to board ship to flee the pestilence. Then I was forgotten, and no one has come these past five days, save the one in the other room who drove off the breakers and thieves. Is he alive still?"

"He is alive."

He nodded and nodded, and even produced a weary smile.

"Xanthippos, I have hard news to tell", I said, choking. "All have perished—the entire family."

A great sigh came from his mouth, and he closed his eyes.

When he had regained his composure he said, "Loukas alone remains."

"Loukas was among those who died."

"Then you have been to Pella. Did you give him proper funeral rites?"

I shook my head, though he could not see it.

"I have not been to Pella. What do you mean?" I asked.

He explained that three days before the first of the household fell ill, the boy had gone to visit his grandmother, who lived in a village on the river Axios, northwest of the city a half-day's journey by foot. A messenger had been sent to fetch him for the ship's departure.

I found a woman alive in a house on the next street block and asked her to care for the old man until my return. She was at first reluctant.

"You would put me into danger?" she complained with a whine. "This plague is a monster, eating the many and leaving the few. Why, it eats even the rats!"

I offered a purse full of coins if she would care for Xanthippos and vowed to give her as much again upon my return, if I found him alive and well. Warming to this incentive, she eagerly promised to hand him over in better condition than he had come to her.

With that, I set off on my journey. As I proceeded through the lowlands, the road was deserted, though plenty of birds and wild creatures were about and some domestic animals wandering without aim. Sheep grazed shepherdless, and more than one billy goat tried to bluff me into a panicked run. Now and then I spied lone human figures in the distance, walking through unharvested grainfields or standing in wary groups by the doors of their cottages. Once I passed a *decuria* of Roman soldiers sitting wearily in the grass by the roadside, unshaven and with their helmets off, among them two who lay groaning in the throes of infection. Were they headed to Thessalonike or away from it, I do not know, did not ask. Though at least six cohorts of Romans were usually in Macedonia, and doubtless a portion of them garrisoned in Thessalonike, these were the first I had seen. They paid me no mind, and I had no need to ask them for directions to the village, for I knew that it was on the Axios near the road.

Xanthippos had called it Pella, though I understood the reference as a general one. The village, in fact, was named Herakleia. I had visited it once with Timo, and there I had met his mother, who lived alone. She had ever resisted her husband's city life, being more at ease in her crude ancestral home among her lifelong neighbors and their rustic ways. It was a curious arrangement, but there was no enmity between the husband and wife, for Heron visited her frequently, sent his grandchildren to spend summers with her, and had accepted the truth that his wife's spirit would have faded in a fine home in city streets.

Despite its heroic name, the village was no more than a cluster of cottages sitting among its fields and orchards. It was known colloquially as "little Pella" or the "small toe of Pella", though the city was still a good many hours' walk beyond it. The road was its shin, and great Pella its head. The afternoon was far on by the time I came to the bridge over the river and spotted the roofs of Herakleia on the other side, at a distance of three stadia upstream. I crossed the bridge and turned off the road onto a footpath that brought me along beside the water. It was a bright day, with breezes blowing down out of the mountains in the north, with many birds flying about and singing.

As I came to the first houses, I saw the smoke of cook fires rising from some. Two children played in the dooryard of one. They were pale and thin but otherwise well. A woman's voice called from somewhere and was answered by another, hens clucked and pecked about, the dogs barked at me—all seemed normal. Try as I might, I could not remember which cottage was the grandmother's, for they all looked much alike. As I walked along the path between the dozen or so homes, I noticed that many of them seemed lifeless, their windows shuttered. A man carrying a pitchfork and a bucket of grain came out of a shed and stopped, startled by the sight of me.

"I am looking for the wife of Heron", I said. "Tell me, which is her house?"

Listlessly, he pointed to a cottage that stood on the edge of the village, shuttered and smokeless.

"Has the plague come to Herakleia?" I asked. "I am a physician and might help if there be any ill here."

"It did not pass us by", he answered with chin on his chest, his eyes staring at his feet. "Near half of us the gods struck down, and the few who recovered are now walking about. No physician is needed here."

"Then Heron's wife is among the living!"

He shook his head. "Old Pellene is dead. And so is the boy who was with her."

"Are you certain?" I cried.

"Three days have passed since we last saw the boy. Now the house is shuttered. No smoke and no face appears."

Stricken, I grew angry. "Did you not go to see if they needed your aid?"

"Save your wrath for an enemy. The stench of death comes from the place. We dare not enter a plague house to take the bodies for burning unless it be our own. We do what we can, for grief is lord in all houses, and there have been many to burn, and small ones to feed, though we have little strength for either task. Heron or his sons will come and do it."

"All Heron's kin are dead", I murmured and left him.

Like the entire village, the house of Pellene seemed normal to the eyes. Red hens pecked at seeds in the front yard, and a cherry tree loaded with fruit swayed heavily in the breeze. The stench of death was indeed upon the place. I tried the door latch, but it was locked from within. The window shutters would not give way to my hand. I found a thick length of firewood in a stack by the front step, and battered upon a window. It gave way with a crash, and I climbed inside the house.

It was the kitchen, and here I found the source of the smell. On a bed beside a brick oven, the woman lay curled in fetal position, as if asleep. Beside her on a low wooden table sat a bowl of uneaten fruit and a cup and water jug, half-empty and stagnant. Beside the open oven, a bundle of sticks lay unused. A pile of dirty rags had been heaped by the door, stained by blood and the effluent of the sickness. Someone had tended her during her dying hours.

It was a two-room dwelling, and I found him in the second chamber. The stench of death was as strong here as in the other room. I unlatched the shutters and threw them open, letting in light and fresh air. The body lay motionless on a floor pallet, arms extended down the sides, mouth open, lips cracked. Blood had run from the mouth and ears and eyes and had dried. A cloud of flies buzzed around the face. Quickly, I opened the other shutters throughout the house, and finally I unlocked the door and left it open. That done, holding my breath, I wrapped the woman's body in the sheet on which she lay and dragged it outside and into the backyard, where I left it near a pile of deadwood saved for the cooking fires. I returned to the house for the other body, intending to burn them both, grandmother and grandson together.

As I entered the boy's room, I heard a groan.

For two weeks I lived in that house of death, wrestling hour by hour to change it to a house of life. I slept little, if at all. During the first week, he held to life by a thread. I lanced the swollen black buboes beneath the armpits, draining off the poison, yet they filled up again and again. I poured water through a reed inserted deeply into his throat, for he was unconscious and could not swallow. To the water I added drops of *origanon* oil, as well as herbal tinctures. Also the compound *theriake*, which I rarely use, but I was desperate. One of its virtuous ingredients may have helped the boy, but I do not know this for certain, since nothing I gave him seemed to have any notable effects.

Water, and again water. I could not understand why he did not die.

But he did not die, and why he did not must be left to the realm of mystery that the gods hold ever over us, sometimes as horror and sometimes as blessing, and never with explanation. Loukas and I hovered between the two, night after night, bound to each other by this wrestling match that was as much *psyche* or *pneuma* as it was *soma*. With my whole soul I willed him to live, and though I knew full well that human will is a reed in the wind, it was what I had to give. And I gave everything. I fought for him, and he fought alongside me, though he did not know of it, for his soul had wandered far to the west and south, to the place where Titans battle on the heights of Olympos.

In the second week, he opened his eyes, and a little color returned to his face. The poisonous secretions began to dry up. Now and then he was able to swallow water on his own, and a wet corn mash that I washed down his throat. But consciousness, if that is what it was, seemed thin, and quickly faded out again. He spoke no words; his eyes noted things through a screen of confusion and seemed without thought or questioning.

Toward the end of the second week, I gathered his grandmother's ashes and pieces of bone, put them into a clay jar, and capped it. I located a farmer who owned land beyond the village, a man with a donkey and cart. For a fee he agreed to take us to Thessalonike. I carried the boy to the cart and laid him on a bed of fleeces. We left Herakleia in the cool of the evening and arrived before dawn at the house where Xanthippos lay. He was alive and clear in mind but still weak. I paid the woman as I had promised, offering a little extra if she would feed us while I sought a ship to take us away. She agreed. And so we spent a third week in the pestilential city.

During that period I gathered the bones of Thea and her kin from the cooled ashes of her house. I will not write about what I felt as I did this. I will take it to my grave, for of all the woes that have befallen me in my life, before and since, this was the worst. Among the bones were three small skulls and three large ones. Heron, I think, had been with them. To this day I know nothing more. After I had searched out the family tomb, I interred the jars of their ashes there, and with many tears I bid my beloved sister farewell until we should meet again.

Near the end of the third week, Loukas began to revive a little more. He sat up in bed for short periods, saying nothing, gazing out a window at the empty sunlit wall of a neighboring house.

"Do you know where you are?" I said, but he merely shook his head.

When I asked him if he remembered his name, his lips and tongue began to shape an *L* sound but could not complete it.

"I am your uncle, your mother's brother", I said. But his eyes registered little comprehension, and he slipped back into sleep.

Ten more days passed, and then good fortune seemed to smile on us again. A cargo ship out of Poteidaia, bound for Piraeus, was blown off course by a storm and took shelter in the bay at Thessalonike. I met its captain by a tavern on the waterfront street and asked if he would accept three passengers. For a stout fee, he readily agreed. The ship had a deck hut for such purposes, he said, and his cook could feed us on the voyage.

By then, I was getting Loukas out of bed each day, no more than a few minutes at a time. I would make him take hesitant steps on wobbling legs, across the room and back again, holding onto him all the while, until he could endure no more and fell onto the bed with exhausted relief. He slept a lot. And drank much water. Still, he did not speak.

Finally, one morning when the storm winds had abated and the sky had cleared, the captain sent a message that he was in haste to set sail and would wait no more than an hour before pulling the anchor. We were living a few streets from the harbor. I could not find anyone with a cart to help me bring Xanthippos and Loukas to the wharf, and no man I spoke to in this ravaged city was willing to carry a body that had been struck by the plague. In the end I was forced by necessity to get Loukas upright and make him walk all the way. It was a hard risk, but he did it. Xanthippos was another matter. As I hoisted him onto my shoulders and he wrapped his arms around my neck, I found that he weighed little more than a bird. So with him on my back, and my arm around the boy beside me to keep him from falling, we made our wretched way to the harbor.

The ship had been brought in close to the wharf and was joined to it by wide wooden planks. As I put my foot to it, Loukas took my hand in his and held it tightly. And in that manner, with tears and stricken hearts, we entered the unknown, blind and powerless before the revelations of mysterious fate that were yet to come.

*

[Journal entry, June 8, A.D. 65]

Gortyna
Thargelion—Iunius

I may resume remembering now. Renewed sorrows have poured out in the interim since I last made an entry in this journal. I could not write any more while the unexpected waters flowed. Now I am better. Or to shift my metaphors to ones most suitable to me: An abscess unhealed, which the skin too soon covered those many years ago, broke open again. But I prefer the image of water to that of damaged flesh. Regardless of how one expresses it, grieving heals us, and in the flowing of sorrows long past there is, strangely, much consolation.

The weather on our voyage was the finest. Fair winds blew us to the south, and clear skies arched overhead. We spent the first three days in the open air, under an awning, Loukas sleeping on a bed of blankets between me and Xanthippos, who sat with his back to the rail, his head turned upward to the sun.

"I see the light and the darkness", he said.

"But no objects clearly", I commented, stating the obvious, for throughout the years I knew him, he had only been able to distinguish night from day—that much entered him through his eyes.

"I mean the light and darkness that is in the world", he said, as if explaining to a child a most certain, most adult thing.

"I see", I murmured stupidly, though I did not really understand his meaning.

"The light will win", he went on. "It will win, and you must not doubt it. No human eyes can foresee the ways in which the war will be won."

Now I was sure his mind was wandering, for no war was abroad in the world during those days, none that we knew about.

He put his hand to Loukas' sleeping brow and held it there.

"Who can foresee", he whispered. "Who can foresee?"

Then he fell asleep, which was his growing habit.

He died in the night, four days into the voyage, when we were far out on the Aegean. I learned of it in the morning when I shook his shoulder to awaken him for breakfast. In death his eyes were open, and there was a smile on his lips.

The captain would not allow me to burn the body on his wooden bark nor keep it until we reached Piraeus. I wrapped Xanthippos in a sheet, and kissed him, and dropped him into the sea.

That night I slept outside the passenger hut. The air was warm, the breeze slight. Loukas had begun to cough, with a rasping dangerously low, and I feared that the lung sickness had begun. His color had worsened earlier in the day, and the brown-tanned skin of his face was bloodless, green in hue at first, then blue about the lips. He did not open his eyes and in his sleep appeared to be sinking back into unconsciousness. Throughout the night, from the moment when Hesperos the shepherd star appeared, until dawn, I held the blue-skinned survivor in my arms, defying the death gods who would seize him, the lines from *Agamemnon* burning through me like black fire.

> The god of war, money-changer of dead bodies,
> held the balance of his spear in the fighting,
> and from the corpse-fires at Ilium
> sent to their beloveds the dust
> heavy and bitter with tears shed
> packing full the urns with
> ashes that once were men.

I tried to pray, though I did not know to whom or to what I was praying. The following day, he began to revive; the cough declined, and color returned to him. He slept more easily. We reached Piraeus, and there we boarded an empty corn ship bound for the granaries of Egypt that would stop at Fair Havens on the way. A week after that, we were home. The women took the boy from me and did what was needed, and in time he fully recovered his physical health and could begin the long, slow healing of the deeper wounds.

*

I remember the way Paeonia was with me the night after my return. It seemed a dream to me that I was in my own bed, beside my beloved, after all that had happened. Three months I had been gone, yet it felt as if years had passed.

After our embraces and murmured conversations, after I had described to her everything about my journey in a quiet and dispassionate voice, I thought that we would now sleep together in the sleep-of-peace.

We fell into contented silence, and I sensed she was drifting off into dreams. But I could not sleep and lay awake listening to the night birds of Crete.

Then she put her arms around me again and her lips close to my ear.

"Never have you shown your tears to me, Theophilos", she whispered. "Do you have tears?"

"I have tears, my wife. Yet it is men's lot to save their tears for the night and solitude, that they may retain their strength for others' sake."

"Is it so? Is it necessary?"

"Yes."

"We have been married these many years, and lost three babies, and other kinsmen too. And you have seen more pitiful things than that among those not of our family, and death in many guises. If a woman were to see what you have seen, she would become a fountain." She kissed me on the cheek and stroked my head. "Now I see that you are the strongest of men."

"No, I am ordinary."

"Ordinary. That word is meaningless."

"I am glad to be by your side. It is the greatest treasure of my life."

"You mean it. I hear it in your words and also beneath your speech."

"I mean it. It is true."

"That is what you are to me", she said.

"I know it."

"It is what I would be for you always."

By such small words the greatest truths are communicated. We held each other very closely.

I think I fell asleep shortly after. From time to time I would awaken a little and see her lying on her side, her head raised on her elbow, regarding me. The moon was shining full through the window.

Toward dawn, she whispered into my ear again:

"My sleeping Theophilos, I am sorry for the loss of your Thea. I am sorry for all your losses, for though you do not think it so, they are mine too. If your soul hears me now, be assured you are not alone."

For a moment I felt it best that she presume I was asleep, for what she had done was beautiful and dear and very deep. But I could not help myself. I broke into sobs and wept until the first cockcrow as she held me all the while.

Thereafter our love was friendship too, and our life changed much.

*

[Journal entry, June 10, A.D. 65]

Gortyna
Thargelion—Iunius

This morning I awoke later than usual. I roused to the sounds of women talking loudly in the kitchen. There were several voices and a good deal of laughter. I got up and went to investigate.

There they were, gathered around the worktable, chopping vegetables, clucking like a flock of hens, giggling, all talking at once. Paeonia, Mila, Theodosia—who was visiting for two days with Leandros, who has business in the city and was for the moment nowhere in sight—Philippia, Helena, and their cousin little Thea. And last but not least, Calliope, who was in thick with them.

I cleared my throat and glanced at the bread cupboard, hoping that one of them might get the point. They all turned their heads to me and fell silent for a moment, then burst into unstoppable hilarity. While they were thus engaged in their symposium, I fixed myself a plate of bread and cheese and a cup of goat's milk.

When the tumult had subsided a little, I asked them what had caused their laughter. Paeonia answered for all.

"We were discussing the ways of Roman women."

"Oh, I see", I nodded somberly, not seeing.

"Mila asked why Greeks and Romans so seldom mingle. I told her that we live side by side on the same streets as fellow citizens under the *imperium*, yet in our deepest selves we keep our Greek soul." She used the word *pneuma*, not *psyche*.

"And that is why we do not much enjoy each other's company", said Theodosia. "In Phoenix it is somewhat different. Leandros has Roman friends, and I do too, though not close ones. But that is business, not the way of the capitol, where sour politics is mixed with everything, like the vinegar they mix into their wine."

"Do you share meals, do you invite them to your home?"

"Not often", she frowned. "Even less do they accept an invitation, though they are gracious when they come. Our houses and food are too simple for them, I think.

But the Roman women in Phoenix are pleasant. Not like here."

"Yes, sad to say", I nodded like one with some authority on the matter. "Gortyna's Roman women are richer and more complicated."

"Papa," said Mila, "why is it this way even with those Romans who have lived here for generations?"

"Well, the world is Roman now", I explained.

They fell silent; then, after no more than the briefest pause, their several eyes all met at once and they erupted again.

A ridiculous scene.

"Where are the boys?" I asked Theodosia.

"They went with their father", she replied. "Today he is selling 'cedar of the gods' to a merchant, and he wants them to learn about the trade."

"And Cleon—at school, of course."

"Yes, he's there", answered Mila with a smile.

"And Tranquilatus. Has anyone seen Traquilatus this morning?"

"In the garden", several voices answered.

Once more they went red in the face, tears of hilarity spilling from their eyes.

"Well, I leave you to your discussion", I mumbled. "I do not understand Roman women and have nothing more to contribute to the subject."

Calliope jumped in at that moment and cackled, "It is not just Roman women you fail to understand, Master. *All* women are mysterious to you!"

It bordered on the insolent, but the entire scene was already a loss.

"You say rightly, Calliope", I nodded, using my sage tone. "Though I hold womankind as more splendid than men, and as the summit of all living things, yet I do not understand you, not one of you, and I never have, and likely never will."

They grinned in appreciation, bestowing fond looks on me.

I sighed. Not wanting to depart without a final word of summation that would restore my dignity a little, I said, "I am sure that we men are the same in your eyes."

Astoundingly, they all, young and old alike, burst into wild laugher.

"Oh, no, my dear", said Paeonia. "Men are the easiest book to read. Men are transparent."

And so I beat a hasty retreat, leaving them nodding to themselves in mutual affirmation.

I sought out Tranquilatus and found him on his knees in the garden, cutting grass with shears.

"Have you been into the kitchen for your breakfast?" I asked.

He shook his head and got to his feet. After searching his mind, rubbing his chin, and casting careful glances at me, he muttered in his crude country accent, "Nay, Master, that is not a good place for a man to be this morn."

*

I am remembering something today. It happened twenty-five years ago, during the year after Loukas came to live with us. He was then about twelve years old. Largely recovered from the plague, he was growing stronger and looked healthy enough, if a little thin for his age. At the time I was mainly worried about his inner life, of which I knew next to nothing, for he was grieving still, and silent unless a persistent member of the family dug some minimal responses out of him. He had not yet begun to call us father and mother.

On a certain night in midwinter, however, there was a breakthrough. I was roused from my sleep by an urgent hand shaking my shoulder. I grumbled myself awake and sat up to find Loukas kneeling by the bed.

"Uncle, you must see something", he whispered. "Come with me."

This unusual behavior intrigued me sufficiently to get me out from under the covers and into some clothes while the boy danced on tiptoe, anxiously whispering that I should hurry, hurry, lest I miss whatever marvel he wanted to show me.

He led me into the garden and up a ladder onto the roof—in those days I was still young enough to attempt such foolishness.

He stood on the apex of tiles, his bare feet planted on either side of the crest, head tilted back, pointing upward to a cascade of falling stars.

I was moved by the sight, for never in my life had I seen the winter shower fall with such a dazzling display, the fire arrows more numerous than I had ever seen, and brighter too—a rain of light.

"O beautiful, beautiful", Loukas gasped.

The shower continued for longer than usual, primarily white stars, mixed from time to time with a flare of orange or blue, and once a long, slow spear of green that dissolved near the horizon.

We sat down on the tiles and then lay on our backs. Though it was a moonless night, the air was so absolutely clear that the sky was choked with stars, and we could see each other's faces. I pointed out to him some of the constellations, comparing their Greek and Roman names. He knew all the Greek and was curious about the Roman adaptations.

He asked me which star was my favorite, and I pointed to the polestar in the north.

"It is dimmer than the others", he replied dubiously. "Why is it your favorite?"

"It is quiet and draws no attention to itself. It is humble and steadfast, yet all the lights in the heavens, the great and the small, revolve around it in unceasing motion. Why is that, do you think?"

"I do not know, Uncle."

"Nor do I, yet it is a great puzzle, is it not?"

"It is."

"Tell me, Loukas, do you have a favorite?"

"Chiron", he said without hesitation.

"Ah, you mean the constellation the Romans call Sagittarius."

"Yes."

Probing to see how much Timo had taught him, I asked, "So, do you like centaurs?"

"No, Uncle, I do not like them, for they are rude, unthinking, and very violent. They are cheaters, always breaking their promises. They also drink too much. But I like Chiron."

"Yes, he is the only likable centaur ever made by the gods."

"He was kind and wise."

"Did you know that Chiron was educated by Apollo?"

"I knew that."

"Did you know that many sons of kings were sent to Chiron to be trained in the skill and the art of healing? Among his students were Heracles and Aesclepios."

"Really? Your god?"

I chuckled, "Well, Aesclepios is not quite my god. He is a . . ."

"He is your mentor in the heavens?"

"Yes, something like that."

"That is very interesting", said Loukas with furrowed brow, chewing on a thought.

"How so?" I asked.

"I am thinking of Heracles and his nephew Iolaus, who was his constant follower. And now I see that they are all connected, Heracles and Iolaus and Aesclepios and Chiron."

"They were good friends, and our friends too. We can think of them when we see their stars. But surely you know the sad ending of that tale?"

"You mean the arrow? It should not have happened."

"Why shouldn't it have happened?"

Loukas' voice trembled with hurt and vehemence: "It is a terrible thing! Heracles shot Chiron by accident, the centaur whom he loved so much!"

"Yes, a terrible mistake", I nodded. "Life is full of terrible mistakes."

"But it should not be so!" he protested.

Correct, my very young man: It should not be so. But what can one do with centaurs? They are a mad and selfish lot. According to the legend, Heracles had traveled far one day and was very thirsty. Arriving at a friend's house, he asked him for a drink of wine, and the friend opened a large amphora of fine wine that he stored there. Heracles did not know that it belonged to all the centaurs. When the wine's aroma flowed out over the countryside, the centaurs realized that someone was into their jar and galloped up to the house, furiously demanding an explanation: Why had he dared to open the wine without first consulting them? The centaurs flew into a rage and began to attack, but Heracles killed many of them and drove off the rest, commanding them never to return. Chiron was nearby, observing the melee, although he had not taken part in it. Heracles deeply respected the greatest of centaurs, but he could not recognize his friend from a distance and accidentally shot him with one of his poisoned arrows. In the end, Chiron the healer could not heal himself. Seeing these events and knowing of his son Heracles' grief over what he had done, Zeus gave Chiron a throne among the stars.

I saw that Loukas was reliving the tale as if he were inside it. When he spoke at last, his voice was strained, as if he were struggling to grasp an elusive thought:

"Uncle, when our *eyes* look at a thing in a certain way, our mind gives it a name, a meaning. But when our *mind* considers it another way, our eyes change and see it differently."

"This is quite true."

"It seems that our minds are unreliable."

"Or our eyes are unreliable. Or both, for they are united."

Loukas paused, then said: "Yet the mind may correct what the eyes tell it, if it is a wise and trained mind."

I smiled to myself. Timo had taught him much—or perhaps it had been Xanthippos. Yes, Xanthippos, who had always sought to move my mind's interpretations beyond the most obvious. It had been he, I now recalled, who first dislodged me from my belief that the world was flat.

I said: "Do you know that our friend Xanthippos once told me about a mariner he met who had sailed on great seas to the west and south of Africa? Did he ever mention him?"

"I do not remember it", said Loukas, shaking his head.

"Well, the mariner told him that the sky above the southern seas is different from ours, and among those stars there is another man-horse."

"Is there?" said the boy. "Well, I prefer my Chiron."

"Yet your Chiron could be seen as a man, not a centaur. He looks like a warrior to me."

"He looks like a centaur to me."

"I think he is the centaur's slayer."

"Uncle," Loukas declared emphatically, "that is the centaur enthroned by Zeus."

He turned a swift glance toward me, worried, I think, that he had argued disrespectfully.

"It is good that you exercise your thoughts freely, Loukas", I said, hiding my smiles. "It is this faculty in men that keeps us from becoming a herd of maddened centaurs."

He said nothing in reply and resumed his observation of the stars. I silently rejoiced, for his imprisonment in mute grief had been broken and our dialogues begun.

We sat together without further speech until Loukas began to shiver with the night chill. I threw my *himation* over him and told him to go down to bed. I remained on the roof a while longer, feeling keenly the absence of Thea and Timo, but glad to be the steward of their son.

Then it struck me that blameless Iolaus, nephew of Heracles, had been condemned to ever wander as an exile.

*

My eyes are drawn to the white stone from Iraklion, again and again. Loukas' name scratched so clumsily on it speaks to me like a word from a mouth. Where is he now, and how is he faring?

Will I die soon? Is that why so many old memories continue to press forward to center stage?

Picture after picture, scene after scene, fragments of our dialogues, some banal, some loaded with meanings that became apparent only years after they were spoken. The women are correct about this. Not only do I fail to comprehend one half of the human race, but it seems to me now that I fail to understand most everything, including myself. Man is a mystery to himself, and if he begins to reflect on his own nature he is soon bogged down in a multitude of unanswered questions. Who are we? Where have we come from? Where are we going? All the philosophers ask these questions—as do physicians and even the most brainless magician, I would guess. From goat boy to emperor, man ponders his existence and wonders.

How old was Loukas when I first discovered the little shrine he had made in his bedroom? Eighteen perhaps. Until then, he had been neither more nor less religious than any other boy of his age. But he had displayed no interest in gods such as Eros or Hermes, which are popular among youths and young men. Yet here now was a poorly carved marble of Apollo, one of those items produced in great quantities and in various questionable manifestations by the vendors at the temple of Pythian Apollo. It sat upright on the floor, no more than a foot in height, perched atop an oval white stone that he must have retrieved from the river. About its feet the stumps of burned-out candles sat in hardened puddles of bees-wax. What had he been praying about? And why to Apollo?

At the next opportunity, I asked him for an explanation. He was hesitant at first to give an answer, but I think this was more because he was not entirely certain about his attraction.

"Apollo is associated with the sun", he mused. "Thus, he is a son of light. He is a healer too—like you, Father, and like Aesclepios, and in his own way Hermes the messenger. But he is more than they are. On Mount Parnassos he killed the dragon Python, the child eater who would have devoured Leto's offspring in the womb."

"A good god", I said. "A good choice you make, Loukas."

He nodded, but said no more. Though capable of garrulous talk, he was in the habit of keeping his deepest thoughts to himself. Or it may be that he held them close whenever he had not yet worked through a matter.

"'I sprang upon the ship in the form of a dolphin'", I said, quoting a line from the Homeric hymn to Pythian Apollo.

"'Pray to me as Apollo of the Dolphins, and the altar itself shall be called the Dolphins'", he replied, giving the responding line.

"Someday we must go to Delphi, Loukas, if time and the fates permit. Apollo in that place is ever the best friend of Cretans. Is that why you like him so much?"

"The story interests me, certainly. It has great charm. When the god noticed a Cretan ship sailing from Knossos to Pylos, he turned himself into a dolphin and brought the vessel to Parnassos, and having become priests of Apollo, the mariners called the city Delphi, in honor of the god. But it is not that which draws me to him."

"What then?"

"I think it is the many aspects combined in him. He is light and healer and rescuer and guide. He defends the small and weak. He lifts them up and casts down their vilest enemies. And more than this, he is the god of prophecy and inspiration."

"A characteristic he shares with other gods."

"But none are of his quality."

"True."

I left him to his prayers. He said no more about it, and in his manner of silence regarding matters most profound to him, I realized that he was very much the son of Timo.

Not long after, I obtained a copy of Cicero's treatise on the nature of the gods, and he devoured it, but I regret to say that we did not discuss it at length. Or if we did, I have forgotten what we said. Sometimes my failing memory makes me angry at myself. Today I experience one such moment. We forget important events that offer us keys, and then we compound our forgetfulness by forgetting there ever was a key and ever was a door.

I do recall him asking me about my devotion to Aesclepios.

"Father, is he like a person to you? Do you pray to him and worship him?"

"A complicated question", I replied. "In a sense he is like a person to me. But if he ever existed, he is long dead and beyond my reach. I do not pray to him and do not worship him."

"But why, then, do you keep such a fine statue of him in our garden?"

"He is a symbol for me. A representative of my vocation."

Loukas took the little Apollo with him to Alexandria, but when he returned from there he no longer had it with him. I noticed this quite by chance a few days after his homecoming. The oval stone in his room remained bare. When I asked about the statue, he said that he had given it away. In the ensuing years no replacement filled the empty space.

Now, more pictures from the past:

I see him in this very room, arguing with me about bloodletting. I have never held with the practice, since it is based on a theory that is disproved more often than it is spuriously "proved". Almost every physician still does it, but how many of them really understand why they do it? It is a tradition based in very old medicine from Babylon, Assyria, and elsewhere, originating perhaps farther back in the superstitions of numerous primitive peoples.

One rightly drains poisonous substances from the body, because poison is invasion. One should not drain good blood from the body, because blood, if it is red, is health and life. Loukas returned from Alexandria with a head full of excellent knowledge, and also a few inconsistent notions, some of which were true science based on observation and some of which were derived from common practice and superficial theory. Among the latter was the belief that many ill conditions were caused by *plethora*, an excess of blood, and could be healed by decreasing the volume of blood in the body. I quickly took charge of this error in his thinking and required of him a careful reading of Erasistratus, who was opposed to violent measures and rarely employed bloodletting, preferring instead to concentrate on fasting, regular diet, and vapor baths. His students, building upon their master's wisdom, later rejected bloodletting altogether. I was sorry to learn that Loukas had not been influenced by them. However, with time, he changed his mind on the matter and never thereafter changed it back again.

I see his face again as if it is physically present before me. He was in his midtwenties then, the same age as I was when I made my way northward on foot to find my new mentor Xanthippos of Thessalonike. Loukas, despite his sojourn among the bearded Alexandrian philosophers, had continued his custom of short hair and a close-shaven face. Taller than I by a head and very sturdy from his days of running, he was being considered by uncountable mothers in Gortyna's Greek middle class as a prize match for their daughters. While I knew that he had been struck by the sight of a few young women from among their ranks, he had as yet made no steps in that direction. For the present, he was all mind and all dedication.

Some things he said that day stand out:

"Father, in your studies of the human body, have you not witnessed the power of the mind over the flesh?"

"I have often pointed out the phenomenon to you, if you recall."

"Yes, and that is why I keep an eye open to it. It seems to me there is a pattern: A man with a sick body and a healthy mind recovers his health more quickly and completely than a man with a sick mind in a body that is not nearly as ill."

"True", I nodded.

"But what is this power of the mind? Might it heal all things, if it were to apply its powers rightly?"

"Not all", I said, remembering much, remembering especially the tragedies of Herakleia and Thessalonike, though I did not speak of them. "You wish to advance a theory, Loukas, one that is speculative and against which there is copious evidence. A man's powers, whatever they may be, however

123

greatly they may be developed, always have their limitations while they thrive, and must come in the end to nothing. Death speaks the last word for all."

"Does it?" he murmured, as if to himself. Looking up, he met my eyes. His own expressed a mixture of puzzlement, guilelessness, and earnest goodness. He said:

"But what is love?"

"Love? That needs no explanation."

"Is it a power of the body and its emotions only? Or is it a power of the mind that flows into the body? Or is it a power of the soul that radiates through every region of our being at once and continuously?"

"It is all three, I believe."

"That is not possible", he protested.

"Why do you think it is not possible?"

"Because a person is like three countries of an empire, each with different languages and customs, and at times they wage war against each other. Thus, the parts are separate entities."

"I do not see it that way", I replied. "All dimensions of a man's being are one, with different faces exposed to us. We wrongly conclude that because the various exposures function differently, and appear differently, they are separate. The war, as you call it, is not *cause* but rather is *effect*. When one dimension is ill, the others suffer."

"It makes sense what you say", he mused, furrowing his brow and tapping a finger to his lips. "Yes, I can see it—though it is but a theory."

"Agreed", I shrugged.

He stood and paced about the surgery, immersed in his private thoughts. I let him be.

Returning to the stool beside my chair, he sat down at my feet like the small boy he once had been. Absentmindedly, he took my hand and held it tightly for a moment. It seemed like only a few years ago that this hand, now so large, had clung to mine as we boarded a ship to escape the plague city.

"But what, really, is love?" he asked, as if speaking to himself again. "There is nothing like it."

Despite myself, I laughed. "That is so. There is nothing like it."

Then he dropped my hand and asked me unconnected questions. For a time we discussed the theory of atomism, which strives to explain the structure of the material world. Neither of us had much attraction to the atomic theories of the Epicureans; we preferred the rationalist atomism of Erasistratus. In any event, Loukas eventually could not keep his eyelids open, and I sent him off to his bed.

As I went through the room blowing out lamps, it suddenly struck me that he was in love with someone. The young woman, whoever she might be, was out there somewhere in sleeping Gortyna.

*

I did not probe. He would tell his mother and me about it when he was ready. After all, our permission and our services in the rituals of matchmaking would be required if he was serious about her. Was it that year he told us or during the following, when he had begun to work beside me in the surgery? Yes, it must have been the following year because he was then doing difficult procedures alone, under my watchful eye of course, but advancing daily in skill to meet his knowledge. I think it was midsummer when I began to notice the change. He had developed shadows beneath his lower eyelids, and his mouth was often tight, as if he were suffering pain. He was quieter too, said little at boisterous family gatherings, which was quite unlike him.

Whenever I asked him if he was ill, he would smile and deny it. When I asked if he felt overworked, he invariably said no. But I observed closely and noted his deepening fatigue.

One night I could not sleep—I cannot recall the reason now—and lay awake listening to the autumn wind blowing around outside the compound walls. The night was cool but not enough for shuttering the windows. Through the open doorway of our bedroom I saw a spark of lamplight in the hall, passing from room to room. The girls had been married by then, so I knew it was Loukas roaming about restlessly in the dark.

I got up and went to find him. He had extinguished the lamp at that point, and I shuffled blindly through the house, knocking my shins on furniture. Finally I saw his shadow against the square of moonlight in the alcove where Paeonia keeps her weaving loom. It is a cramped space, but with a large window opening upon the garden. He stood by the window, staring out, motionless.

"You are awake", I said in a low voice so as not to startle him.

"Yes, Father," he whispered, "I am awake."

"Are you unwell?"

When he did not reply, I stepped forward and stood beside him. The moon was full, low in the sky, the color of an orange from the pall of wood smoke hovering over the city.

We did not speak for a time. Then, in a shaken voice, he murmured lines from Sappho:

> The moon has set
> and the Pleiades,
> mid-night has come and gone;
> and I lie here unsleeping, alone,
> O I am sick with love.

And so I brought him into the kitchen, where I lit a fire and made him a pot of warm milk, and probed some more.

She was the sister of a friend he had run with as a youth, during the time they had dreamed of Olympics. He had not noticed her then because she had been a little willow of a girl, but now she was a woman. He met her shortly after his return from Alexandria when paying a call upon his friend to renew their bond. She had sat with them on the summer porch of their family home and served them peppermint tea and honey cakes. The discussion between the three had been about travel, and city affairs, and poetry. She had quoted something from Sappho and argued that she believed the poet was a man, not a woman as all believed. Her brother teased her strongly about it and made her laugh, but she argued against him well, quoting from other poets and poetesses of the past. And all the while, as Loukas listened to her mind, he was falling into awe over her beauty and character and intelligence. He let not a spark of it show.

"Did you lower your eyes when she looked at you?" I asked.

"I think I may have", he answered in a puzzled tone, cocking his head with curiosity. "Yes, yes, I did. It was involuntary. Why do you ask?"

"No reason."

"I felt so foolish doing that, as if I were a timid boy. I'm sure they could hear the big drum booming inside my chest."

"I'm sure they heard nothing."

"I hope not", he sighed. "Then again, I hope *she* did."

"Have you spoken together about it?"

He shook his head. "If you mean have we spoken together about my feelings—no."

"And what is her manner with you?"

"Pleasant and at ease. I am her brother's friend; that is all. And as brother to her brother, I am her brother also."

"She does not lower her eyes when you look at her?"

"Never. When she looks directly at me, she laughs. I must seem very ugly to her in a humorous way. Like Socrates or a theater clown. Am I so ugly?"

"Quite the opposite. I can think of forty or fifty maidens in this city who sigh over the very thought of you."

At this, his mouth hung open stupidly, and he stared at me as if I had made an unkind joke.

"I do not understand what you are saying", he said. "I have never noticed anything like that. You invent it to salve my shame."

"There is no need for shame."

"And what's this about blinking and lowering eyes? You make no sense at all."

"I make perfect sense, but you are presently senseless. You have fallen under the tyrant who rules us all."

He stared at me with resentment, and for a moment I thought he would become angry. But then his face softened, and he smiled ruefully.

"More milk?" I asked, offering the pot.

"Yes, if you please, Father."

"Wipe your chin, Loukas. You are dribbling your milk, and it makes you look quite ugly."

That made him laugh. I took him into the library room and lit the lamps, and when he had settled down to nurse from his cup, I read aloud a few lines from the comedians. They did not make him laugh, but he smiled at the wit, and not long after he went off to bed and slept until morning.

Oh, I must stop here. Paeonia is calling me to our bed. The Pleiades have not set, and I am not sick with love, but I know where good love is to be found.

Before blowing out the lamps, however, I will add just this to round off the story:

He never married the young woman. She married some-one else, and theirs is a happy union, with several children and a modest home. Loukas recovered from his spell. He fell under the tyrant a few more times during the following years—different women, very fine all of them, but with none did he make a match. His practice grew and grew as mine declined, and he became much sought after socially and professionally. Yet he kept to a quiet life, and seemed, all told, to be content with it.

Was he lonely? Yes, at times. But on the whole, he was happy. He had his work and his family and his collection of medical and philosophical books, which he enlarged contin-ually. He was at risk of becoming a pedant or a recluse, but his warm spirit would not let him sink for long in those direc-tions. He loved his friends and occasionally drank with them, always in moderation. Well into his late twenties, he still ran around the city walls, alone.

I really must go now. One breath and the lamp flame is out.

*

[Journal entry, June 12, A.D. 65]

Gortyna
Thargelion—Iunius

From time to time in the years leading up to his departure, Loukas frequented the harbors at Fair Havens in the south and Iraklion in the north. He did medical work there for people who had fallen ill on ships. It began when he was asked one day by someone in the city—I never learned who—to accom-pany him to the havens to see a man who was dangerously ill and could not be brought to the city by cart.

Loukas returned days later, exhausted and dispirited.

"It was a slave ship," he explained, "held over there by the weather."

"The captain paid you well, I suppose."

"From the captain I received nothing at all, for it was not he who required the service. He permitted me to go down into the holds among the captives only because he feared to lose his cargo."

"Who brought you to him?"

"A man of Gortyna whom I met last year and have come to know."

"The ship owner?"

"No, the owner is in Ostia. The man who brought me to the slaves knew none of them. It is a thing he does—though he does not speak his thoughts to owners and their shipmen. He is an honorable fellow. He does it for the sake of goodness. It is his philosophy."

"Ah, a philosopher!"

"In a sense but not formally. He is from Cilicia and resides for a time in Crete. He travels about the island, though I do not know for certain what he does."

"So it is he who pays you."

"He pays me nothing, but he would if he could."

"Do you trust him?"

"Yes", Loukas nodded, and seemed reluctant to justify it.

A great deal about this relationship worried me. The lack of payment was the least of the matter. My concern was mainly for the change that came over Loukas during that stage of his life. He grew more troubled over the human condition with all its sufferings, though he had seen plenty since childhood, and as a young physician had developed a healthy detachment. In addition, he was now more silent than ever, as if his thoughts were continually in diverse places. He had always done some service for free, for the poorest especially, who could not pay him. But now he was traveling farther afield in order to do so.

It cut into his time in our surgery and meant additional loss of income for him at considerable expenditure of energy.

When I voiced this argument, he replied, "Do I need more money? What is the worth of a man?"

"But do you mean *any* kind of man?" I said, then recalled with a start that my grandfather had once been a slave. How easily I had forgotten.

"Any and all", he replied firmly, his facial expression telling me that I should not press for further explanations.

Over the course of three years, he asked me a few times to accompany him, but I told him that I was growing too old to make the journey. In truth, I felt too old to crack open my heart again over human misery at its worst and then struggle to repress it, like ashes in an overfull burial urn; too old to go down into the dark bowels of an evil ship and labor to rescue those who would live only to die under the lash. Too old to face my dismay, which could so easily awaken in such company.

And so he continued to serve the slaves without my aid, and I must admit that the time he spent with them and other unfortunates was no more than a quarter of his time spent on regular patients. But it was the prologue to his departure for Syria, and almost certainly its preparation. I remember the evening when he brought his mother and me into our library and sat us down before him, clasping and unclasping his hands in uncertainty, his face pleading with us to understand what was incomprehensible even to himself:

"I must go on a journey", he simply said. "There is more I must learn."

He told us where he would be going and how he would travel and reassured us that he would write to us often. He did not know how long he would be gone, but he thought it would be no more than a year.

That was ten years ago.

As I write, I am looking at the white stone on which he scratched his name. I gaze at it more and more these days—so obvious and mundane its history, yet mysterious too. Why is it mysterious? And how is it that, in this gazing, I have learned what reason alone could not tell me?

I am now certain of what I must do.

*

[Journal entry, June 14, A.D. 65]

Gortyna
Thargelion—Iunius

Midmonth, and the winds have changed. Soon it will be Scirophorion by our old calendar. I spoke with Gaius yesterday.

"I wish to accept the favor you offered, my friend, the one you made last year."

"Are the dice cast, then?" he asked. "Or is it only a throw in the mind?"

"I am resolved. And with your help, I will win the game."

"I have already shipped last year's vintage to Ostia and Alexandria. But a wine ship departs from the havens three days from now, bound for Syria, if it is not too early for you. I will speak to the captain, who owes me much. The voyage will cost you nothing in terms of gold or silver."

"That is a great favor."

"My life-debt to you can never be repaid. And in truth, Theophilos, it is a debt I do not wish to be free of. Even so, I can do this little thing for you."

*

Everyone is here. Two days from now I go.

Last night, the family gathered in the garden to have supper. As the sky overhead faded to rose and jade, we lit oil lanterns and hung them from tree branches. We sat on the grass together and ate, Paeonia and I, our daughters and their husbands, and the grandchildren. The mood upon us was not unhappy, and I think this was because we felt it best to avoid discussion of the pending separation. The children ate like little animals, climbed trees, laughed and cried, teased each other, and hugged in forgiveness or affection. I soaked up the antics with my eyes, knowing that it would be months before I saw them again.

Still, despite their play, despite the companionable conversations between the six adults, despite the sweetness of the air, the perfumes of the garden, and the good feast my wife and Calliope had made, a sadness loomed over us. It is this way with every man's voyage, for the parabola between departure and return is not fixed—it may be altered by fortune good and ill, and all know it.

As if to fill the silences that appeared among us as we drank our wine after supper, Cleon and Leandros grew loud and male in a pretentious manner that, despite its theatric style, we all enjoyed. Cleon described a harsh row he had had with the mother of one of his students, a spoiled Roman boy whom she had sent to his school in the hope that a firm Greek teacher with a rod of discipline would supply what she and her husband had omitted in their son's upbringing. Cleon forthrightly told her that her hope had proven groundless. Now all blame was being shifted onto him. He laughed it off, since the waiting list for entry to his school is overfull.

Then Leandros told a story about a poor business dealing he had suffered in Gortyna that morning. He rambled long and detailed about it, but no one minded, and we were glad for the distraction from our private thoughts. At the completion of his tale, which did not end badly, he too laughed off the vagaries of fortune.

A little argument between cousins broke into our attention, and mothers pulled children onto their laps and began negotiations. For this reason I did not notice Leandros get up and stroll to the compound gate and unlatch it. He returned to the group and sat down again. Then Cleon ambled away and returned with two torches, which he lit from a lantern and stuck firmly into the soft soil of flower beds, one on each side of our circle.

Their argument resolved, the children ran off to play, leaving us in silence. This silence grew more solemn minute by minute, and I could think of nothing to say to break it. I noted wetness in Paeonia's eyes and in my daughters' eyes too. Mila frowned to herself; Theodosia watched the first stars appear above us.

Then, without warning, my sons-in-law locked eyes, nodded, and leaped to their feet. Quickly they scooped up their wives in their arms, threw them over their shoulders, grabbed a torch apiece, and lumbered toward the gate. Cleon pushed it open with the sole of his foot, and they ran out into the street with their wives kicking wildly and pounding their men's backs with fists, not knowing whether to scream or laugh hysterically. They did both, and soon everyone in the neighborhood knew it. The children ran after them and halted in the open gateway, jumping up and down with glee and giggles, cheering their fathers on, as the *marathonistai* ran up and down the street bellowing like stags and waving their Olympic torches.

Paeonia and I remained seated on the grass, watching the performance from a safe distance. Her eyes glistened now with delight, sorrow banished for a while. I reached for her hand and said:

"My arms are still strong. Should we?"

"But that poor back of yours", she smiled. "It would not be wise to risk it."

"Perhaps you are right. Neither are my knees what they once were."

"You were never a good runner, Theophilos", she laughed. "Yet always a good plodder."

So we got up and went to the gate with our arms around each other. The younger children clung to our legs as we watched with them their admirable parents. The boys Niko and Daemo—my Icarus and Icarus—trotted along behind their father in imitation, strutting and shouting and convulsing with laughter, having the time of their lives. Before long, the men used up a portion of their strength and returned with glowing, exultant faces, their wives clinging to them tightly lest they be dropped to the pavement.

Everyone collapsed back onto the grass, the men still roaring over their great joke, and their women beaming with pride. Calliope toddled in with a jug, scolded us for making scandal, and filled our cups. Paeonia bade her stay with us, and so our cook and scourge did what she had never permitted herself to do before. She sat among us and sipped from her cup and told stories about what men were like when she was young and beautiful—a race of heroes, a race of gods, if half of what she said were true, which it clearly is not, since memory, as we all know, filters experience as the loose-weave cloth filters new wine and permits it to age as it should. We gave no more thought to the sadness that had nearly gripped us in its soft embrace, and I do not know how much of the night was gone when we all went off to bed carrying sleeping children in our arms.

*

[Journal entry, June 16, A.D. 65]

At sea
Scirophorion—Iunius

Yesterday evening, as I packed my baggage, Paeonia hovered nearby, not saying much, "improving" certain details of my choice of clothing and reading material. It was unnecessary help, but it kept us side-by-side and busy. Throughout, her eyes were full of anxiety, but she suppressed it for my sake. Later, we slept a little. She woke me up before dawn, spilling tears, to tell me that she had had a terrible dream. The same as before—I ran into a burning house to save children.

I assured her that the dream was no more than a form produced by her fears. I reminded her, as well, that the deeps of her mind had simply borrowed an event from the past—the time in Thessalonike when I had tried to run into a burning house to save the children, to save anyone I might find inside.

"You were stopped that time", she said. "The next time, you may not be stopped."

"It could happen", I shrugged. "There are always fires. But there is a greater danger: Man seeks certainty in an uncertain world, and thus he consults oracles and diviners and would even turn the phantasms of his dreaming mind into messages from the gods. If we live that way, we will soon run around and around in circles, the slave of every phantom our lower emotions throw onto the stage."

"You live too much by reason, Theophilos."

"I hardly live by reason at all, my good wife, though I strive to do so."

"No, you are all mind—all mind and work."

"Do you really believe that of me?" I scolded affectionately.

"Every day, I see the proof of it."

"I *must* work and I must think, if I would bring home the food that feeds us all."

"Yes, but you love it more than you love us."

"No, no, no," I whispered, hurt now, "you do not understand me. You see the surface of me and make a quick judgment. Do you not read my heart, you who read men as the simplest of books? Am I no longer transparent to you?"

"You are transparent, and that is why I see it."

What could I say in reply? She was wrong, but so great was her need to be right at this moment, so that she might release her anger-fear, that I ceased my self-defense.

I took her hand, cool and trembling. She let me hold it.

"Only once did I go away from you", I whispered into her ear. "I did not love to go away from you. I loved to return to you. And I brought you back a son."

She burst out weeping.

"Now I must go away again. And it is my hope to bring him home to you a second time."

At cock's crow she dried her eyes and got up. I lay in bed awhile and listened to her clanking pots in the kitchen. I smelled the homely incense of woodsmoke, then the scent of food cooking.

We ate breakfast alone together, picking at the food, holding hands. I noticed with a start that her hair was now completely gray. How had it escaped my notice, this metamorphosis? Her wrinkled hands, the lines of her face—lines that are carved only by long sacrifices, by the slow accumulation of wisdom in the women's way. Much love was written there, a deep love, its languages half-known to me but sustaining me always.

Not long after, Leandros brought his four-wheel lumber wagon around to the house. To our surprise, he had borrowed a horse from somewhere and had tied his two donkeys to our gatepost, where they would remain until his return. On the wagon bed sat Theodosia, with Thea asleep in her lap and Niko and Daemo still rubbing their eyes. Cleon and Mila sat there too, with their Philippia and Helena scurrying about like squirrels eager for the day's adventure. The women had brought food baskets and small amphorae. Paeonia and I climbed up with them, and Leandros took the driver's seat.

So, with hardly a look back, off we went to the havens by the sea.

*

This ship I ride upon is the *Isis of Iunius*—the present month and the name of the owner are the same. The vessel is 160 foot-lengths from bow to stern, about 30 wide at midship. A freighter, it is carrying hides from Spain, a half hold of Cretan wine in large amphorae, stacks of tin sheets, and boxes of a black stone that can be burned as fuel, I am told, from the great island in the northern seas beyond the western mouth of *mare nostrum*, as the captain calls it. The hold is not full; the ship moves swiftly toward Syria. It is a Roman war trireme, one of those older ones that are sometimes sold off by the imperial navy to commercial shippers. The hull is solid but much battered. There are no oarsmen on the three levels, no slaves aboard, as far as I know. The sails do it all—good new sails stretching roundly before the wind. The blade at the prow slices the water in a way that no other ship can do. The Roman lion carved on the bowsprit is gilded and proudly rampant, yet the hubris cannot disguise the fact that the ship's design is a replica of our Greek trireme. No better has ever been invented.

I have a cubicle of my own to sleep in, one of several in the forward deck house. There are few passengers. The lamp swings above me as I write.

Is it only a few hours since I embarked? The helmsman permitted me to stand aft of him at the rearmost rail, as the *Isis* like a great whale eased away from shore and then slowly gathered the wind and began its voyage eastward on the sea-road. My eyes were fixed on the dock all the while, and my family looked back at me. In the purple shadows of the hills surrounding the havens, their *chitons* were as white as statues glowing in moonlight on the Parthenon. Side by side they stood, their arms touching or around each other, their bodies still and attentive, watching me recede, with the thought in the minds of all that we might not see each other again. They shrank and shrank, as I must have done in their eyes. And when they were too small to be seen, I turned away, blinded.

*

[Journal entry, July 1, A.D. 65]

At sea
Scirophorion—Iulius

Dolphins this morning, diving and leaping beside the ship.

We are a week into the journey, and I have slept well thus far. No seasickness. At the same time, I have felt little desire to write in my journal. I have brought it with me in its entirety—three scrolls to date—on the chance that Loukas may be interested in reading it, since much of it concerns his life. Now, with time on my hands, there is a good deal I would like to add to the text, but the ink is long dried and I habitually use every bit of space on a page for economy's sake. There is also much I would like to delete, since upon rereading it I am embarrassed by its rambling, bordering on incoherence, hopping this way and that over decades of time and masses of geography. But I will leave it untouched. I am what I am, and it is what it is. I will begin a fourth scroll when I arrive in Judaea.

*

I have noticed the frequency with which the concept of death arises in the text. It worries me a little, yet I remind myself that I am not obsessed by the matter and often go for days without thinking of it, until the next threat of mortality falls into my hands and demands a miraculous rescue.

I have fought death throughout my entire life, in my struggle to overcome my personal bouts with illness, in my battles to save my beloved ones, in my vocation as a physician. With every thrust and parry, I beat death back only to have it come at me from another quarter. Year after year, the small ranks of the body's friends resist the vast host of its enemy—both sides clashing with weapons old and new, and all the while I know that the foe will win in the end, for all men fall before it, and those who live to fight another day are merely granted the choice of the field where they will fertilize the soil with their lifeblood.

I think of lines at the end of Euripides' drama *Hippolytus*. The brave chaste man, in character not unlike Loukas, is dying unjustly. The goddess Artemis, his beloved to whom he consecrated his life and for whom he endured exile, speaks her final words to him:

> Farewell! I may not watch man's
> Fleeting breath,
> Nor pollute my eyes with the
> Effluence of death.
> For that terror is now upon you.

She delivers this cold evidence of divine indifference, then vanishes away to her remote, inaccessible paradise. Here is the loneliness of a world under the power of death. The play is honest. This is our fate. Fickle gods!

I see once more my three children who died, the little daughter who slipped into the midwife's hands from her mother's body-gate and took a few breaths then ceased to move, though I breathed into her tiny mouth again and again until even weeping Paeonia screamed at me to stop, for there was no more hope. And the two boys who were born without life, my sons whom I would never know. And my Thea, apple of my eye, and Timo my brother-friend, and Xanthippos my little father. So many more, so many, many more. I see their faces before me now and ask what I have asked myself a thousand times before: Why did I not possess the skill and knowledge, the time and strength, that might have saved them? I know the answer to this question. I know all the answers to this riddle that mysterious fortune sets us. Yet I know it and do not know it. As we near the end, we suspect that we know little. At the utmost end, perhaps we discover that we know nothing. I seek to understand these things, and fail, yet I cannot stop myself from trying. It is my lot to fight.

*

Today, some isolated thoughts, to finish the last few pages of this scroll:

On his voyage through life, a man simultaneously looks ahead and behind. The past is interpreted, the future anticipated, yet neither viewpoint gives more than a glimpse of the real. Both past and future recede before our eyes as we stare at them, for we are in motion. I exaggerate, of course. We can reflect much, and learn much from the reflection.

*

A medical note, lest this journal leave a trail of misleading information for future generations of physicians, if there be any to read it with interest. I mentioned earlier in this book that when I found Loukas ill in Herakleia, I gave him the compound *theriake* dissolved in water. I should reemphasize that it seemed to do him no good—nor harm, for that matter. Generally I use it only as a last resort and always employ a version of the compound without the powder of ground adder snake, since, to my mind, the use of this and similar elements is merely the product of superstition. The theory behind *theriake* is that among the usual sixty and more elements in the compound, at least one might hit the target. It most often fails to do so, though it seems successful at times—but whether the occasional success is the result of other factors in the body's natural healing process or something in the medicine itself, I do not know. Enough about this!

*

Well, maybe a little more. As the sea passes by, whispering its secret language, the aphorisms of Hippocrates I memorized in my youth return to me again and again, sometimes with no apparent connection to my thoughts, and sometimes in connection with past events. Seeing in my mind's eye the body of Loukas at Herakleia, for example, I hear long-forgotten words speak inwardly:

"Old persons bear fasting most easily; next, adults; and young people yet less; least of all children, and of these least again those who are particularly lively."

The body that lay in death's grip during those weeks was far from lively, and only later did I learn how very lively he was by nature. I am glad now for the wet corn mash I poured down his open throat.

And this: "Life is short, and the Art long; the occasion fleeting; experience fallacious, and judgment difficult."

*

Oh, before I forget, more about books: The day before my departure from Crete, I made some gifts to my children from my library. Tranquilatus loaded the boxed rolls onto the garden handcart, the squeaky one with the single metal wheel, and we walked together through the city to Cleon's house, where Theodosia and Leandros were temporarily living during their stay in Gortyna. While I know that neither of my daughters is bookish by nature, except for Theo's affection for

142

older Attic poetry, I had a book of such poems for her in a single scroll. I had a book for Mila as well, a lovely short meditation written on *hieratica* papyrus, rolled on an ivory spool. The subject, a philosophy of motherhood—practical and inspiring.

When I arrived, I found the two couples sitting together chatting on benches in the dooryard. Surprised, all stood to greet me. They looked rather fatigued from the Olympics the night before, and we made some good jests about it. When I gave my girls their gifts, they flung themselves upon me and nearly suffocated me in kisses and tears—more of the latter than the former. The husbands stood nearby, observing.

Cleon is the scholar, and thus the largest gift went to him; Thucydides on the Peloponnesian War. Cleon has often visited my library to read from it and has not yet reached the end of its six massive rolls, a hundred pages each. If I had unrolled this book from my own front door to his, I would have walked on a carpet of papyrus all the way. He bowed his head when I showed him. Then, standing straight, he looked me in the eye and said:

"Father, this is your great treasure, and now I will hold it as my great treasure, and keep it in trust for us both. I will guard it with my life and pass it down to your descendants."

Leandros watched with a smile and his arms crossed, perhaps expecting nothing for himself, for of the two he is less like me in interests. But I had come prepared. I gave him the book I have been writing nearly continuously since my fortieth year, my own examinations of the trees and flora of Crete, with my drawings to illustrate each species—root, trunk, branch, seed, and fruit—with colors too. They are very good drawings, I might add. The book is a single scroll, middle-sized, and I unrolled it a little for him to see, then placed it into his hands. Straightening himself, head bowed, he said:

"Father, I accept this book that comes from your pen, your eye, your excellent mind, and your excellent heart, as a treasure I will guard with my life and pass down to your descendants."

After sending Tranquilatus home with the cart, I sat with them awhile, sipping a cup of mulled wine. As the sky turned red over the Plain of Phaestos, my sons-in-law walked back with me to see me safely home. At the gate, Leandros said, "Do you fear you will not return? Is that why you now give us such an inheritance?"

I did not say to him, "Life is short, and Art is long", though I should have. As I mentioned before, I do not tell lies easily, and so I said nothing in reply to his question. Instead, I thanked them both for loving my daughters so well and told them that if perchance I were delayed in my return, I would yet be at peace knowing that brave souls guard my family. They nodded somberly, clasped hands with me, and left.

*

For an hour last night I stood with the captain on the roof of the aft cabin as he took readings of the stars. He explained to me a few principles of stellar navigation, which is fascinating, I find. At one point he said:

"Master Theophilos, I have often thought that each man's life is a sea voyage. If he makes a mistake in navigation at the beginning, it appears to him as unimportant—a degree or two off, he thinks. Yet if he does not correct his course, that erroneous degree or two will translate itself into missing his destination port by vast distances. The error can extend his journey by weeks or months as he tries to find the port; indeed, he might never arrive there."

"A principle of mathematics, well known", I commented.

"Aye, and a rule of life well known, but not by all. Many a sea war has been lost, I would wager, because of that unimportant degree or two."

A good insight, an intriguing metaphor.

Now as I write in my journal, another: The rod or tube upon which a book is rolled, to which its endpiece is affixed, is called the *umbilicus*. A whimsical image, but there is a sublayer of truth within the name. A man's life—each man's life—is a book. There is material for further meditation here—but later.

And another: The sea is time and fate and mystery. It is calm weather and storms. Man's life is more storm than calm.

Would it be pretentious of me to coin a phrase? *"Man is metaphor maker."* He is like this because he senses in his very nature that the story in which he lives—as my father once emphatically told me—is an epic one, and this epic *is* the Great Metaphor.

*

[Journal entry, July 9, A.D. 65]

At sea
Scirophorion—Iulius

The days are stretching long, but I am resting. I did not realize how fatigued I was during the time leading up to departure. There is little for me to do now. I have set a sailor's broken arm bone after he fell from rigging. I also helped a fellow passenger, a Greek woman traveling to join her husband, a Roman official on Cyprus. She had lost much body water from dysentery, but she followed my advice and is improving. Other than that, nothing to write about. I walk the long deck back and forth each day to keep my lungs healthy and my limbs doddering along at a respectable old man's pace. I feel well in my flesh, but my thoughts constantly turn back to Crete. This is not to negate the rising anticipation of reunion with Loukas. But the sadness is there. I long for a child's quarrel, a girl's laugh, a boy's prank, a night-bird song, the face of my Paeonia.

There is a storm under way. The trireme handles it well. But the deck is heaving mightily, and I hear groans of seasickness from other cubicles in the deckhouse. The captain ordered all passengers to their cabins earlier today. As darkness fell, I made my way by stealth to the stern and climbed the ladder to the deckhouse roof. The man at the rudder cast a censorious look at me but decided to turn a blind eye. The sky above us roiled with turbulent clouds, beyond which stars and a fractured moon appeared and disappeared again. There was little to see, and the deck lamps swayed and flickered too brightly. So I went forward to the house at the bow, climbed to its roof, and held fast to its rigging. As I rode the great ship, I felt it plunging beneath my feet to the abyss below and then lifting me high into the clouds, and all the while the wind wailed like the sirens who would have dragged Odysseus to a watery grave. And though I was not tied to the mast, I held fast to the rigging and shouted the lines from Horace that came to me, his ode to Vergil's ship, on the presumption of human adventure:

> Encased in stubborn oak and threefold brass
> The breast of him who foremost dared
> Adventure in his fragile bark to pass
> Out onto the cruel sea—

And when my voice failed and I could shout no more, my own thoughts became a chorus: O human race, on waves of fate, the worst of you will plunge to crime and guile, the best of you will rise on the crest of presumption; as knowing or unknowing, defiling or abandoning, you leave your innocence in your wake.

I found myself laughing into the wind as I climbed back down to the deck, for it struck me that my musings approached the quality of verse. Is it possible, I thought, that I have composed an actual poem?

Then I slipped from the ladder and fell not far but was thrown by a roll of the ship toward the railing, and was saved by a hair from being washed overboard because I grabbed a cord of hemp that fate had unknotted and cast toward me. I pulled myself to safety and staggered obediently to my cubicle, and there I lay throughout the night, awake with wonder.

*

[Journal entry, July 14, A.D. 65]

Caesarea Maritima
Scirophorion—Iulius

Loukas will come down from Jerusalem four days from now, I am told. Neither he nor any of his friends in this city knew that I was coming to Judaea. But I was welcomed generously because of what he has told them about his early years. The respect I receive is due, in part, to the ways of this group of people, and as much or more because I am the father of Loukas.

I have had a good supper of bread and fish. My sea legs are becoming land legs again, though I am tired from the journey. My room, which is scarcely larger than the ship's cabin, is situated on the second floor of a brick house on the inland side, beyond the city walls. From my window, I can see a nearby cluster of palm trees and a very large grove of olives. The latter remind me of home, though Caesarea is markedly different from Gortyna.

Let me describe this wonder. When we sighted land a day and a half from port, I beheld only a vast coast stretching from horizon to horizon, from north to south, baked brown by the sun, peppered here and there by patches of green. It seemed deserted and barren.

Closer and closer we came, and during the night watch, I saw a spark appear above the waves. The helmsman turned the rudder a degree or two, pointing the bow toward it.

"Caesarea", he said. "You Greeks call it Sebastos."

The next morning there appeared an even greater light on the shore, still distant but steadily growing—a blaze of white that dazzled the eyes. By midmorning I could make out its buildings and the astounding harbor, which was made seventy-five years ago by a king of this land named Herod the Great. He spent twelve years building it as a gift to his patron Caesar Augustus. It seems a royal city, still fresh and new. Everywhere one looks, there is brightest, unblemished marble. Here the procurator of Judaea has his seat of government.

As one approaches by water, a tower stands higher than all rooftops—Strato's Tower, it is called. From the body of the city, immense jetties reach out like arms embracing the sea, surrounding a tranquil harbor of green-turquoise. Where the arms meet, there is a gap for ships to pass through, guarded by the great tower, on which fires are kept burning for guiding ships at night. We dropped anchor inside the embrace of the jetties, and then a small boat brought passengers to the grand promenade ringing the shore. Even this is floored with marble, though north and south of the city core it changes to less valuable stone. Nevertheless, the entire effect is one of grandeur and wealth. When I climbed up from the lower wharf—again, on steps of marble—I noted large numbers of soldiers continuously embarking and disembarking from the six war triremes anchored beside the higher piers. The departing soldiers looked weary and overheated, and with them they carried a few litters on which lay wounded or perhaps ill men. Numerous smaller vessels bobbed about between the great ships, fishermen's craft, and private boats of finer design, gilded or multicolored.

As I stepped onto the promenade, I was blinded by the sun beating down directly on all this splendor. With a hand shielding my brow, I looked up a flight of wide steps leading from the pier to a temple facing the harbor, its roof rising above all other public buildings around it. Turning aside, I entered the first street that would lead me into the city, and there I asked directions from a shopkeeper, a man in a striped red and black robe selling sweet breads folded over mashed dates. He spoke some Latin, but the little he knew was crude. In a friendly manner he explained that the Street of Silversmiths is beyond the city walls because the Romans have made a law against too much noise in Caesar's city. No horses or donkeys or wheels are allowed here during daylight hours, and the banging of hammers is banished to the outlying districts at all times, night or day. I would come to the silversmiths without fail, he said, if I went in the direction he pointed. And so indeed I did.

After traversing block after block of wealthy homes, I entered a less prosperous district of mixed marble and stone and passed through it until I reached the city's eastern gate. The soldiers on guard did not question me, and so I walked through the walls and into a meaner maze of brickwork and stone, with many a broken roof tile. I had reached the suburbs, and though here the building materials were decidedly of the humblest sort, the shops and residences were still three and four stories high. I had seen no beggars at the harbor, nor since, but now I noticed several, none of whom appeared to be Roman or Greek but were of diverse races. Some of them were children, and among these were a few who had been mutilated to invite pity. Latin is a universal language, it seems, and as I passed each beggar he would invariably hold out his hand and cry in a pleading tone, *"Da! Da!"*—Give! Give!

I gave what I could and kept going. Soon I heard the tapping-clanging of silversmiths and followed the sound until I reached its source. Turning onto the street, I proceeded with no one troubling me, searching for a sign with the name Diodorus inscribed on it. I found it three blocks farther along.

The house in which I am staying is overseen by a husband and wife, a Jewish couple who sell seafood for a living, I think, since there is a symbol of a fish scratched on the doorpost. They opened the door cautiously at first, but when I explained who I was, they bowed and let me in. There is no Diodorus here; he is the owner but lives elsewhere.

I will save myself a lot of needless effort by passing over much that followed. At least let me say that this house is something of an inn, though not open to any who happen by on the street. The ten who live here seem to know each other well, though five are Jews, two are Greek-born from Corinth, one is a darker man of Egypt, and two are native Judaeans of Greek race. There are others who come and go, but they do not sleep here. We eat together—very simple food, much like ours at home. They are warmhearted people. All are Greek speakers in varying degrees of competence. They asked me many questions about the boyhood of Loukas. I told them some amusing stories that made them laugh, and I noted that their laughter was affectionate. He is loved here; that is plain to see. They were not surprised when I mentioned that he had been a fine runner in his youth. "He is a fine *walker* now!" said one. It was the cause of some interest when I said that my son could recite from memory great quantities of poetry.

"He *is* good with words", one of the Jews commented.

"When he *does* speak", said another.

"From his roots in silence, his words flower and bear fruit", said a third. And every head in the room nodded in agreement.

He is not only loved; it seems he is greatly respected.

As I write this, they are singing together in the room below. I am very tired. I must sleep, since Loukas will be here soon. Three more days.

*

[Journal entry, July 19, A.D. 65]

Caesarea
Hecatombaion—Iulius

He is sleeping now, having walked all the way from Jerusalem. We share a room that is nearly filled by its two cots and a little desk. His physician's bag is on the floor in a corner, his walking stick beside it. Another bag holds blank papyrus rolls, some books, his pens, a small jar of ink.

I am listening to him snore. It makes me smile—so many memories. How many times in our lives have I remained awake beside him while he slept this sleep of trust? Countless nights in Gortyna, the dark sleep of Herakleia, the troubled sleep on the ship that bore us away from Thessalonike. Sleep, sleep, the little training for death, and all the while a physician sits nearby, awake in the night.

This morning we met again after ten years apart. It was like this:

I came down the stairs into the kitchen, and the woman tending the stove nodded with a smile toward the garden. I saw the figure sitting on the grass beneath an almond tree near the back wall of the enclosure but for a moment failed to recognize him. He was speaking with two other men of the household, and it looked to be about a serious matter. When

I stepped outside, he rose swiftly to his feet, his face naked as always—surprised, joy-filled, hesitant.

What did I feel? Love, fear, confusion. There are no words for it, and I had none to speak to him at that moment. This stranger in a Judaean robe striding toward me with outstretched arms, as tall as he was before, but bowed a degree by the weight of years. Then I saw my Loukas simultaneously as the boy, the youth, the young man—and stepping forth from them, as if from a dream, this older man now thirty-eight years of age. Balding, his great thatch of black hair had receded to a fringe on the crown of his forehead, threaded with gray. But the face was still young and open. As he threw his arms about me and kissed my old cheeks, tears ran from his eyes. He would not let me go, not even to preserve my dignity.

Well, it was a good feeling.

Finally, collecting himself, he introduced me to the others, though of course during the previous four days we had already met and had enjoyed some pleasant discussions.

"This is Theophilos son of Ariston of Gortyna", he said. "He is the father of my heart."

Later, he declared that I had not aged a day. I suppose this is so—my abiding curse (or blessing?) my too-young appearance. I reminded him that I was born in the twenty-ninth year of the reign of Caesar Augustus.

"Despite your white hairs, who could believe it?" Loukas laughed, shaking my shoulder with his hand, his eyes glinting with boyish mischief. "You have seen the sun circle about the earth sixty-six times!"

"A few circlings too many, I think."

"*Ooo-ooo*, Theophilos!" he frowned in jest. "How can you say such a thing? If you were not here, who would correct my poor philosophy?"

"You would find others with better minds than mine."

"But no better heart."

"Do not flatter me", I scowled, lifting my wrinkled hand. "Is this not the hand that once caned you for stealing the neighbor's pears?"

"But that was very good for me", he grinned. "I am grateful for the caning." His smiled faded a little, and his eyes searched out the window. "Though I regret the theft."

From his youth onward he had been an exemplary and honest boy, and it surprised me that he would rue so small a misdemeanor. But I did not think overmuch about it.

"They tell me you walk a great deal", I said.

"Ah, yes, I do", he nodded. "I am collecting more stories of the Kyrios."

"Will you ever be finished?"

"You mean, will I ever come home?"

"That too."

He did not answer the question. In fact, he changed the subject.

"So I hear you are running around Gortyna's walls again."

"Nonsense! Who told you that?"

"You did, in a letter."

"I did not! I *walk* around the walls, one or two days a week at most."

"That is a pity, for I was about to invite you to run with me to Jerusalem."

"Jerusalem. I would like to see it. But I fear I have little time for it. I had hoped to visit with you in this splendid city and return to your mother by next month."

"Well, we need not run to Jerusalem, Father, but we can surely walk together. There are several places I would like to show you. Especially we must walk by the sea." Suddenly, his face lit up, and something of his old childlike innocence shone forth. "We can make a little theater and listen to the waves chanting their poems."

I nodded and smiled, saying nothing, for I was overcome.

*

[Journal entry, July 23, A.D. 65]

Caesarea

Hecatombaion—Iulius

We did walk together by the sea. One afternoon we made a little theater out of small rubble at a place on the shore, an hour's walk north of here. But we did not turn to the darker tales of Aeschylus as we once had done. I recited something reflective but not tragic, a long poem. For my own amusement, I inserted into it the verse I had composed on the ship—about waves of fate and human presumption—hoping he would be deceived into thinking they were the poet's words. When I spoke those lines, he cocked his head with curiosity but made no comment. After that, he recited something comedic, and we laughed, then lapsed into silence. For a while we sat and watched the ships heading in and out of the distant harbor. At a certain moment we both seemed to know it was time to leave. We got up and walked back to the city in peace, with no further conversation.

When we arrived home, we found the others singing in the kitchen, a kind of prayer-song in a language I do not know. Loukas seemed to know it. Later he told me that part of it was sung in the formal Hebrew language of the Jews and another part sung in Aramaic, which is the common language of Jews throughout the land. It was a beautiful sound, though its meaning was incomprehensible to me. Apparently, they sing in many languages, often in Greek and sometimes, though seldom, in Latin.

Afterward, they did something quite surprising. They all went into the garden and washed each other's feet. They invited me to come too. I was reluctant at first, for it seems to me that one need not do a thing which another can do very well for himself. Loukas washed mine. The Egyptian washed the feet of a Jew. That man washed the Egyptian's. Well, it would be hard to sort out, if I were to describe it all, but in summation I can say that every foot was washed. It was done in a kind of restful silence. I did not mind it, though I feel more accustomed to giving such low service to the bodies of others and am uncomfortable when it is done to me. I hope I do not linger long with illness when I come to advanced old age. I would hate to be a burden. I hope I die walking.

There were numerous other companionable things that Loukas and I did together during my time with him, and we had good conversations too. He led me around to many interesting sites. I was impressed by the arched aqueduct that brings water to the city from a mountain named Karmel in the north—a great distance away. The Romans overwhelm the eye with their massive construction projects; the emotions reel in amazement, making one respect them for their skills. Even so, they impress by engineering and practicality, and oftentimes the eye is starved for the presence of beauty. I have seen our old Greek wonders, and though they are not as titanic as these, the form of beauty was always woven into their functions as a single unified whole. I should note, however, that the great theater on the south side of the city is quite beautiful, larger than ours in Gortyna, and newer too.

But this book is nearing its final pages, and so I will now record our most significant and disturbing exchange.

*

One night we sat in the garden very late, for the day's heat had been merciless, and though the sun had set, the rooms on the upper floors were like ovens. A light dew settled on the grass, and a breeze from the sea stirred the almond branches, the little seeds clicking pleasantly.

Until now we had not discussed the cause of his continuing interest in these people. While it was clear to me that he had adopted some of their customs, I still could not decide whether his behavior was merely sympathetic or was due to profound conviction. I had arrived in Judaea not knowing what to expect but had soon been reassured by their quiet nonfanatical ways. I had found them to be as Gaius had described—harmless. Even so, I wondered how long Loukas would tarry among them. Was their cult and their history really so important? Why had he given so much of himself to it?

I also wondered why he had not raised the subject with me. Was he hiding something? No, I told myself, that is not his way. More likely he thinks I will not understand what he would tell me, and so he bides his time until he thinks I am ready to hear it.

That night, it seemed that the time had come.

We ate a tasty bread with salted ewe's cheese and sipped some green Judaean wine that had not yet properly aged. Then I said:

"These are good people, your friends."

"Indeed, they are the best", he replied.

"Yet such diverse races and manners there are among them. What keeps you together?"

"It is the *koinonia*—which is given to us."

"But what gives you this union, as you call it?"

"It is given by the Kyrios."

"Ah, you mean the Christos, the anointed one whose life you wrote about in your chronicle."

"Yes, but more than him. It is difficult to explain it to you in a way that can be understood by the mind."

"Do you underestimate my mind?"

"No, but I know that some truths are so vast, so deep, that they are not comprehensible to the mind alone. When we speak of them, our words convey little more than impressions, and as you would be the first to say, impressions are unreliable."

"Even so, why not tell me one such truth, and we might put it to the test of understanding?"

Loukas hesitated a moment, then said:

"The Kyrios, our Iesous, is one with the Father and the Holy Spirit."

"They live together?" I asked, puzzled. "But which of them is the god?"

"All three."

"Then you have three gods. I thought the Jews believe there is only one."

"They are three in one."

I shook my head. "Loukas, the logic of that escapes me."

"You reverence logic, Theophilos, yet logic does not contain the whole *kosmos*. A city, for example, is logical. The sea is not."

I was startled by this, for my own father had said much the same thing to me more than fifty years ago. Had I once told Loukas about it, and was he now repeating it back to me?

Leaning toward me earnestly, with a look of yearning, he said, "I know how difficult it seems. But did you not once say to me that a man is a single unified being with several dimensions? Did you not tell me that he is not an empire with three separate nations held together by force?"

"I might have said something like that about the body, mind, and spirit."

"So, you see it! If man can be one thing when viewed in a certain way, and three things when we consider him in another way, is it possible his Creator is also like that?"

I nodded and said, "Yes, I can see it—though it is no more than a theory."

For a moment I felt haunted, as if we had had this conversation before, but of course that was not so.

"Yet this too is no more than an imperfect figure of the reality", he continued. "They are not three gods in alliance. Neither are they one god with three manifestations, like an actor with several masks."

"You confuse me totally", I said with a shake of the head and a click of the tongue.

"They are three Persons in one Godhead", he declared emphatically. "But to attempt a convincing explanation, as if the infinite Creator could be examined scientifically, is to try to contain an ocean in a cup."

"Then why this futile discussion on the matter?"

"I have prayed and prayed, for years I have prayed, that you and Mother and all who are beloved to me will come to know the joy the Father offers us through the Son."

"It seems to me that he offers much suffering to those who follow his son."

"Yes, in the world we will have troubles, yet he has overcome the world."

"How can you say this, Loukas? Look, look at the world, my son!"

"You do not yet understand."

"I understand that you have been beguiled."

"There is no place for guile in his kingdom. He does not force me to love him, for in truth that would not be love. He invites us to a wedding banquet, Theophilos, one that is most glorious and without end."

"One cannot eat and drink the air of dreams! By what roads have you come to this mystical belief?"

"In Antioch I was born."

I stared at him as if he had lost his sanity.

"In the first year after I went away from you, I journeyed to Antioch, where Paul was staying for a time. There I was baptized and there I was born again."

"Why did you not say anything about this? You wrote letters to me from that city. You mentioned its marvelous buildings and the river Orontes and said you had good friends and a teacher. But you did not tell what kind of friendship and teaching, and now I see why."

"Would you have understood me if I had explained?"

"You might have made an effort at it."

"Oh no, my dear Theophilos, that never would have succeeded. From the beginning, it has been my desire that you should come to these lands and see for yourself. I know your great intellect. Your logic and vast knowledge would have absorbed whatever I said in a letter and put it away like a new book in the library of your mind. An oddity, no more than a curious tale to be fitted into your cosmology. You would have presumed you understood when you understood little or nothing."

"And last year you changed your mind about me?"

"I sent you my record of the Kyrios because he told me the time had come."

"He told you the time had come?" I laughed. "Well, here I am before you. But I am here because of love, not for a diet of new myths. You say that your Christos has overcome and not overcome. Do you not see the contradiction in this? Besides, the Romans killed him."

"He lives."

"The realm of spirits and ghosts is known to all peoples. If he walks in the Isles of the Blessed, well then, he lives. But I cannot accept what you wrote in your chronicle. When the lifeblood leaves a man, none can put it back into him again."

"It did leave him."

Loukas then described in medical terms the details of the Christos' crucifixion, as it had been told to him. It ended in blood and water spewing from a lance wound through the heart. The water was significant, and it puzzled me because this unexpected detail would have meant little or nothing to most who saw it.

"So he was dead, according to those who told you about it."

"Yes, he was dead—fully dead. The body was stiffening as they laid it into the tomb."

"And three days later he was alive again, you say. But in what sense alive? Are there not many who grieve over a death, and then see their beloved alive again? Yet it is a phantasm of their heart's longing. The imagination is a powerful force."

"It was not like that", said Loukas, shaking his head emphatically. "He walked with them, they spoke together, he let them touch his wounds. He ate meals with them. He cooked breakfast for them on the shore of a lake that is east of here."

"He cooked breakfast? If that is so, he never died. His death was the illusion."

"His death was no illusion. And his return from death was no illusion."

"Did you see either of the two with your own eyes? Did you see one of them, perhaps, or both of them, or neither?"

"You know the answer to that."

"Yes, and I will ask it again and again, for our human minds cannot be trusted. Neither the teller's nor the listener's minds. We cannot hang our lives upon a thread of someone's story."

"Oh, it is far more than a story, though it must be related by stories. But I have seen with my own eyes what happened to his mother."

"Ah, yes, you mentioned her in one of your letters. She too rose from the dead, apparently."

"Myriam died, Theophilos. I attended her when she died. It was real death. I helped carry the body into the tomb. I watched as the stone was rolled over the entrance, and I observed the sealing. Myriam's son Yochanan sealed it with wax and inscribed it. When we returned days later to open the tomb for an *apostoloi* who had arrived too late, we went inside, intending to lay fresh flowers and spices by the body. We found the stone still sealed as we had left it. But when we opened it, there was no body within."

"Another missing body", I muttered, frowning, my eyes communicating what I thought about this tale.

At that point, he abruptly rose to his feet and went into the house. I wondered if I had offended him by my doubts, for now I knew how strong was his belief. Yes, strong—but how deep, really?

He returned bearing a tray with three small clay lamps and a larger brass one, their wicks burning brightly. He set the tray on the grass between us and gently pushed the clay lamps together until they touched. These had a single flame each. The brass one had three flame spouts.

When he had settled himself, I saw by the light that his face was tranquil. I had expected to find anger there or at least some irritation. But there was none.

He pointed to the lamps and said, "Three separate entities pushed together are not the same as one entity with three manifestations. Though the metaphor is flawed, do you see the difference?"

"I see six flames, that is certain. These old eyes of mine have seen much, Loukas. They are good eyes."

"Yes, they are good eyes. I know it."

"Yet it seems you no longer trust my eyes."

He smiled and said, "I revere your eyes greatly, for without them I would have died long ago. Yet I have met men with other sight. Their eyes are true and good—as are yours—but they have seen more than you."

"You love them, this I can see plainly. It makes me doubt your story more than ever, for a man's mind is influenced most by those whose opinion he values."

"True, man is easily influenced. But I have seen evidence."

"More empty tombs?"

He closed his eyes and tapped the lids with his fingers. "I put a case to you: Let us imagine that I have never met your mentor Xanthippos. Let us say that he has died, and you tell me remarkable stories about his life. I accept your stories; I believe they are true because of your testimony."

"You should not trust me *that* much", I said, and he laughed, as I had hoped he would.

"I know that your testimony is trustworthy, because it has never failed me. You pulled me from the mouth of death. But what if many witnesses who had known your friend were now giving wondrous accounts of him, and all tales matched? And then what would you say if those friends put their hands upon the lame and asked of God a healing in the name of Xanthippos? And then the lame walked, and the blind were given their sight, and the mad became sane, and those possessed by evil spirits were set free, and those in all manner of darkness were changed, their lives now filled with light, and moreover light poured from them too? And when they in turn prayed over others in the name of Xanthippos, the same miracles occurred?"

"I would say that the gods were generous and wished to honor the man Xanthippos."

"I do not think you would say that." Once more Loukas shook his head. "You do not believe in the gods."

"Well, in a fashion I do. At times it seems to me they may be real. At least our thoughts of them represent some force or majesty that is in a realm beyond us."

"Yet they behave like beasts at times. In fact, worse than beasts, for they are ourselves writ large on a theater stage."

"I know. They are sometimes a sorry lot."

"I ask a serious question, Theophilos. I ask you to shift your mind's eye, your soul's eye, and see farther. Because what I have told you has happened, and I have seen it with my own eyes. I have seen the lame walk and the blind given sight and those without hope restored to fullness of life. It is done in the name of Iesous. It is done abundantly in his name, and it is done not at all in the name of any other."

"Science has explanations for what we call miracles. And when it cannot explain a phenomenon, it is because we do not yet have full knowledge of the forces in nature. All men of intelligence agree about that."

I expected a reaction. I expected a copious dialogue to ensue. Instead, to my surprise, he merely gazed at me with affection and sympathy. It made me very uncomfortable.

"I have seen the dead raised to life", he said quietly.

This now took me aback.

"You saw what you desired to see. They were not dead or else they were not truly alive."

"They were both. I saw both." And again he touched his fingers to his eyes.

"Loukas, Loukas", I sighed. "Man is ever yearning to overcome his great enemy, and he clings to splinters of hope as a survivor from a sinking ship, but these are illusions. Death is the victor. Death has overcome the world, and it will always be so. We can resist him for a time, and in this lies our heroism, our true greatness. But he will not be overcome."

"He is already overcome, and his last defeat awaits him."

"So you say", I murmured sadly, for it seemed we had progressed no farther than when we began. I wished to end the conversation, to go to bed, to weep, to sleep, and then to dream of the Blessed Isles, which do not exist yet may console us for a time before the end.

"There are many witnesses", Loukas said. "Will you not come with me and meet them?"

Then did old words of defeat arise in my heart again, from a time years past when he had wanted me to go with him down into the bowels of evil ships to heal the enslaved. Now, as then, I could not. I could not face my broken heart, and beneath it my dismay, and still deeper I saw waiting for me my despair over the fate of man that I keep ever within its urn.

"Come with me and see", he said again.

I said nothing. I could say nothing.

He took my hand, firmly and tenderly. And in the holding I felt the world turn, and I was the child and he the father, and both of us were going out into the dark earth from a burning city.

And when at last the night had grown cool, he drew me to my feet.

"Come", he said once more. "And we will make a breakfast on the shore of eternity."

*

[Journal entry, July 29, A.D. 65]

Nazareth
Hecatombaion—Iulius

I am not happy about this. I have agreed to Loukas' proposal only for the purpose of proving my unprejudiced mind to him, which may lend itself to a better dialogue. In time he may hear my objections with unstopped ears and then begin to reconsider the fallacies that have ensnared him.

In the end we did not go to Jerusalem. He decided that we should go first to the place where it all began. He rented a donkey and made me ride upon it as he and two companions walked along beside me. The journey northward into the high hills of the interior took five days. The Jews who came with us are both Galileans, their speech plain and soft, not unlike the musical Hebrew that I have heard at Caesarea. These languages remain impenetrable to me, but Loukas has a passing knowledge of both. One of the Jews speaks good Greek. They call this upland region "mountains", though they are no more than high hills. Clearly the poor fellows have never seen real mountains, and doubtless the white peaks of Crete and the soaring ranges of Thessaly would make them stagger with wonder.

Now we are here. For sleeping, Loukas and I are to share a straw mat on the floor of a one-room inn—though it hardly deserves the name. The building is on the outskirts of the town, a shelter of unmortared stones with rough-hewn timber as its roof beams and over all a thatch of grass. There is a well nearby with clearest spring water. The food is plain but good, brought to us by the woman who owns the inn. She addresses Loukas as *adon*, "master". He calls her *marttha*, which means "lady", but who she is I do not yet know.

Though it lacks the red tiles of civilization, Nazareth is nevertheless a pretty place. Inhabited by fewer than a thousand people, it is scattered about a hillside overlooking a lush green valley, which these people call Jezreel. The air is milder than it was on the coast. There are plenty of trees round-about or standing here and there between the houses— olives, almonds, and figs, but no dates as far as I can see. A single cinnamon cassia tree, ancient and solitary, shades the inn's front door, spreading its perfume on weary travelers. Below us, a copse of tough little oaks stands guard by a road that comes from somewhere and goes somewhere else, a traders' route centuries old.

Each house has its walled kitchen garden, and clustering about many are sheds and shops. There are only a few larger buildings, including a substantial synagogue of simple stonework and unadorned pillars. In the streets numerous goats wander about, and mongrel dogs will bark at anyone whom the curs have judged to be an interloper. Flocks of sheep move at a leisurely pace over the surrounding hills.

Loukas is busy negotiating meetings for me with local people. He must return to Jerusalem tomorrow and will meet with me there four weeks from now. I feel extremely irritated by this unexpected change in plans. However, he promises that when we are reunited in the city he will conduct me through the next stage of my journey.

"Dear Theophilos", he said last night. "I know you will listen to what these people will tell you, some of whom are favorable and some of whom are not. Sift and weigh, and write it down in your books, if you will."

"Indeed I shall", I said like a magistrate who cannot be swayed by influence.

With a swift look into my eyes, and a whiff of his boyhood humor, he said, "Good. You can call them your examinations. I will read your prognosis with interest."

"My *diagnosis*."

With a smile he blew out the lamp, and we went to sleep.

So, it turns out that I am to be left in this place without his protection or guidance. Despite my protests, he assures me that I am in good hands, for one of the Jews, the Greek speaker whom I mentioned, a man named Aharon Ben Issachar, will stay with me to act as my interpreter.

What folly, all this! I have made a great mistake entangling myself in it. But I will persevere for his sake, and who can foresee what will come of it?

Now I have reached the end of this book. There is only enough space to bring it to a close with these few words of explanation. I breathe uneasy sighs. I am in a strange land among very strange people. Yet I am alive and more or less in my right mind, and with my own hand I can still put a pen to the final page.

I am
Theophilos of Aristonides of Gortyna.

EXAMINATIONS

Here I begin a fresh scroll.

I wrote the above line in the first rays of sunrise as I sat on a bench beneath the cinnamon tree. I stared at the blank page and wondered what would be written here by the time I had reached the final leaf. Doubtless it would be a compound of human opinions, distorted memories, imaginings presented as experience, and all manner of things that people spew out of their mouths when they are asked a simple question.

Then I saw by my irritable feelings that anger brewed in me. This was not good. This would not be helpful to my task, for I honestly intended to make an accurate record of what people said, regardless of how far from reason they might be.

No emotion, Theophilos, I admonished myself. *No emotion!*

I resolved to treat the matter as if I were a physician ministering to the ill. I would carefully write down the words of people who had known the Christos, and I would weigh their accounts—should I say, their symptoms—in the interest of making an informed diagnosis. And if such diagnosis were insufficient for a conclusion, then I would make incisions for the purpose of biopsy, to see if the flesh was infected deeply or merely suffered a surface ailment. My mind and my tongue would be the scalpel.

Loukas had left for Jerusalem before dawn, and I now regretted that my parting with him was rather cool, indeed quite formal. I did not respond in kind to his warm words of encouragement nor to his avowal of how highly he esteemed my capacity for honest inquiry. He kissed my cheek upon departure, and I returned the gesture woodenly.

I have accepted this challenge for no other reason than that it may prove to him how misled he is. He cannot hereafter argue that I was unwilling to examine the so-called facts on which he has based his new way of life. As burdensome as this investigation is for me, it is a sacrifice I am willing to make for the sake of his ultimate good.

When the sun rose entirely above the eastern hills, the burning orb coaxed the dew off the tree and began to scatter its strong perfume all about. A thin golden mist hovered in the valley below. The "marttha" of the house brought me a cup of water, a basket of hot bread, and a bowl of salty milk curds. She bowed to me and went away. I ate the breakfast distractedly as I awaited Aharon Ben Issachar's arrival.

My translator, my guide across the Styx, made his appearance soon after and greeted me with kindly deference. Since we were to be companioned for some weeks, I took a closer look at him:

At first glance he was a typical Jew about forty years of age, long-haired, long-bearded. The skin of his face and hands was light brown, his eyes dark brown, the dome of his skull indicating the potential for developed thought. His hands were disproportionately large, well accustomed to physical labor. He carried his body with dignity but without affectation. His robes were simple woven material, tawny in color, girded by a belt of braided wool. His calves and ankles were sun-darkened, the wide feet bound in heavy sandals that looked as if they were designed for lengthy and arduous walking. Around his shoulders dangled a long narrow scarf, which, I presumed, could be wrapped about his head as protection from wind and sun. Unlike other male Jews of the region, he usually wore no cap or cloth headgear. Suspended by his hip, on a strap that crossed his chest, was a satchel that contained I knew not what. Food perhaps.

"So, Aharon," I commenced in a disinterested tone, "we are to meet people who can tell us something about the Christos."

His head dipped at his hero's name, and he said, "Yes, there are many here who knew him from childhood onward, and they would tell you much about him. From my own experience I can tell you only a little, for I was still a boy when he died and am not from this town."

"Yet you are a follower of his new religious way."

"Yes, I am, though it would be more correct to say that what he taught us is both new and the fulfillment of the old."

"Ah", I nodded without commitment. "Did you ever meet him?"

"Yes, in my hometown, Capernaum, which is to the east of here. But as I said, I was very young and did not understand at the time what was occurring before my eyes."

"And now you understand it?"

He smiled. "As much as a man may understand the ways of the Most High."

There was nothing I could reply to this, so I stood up in a brisk, determined manner, inhaled, and glanced down the slope to the center of Nazareth, implying that we must not let ourselves be mired in philosophizing.

"Perhaps we should begin", I suggested.

"Of course", Aharon replied. "Whenever you are ready."

As I shouldered my physician's kit, after first placing this scroll, my stylus, and my ink bottle into it, he said, "There are several people who have agreed to meet with you. The first is—"

"Are they believers in the Christos?" I interrupted.

"Yes", he said, scanning my eyes curiously.

"I would prefer a different method of research. It would be best, I believe, to discuss the matter with a broad variety of people in this town."

"As you wish", he replied without great enthusiasm. "Whom would you like to meet?"

"Anyone and everyone. Why don't we simply stroll along the main street and ask the first passerby we come to. I expect that all those of a certain age knew him, and those who did not know him have surely heard about him."

"It will be as you choose", said Aharon evenly. "And I will translate for you, if you wish."

"I would be grateful", I said, looking into his eyes. "I feel sure that you will translate accurately, even the words of those who are not followers of the Christos."

He nodded in affirmation, but there was a sudden hurt in his eyes, as if I had questioned his honesty. I suppose that in a veiled way I *was* warning him to be honest. Doubtless, some of the sadness that washed across his face, swiftly come and swiftly gone, was also due to his realization that I am very unlike Loukas. I instantly regretted inflicting this offense, unwitting as it was, but I also saw that the thoughtlessness on my part had its root in my anxiety to avoid delusion.

We walked side by side from the inn and turned onto the main street. It was not crowded, but there were more than enough people to serve my purpose. Even so, as I approached this one or that one, he or she would invariably swerve away to avoid meeting me.

"It is your Greek appearance", Aharon explained. "In the cities it is different, for there one finds many Greeks, but here people feel some suspicion."

"Would it be better if you were to make the first approach?" I asked.

"It would."

Coming to a well in a small public courtyard, Aharon spoke to three women who were filling their jars with water. Two glanced at me nervously, finished their business, and departed. The one who remained eyed me guardedly, but Aharon continued to engage her attention with whatever he was saying, until at last she shrugged. Lifting her full jar to her shoulder, she indicated with a tilt of her head that we should follow her. We were led from the courtyard to a side street, and a short distance along it we came to an open gate, which I took to be the woman's. As we entered the dusty little compound I saw that her house was not unlike the dwellings of Xanthippos and Pellene. She perched herself on the doorstep and pointed to a rough garden bench, on which Aharon and I sat down. My first examination followed.

Nazareth
The housewife Tzipporah

She is at least seventy years of age, a widow, indistinguishable in appearance and way of life from numerous other women in this town. In her face can be read a mixture of irritability and eagerness. She wishes to tell her story.

Aharon translates aloud. I write as quickly as I can and in the process find myself resorting to this Tironian shorthand. The more I use, the more returns to me. Frequently, I must stop the woman with an upheld hand in order to complete transcribing her words, which do not emerge slowly and in low murmurs as is usual with these people. No, she is fast and intense. I wonder why it is so, especially since most of the Nazareans I have met so far seem indisposed to speak with me. From time to time, Aharon himself raises a hand to her and then turns to me with explanations of a phrase or a word. I write down what she says, omitting our interruptions:

So, you want to know about him. Well, people have come and gone and come again asking the same questions over and over. This is the first time anyone has bothered to ask me, and I can tell you much. I can tell you things about him that no one wants to hear because some say he was the *meshiha*, and some say not, but most who live here think not. And who better to know a man than the ones he lived with all his life! But the others, you Greeks and some of our own from Jerusalem and eastern Galilee, they like to make him bigger than he was, because they need him for their own purposes. It has always been that way with us. It's a bad habit we have. A *meshiha* arises among us and the Babylonians strike him down, or the Syrians, or the Romans. And still no kingdom restored. Each of them leaves a trail of worse woes behind him. And who cleans up the mess? We do. Always it's this way.

Yeshua Bar Yosef? What was he like? Let me tell you about him. I was ten years old when he and his parents came back from the south. Some say they went to Egypt. Why to Egypt? I ask myself. Why would a good Jew go down to the land of our bondage unless he is flying from shame? No one ever thinks to ask about that!

I have held my peace all these years while the world talks and talks and talks. If anyone had asked me, I would have told them the plain facts. But no—they all want what they want. Do you think we are fools, just because we live in a little town in the hills far from the big cities? We have a fine synagogue, and rabbis who studied in Jerusalem, and plenty of lettered men among us as well. And those who cannot read scrolls are not lacking in good sense. We know about people. We keep an eye on each other's ways, and that has kept us from harm since Mosheh brought us out of Egypt.

Maybe you heard about what happened here. When he started calling himself *meshiha*, our elders knew he was speaking blasphemy and would have thrown him from the brow of the hill—over there—but he ran off. He ran far away and did not come back. Then the Romans killed him. Yes, another *meshiha*, but a bad one, talking blasphemy and dying on a cross. I do not say that any Jew deserves to die in that way, but he brought it upon himself.

Some will tell you he came back from the dead. A few such live here among us, the gullible who would believe anything.

Yeshua was ordinary in every way. You would not notice him unless you needed a bench made or a roof timber cut. I saw him nearly every day from his childhood until he started roving about preaching. Suddenly he was a preacher, after he hardly put two words together during all those long years he worked in his father's shop. Carpenters they both were. Of course, I don't want to be harsh. He wasn't so bad when he was younger. He did nobody harm, not that I heard about.

You ask about his childhood. There is nothing unusual there. He was like other boys, though maybe a bit quieter than most. When I was a girl, our mothers sometimes talked together at the well, his and mine, as they were getting water. He sang songs to himself. I forget what those were about, his own things he made up. He had friends, other boys his age. They played kickball in their street with a sheepskin. But he wasn't noisy like some of those lads. The children of Nazareth are very well behaved, I should tell you right now. There are no thieves among them and never have been. Now and then a stupid one or a too-smart one will be insolent to his parents, but we put a stop to that. There is a saying among us: "When a thistle blooms, pluck its flower swiftly, even though it hurts your hand." I say more—I say *burn* that thistle because even a plucked one makes its seeds and the wind blows them all over the fields. You should see how hard we work to get rid of them down in the fields of Jezreel. My husband and I had a plot of wheat and barley there, though I had to sell it after he died. Life is harder now, but I get by. I could tell you a lot about good wheat and bad thistles.

Was Yeshua wheat or thistle? Maybe a mixture of both. I liked him in the early years, and now it makes me sad when I think about it because he went so wrong in the end. He might have had a good life here, done well in his trade, raised a family. But that is always a problem with our young men. They spend every spare hour in the synagogue reading the Torah, studying the Law, praying all the time, and then a madness strikes them and they go off thinking they will save Israel.

I remember one thing that happened when he was a little boy. Talking about thistles brings it to mind. He was about five years old. I was twelve. That day I was filling water jars with my mother at the well. The mother of Yeshua—Miryam was her name—was filling her jar too. The women chatted together for a bit. Miryam's little boy was hopping about in the dust like a sparrow, playing some kind of game, singing silly songs—you know the way children do. I was bored by the adults and so I watched him.

He spied a thistle plant blooming against the back wall of a house and went over to it, very interested, as if it were a rose of Sharon. He held the prickly bloom in his hand and stared at it. I wondered if he was addled in his wits, for everyone knows thistles and hates them, and I would guess that he had seen more than enough of them even at so young an age. But you would think he had never seen one before. For the longest time he stood very quietly without moving, holding it. It makes me wince just thinking about it. Then his mother noticed and put down her jug and went to him. I went too. He turned to her and showed her the blossom he held in his hand. There were drops of blood on his fingertips. She said something to him, and he let it go. She wiped his hand with her apron.

Then he did the strangest thing. He bent over and kissed the blossom, and that must have hurt him. When he straightened up he turned toward the wall of the synagogue, which is just down the street from the well. He bowed to it. Then he smiled. He had a nice smile. His eyes were nice too. So you understand why I am sad when I think about him sometimes, the way he was. A good boy. But a little bit crazy, as you can well see by my story.

Nazareth
Joash Bar Eliazar, the rabbi of the town synagogue

In the afternoon we happen to pass by the open portal of the synagogue, where a man near fifty years of age is standing in the shade of a pillar reading from a small scroll. Aharon approaches him and speaks in low murmurs. The man ponders what is being said to him. Finally he shoots a swift glance in my direction and nods, once, and heaves a visible sigh.

Courteous introductions are made. I learn that he is the rabbi—the main teacher—of the synagogue. The day is so hot that the soles of our feet are blistering within their sandals, but it seems I am not to enter the cool of the building. Because I am a Gentile, it is forbidden. Yet he is not unfeeling and invites Aharon and me to converse with him in the shade of a terebinth tree across the street. There we sit down on the ground and begin. He speaks in the low-pitched ponderous tones of a scholar. He apologizes that he knows little Greek and asks if we prefer to hear him in Hebrew or in Aramaic. Aharon chooses the latter.

The rabbi says:

Please accept my welcome to you. It is my wish that the guardian of Loukas of Antioch be at home among us. Yet I am sure you understand that our people suffer from prejudices and division. Please do not be offended by the attitude of some toward you. The Romans have created much fear, as have all conquerors before them.

179

Galilee is ever the land of unrest, especially the region north of here in the uncharted highlands covered with forest and riven by cuts in the earth, with caves where men may hide in times of peril. Thus, it is a place for both refuge and fomenting rebellion. For that reason the Romans are thick among us, coming and going, arresting those whom they suspect. Zealots in the hills are a growing problem. They love Israel but are thoughtless about the fate of our people. Too readily would they sacrifice other lives for the sake of all—that is how they see it, that is what they think they are doing. But I say it is better that the nation should suffer than to bring about the unjust death of one man. In times past the Most High permitted alien nations to come over us so that we might be purified of our sins and learn again what we so easily forget: that the Lord alone is our strength. The Lord is also a God of justice, and no innocent blood will go unseen by him.

You ask me about Yeshua Bar Yosef. I will tell you. But first I wish to make clear that I do not believe that he was the *meshiha*. I am a faithful Jew, of the Pharisees, though I cannot agree with everything the Sanhedrin has done, then and now. The people of Israel will survive everything. The political zealots and the religious preachers, even those who may have a spark of the prophetic gift we once knew in times past, all of them mix their own thoughts with the truths of the Torah. It is in this mixture where we become lost, and from it injustice spreads. Our entire history is full of this confusion, though at times the Lord raised up prophets and teachers, and now and then a righteous king, and there was peace for a time.

The execution of Yeshua Bar Yosef was unjust in every way. The Sanhedrin violated the Torah by turning him over to a pagan judge and a death of shame. Though the elders' knowledge was great, their eyes were blind to the fullness of the

Torah, to its deeper intention. Yet are we not all blind, each in his own way? That is why we must study what has been given from above and follow the Law to perfection. In no other way can a man be saved.

No, he was not a Zealot. He was zealous for the House of the Lord. Not once during the time I knew him did he speak a word that would promote insurrection. Always, he drew his followers to the ways of peace. Also, you must try to understand that there were two distinct periods of his life: the years he lived in this town, when few, if any, paid him attention; and the years when he went forth from us and journeyed about all Israel and into Samaria as well, preaching what he called his "good announcements".

Yes, I do remember the day the whole synagogue rose up in anger and brought him to the brow of the hill. That year I had become a man and prayed among the men. I was thirteen years old. By then we had begun to hear reports about certain wonders Yeshua was doing in other places, and most of us doubted it. Yet all were curious, for here was the carpenter's son becoming famous.

One Sabbath day he returned from his journeys without warning, entered the synagogue, and sat down among us. My father was the elder that year, and he called upon Yeshua to read from the scroll of the prophet Isaiah. He stood and took the scroll, unrolled it, and read the passage about the Lord's year of favor when the poor and the afflicted will be raised up from their sufferings. It is a prophecy about the *meshiha* who is to come. Even now, more than thirty years later, I remember what I felt as I listened to him. He spoke with strength, but not with the force that is usually seen in speakers who wish to impress. He let the words themselves be the power, and his heart was wholly in them. Indeed, my own heart leaped within me, though I was unsure of his meaning.

He sat down and began to explain the passage to us. His words were gracious and simple, and as he spoke I learned why his reputation was growing far and wide. Neither before nor since have I heard any other man speak as he did. I think most of us were moved. There was great stillness in the room.

Yet he would not leave it at that. He said:

"This text is being fulfilled today even as you listen."

Then puzzled looks crossed many faces. What did he mean? Was it being fulfilled elsewhere in Israel? Was there a great event under way that we had not heard about? And some began to frown and whisper, for they remembered that he was a man with callouses on his hands, and no son of scholars and priests. We all had known his father, Yosef Bar Yaakov, a just man but in no way outstanding beyond his righteousness.

Then Yeshua made a great mistake. He seemed to know the grumblings in the hearts of some, and he spoke directly to it. He told them exactly what they were thinking, and this made them angry. A few elders rose to their feet, as they began to understand him.

"I tell you solemnly", he said in a voice so quiet, so gentle, that none should have taken offense at it. "I tell you solemnly that no prophet is ever accepted among his own people."

If he had left it at that, the situation would not have turned out as it did. But he went on to declare that in times past certain prophets had been sent by the Most High to those outside the household of Israel. He cited Elijah and Elisha, who are especially beloved to us, for Karmel is near and these two are considered foremost because of their wondrous doings. All in the synagogue were enraged by this, save me and my father and a scattering of others. All sprang to their feet as the crowd began roaring and shaking their fists. Then they swept him out into the street and from there to the brow of the hill.

They would have thrown him over to his death, but he slipped through them and walked away.

Now all these years later, I see that it was a temper of the moment. He had stripped bare not only their thoughts but also their pride. Even so, I still ask myself why they were so angry. It was a shock to me at the time, and I still puzzle over their reaction.

When the dust had settled on the hill, my father took me apart and explained a little of what had happened, though I think he too was greatly perplexed by it. He said:

"The spirit of the Most High is indeed upon this man. Yet I wonder, has this spirit come in fullness? Is it yet to age like wine? Or will it spoil and become vinegar? He has called himself the anointed, and this is a thing so immense that no man should say it of himself."

"Is he the *meshiha* we are promised, Father?" I asked.

"This is what he says today through the scripture and in his explanation."

"Do you think he is the *meshiha*?" I pressed for an answer, for my heart hoped that he was.

But my father would not reply. He was greatly troubled, and we went home in uncertainty with secret questions in our thoughts. I never again saw Yeshua Bar Yosef, but reports of him continued to reach us long after by word of mouth.

You ask me, what was he like when he was younger? There is not much I can tell you about that. At least there is nothing beyond the ordinary tales one might tell about a laborer. I remember his father's shop, where they both worked side by side. I loved the smell of wood shavings, so I went there whenever I could. Yosef was a solemn man, devoted to the sacred texts, but he also had a twinkle in his eye. You know the type—small proverbs and much kindness. His jokes were whimsical and never mean. They always had a hidden point to make.

Never a mocking belly laugh would you hear from him. But a smile now and then, and many a small gift to be had.

A few years before his son went away from Nazareth, I was sitting at the doorway of their woodshed while Yeshua trimmed and squared a trunk of olive. Behind him, his father watched. I watched too, content just to be there. A good feeling. I should have mentioned before that whenever I was around them I felt the world was no longer dangerous, that life was very good. Later, when he went away, it was as if he became a stranger, because what he did and taught were things I had not seen him do before. Of course, I was just a boy at the time. I was eleven or twelve years old when he went away.

What had I begun to tell you? Oh yes, the gift. Well, I was eight years old, just sitting there in the sunshine, and it was the light of spring, a beautiful light, and all the almond trees throughout the village were rich with blossoms in a way I had not seen them bloom until then—an abundance of flowers and later an abundant harvest. Even now I recall what I thought that day. Perhaps I merely felt it, but here is its meaning:

This is how life should be. This is how I would always like to live, with these people.

Part of what I felt had to do with the mother of this family—Miryam—whom I believe you never met because she went away to Jerusalem and later to a city in Asia. Loukas tells me that she has passed away into the hands of the Most High. She sleeps in the bosom of Abraham, and that is a place she well deserves to be after the trials she has borne in her life. I remember many gifts from her. When I was a boy I could not stay away from the place, both house and shed. I would offer to sweep the shavings off the work floor, and they let me do it. I would carry firewood to her door unasked, and she let me do it, rewarding me with small cakes of pressed barley and honey with poppy seed. I can taste it now. My wife makes it too. Maybe they liked me especially for working unbidden and demanding no wages. They had few coins, you can be sure. But food and kindness they gave me aplenty. I did not ask myself why I did these things.

What was I saying? Oh yes, that day I was sitting by the doorpost watching the men at work. The blossoming almond trees were colored a richest rose, like trees in flames, like burning bushes.

Yosef went to the doorway to smell the air, and he turned to his son.

"The watching tree is awake", he said.

That is what we call the almond in this country because it is the first to bloom. It is the watchman of spring.

"After the watching tree, Father," Yeshua replied, "the fig will come."

Yosef nodded. "Yes, and a bountiful harvest it will be, if the harvesters are awake."

It seemed a riddle to me, what they said to each other. Yosef then mentioned Jeremiah and his good figs and bad figs, and only when I later began to study the prophets with attention did I learn his meaning.

Noticing me sitting there with big eyes and my mouth open like a fish, father and son smiled at me. Yeshua returned to his work, sweating hard, and Yosef went to a shelf on the wall and took something down. It was a little flute he had made of olive, dark with oiling and very smooth. He gave it to me. I put it to my lips and blew a note. Yeshua put aside his tools and knelt down beside me. Guiding my fingers, he positioned them on the holes. "Like this", he said. I blew three different notes. So sweet were those notes to my ears, because they had come from my very self. Of course, it was poor music; the notes were not right, but they sounded fine to me. Just last year, I gave it to one of my grandsons. He plays it now.

Yeshua said to me, "Now you are like King David, Joash. Once he was in the fields with the sheep and put his breath of life into a reed such as this. And thereafter was all Israel changed." He said it as a small jest, but there was seriousness in it too.

"Joash Bar Eliazar," said Yosef, "even King David had to eat sometimes. Go and ask Miryam if she will give you bread."

"And a bite of poppy cake", said Yeshua.

And that is why I have not ceased to think well of them.

I believe that he misunderstood a light from the Most High, then took it farther than he should have. He was a just man and he was great in heart. And it may be that when I have reached the last day of my life I still will not have met any as good as he was. His teachings have wisdom. I think we should ponder what he taught, for it gives life to the Torah. Not all of it, because in part it goes beyond the Law. People say he went against the teachings of Mosheh. I do not interpret it that way. He went through and beyond Mosheh. But, as I said, it was a little too far.

Please do not repeat what I have told you. It would make difficulties for me.

Nazareth
The basket weaver Yonah

He is called "Yonah the Leper" by the people of Nazareth, despite the fact that throughout the latter part of his life he has not suffered from the disease. We encounter him in his "shop", which is no more than three low stone walls covered by thatch, extended by a two-poled awning of tent cloth. He sits cross-legged in the shade, weaving baskets from strips of reed. He looks up when we enter but does not rise, for his body is extremely frail.

To my practiced eye he does not seem to be a leper. Toes are missing from one of his bare feet, but otherwise he is clean. When I politely make a gesture that he should remain seated, he reaches up and seizes my hand, pulls me down to a sitting position on the rug beside him, and then to my discomfort strokes my cheeks with a hand that looks older than a hand can possibly be. He is skin and bones, yet there is a flickering fire inside that keeps him going. His eyes are full of warm feelings of the better sort. Though a temper is also somewhere in there, its extremes are somewhat moderated by age. At times during his discourse he expresses the sweetest affection for us, and the next minute he bursts out with weeping or reproaches. I record it exactly as it was spoken, and the reader must imagine the rest.

Yonah is very proud that during his long life he has visited Jerusalem and Caesarea and also went once to Damascus when he was a young man, before he contracted leprosy. He tells us his life story not in chronological order, but he is sufficiently clear to make himself understood. He tries out a few words of *koine* and grins with pleasure when I rather falsely nod and smile as if I understand what he means to say. He is really understandable only in Aramaic.

He says:

It is good to have visitors. Aharon Ben Issachar, I know you well, and you, sir, are the father of Loukas, so I hear—welcome to you both. You want to ask about our Yeshua, and I can tell you a startling thing or two. But first let me explain why I am called Yonah the Leper. I do not like that name because it doesn't help basket sales, you can be sure. But on the other hand, I like it because it lets me tell my story. People sometimes ask about it.

I want to tell you a thing that may surprise you. I was a very, very handsome young man. No, don't laugh, I was! The mamas of Nazareth all wanted me for their daughters, and I can tell you I was a fine match for the best. My mother and father had a vineyard—see it, along the side of the hill toward Jezreel. That small house was ours when I was young. We also had a flock of the fat-tail sheep. We were not rich, but back then nobody was rich here, nor is anyone now. But as I told you, without puffing it up, I was extremely good to look at. Taller than most and very strong too. A young David or maybe a Samson, with the best of both combined. Yes, gentlemen, so much so that I was as vain as a Persian rooster, always preening my feathers and loving the way every eye would turn my way. Was I a sinner about it? No. Well, not in any big way. I was just accustomed to adore my face in the water and the thoughts in my stupid head.

So, there I was, about to be married to a fine girl, and both of our families rejoicing. Oh, before I get too far into this story, I should tell you that she is an old woman now with twenty-five grandchildren, and they all live in Sepphoris, north of here. I visit them sometimes, since they are in the discipleship of Yeshua, and I was baptized with them. She and her husband are my friends. But I am getting ahead of myself.

So there we were, ready for marriage. The date was set and the invitations sent out. Then one morning I woke up and saw the white spot on my foot. It grew and grew and began to stink. We tried everything to stop it. Then more spots appeared, my face, my hands, here and there. The wedding was delayed. And delayed and delayed. Finally the agreement was broken altogether.

According to the Law, I had to go outside the community. My parents sold some of their land, built a one-room stone house up in the hills, and hired physicians. None of them could do a thing for me. They looked on from a distance and gave advice, sold us medicines, but none came near me.

When it seemed that things could not get worse, my mother died of a fever she caught while journeying through the wetlands—those eastern swamps that we had before the Romans drained them. I kept to my hut and was afraid for other eyes to see the ruination of my body. The sickness spread and spread and ate deep into my flesh. It began to cripple my feet. Then my father died the year after my mother. He was taken by brain fever during the terrible summer when it seemed that the sun would burn up the earth. You are too young, Aharon, to remember it, though maybe you, father of Loukas, will remember that year.

So I was alone. And very ill and very frightened. But I was able to sell the house and lands and flock. Even the stone hut had to go. With the money, I hired more physicians and herbalists, medicine merchants, and every other kind of help we lepers seek in order to delay our hopeless end. There was plenty of advice shouted from a distance, but none of it was any use and still no physician would come near me. When everything had been spent, I was left with nothing. Other branches of my family were scattered throughout Israel, and none had replied to my messages pleading for help. Truly I was alone, and now I was unable to walk far. I covered myself in bandages and went higher up into the rocky places beyond the town, and there I made a shelter of stone with a bit of canvas as a roof. There was a trickle from a nearby spring, and that kept me alive, I suppose.

Did the people of Nazareth care? Some did in the beginning; some remembered me, the handsome one. They felt pity, but when you are no longer seen with the eyes, few will turn their thoughts to you. It's a big place, Nazareth. You can't remember everyone's names, not now, not then. Hundreds and hundreds of people, from several tribes too, not only the Issachar to whom the prophets apportioned Galilee. Besides, everyone has troubles of their own, and lepers are no new thing. People want you to go away and die quickly. Be it slow or quick, above all they want you to go away, and stay away—far, far away so you will not frighten them with how you look and how you smell.

It is terrible, the smell. Imagine living inside the body of a rotting corpse. Think about this. Then add to it the truth that every morning when you wake up, you do not wake to pains of the flesh but to something worse. You wake up and for the thousandth time realize that the corpse is you. Yes, and then there comes a time when the blackness of it is so deep that you would kill yourself if a knife came to hand. You try to starve yourself, but it is too slow. To kill yourself that way you must persevere in it, with a strong will. And when you are sick and eaten away, you have no will to speak of. You can only shuffle here and there in the hope that someone will throw you a crust from a safe distance. But mostly you lie down in remote places and sleep. You wait to die.

So there I was, about twenty-five or twenty-six years old, sitting in the shadow of a rock, in the hills above what had been my home, just looking out over Jezreel, which was covered with a mist in the sunrise. A place where no one could find me. My feet were half-rotted by then, and I could not walk. I could no longer go down to the edge of the village to beg a crust of bread. The end had come, and I was very glad of it.

That is the day I met Yeshua for the first time. Suddenly, below me I saw a small figure climbing this way and that through the stubble and stones. I was well hidden and knew that he could not find me even were he to search for days amid all the jumble of rock on the hill. Even by accident he would not come anywhere near. But he came closer and closer and closer. I saw that his head was down, watching his feet, not looking where they led him. He just walked step by step toward me, though not a soul on earth could have seen me. He stopped not a pace in front of me and spoke my name.

"Yonah", he said.

Never will I forget the sound of that word, the way he spoke it. There is nothing like it. I cannot describe it to you. You would have to hear it with your own ears.

So when I heard my name called, I looked up from those feet in the sandals before me, and there I beheld a young man of sixteen or seventeen years. I had never seen him before and could not guess how he knew me, or how he had found my dwelling place in the rocks.

I hid my face in shame, for I did not want him to look at the horror that I had become. I covered my head with a rag.

You will not believe me. You will not believe what I will tell you now.

No, no, he did not heal me then. That came later, years later, when he had begun to go about healing and preaching. But from the day of our first meeting when he was just a lad, the disease progressed no farther—but this is not what I want to tell you. This is not the thing you will find hard to believe. But I will tell you nevertheless, and it is true.

Forgive me; I did not mean to shout at you, nor to cry so much. People's hearts are very hard. They do not believe you when you tell them a true thing, even when it is the greatest thing in the world. It's all right; I won't shout at you again. It's just that I saw the look in your eyes, sir, one that I know very well. But we all are blind, we all are hardhearted, and me most of all. When I think of what he did for me, I can hardly speak.

This is how it was:

I begged him to go away because the sight of me was very bad and the smell was worse. In the eyes of another we see our true selves reflected. And his eyes were a mirror clearer than any I have ever known.

He said nothing. He dropped to his knees in front of me. He pulled the cloth from my head. Then he put his arms around me and kissed my cheeks and my forehead.

Then we sat together in silence. He said not another word until he was ready to go. Unslinging a bag from his shoulder, he removed a loaf of bread from it and a clay jug of milk. He put them on the ground near me.

"Yonah", he said. "Tomorrow I will bring you another."

And so he did. Year after year he did it. Many other good things he brought me, and in time I let him carry me down the hill on holy days, but only before dawn or after dark, for he respected my need to be unseen. We would pray together to the Most High outside the wall of the synagogue while others prayed or sang within. Did you know he called the Most High his Father? He did it that way even when he was young.

You ask me, when was I healed? Later, after he had gone out into the world, I met him on the road to Sepphoris, during the time he was becoming known as a prophet throughout Israel. I had taken to wandering about the region because I was able to hobble a little. He had made me a sturdy crutch before he left. So, on the day I met him again, he noticed me in my rags by the side of the road, and though my face was covered, he knew me. He took me aside from the people and removed the cloth from my head. He put his hands upon me, but then he had to go away because there were many people clamoring for his attention. And when they had all gone, I felt my face and my feet and my hands. They were no longer a leper's.

Here I am now. I have lived by the labor of my hands these thirty years and more, ever since. I have never married. I would have liked to, but I have everything. I am the richest man in Galilee. I am so happy. Always I am happy. Pardon me if I shout and cry too much—it doesn't mean anything. When they crucified him it broke my heart, worse than the darkest leper years, but only for a short while. After he rose up, my life was better than ever it was before.

I tell you, he gave me the best gift in the world, and none can take it from me.

In a dream he came to me. It was after he had risen from the dead but before he had gone up into paradise. I confuse my times a little. I am getting too old. But I feel very young.

In that dream he said I must return to Nazareth, his home. He loved it, even though its heart was hard. He asked me to live here always so that I might bear witness. And so I have done. He left some wounds on my feet as a sign for others. As you can see, not all my toes are with us. He told me that I must weave my anger and sorrow into a basket—a basket emptied so that it might be filled with praise. He promised to help in this, and so he has done, though you can see for yourself that I am not yet perfect.

Do you understand now? If my health were taken away again, I would still be happy. I would see the sun and all the good growing things of the earth, and the faces of children. I would smell the breeze and taste the honeycomb, like gold on the tongue, and warm bread from the oven, and pure water from the rocks—and all of it would still be beautiful to me. And if that too were taken from me, I would have my thoughts within, and memories of him. And if my life itself were taken away from me, there would remain in my soul the print of a kiss.

Will you let me pour you some water? I'm sorry, I have only one cup, but we can share it around. And you, sir, please accept this basket from me. No, no, put away your coins. It is a gift.

Nazareth
The housewife Avigayil

We meet her in the street on which Yeshua once lived. She is about sixty years of age, a calm and dignified woman. She knows my translator personally and greets him with a pleasant expression. They exchange news about people known to them both. She glances at me curiously, and Aharon introduces us. Her mother was related to Yosef, the father of Yeshua. She and her husband live in the house once owned by him. She invites us in to see it.

It is like most others in the village—a central space with kitchen and pantry shelves; large clay pots and wooden bins for storing dried food; sturdy benches on which three people could sit with ease, made more comfortable by sheepskins thrown over them; a low wooden table; and various other normal household things. The woodshed and bread oven are out back, visible through an open doorway at the rear of the house. Behind three striped cloths are small sleeping rooms. Little remains here that once belonged to the former owners. We are served a good meal of mashed lentils in clay bowls, into which we dip our fingers. There are onions, bread and cheese, milk, and also two small silver cups of wine because we are guests.

She says:

Yes, I am a kin to Yeshua, as are my sisters and my brother, and other branches of the family.

We were all very sad when he was taken by the Romans and put to death. I believe that the Most High brought him forth from the tomb. Some say he rose to the fullness of life. Some say he came back in spirit only, others that nothing of him was seen and that a false tale has been spread and his bones lie hidden in a grave at Jerusalem. Among his brothers and sisters—I mean the children of his aunts and uncles— there are some who say this is so. Others in our family believe what his followers teach about him. My husband takes a little of this and a little of that. I am one who believes it all, though I did not see Yeshua with my eyes after his death. His mother Myriam did see him, and she told me how it was. Three days after his death, she saw him and felt his hand warm on her face.

With my eyes I have seen no miracles. Not when he was living here, nor later when he moved about the countryside. But I feel him very close. We knew each other from child-hood. Though I was a bit younger than he, I remember many things about him. There is too much to tell you. I believe everything about him. Everything. I know people whom he healed. I knew them when they were under the heel of the adversary, and I knew them after they were set free. It is true, all of it. I do not understand why it is so difficult for people to believe it.

If it were granted to me, I would go down to Caesarea or Capernaum, to the houses where his followers live. They pray to the Father of us all in the name of my brother. Wondrous things happen when they pray in this way. Once I met his friend Shimon, who is now called Kepha. I know Yochanan too, since he comes here now and then and sits in this house with me and listens to me tell my stories about when Yeshua was a boy, and also about Myriam and Yosef, who are now gone to the Father of us all. He told me that he once put his ear to Yeshua's chest and listened to his heartbeat. Yochanan said that a man cannot really hear his own heart beating, that he can hear only another's, and that the Lord himself made us this way from the beginning. It is so. Sometimes I take my granddaughter, who visits me because I am teaching her to cook properly, and I sit her down on my lap. She puts her ear to my breast and listens. And then I put my ear to her little heart and listen to it. It makes us laugh and brings us very close.

As I said, I would like to be closer to the ones who pray in his name, for there are not many in this town who believe. But my place is here with my husband, Nahum. Indeed, he is a comfort to me. Our children and grandchildren live here also, and in other villages nearby, so it would be hard to go away from them. Children need to see that they are part of a history and that the story of their family is a living thing. God tells it, a new story in each generation, and each must hold hands across the sea of time, joining together the ones who went before and the ones who come after. Our part in it cannot be done by another. It is given from above. Little do we understand this in the beginning, but time teaches us many things we did not expect to learn. That is life. It is the same everywhere.

What can I tell you that you do not already know?

Today, I am remembering something. It is a small thought but very dear to me.

It is about Yosef Bar Yaakov. I was three or four years old at the time. The children of our family went often to the home of Myriam and Yosef because they were so good to us. Miryam always had a handful of dates, or a barley cake to break into pieces for us, though sometimes the pieces were small because we were many. Yosef made toys for us and also brought us firewood. He was a very strong man. His arms were like trees.

And in the manner of such strong men, he was gentle in his ways, and through all the years I knew him, not once did I hear an angry word from his mouth, though you can be sure that many deserved it.

If I close my eyes, I can see clearly how it was that day. I can hear it too. Yeshua was about five years old. He was playing with my brother and me. We were making little hills of dirt in the yard in front of the woodshed, and we made our fingers act like people walking about the heights and climbing them, and falling down them. Giggling and giggling we were. Yosef came out from his shop and watched us awhile. When Yeshua noticed his father standing there, he jumped to his feet, dusted off his hands, and lifted his arms as if he were a little staggerer who had just learned to walk and wanted to be picked up. Yosef picked him up and threw him into the air. So high was he thrown that I gasped and covered my mouth with my hand, and my brother took a few steps back with open mouth. Yosef caught him, of course. With a big smile, he threw the boy up into the air again. Yeshua's laughter rang and rang. If it had been me flying up there with the birds, I would have screamed in terror. Not Yeshua! No, his laughter just grew and grew and grew until it seemed to fill the whole street.

"More, Abba, more", he cried. And so Yosef tossed him again.

He had no fear, that boy. None at all. But in time his father grew weary and put him back down on the ground. Then Yosef knelt beside us, and with his big fingers he made a little man go walking up one of the humps of dirt we had made.

"Here we are", he said in that joking manner of his. "Here we are climbing Mount Zion together."

It is things like that I remember best. You must talk with my sister Avi. She can tell you stories too.

Nazareth
The housewife Avital

A woman in her midsixties, she is the elder sister of Avigayil, the firstborn of a family of five girls and one boy. At first hesitant to admit a foreigner into her house, she listens to her sister's request, then opens the door wide. She offers us milk and bread. Her house is poorer than Avigayil's, and it is plain to see that she has suffered a great deal in her life. The suffering may have come from external causes, or it may have come from a personal habit of bitterness regarding life's trials. It may be both. She is suspicious yet capable of tolerance. When Avigayil reassures her that I am a friend of those who knew Yeshua Bar Yosef, her tension eases, yet she remains cautious. Later, I learn from my translator that she lost two sons to Roman justice. Her husband is a good man, but he squandered the bit of land they owned by incurring debt. He is away just now, hiring himself out for a harvest down in the southern part of Jezreel. Her younger sister helps with food and what coins she can spare.

She says:

You ask me about Yeshua? I don't think there is much I can tell you that others would not tell better. But I can say this: He was always good to me and my sisters. He would not let people with bad mouths say things against us. The bad things were all in their minds. But our mother died young, and we were left to raise ourselves, more or less. My father's name was Hiram. He was crippled by a stone wall that fell on him. He tried to build it around our garden to keep out the goats. People are not careful about their goats—they let them wander all over, eating other people's food. The stones fell on him in the year after our mother's death. The wall was never finished. From time to time I still put a stone on top, but it is no good. The goats just jump over and eat what they will. I keep them away by throwing sharp stones at them. They know me well, those goats.

My father never fully recovered from the fallen wall and also from our loss. He did not work much. It was a hard time. We were without a guide to help us make our way in life. You know how people are—some, not all. They see a weakness and kick it with their foot. Or they see a weakness and rush to help. Both kinds live side by side in this world. Both kinds, and you never know which one a person will turn out to be. How can you trust people when they are this way?

My father was of the tribe of Levi. Many times he said to me, "Avital, you must always keep in mind that Mosheh gave no inheritance to the tribe of Levi because we were to be the priests." My father was not a priest, but he was from that line. "The Lord, the God of Israel, gave us no inheritance because the Lord himself is our inheritance", he often said. He praised the name of the Lord until the day of his death, and did what he could to feed us, with the help of others. But he was weak in body and later in mind. And when it was seen by some, they kicked him again. And when he was gone, they kicked at his daughters. I do not understand why they did that. I do not understand people.

Why are you writing my words onto that paper? Who will read it? What is it for? I have spoken with others who want to make a story about Yeshua's life. That is enough. I did not see any miracles. I saw only that he had courage. Whenever someone said a thing against my father, if Yeshua heard it he would step in front of that person and look into his eyes. He would say nothing with his mouth, but the people would turn away in shame. I do not want you to misunderstand me. He was not a boy with strange powers. He was not a magician. He was—he was just ordinary. But there was a thing in him. I do not have words for it. If an evil came out of the woods or out of a man's mouth, Yeshua would quietly step in front of it and take it on himself. He did not strike back, neither with his fists nor his mouth. Never.

We loved him. I can say that now. He was a brother to us. I cried a lot when he was killed. I think most of us who knew him cried until we could cry no more. But there were some who rejoiced when the news reached us. They strode up and down in front of the synagogue telling any and all who would listen that they had prophesied years ago that the son of Yosef Bar Yaakov would come to a bad end. And it is interesting to me that those "prophets" were the very ones whom he had shamed. He did not intend to heap shame upon them. He merely stood in their way. So you see, that is how people are.

You ask about Miryam. I loved her very much too, and I pleaded with her not to go away to Jerusalem. I really begged her. But she said she had to go because that is what the Most High desired of her. I said to her: "Does the Most High desire that we be left here alone without you?" She said: "You are not alone, and from now on you will never again be abandoned."

That is the way she was. Wise. You would not look twice at her in a crowd of women at the well, though she must have looked nice enough when she was younger. She was like a mother to me and my sisters. Myriam taught us a lot about weaving and sewing. Cooking too, though she kept it simple, except for feast days. It was just us girls left at home because my little brother Ezer was sent away to live with our uncle who is in Cana. He was not a bad boy, but he nearly went crazy living in a house of women. I could not make him obey me, and my uncle needed a boy for his sheep, so he asked for Ezer and we sent him to him. He grew up very well. He is married and still lives in Cana with his wife and their children. He has grandchildren also. It did not turn out badly for him. All of us sisters went to his wedding. Myriam and Yeshua went too. Yosef had died by then. I remember that wedding so well; a very good time we had. But it was many years ago. Ezer still sends me food and other help from time to time.

You are a Greek, sir. I can see by your clothing and your book and pen, and most of all by your face, that you have not suffered as we have suffered in this country. You are a wealthy man, and I do not fault you for it. But it seems to me that you are like many who have never known want. You provide for yourself. You don't need other people. And none dare insult you.

Let me tell you a little story. It is about people who live down here at the bottom of the world, far below the rich palaces of Jerusalem. I will make a picture for you, and perhaps in your mind you will see it.

Suppose you live in a small town in the hill country, far from the big cities. And suppose that just down the street from you there lives a quiet sort of family about whom there is nothing unusual, except that they are devoted to each other and very devoted to the Most High. The father is a carpenter who makes furniture and house beams in his shop. The mother is—well, she is a mother. Their son is a polite sort of boy. He helps his father in the shop, is serious by nature, and never says much but is ever ready to smile. He is often in the synagogue studying the sacred books.

You meet him sometimes when you are climbing in the unclaimed places looking for a wild tree from which you can pick some fruit. You pass through the thorns and bushes, and there you find him kneeling beside a rock watching a snake, or there he is gazing up into a tree branch listening to newborns chirping in their nest. Or maybe he is holding a seed-pod in his hand, thinking about its design. There is a cross in it, a deep black cross, and beneath the cross is the seed. That's him—just listening, just looking. He notices you, smiles, then seems to gaze at you as if *you* are as wonderful as the world. He is not shy, just quiet. Like his father, he carves small wooden toys as gifts for the other children in the neighborhood. There is something special about him, but you cannot say exactly what it is. It's just there, like a seed in a pod.

Suppose the mother of that family is busy baking cakes one day in preparation for a holy day. In your own home you do not have enough grain for grinding into flour. You do not know how you can fill every small belly in the house. But you have the hens, and if they are laying that day, you will be able to eat something. Suppose the woman sends a message asking you if she can borrow an egg. You have only one egg, and it would hurt to part with it. You bring it over to her house. She invites you in for a cup of milk. You do not refuse because you are hungry and thirsty. Most of all, you are hungry and thirsty for the way she looks at you. You go in and sit at the table in her kitchen. Everything inside their house is simple—well made but simple. The air is full of peace. You listen to the sound of two hammers tapping away in the workshop next door. The mother serves you more milk and also buttered bread. Like her husband and child, she is a quiet person, but you do not feel uncomfortable in her silence because it is as if she is always speaking—speaking with her eyes. Without being told, you know you are welcome. You are at home.

You sip the milk and nibble the bread as you observe the care she takes over every detail in the making of the cake. You can see that she wants it to be right.

"You are making cakes?" you ask, knowing the answer.

She nods and smiles—the smile going deep into your heart. There is no smile like it in the world, at least not that you have ever seen before.

So you get up and go home. And you know that later in the day you will find a surprise package on your doorstep, or maybe it will be delivered by the lady's son, with a smile and a look. And so it is. When you unwrap the package, you find within it a splendid cake and a small wooden toy.

Can you understand this? Can you understand *us*?

Look, I will show you one of their gifts. When Myriam departed for Jerusalem, the last time I saw her, she gave it to me so that I might remember her. Her father made this distaff and spindle. A righteous man, Yoachim, married to a righteous woman, Anah. He made this for Myriam at her birth. It is very old. With this, with her own hands, she made wool yarn and wove it into her son's garments. And she gave it to me—me, who does not deserve such a precious thing. When we parted, I asked her why she gave it to me and not to other women in our family who are more warmhearted, for few are fond of my stiff ways. She said: "Avital, I give it to you because you are mother of many. From your youngest years you carried your family in your arms, and you were very young for such a task. Yet many are the righteous souls, yet unborn, who will come from you."

I am sorry, but I have chores to do now. Please do not think me rude. I have told you my story.

Nazareth
Zakhhay the fool

I stumble across him quite by accident. As Aharon and I make our way back to the inn, I take a little side lane that will bring us close to the edge of the town, where there are green pastures and fresher air. The heat of the day has filled the atmosphere with the potent stench of animal droppings and the offal piles of households. I am fatigued and would love nothing more than to return to a city—any city would suit me well.

Along this lane, we come upon what looks at first to be a log fallen across our path. In fact, it is a huge-bodied man lying on his side earnestly observing a dung beetle roll its ball through the dust.

Aharon drops to his knees beside him and shakes his shoulder. With a grin of recognition, the man lurches to his feet and throws his arms around Aharon, who laughs with a curious mix of embarrassment and delight.

An attempt at introduction is made, but I doubt the poor fellow catches my name. I soon realize that he is a half-wit and that whatever he says is fairly meaningless. Regardless, he makes it known to us that he wants us to come with him. Grabbing Aharon by the sleeve, he drags him away, and I follow with some reluctance. Clearly, no useful examination will be forthcoming.

We enter a barnyard at the base of a hill and approach a crude log structure thatched with straw. A woman slowly gets up from the ground, where she has been sitting before a hollowed stone grinding corn, and stares at us with surprise. She is the man's mother, and this is where they live.

Her name is Naomy. From her we learn that her son's real name is Zakhhay Bar Lamech, though she calls him Zakiu or Zaho, as if he were a little boy. He is about forty-five years old, born a few years before Yeshua departed from Nazareth to go about his public preaching. Not once in his life has he left the village and its immediate region. They have always lived in this house, she says. It belongs to someone else, who lets them live here out of generosity. It was built originally as a shepherd's shelter, very crude, though she has improved it to make a home.

The woman explains that she did not really know the family of Yosef Bar Yaakov well, but her boy was a great friend of the carpenter's son. She does not understand the troubles that came later because of him, but she liked him because he often came to see Zaho. Yeshua was always very respectful to her, she says, not like some others in town. Then and now, people call her son bad names. It hurts her feelings, but she is glad that her son does not understand what they are saying. They speak this way not only because he is a fool but also because of his trade. He makes bricks of donkey droppings, dries them in the sun, and sells them. People use this kind of fuel for purposes other than cooking. It brings in a few coins. Indeed, her house, inside and outside, smells like a stable. The mother's and son's clothing also smells strongly of it.

Zakhhay is capable of putting a few words together, but mostly he babbles, and his mother interprets his personal language into Aramaic, and then it comes to me through my translator. It is a long process.

The son taps his chest with his forefinger again and again, then he taps the palm of one hand, and then the other. He looks keenly at me to see if I understand what he means. It makes no sense to me. He lurches across the yard and sits down on a rock by the roadway. He stares down the road, looks back at me, then stares up at the sky. Then he laughs and laughs, a great bearded hulk of a man, none too clean, unpleasant in appearance, though he is not threatening. He repeats his gestures three times, then remains seated on the rock looking at the sky. His only words, "Yeshua, Yeshua."

The mother watches all this, then turns to me and says:

He is trying to tell you he is waiting for his friend.

My husband Lamech was a good man, though he was made low. We had one child, and him you see before you. There are no fools on my side of the family, and there were none on Lamech's side. My husband may have been slow of wit, but he was no fool. He worked hard to feed us, and never a word of complaint did I hear from him—not a one from our wedding until the day he died. I do not know why the Most High takes some away early from this life. It is not my place to question his will. Why so many women and children die at birth, this you must ask our mother Eve, she whom we call *hawwah*, which means "mother of all the living". My son was born with blue skin and without the breath of life. Lamech breathed life into him when the child came forth from me. But it was not enough, and ever since then he did not grow in the way other children have grown. His body is now big, but his thoughts are small. His name means "pure", and so he is.

I did not know Yeshua or his parents at first, only to see them at the well or the market. Lamech would carry my boy to the synagogue for prayers when he was little, but in time it became plain for all to see that there was something wrong with him. When the boy's father died, I did not have the heart to take him there for prayers, since people talk, and besides, I could enter only for the prayer of the women. I think I saw Yeshua a few times before I was married. I must have, though there was nothing to make him stick in my thoughts. Later, when Zaho and I were alone, he began to come past our house. His mother sent me a loaf of bread now and then, since I was a widow. He always called me *marttha*, "lady"—it was no matter to him that our home was a sheep shed.

He would kneel down and talk to my boy, and help him to stand up, though he always fell down again. It was a lovely thing to watch them together, that big strong man and my small afflicted one.

Once I asked Yeshua: "Why do you love my child so much? He is ugly, and his body and mind are weak."

"I love Zakhhay because he is pure", said Yeshua to me. "Yes, he is pure", I said. "But few can see it."

Then he said a thing that stuck in my thoughts, and I remember it often. I think about it most when Zaho makes a mistake down in the town, and people become impatient with him. I should tell you that many among us have pity, and this is good. But none respect my boy, for he is a dung gatherer.

Yeshua said to me:

"He is very beautiful in the eyes of the Most High. The Father sees him and loves him greatly."

A woman can feel two things at once, you know. When he said what he said, I felt both a sudden joy and a very deep pain. I do not understand it even now. But the pain became less as the years went on, and the joy increased, and it remains with me. There are sorrows still, though never the black grief.

But back then, when he said that thing, my heart was cut into two pieces. I said bitterly, "The Most High, praise to his name, does not have to wipe Zaho's drool and his hind end. He does not have to carry him before the mocking eyes of others."

Yeshua picked up my boy in his arms and said, "He does carry him."

When he was six or seven, Zaho began to crawl about the yard. Then he sometimes crawled away and got lost, and I was in great fear to find him. Do you know how many people returned him to me with a scold, as if I were a bad mother? Many. Whenever Yeshua brought him back to me, it was always with a smile and never a word of blame.

When he was about nine years of age, he began to walk. Yeshua would come by from time to time and stand him up and put an arm around him, and they would hobble about the yard a bit. Later, down the street they went together. Soon, my Zaho was stumbling along by himself, going here and there, into the town and up into the pasture, getting into trouble through no fault of his own.

He learned to speak a few words. "Mamma". "Milk". "Bread". "Go" and "come". He was always happy. I never heard him cry much in his life. Only when he was a baby and needed a nursing.

When my boy was about ten years old, Yeshua came to me one day and said, "Marttha Naomy, soon I must go away. It will be long before I return. May I take Zakhhay to the synagogue for prayers?"

Of course, I let them go. What could I say? How can one refuse a request from a man like that? So they went down to pray and then came home again. And that day my son was happier than ever before, though nothing else changed in him that I could see.

In the month of Shivat of that year, Yeshua brought to our house two things he had made in his shop. One, a little wooden shovel, all of a piece. The other, a box, the size of a brick. Like a tiny house, four walls without roof or floor. He gave them to Zaho, who hopped about in the yard singing and laughing. He was so happy to have such gifts, though he did not know what they were for.

Yeshua showed him how the gifts were to be used. With the shovel, he gathered donkey droppings and put them into the box. Then he knelt and sprinkled straw over them and with his bare hands pressed the droppings flat inside. To this he added more straw and pressed again. With that, he took the box and tapped it out onto a hot stone in the sun. Then he made another.

"No dog droppings", he said to Zaho, and a little lamp seemed to light up within my boy's eyes. "No hen or human manure. You must use only what the donkeys leave, for it has much straw in it. You must wash afterward. And do not put your fingers into your eyes."

Then we both watched as Zaho tried to make one of the bricks. It was a sorry mess, I can tell you. But in the days and weeks that came after, Yeshua showed him again and again what must be done. And in time, Zaho understood it all. His bricks are very fine, you know. They are good for some kinds of burning, but as I said, not for cooking. It makes a smell in the food. Not everyone wants them, but enough people buy them so that we can eat.

Oh, I almost forgot about another gift he gave my son. It was a bag made of sackcloth. Yeshua told Zaho that every week on the day before the Sabbath, he should go about the town and fill the sack with dog droppings. He must use the little shovel to scoop them up and must take care not to touch them with his hands. Also, he should wash his hands and fingernails very carefully afterward and make sure he was finished before sunset because that is the beginning of the Sabbath. And so Zaho learned to do this too. The tanners pay us well for a full bag. It is a job that everyone hates—the smell, you understand. They use it to cure hides for leather.

I do not know how Yeshua told my boy that he was going away, but Zaho knew it somehow. Yeshua came to see us on the day he left. He told us that he must go far to the south, to the great river we call Jordan where Mosheh could not cross, the place where our people crossed over into the land of milk and honey and brought down the wicked city by the sound of a trumpet.

"Marttha Naomy", he said to me. "Marthha Naomy, in paradise we will see with new eyes. In this world it is man's way to love what we see with the eyes of the flesh. It will not always be so. The time will come when we will see what our Father sees, for each man is like all others, yet each is unlike all others. We will love both our sameness and our differences, which will be as one thing, and it will be beautiful to the eyes of the soul."

"An ugly trade you taught him", I said. I am ashamed to tell you this, for I was a terrible grumbler in those days.

"Marttha Naomy", he answered. "For a brief time your son will gather what is loathsome to man. But it is just earth. From his labors will come warmth and leather for others and food for yourselves. But know this: In eternity, Zakhhay will wear a crown."

I did not understand him. And to this day I do not understand what he meant. But it gave new heart to me.

When Yeshua walked away down the road that last time, Zaho sat on the stone by the edge of the yard and watched him go. He sat there all day. For days he sat there, waiting. Then he got up and began to make the bricks. That was many years ago.

I am happy. Zaho is very happy.

*

I will make a break in the examinations.

I have listened to too much talking (everything is said twice, and then inscribed), and there is no opportunity to fully open my own thoughts to others.

I am writing by lamplight as I sit beneath the cinnamon acacia outside the door of the inn. My chair is a wooden stump hacked into its present shape by rough tools. The table is a slab of crude boards pegged to upright beams. The stars are out in force, insects and night birds are singing in the hot windless air, the flame of the lamp stands straight, trembling only when I turn my face toward it.

The innkeeper speaks a little Greek. When she brought me supper, she told me that her name is Deborah, and she offered a bit of local color by explaining that the word means "bee". She *is* a buzzing person, sturdy and competent, ever bustling about her duties, circling small tasks as if they were flowers, then striking off into the distance in a straight line. I asked her if she had known Yeshua, and in response she related a number of things, normal encounters that are better represented by the other accounts I have written here. My scroll's length is limited, and I must take care not to fill it up with duplications. She is a strong believer in the new religion (my expression, not hers).

Our conversation has stirred my inner attention in the general direction of women. I am missing the feminine presence in its most familiar form, that is, in the language and visual styles and customs of my native culture. When we are too long without their company, we men grow uneasy, afflicted with a sense of the *kosmos* thrown off balance, or at least of an ethos incomplete. Though it is indispensable for us to go away from them, to thrive in the company of men for a time, we always return to our women. It is more than sex, more than food that draws us. The need is deeper, far deeper than that.

There are a few beautiful young women in the town. We pass each other in the streets, our eyes meeting without connection, no more than an instant's exposure. Beautiful *faces*, I should say, for bodies here are heaped in robes as protection against the burning sun and the ever-present burning in men's eyes.

Do my eyes burn? If they do, it is not with lust but rather with a yearning for the consolations of loveliness. I miss Paeonia greatly, and my daughters. What is this longing in my heart, my thoughts? It is loneliness, of course. But what is loneliness? Is it the sense of incompletion, like a severing or clamping of arterial flow, when love cannot express itself or receive the expressed love of others? What binds two souls together like this? Animals mate but rarely abide in each other's company beyond the demands of necessity. What binds a family together into one thing? What binds a group of families together, and then binds these gatherings into a town, and the towns into a nation? At the core of it all is need, dependency, the desire for reassurance in a perilous world. But it is more than that.

Well, I have no one to blame but myself for my present sense of apartness. I freely chose to be a sojourner in an alien land, to feel rootless for a time.

Oh, look at me now; I am using up good papyrus on a musing!

What have I learned so far? There has been a great deal to take in at once. My mind recognizes the usual variations, opinions about an individual who is pondered after a lapse of three decades. The wine filter of memory. This Christos—Yeshua, as they invariably call him here—left few people unaffected, for good or ill. He was kind, that is plain to see. He was a man of honor, that is also plain to see. But kindness and honor, as important as they are, can be found everywhere. Though men with these qualities are always a minority in human affairs, they are omnipresent in the world. Man is neither animal nor monster. But neither is he a god.

Every person I have met here is sincere. So far, I have sensed not a whiff of false motive, no attempt to persuade me or dissuade me by the usual human devices.

My anger has subsided. However, maintaining vigilance against illusion demands constant effort, generating both strain and stimulation. I am more and more intrigued by whatever has occurred in this place, and how it has affected human thoughts and behavior. What will tomorrow bring?

I will end this record for the day.

Nazareth
Barak the "prophet"

As Aharon and I walk toward the synagogue, we see a man leaving it. He notices us and approaches with hands clasped and humble steps. "Come, let me introduce you to a false prophet", whispers Aharon. Introductions are made. Barak is gray bearded with a not unintelligent face and a respectful manner, but there is subtlety here. A wily glint is barely visible beneath a veil of sincerity. Too easily could one mistake it for humility. Instinctively, I feel first aversion, then danger, though there is nothing apparent to cause these emotions. Explanations of my presence in the town are not needed because Barak seems to know everything about me already. Indeed, my companion and I say not a word as the following discourse is recited:

Welcome, sir. Welcome to you also, Aharon Ben Issachar. Nazareth has not been blessed by your presence as often as it was before. You travel near and far, I hear. But now I see that you bring us a noble visitor from the Greek lands, a physician, a learned one who is interested in the great happenings that occurred among us. I would like to tell you of the astounding events I saw with my own eyes, but I am short of time, for I am just now on my way to distribute alms to the poor. There are many poor here—so many. Widows and orphans, fools and madmen. You, Aharon, since your name is that of the prophet who upheld the arms of Mosheh at the great battle, you will understand that arms cannot be lifted to the Most High without food in the belly. I hold up the arms of the poor to him, and I fill those empty hands, that they might make supplication for the people of Israel so that the Canaanites, the Philistines, and the Egyptians of our times will be cast down. The blood of the innocent cries out to the Lord, and our soil is ever wet with it. Soon he will send the *meshiha* to us, with the sword and the crown, and then will all our enemies be no more, and the glory we once knew in the days of the kings will be as the moon is to the sun, for the true king is coming, as our ancestors the prophets foretold.

213

Yet I have a minute to spare.

I hear that you inquire about the life of Yeshua Bar Yosef, sir, whom I knew when we were boys together. That he was a prophet none can deny. With my own eyes I saw miracles. Let me tell you some, though there be countless to relate. A few will do, for these are exceedingly marvelous.

From his birth he was set apart for a work of the Lord. When we were small, just crawling about unweaned the both of us, I often saw him make wonders and signs, which he did so that his generation might know his stature. From birth he could speak with many words and knew all things. Before I could write *aleph* to *zayin*, he told me that he was the fore-runner of one who would come to rescue Israel from all its woes, the *meshiha*. He himself was not the *meshiha*, he said, but a servant of the *meshiha* who would be revealed.

Sad it is, sad it is, that the messenger is often mistaken for the one who sends him. So too the messenger of a king is often struck down in place of his lord. And that is the case with our own poor Yeshua Bar Yosef. I regret the loss of him. Yet with his blood he testified to the evil of Rome, and his dust, wherever it now lies, will rise up one day, as the prophet Ezekiel foretold, with all those who lie in the valley of dry bones.

In the beginning, he told me all that would come to pass. And lest I doubt it, he showed me his powers. We were about five years of age at the time.

"Barak, my brother", he said to me that day. "I am of the company of prophets, and you also shall be with me in that company. See, I now give you a sign that you may believe in me, and yet believe more in the one for whom I will bear witness."

He knelt down on the ground and formed from the dirt a shape like a turtle. Then he breathed on it, and it began to move. It was a turtle, alive and true. Then he made another shape, a bird this time. He breathed on it and lifted it up, and it flew from his fingers into the sky. Then a snake, and it slithered away. And after that a tree, which he breathed upon, making it grow and grow before my eyes, to flower and bear fruit. A fruit that tastes like no other, wet and sweet. I ate it, and it was good.

I remember well another time. Some boys of our town were teasing us in the street, older boys, hard and cruel. One struck me with his fist, and the fist turned black, withering upon his arm. Another struck Yeshua's cheek. In an instant, that one fell dead at his feet. Then did the others drop to their knees and beg for mercy. And Yeshua did not kill them on the spot but let them run away. The next day each one died of plague.

There is more I might tell you, but the morning is getting on and I must serve the poor, and this is the will of the Most High. Sir, do not doubt that the one foretold by Yeshua is near. Even now there are other prophets alive in Israel who give testimony for the One who will come. They move among the people with deep teaching and doing wonders. There is Yael of Ptolemais and Menander of Caparattaea and others like them, though the greatest is Shimon of Ghitto in Samaria, who is called the Great Power of God. He astounds all who see his works in Judaea and as far away as Rome, for he has been there too, and the people of that city reverence him. So, you see, there are others who now do what Yeshua once did, and thus it is not all loss. Soon Jerusalem will be restored, the mighty city of Zion lifted up above the whole world, for the King of Kings will break all other crowns, and Israel shall dwell in peace and plenty.

I must go. There is work to be done. If you would like to give me some coins for the poor, I know they will make supplication for you.

*

A final note of explanation: When Barak has rounded a corner, my translator turns to me and sheds more light on the matter.

Aharon says:

"This man told us lies from start to finish. That is not how Yeshua was. The healings and other signs, as far as we know, began when he left Nazareth to preach the good news. Until then, people here thought of him as nothing special. He was the carpenter's son, a devout Jew, but no more than that. Those with eyes to see understood that his heart and soul were very great and his deeds always good. There was sacrifice and love in everything he did. But he did not make a display. No one really knew his full stature.

"Yeshua was the true power of the Most High. He is the Son of the Father. He was with the Father before the beginning of time and was born among us and lived with us for a short span of years, so that the Father might speak to us through him and reveal his hidden face in a living man. Now Yeshua has ascended to the Father and the Holy Spirit, and he will come again in glory to judge the living and the dead. Until the harvest at the end of the world, as he warned us, there will be weeds sown by Satan among the wheat.

"This man whom we just met sows weeds in the fields of the Lord and covers it with a semblance of virtue, for he falsely divides the true worship of God from the true service to man. He is a disciple of Shimon the Magos, who calls himself the Great Power of God. Just like his master, he is as subtle as a snake and as harmful as a snake.

"I wonder how many of the coins he begs reach the hands of the poor. An important part of our life as followers of Yeshua is to care for the poor. We give what we can as alms, but for the most part we too are as poor. The poorest of the poor are most beloved of God, and so we pay close attention to their needs. Our father in faith, Shimon Kepha, says to us: We have no gold or silver, but what we have, we give."

"Two Shimons", I say.

"Yes, two Shimons", nods Aharon. "One is a rock, and one is a desert mirage."

Cana
Ezer Bar Hiram

I am surely rewarded for the aggravations I have endured in Nazareth by a precious windfall of medicine. On the day before my departure for the village of Cana and regions beyond, Aharon obtained for me a bag of dried cassia buds, which are much like cloves. *Kiddah* is the Hebrew word for the fragrant cassia. These people also use the smaller leaves for a salve that is like *senna*, and the pods are mixed with leaves to make a purgative.

My mood improves.

Cana is on the far side of the Jezreel Valley, lower down on the hill facing Nazareth. Aharon and I cross over and reach our destination within three hours. We travel first on a dusty path that bends toward the northeast arm of the valley. Aharon wants to avoid Sepphoris. It is visible on our left, a fairly large city with a Roman fortress, the former capital of Galilee. The new capital is Tiberias, to the east of here, where a larger garrison of soldiers, a full legion, is stationed.

I learn that Florus, the procurator of Judaea, has lately been rounding up bands of thieves in the hills and also the seditious of various parties. There have been gross outrages against Jewish holy places in Jerusalem and Caesarea, but when the Jews protest, they, not the guilty, are brutally punished. The endless provocations are fomenting unrest throughout the land, including some eruptions of counterviolence. There have been an unusual number of crucifixions this year. No one is really safe from Roman suspicion. At this time it is better to avoid Sepphoris altogether, says my guide.

I mention to Aharon that I have found the entire land to be most peaceable and lovely. He stares at me, surprised, then says, "We are protected as we go. Many are praying for your safety on this journey."

About an hour's walk beyond the city, we turn north again and head in a straight course between harvested grainfields.

"You must come and see the valley in spring," says Aharon, "for the fields are then full of flax flowers, as blue as the sky. Galilee is famous for its linen."

It reminds me of the Plain of Phaestos, though the bottom land here is more lavishly productive with grain and garden plots, vineyards, and richly colored flowers. The surrounding hills are greener than ours, with patches of sheep flocks tended by a man or a boy, sometimes a girl—the shepherds walking as slowly as the animals they guard.

Cana is no more than a quarter the size of Nazareth, quieter, less bustling. There are only a few lanes between the houses, no streets as such. Ezer Bar Hiram lives in a house that is large by local standards, six rooms, perhaps seven or eight. The walls are stones carefully fitted together and whitewashed. He and his wife Keturah have raised a family of six children, some of whom are still with them under the one roof. All but the youngest are married. A daughter and her husband live here, so the house is noisy with the comings and goings of grandchildren. Even so, it is a place of peace.

Ezer greets us at the doorway and brings us inside out of the sun. Since it is noontime, we are invited to share the meal. The mother and daughter serve us, then seat themselves with the men, and all begin to eat. Ezer is slow-spoken, in fact ponderous. There are pauses between each part of what he tells us—as if he is rolling and unrolling a scroll in his mind, or more precisely as if he must gather his thoughts like scattered sheep. Despite his age, he is physically robust, and only by his face would one guess the number of his years.

As he begins to speak, a fine-looking young man enters the room. His clothing is patched and dusty—for work, I assume. He bows to his father, then to his mother, and finally to Aharon and me. He washes his hands in a jar of water and dries them on a towel. Then he covers the crown of his head with a striped cloth, takes a piece of bread, and breaks it in two, closing his eyes and praying silently. That done, he removes the cloth, sits down, and begins to eat with us. He says nothing throughout our visit.

Ezer says:

This is my youngest, Hiram. I named him for my father, whose face I barely remember, for he died young. My sister Avital raised the children of our family, and I thank you for your greetings from her. Please give mine to her and to Avigayil when you go back to Nazareth. I was sent here to Cana when I was small because my uncle needed a boy for his sheep. This house was his in those days, though it was just two rooms back then. He was childless and was glad to have me. But I do not forget my sisters.

Sir, do you know that in the Hebrew tongue, this name *hiram* means "helpful brother" and *iram* means "watchful"? So I have named my youngest this, so that he might be both. It is my hope that if he one day marries and has a son, he will name him Ezer, which also means "help". This is what makes for good family and good life. We must help each other. But I do not put my will about this onto him. It is for the Most

High to give a name in the deep wells of a father's heart, and in the mother's heart, for they must raise up a child in the way he should go, to feed and protect and guide him.

A hard blow fell on my family when I was a boy. My parents died young, leaving us to fend for ourselves in the charge of my eldest sister. We were one boy and five girls. But I did not lose heart, and in time the Lord himself smiled on me and gave me five boys and one girl. Do you see the way he is with us? I will look with interest to see if any of my children will have five girls and one boy. If that comes to pass, I will laugh very much, though not like Sarah's laugh. It will be a day to dance with joy like David before the Ark, for then it will be proven to me that, though he is mighty, the Lord's heart is warm as a man's and is full of kindness, just as the scripture says.

On a wedding day, a seed is planted. That single seed may become a mighty tree in the Lord's own time, for a day is as a thousand years to him, and a thousand years is as a day. And then from that single tree, there comes forth a multitude of seeds, and they in turn become a forest. So we must guard the first seed with our lives, giving it water and soil, weeding it and pruning it, and then it grows as it should. But if we become weary or lazy, or if we open the heart to sinful thoughts, the worm bores in and bites the seed, and then the seed dies. The dry-rot and wet-rot can do that too, and all manner of other things could end the little seed. If that happens, the seed comes to nothing, and unseen with the eyes is the forest that will not be.

The Romans are cutting down forests here in Galilee. They say it is to make more land for farming. In truth, it is to remove the hiding places where enemies of the Romans lie in shadows and make their plots. I do not agree with such as they, though they are my own countrymen. The Lord himself will make the increase, in his own way and in his own time, and it is wrong to push his holy hand. You cannot raise children that way, you cannot grow things from the earth that way, you cannot shepherd your flock that way.

I did not mean to talk about this. What had I meant to tell you?

Thank you, my wife. Yes, forgive me.

Sir, you asked about my kinsman Yeshua Bar Yosef. I will tell you. Do you know anything about what happened to him? You do? Good. More than once since that dark year—more than thirty years ago—men came to me with pens and books in their hands to write down the little I could tell them. I will tell you what I told them. It is not much, but it is something.

I remember playing with him in his father's shop when I was small. After that, I went away and saw him only once or twice a year from boy to man. It was always in a crowd of family, so I did not get to know him as well as I might have. My mother was the daughter of a woman whose husband was an uncle of Yosef Bar Yaakov. Here in the mountains, we are all connected in one way or another. The blood gets thinned by marriages and by time, but we know who we are. We keep in memory our ancestors back to Noah. Farther back than that, if you give us a moment to let it awaken again.

After I had become a man, I was betrothed in marriage to Keturah. From near and far the family came to the wedding, and all the people of Cana too—none had been left out. There must have been more than two hundred people, and no house could hold even a small part of them. So there they all were, and after the rabbi blessed us, the guests sat down on blankets upon the grass, though my wife and I and her family sat on benches at a great table in the yard. Ten thousand lamps were lit, it seemed to me, and platter after platter, bowl after bowl, of wondrous foods was carried in, and the feast began. Such singing and dancing! Oh, oh that day! We will never forget it.

There was wine aplenty too, but it turned out that there were *more* than plenty guests. As the night wore on, I asked a friend who was acting as the wine steward to make sure the urns were full enough. I had worked for three years to make that wine, and purchased extra too. But my friend returned to me in great distress to say that it was running low, and the night still stretched long before us.

Myriam and Yeshua were among us. Yosef had gone to the Father of All by then. And it came to pass that Myriam was standing nearby with a group of women and saw my anxious face, and that of the steward, and asked what might be wrong. I would have said nothing, but she was a mother, and I had always missed my own mother; moreover, she had a way of seeing through things. So, without thinking, I told her my trouble. She put a hand to my shoulder just as the steward came up and blurted out the bad news that there was no more wine. Then she went away, and I sat there beside Keturah, ashamed and afraid—I worried myself silly about many things in those days. And she was as worried as I was, because such a lack would not be forgotten by others; the guests might think we respected them little to provide so little, and would go to their homes with hearts not as light as they should have been.

Yeshua had at that time just begun to go about Galilee, and already a few men were following him. He had brought them to our wedding, and they saw what happened next. When I told Yochanan about it years later, he said he was there on the day of my wedding, though he was a youth at the time. I did not remember him. Well, my eyes were elsewhere. He has written about what happened and often tells it to others. And some read the story. This is how it was:

Myriam went to Yeshua and told him the bad news. At first he did not say a thing. Then he said to her, "Woman, my hour has not yet come." His mother smiled, for between the two there was open speech and always kindness. He did not say it unkindly. Yochanan thinks it was because he knew what he was about to do yet wished it to remain a thing unknown by many. She did not press him but turned instead to those who were waiting on the table. She merely said, "Do whatever he tells you."

At the front of the house, there were six jars of water that I had borrowed for the feast, to be used by guests to purify their hands before eating. Those were very large jars, I can tell you, and now that they had been used, you could not drink from them anymore. They had been tipped into the garden and beneath the fruit trees all about the house. Now, as the feast went on, they were empty. Yeshua told the servers to refill them with water from our well. When that had been done, he said, "Draw out some and take it to the man in charge of wine." And they did, bringing it in a dipper to my friend. He tasted it and called to me, and I went to him in haste, for never had I seen his face so astonished.

"Ezer, what have you done?" he cried. "People usually serve the best wine first, and then when the guests have been drinking for a time, they are served poorer vintage. But you have saved the best for last."

This is true. It is what happened. I cannot explain how it came to pass, but there it is, and none can make me change a word.

He was a prophet, and more than a prophet. Elijah made the grain increase for the starving widow and her boy. And I believe someone greater than Elijah was among us.

Some say he was *azazel*, which means "scapegoat". Some call him that because the guilt of our people was put onto him. He suffered for our sins, though he was without sin. There have been many scapegoats before him, but Yeshua was something more. He was the pure lamb sacrificed for our sake.

This lamb arose from our midst, yet he was given from above. Who can explain this?

He was the promised one, our *meshiha*. I think about him always. So do my family and some in the villages hereabout. My youngest, Hiram, travels much to Sepphoris and to other places where they pray in the name of Yeshua and are swiftly answered by the Most High. To make water into wine is a very great thing. It is the greatest thing I have seen in my life. Yet greater things our Yeshua did. I am a small man, and ignorant, and can tell you only what I saw. But I think that my children will see greater things still, and indeed they already have. Hiram hopes to become a disciple of Yochanan. There is a city in the north, a place where the pagans live. Many followers live there now, and Myriam lived there until her last breath. Hiram will live with them too, and soon he will go.

If Keturah and I were younger, we would go with him. But as I said, I am an ignorant man. Besides, there are many here who need me. It is my duty to tend to small ways, and this is the will of the Lord for me.

Capernaum
Binyamin Bar Shimon

After a long day's journey by foot from Cana, we come down from the highlands into a gently sloping region of pastures, orchards, and scattered woods, surrounding a very large lake that people of the region call "the sea". On its northwest shore is Capernaum, a town of about five thousand residents, most of them fishermen and their families. There is a small Roman fort here, a century only, an outpost of the major garrison of a thousand soldiers headquartered at the city named Tiberias, farther south on the west shore. The road from the Jezreel

Valley passes directly beneath the guards on the fort's battlements, then slopes down toward the outskirts. Viewed from this higher ground, Capernaum appears to be about five times as large as Nazareth. On the whole, the houses here are a better quality than those of the hill folk, since the exterior walls are plastered with clay and lime.

Aharon was born and raised in this place. As we walk through the unpaved streets, he is greeted several times, embraced by some. Until now he has been my rather overquiet and humble interpreter, but here he becomes a visiting dignitary. He does not abandon his genuine humility, but it is plain to see that he is respected by all.

We will stay for a few days as guests in a home belonging to a woman named Shoshannah, close to the shore. A breeze is blowing in off the water, refreshing us. We come to the door of her house and I am startled by symbols cut into its wood: a fish, and above it a cross. The fish needs no explanation, but why the sign of infamous death? This is the first I have seen during my time in this land.

Shoshannah answers to Aharon's knock. She is a pretty woman in her midthirties. There are joyful exclamations on both sides. They kiss each other's cheeks, and she welcomes us in. We enter a courtyard surrounded by four walls, each with its open doorways leading into rooms. In the middle of the yard, an oven is puffing smoke, tended by a younger woman—the smell of baking bread is in the air. We are led into the largest room, a kitchen and eating place, filled with stone jars, floored by woven reed mats. There is no furniture other than a low rectangular wood table. Two children are sitting beside it, braiding bits of colored wool, trying to tie a large seed nut to the end of one. Aharon drops to his knees to help them, but they abandon their task and throw themselves into his arms, knocking him over, all of them laughing. An adult-and-child conversation then ensues in their language, and though I understand not a word of it, it is so like all such conversations throughout the world that I feel very much at home. My spirits are elevated by what I see, yet I also feel a powerful longing for my own beloved grandchildren. As the three on the floor continue to babble and roll about, Shoshannah speaks to me. She knows just enough Greek to ask about my family. Too copiously, I tell her about each of them. She recognizes the name of Loukas. She has met him, a very good man—a companion of Paul, she says. In her flow of speech, I hear other names such as Silas, Timotheos, Mattityahu. I do not grasp much of what she tries to tell me.

Whenever she refers to my interpreter, she changes the "Ben" in his name to the Aramaic "Bar". When Aharon is again able to interpret, the woman says that her husband is with his boat out on the sea, and she hopes that he will return by nightfall. We are served leavened bread, smoked fish, grapes, figs, and wine.

If I were to describe all that is told to me by various people in this town, and nearby, I would quickly use up the remaining pages in this scroll. Loukas' chronicle tells the story well enough and does it in his more elegant style. These people recount the same stories and numerous more. In every account, I realize I am listening to events witnessed by the eye. Of course, the stories are filtered through interpretation and memory—with all the flaws implied by this—but seem to be based in fact. Unquestionably, something unprecedented occurred here.

That much I can verify, for in my years of observing human nature, I have come to understand the common characteristics of any true account. Ten men will describe an event witnessed by them in ten different ways, complete with inconsistencies. It is the inconsistencies that ever intrigue me. Long ago, I learned that these are not evidence that a story is untrue.

On the contrary, they are evidence that the original event happened indeed. In everything I hear during my time in Capernaum, I am struck again and again by this flavor or "spice" in the various accounts. What happened here is so remarkable that the minor blurring of the eyes, the small embellishments, are easily picked out. What remains is astounding. I write this, and then my mind springs awake. What have I just written! What remains is astounding only if it actually happened. Thus I am caught in a fracture between the unbelievable story and the characteristics of fact. For the moment, this contradiction must remain unresolved.

I leave much of what could be related to a better hand than mine, that is, to Loukas himself. Here, then, are my own smaller fragments:

Binyamin Bar Shimon speaks:

Sir, I ask your pardon that I was not here to welcome you when you arrived. We were blown farther south on the lake this morning and had a good catch. The heat of the day could have spoiled it, so we put in to Tiberias, the Roman city down there. I do not like that place, since it is very rich and pagan, but it would be wrong to spoil a gift from the Lord. On the dock, I met a Roman who bought the whole catch for a household in the city. When he heard I was from Capernaum, he asked about the stories people spread about Yeshua of Nazareth, the wonder-worker who had done many marvels at Capernaum. I told him some of it before the wind changed, and we have agreed to meet again. But that is why I am so late.

My friend Aharon tells me that you are the father of Loukas, whom I have met three times, for he came here and to villages roundabout, gathering what our townfolk can remember. Your son told me that in many places the Gentiles now believe in our anointed one, as far away as Damascus and Antioch. In Caesarea on the Sea there are followers too. In Jerusalem are many beyond counting—even people of other races and tongues who come from afar to hear about him. But few come here, for Galilee is not an easy place at this time. The Roman soldiers have made numerous arrests because of the Zealots. The people of Capernaum do not make trouble for anyone. We fish as we always have. Yet the region is no longer safe.

My father Shimon was named Kepha by Yeshua. My father left our home when I was still nursing at the breast. So I do not remember his face from the time before he went away. I remember him more from the time after he returned to us. He stayed but awhile and went away again and again, though he always returned. My father has made many healings in the name of Yeshua.

He sends messages to us from other places. He is now in the city of Rome. A letter came from there two months past to the elder of our church in Capernaum. He sent his greetings to his family and asked our prayers that he might cast his net far and deep into the people who are in Rome. Paul is there as well, and they are brothers to each other. After we children were full-grown, my mother left to join him in Rome. She is there now. Some of my sisters pray that they both will soon come home to Bethsaida and live out their final days in peace. But I do not pray this way. I ask that my father will go to all places in the world and bring in a bountiful catch.

Did you know that when Yeshua was on this earth, he told my father he would become a fisher of men? And that is what he has become. Thousands upon thousands now believe in the Lord through him. He also said that my father would be the stone upon which he would build his house. This too is coming to pass.

You would have to meet my father to understand what kind of man he is. Though he is now aging, he is vigorous and full of courage and by nature a person of strong feelings. Great things the Lord does through him, yet my father is always small in his own eyes. Only in latter days did he learn to read. In the beginning, the Holy Spirit taught him through the mouth of Yeshua, and later through the fire of Pentecost, and ever since then he grows and grows in wisdom and authority.

When I was a child, I did not understand why my father could not be with me. I am grateful now that I was blessed with uncles and older brothers to help raise me to manhood. But for years, when I was little, I resented my father for leaving me. My mother understood why he had to leave, for Yeshua had healed her mother, my grandmother, of an illness that would have killed her. There was a strong love between my father and my mother, and if she had been a different kind of woman, she might have become bitter over the separation, yet she did not. By the power of her love, she let him go away into the world. When I was six or seven, she told me that she let him go because the Lord had shown her something important. She had learned that her husband was now closer to her than he was before. I did not understand what she told me, and I was angry about it.

It was when he next returned that I saw how much he suffered to be apart from us. He took me upon his knees and held me close. He said that he was not good enough to be crucified like our Lord, but he had been permitted to share in the sacrifice, for the pain in his heart was like a cross. "What pain?" I asked him. He said, "The pain of not being with you every day of your life."

Then he asked me to carry this cross with him. And I said yes I would, and I knew that he loved me and was with me—indeed, every day of my life.

He is revered by all those in the world who have heard of our Savior. But whenever my father comes to visit us, he sits on the shore and remembers. Sometimes he goes out alone onto the waters and casts a net. At times he will go out with no net, in a storm, and that is a worry to us. Yet he always comes to shore again. Sometimes he sits beside the water and weeps.

*

Capernaum
The paralytic

Aharon takes me to a building about five streets inland from the shore, more like a hut than a proper home.

"This is one of the places where we meet for prayer", he says. "We call it the House of Yeshua. During the time when he lived in Capernaum, he slept and ate here."

We poke our heads inside the door. No one is at home. It is a single-room dwelling with a thatched roof; hanging lamps dangle from the rafters. The place is without furniture save for a wooden table at one end of the room. No one now lives here, Aharon explains, since the house is considered an especially sacred place.

"No beds", I comment.

"He slept on the floor."

The floor, I note, is bare dirt.

"You told me that you met him once."

"Yes, I did. But in those days I was more interested in playing pranks than in miracles."

"Did you see any?"

"I remember one that I saw with my own eyes, though I know of several others that took place here. We lived in this very street when I was young. My mother was upset that thousands of people from the surrounding region were swarming into the town to see Yeshua, choking every street and making it difficult to live a normal life. She was not then a believer in him, though later she was very much so. She died three years ago, in holiness and peace. But that day, being a responsible and practical person, she was greatly irritated by the constant disruptions. She had found me gawking at the edge of the crowd and grabbed me by the hand as she stormed toward this house, intending to tell Yeshua to take his preaching to the outskirts of town. But she ran into a solid wall of people, many hundreds filling every space in these small alleys and lanes. She could not get through to speak to him. I saw that she was furious and might take out her frustration on me, for I was no stranger to swats. I was, I think, about six or seven years old at the time, and too full of life for my own good, as she used to say of me. I shook off her hand, dropped to my hands and knees, and crawled between a forest of legs, closer and closer to the little house in which we now stand. Everyone in the crowd paid me no notice, or if they did they did not care. And that is how I came to see my first miracle.

"A man who had been paralyzed most of his life was being carried on a litter toward the house, but his friends could not get him through. Many were pressing forward, hoping for healings, but Yeshua was inside, talking with people—in fact, some local scribes from the synagogue, whose closed minds he was trying to open. Seeing that it was impossible to get through by the regular route, the friends of the paralytic made their way out of the crowd, still carrying him on the litter. They went around to another street, over some fences, and then they somehow got him up onto the roof, litter and all. That's when I first saw them.

"As they were tearing the thatch off the roof, people down below in the yard noticed and began to shout, pointing and laughing. Then the entire crowd spotted them and roared with both resentment and amusement. I saw it all, delighted by this act of great daring and what looked like a great joke too. Then the friends lowered the paralytic's litter on ropes through the hole in the roof. Not long after, the paralytic came leaping out the front door, shouting and weeping with joy."

"You saw this with your own eyes?"

"With my own eyes."

"How do you know he really was a paralytic? Perhaps it was staged to impress the crowds."

Aharon pauses and quietly examines my eyes, and the sadness I had first seen in Nazareth crosses his face again. In a gentle voice he says:

"The paralytic was my uncle. From my birth until the day he was healed, I had never seen him walk. My father was one of the friends who lowered him into the house."

Rebuked—without an overt rebuke—I look away in embarrassment. He lets me absorb this for a time.

I ask, "How is your uncle now? Did the healing remain with him?"

"For the rest of his life, more than twenty years, he walked as well as any other man. He died after a normal day of hard work."

In holiness and peace? I think to myself, not without a note of skepticism.

Capernaum
Merab and Mikaya

While walking alone by the shore, I meet Merab, known as Mera, a young daughter of Binyamin and Shoshannah. She is working beside a man at the edge of the trees. He is extremely old, trembling in hand and tremendously wrinkled. He is the girl's mother's grandfather. His name is Mikaya. He sits by a metal tub in the shade of a tree, gutting fish and splitting each one into a fork. The girl, who is about eight years old, takes a fish from him and hangs it on a rack of wooden poles in the sun. Beneath the poles, a fire of wet willow wood is making clouds of smoke.

The girl smiles, picks up an ungutted fish from the tub, and points to depressions beside each gill. She puts thumb and forefinger into the depressions and squeezes. The fish's mouth opens wide. The old man comes over with halting steps, takes a coin called the "half *shekel*" from the pocket of his garment, and puts it into the fish's mouth. The girl slides her fingers from the depressions, and the fish's mouth closes over the coin. She presses again, and the mouth opens. She removes the coin and hands it to the old man.

"Shimon", he says, nodding emphatically—and unstoppably, it seems.

"Kepha", says the girl. Then she adds, "Yeshua."

They resume their work. I have no idea what they have been trying to tell me.

Capernaum
Soldiers

I am strolling beside the lake a few stadia south of town, trying to make sense of the number of stories I am hearing, wondering how they fit together in chronology and meaning. Ten Roman soldiers advance toward me on a footpath that skirts the water. I step aside to let them pass, but they detain me for questioning. The foremost among them is low in rank but superior to the others. His manner is officious but not threatening. He says:

"You are a citizen? Yes, the document is good. A physician too, I see by the insignia on your bag. Why are you here? You are wasting your time with those people. They are very ignorant. Do not believe anything they tell you. If you are interested in this land, you should go to Jerusalem or Caesarea. Tiberias would welcome you too, for we are short of physicians. It is because the heat there is worse than in Italy, very humid and stinking with the sulfur springs nearby."

He asks me about my home city, for he has heard of Gortyna. I tell him descriptive things. He wants to know what kind of games we have. I have never attended the games, I say, but it is certain there are gladiatorial combats. Our hippodrome is also a popular spot. My vagueness bores him, and he signals to the others that it is time to move on.

He gives me some final warnings about the "superstitious madness" in Capernaum. The other soldiers make crude jokes about the Jews in that town. I notice that one young soldier neither laughs nor contributes a word. His face is masked. He lowers his eyes during the worst of the banter, then looks away across the lake. The soldiers continue on down the path, and the one who had been so solemn is at the rearguard. He stops and looks back at me. Then he goes on toward Capernaum with his companions.

Capernaum
Achaikos son of Dameon

I am ambling through the marketplace of Capernaum, noting that life goes on as usual despite the supposed miracles that have taken place here. It is a curious thing that the haggling over fruit and vegetable stalls is like that of the smaller market in Nazareth and the numerous multiracial markets of Caesarea. Indeed, it is much like Gortyna's. Here the people are all Jews, with a few rare exceptions such as the two young soldiers, chatting in Latin, who stroll through the crowds, parting them without conscious effort. I pass a very black African, turbaned and robed in white, deep in discussion with a local brass merchant. He is hoping to purchase a lamp on a chain, offering for exchange a handful of small dusty stones, which I would wager are uncut gems. But the merchant laughs at him and gestures that he should go away and try his tricks on someone less gullible. Confused, the African wanders off.

Then I notice a man standing alone by the door of a nearby wine shop. He is in his late forties, taller than any people I have seen here. At first I take him for a Jew since his robes are Judaean. Then I see that he is short-haired, though bearded. His face is fine-featured—in fact, it looks Greek. Moreover, he is quietly reading a book.

A book! How pleasant, how surprising, to find a book in this rustic *polis*, where doubtless a good fishnet is considered to be more valuable than the entire library of Alexandria.

I approach him and clear my throat to catch his attention. He looks up, and his eyes suddenly focus on me, a little surprised. He rolls the book closed.

"Fair morning to you, sir", he says in good *koine*.

"Fair morning to you as well", I reply. "Are you, like me, a visitor to this city?"

"No, Capernaum is my home."

"Yet you are Greek?" I say. "This is surprising."

"Is it?" he smiles. "I suppose it must be by contrast. The ratio of species living in a particular environment, when viewed by a traveler who is not native to that environment, predisposes him to assess their relationships according to alien criteria, does it not?"

I try to absorb the meaning of the question, and fail at it.

Again he smiles. "Would you be so good as to honor me with your company, sir? Would you care to take a cup of wine with me, as my guest?"

The wine shop has a little tavern attached to its back walls, an enclosed courtyard so small that only about six or eight people might squeeze into it. We are the only clients. It is midday, and though the sun's burning rays are deflected by an awning, the walls block the lake's breezes, and I feel that we are to be cooked alive in something like an oven. Even so, it is restful to sit on these benches, sipping rather good wine and nibbling from a bowl of grapes.

He introduces himself as Achaikos son of Dameon. I give him my name, province, and position, and in response to his further inquiry, I explain why I am traveling in this "particular environment".

At this, he leans forward across the small wooden table that separates us and, with eyes thoughtfully pondering mine, asks in a quiet voice:

"You say you seek to learn more about Yeshua of Nazareth?"

I nod.

"You seek the *truth* about him?"

"Yes, of course, I want no less than the truth. If you are able to throw some light on the subject, I would be grateful. But first, I would like to know more about you."

He tells me that he is half-Greek, his father a man from Achaia on the coast of the Peloponnisos who came here as a slave of one of the Romans in charge of Galilee. The father later became a freedman and chose to remain in Capernaum after his manumission because he wished to marry Achaikos' mother, a Jewish woman of this town. He was born here and has lived here all his life.

He says:

I have obtained some learning, and by teaching languages and mathematics I now earn my wages. My school is small because the common people have little interest in these subjects.

In the beginning I was a servant of the Romans, though not under compulsion to be so. My master was the officer in charge of the garrison here, a centurion named Marcus Lapidus. He was a man of virtue, as some of those people can be. He was ever kind to his servants, even before the events I will describe. His whole household, including his wife and son, lived with him here, which is not the usual thing in their army. He died twenty years past, full of years and no longer in the military. He owned a vineyard and lived by the sale of its produce. After he died, his wife and son returned to Italy. But I remember him well. He built the synagogue of Capernaum at his own expense and respected our ways, though he did not become a Jew. I would not be alive now if he had been a different sort of man. Nor would I be alive but for the healing that Yeshua Bar Yosef gave me.

Strange as it may be to your ears, I did not see the face of the one who saved me. He walked in these streets many a time, but the crowds were thick whenever he passed through. I was only eighteen years of age and had duties that kept me busy from morning to night, with one day off for the Sabbath. Now I regret my lack of interest. In those days I was not one to be in the synagogue overmuch or following after every rumor of wonders. I had had my fill of that and dreamed only of migrating to Greece, my father's homeland.

One day I became ill with a fever and fell away from all thought and continued to sink. My master held me in high regard because I was honest and hardworking in every way; moreover, I was a friend to his son, who was about my age. This alone cannot explain what next happened. I believe it was a thing in Marcus' character. He had much power over men but was always just, and in his justice there was no cruelty. He loved the people of this land, and at the time I did not understand his feeling, for I loved them little though I loved my mother. My heart was hard and his was not, yet he was strong. Such are the mysteries of men's souls.

As I said, I had fallen ill, and it was clear that I was close to death. Our family lived in a house beside the master's, upon the hill of vineyards near the fort. That day Yeshua entered the town, and even from the Villa Lapidus all could hear the tumult down by the synagogue. Thousands were in the street, and many were healed that day. Elders of the town had come to report to my master on the disturbance and told him about Yeshua. Without hesitation Marcus asked the elders to go to him and beg a healing for me. They were soon back with the news that he would come.

When Yeshua was not far from the gate, Marcus sent out to him a message through the mouth of his friends, saying, "Sir, I am not worthy that you should enter my house. That is why I did not presume to go to you myself. If you will give the command, my servant will be healed."

Yeshua stood still, in deep thought. The messengers went on. "Sir, the master of this house asks us to tell you that he knows what it is to give an order, for he has soldiers under his authority. If he says to one, 'Go there!' he goes there. If he says to a servant, 'Do this!' he does it."

Yeshua was amazed on hearing this. He turned to the crowd following him and said, "I tell you, I have never found this much faith among the Israelites."

Marcus' friends returned to the house, and there they found me sitting up in bed and asking for something to eat.

All this was told to me after. I remember only sinking deeper and deeper into darkness. My body and soul were in flames. Then in an instant I found myself sitting up, hungry, and ready to put my feet to the floor for a good day's work.

As I said, I did not meet the one who healed me. The whole household believed in him from then on, as did I and my parents. Later, when he was crucified, we were broken in heart. But it did not last long. You must have heard the stories circulating around Judaea and Galilee. It is true. It is all true.

I and my wife and our children are with the brethren here in Capernaum. We have three houses for prayer. It would be better if we were to pray in the synagogue, because Yeshua is the fulfillment of the prophets, but there is resistance. Not everyone understands that he is the new covenant that has come forth from the covenants of Abraham and Mosheh. He is the shoot of the tree of Yishay—indeed, he is the new Tree of Life. The Lord Most High answers powerfully the prayers we make to him in the name of his Son.

When the family of Marcus left this region, they gave their house as a place where the *apostoloi* and all those who follow them may rest from their journeys. It is the largest of our houses of prayer. There we also care for the sick.

The son of Marcus now lives in the city of Puteoli on the coast of Italy. No year passes in which we fail to write to each other. He is one of the brethren there, and his family is also.

I did not see with my own eyes what many have seen. I did not see the thing that was done for me. I was told about it by others. Yet I know this as certain: When I was near dead, a hand touched me and I returned to life.

*

ר

Near Bethsaida

This morning Binyamin and Aharon invite me to accompany them on a short boat ride to a deserted place an hour's walk from town. It is not far from the village of Bethsaida, which was Shimon's birthplace and his home until he went away. We could easily go by foot, for there is a well-trodden path along the shore, parallel to the road above. But Binyamin wants to give one of his sons a pleasurable outing on the water and also desires to try out a new rudder. The boy, who is named for his famous grandfather, is about five years old, a little brown lad full of eagerness. His father unfurls the sail, then sits down on a stern board with the boy beside him. Shimon puts his small hand to the tiller with a grin, convinced that he is the one controlling the craft. Without being noticed, the father keeps his huge hand on it too, doing the work. We three men enjoy the child's delight, his innocence, his unsuspecting lack of guile. The man he will become is hiding within that little frame, and behind his shining eyes there is intelligence waiting to bloom. The years pass swiftly in this life, for it seems that only yesterday we were once like him.

As we near the northern end of the lake, Binyamin says, "Push the rudder this way, Shimon, and it will bring us to shore."

"Can't we go farther?" cries the boy with a yearning look.

"No. That beach over there is where we must go."

"Please, Abba, *please!*"

"If you take us any farther, Shimon," laughs Binyamin, "we will be sailing across rocks and bushes, and we will crash into Grandmother's house. Now, push the rudder a little. Good, you did it just right. See how the boat turns."

"Yes, I see, Abba."

Not long after, Binyamin brings in the sail and drops the anchor a stone's throw from shore. It is fairly shallow there, so we step from the boat and wade through knee-high water to a stretch of sandy beach. Binyamin follows with the boy in his arms.

The beach is bordered by slopes covered with bushes. There are no houses to be seen in any direction. Piper birds run along the edge of the waves, hunting insects and making their distinctive calls. Strangely, there is a bare stone table standing above us in a clearing full of wild grass and numerous flowers of diverse species.

Binyamin shows me a ring of stones by the water, just below the table. Bits of charcoal and fish bones bleached white by the sun give evidence of its purpose.

"Here is a place that is sacred to us", he says. "This cook fire has been guarded and kept as it was thirty years ago. People come here sometimes and make a fire, have a meal of fish. But they do not disturb the stones."

"And what is that?" I ask, pointing to the table.

"On the altar, we make the memorial of Yeshua's last supper on this earth."

"It looks like an altar of sacrifice", I comment.

"It is an altar of sacrifice. But not in the way of the pagans nor solely in our forefathers' tradition. It is a feast of thanksgiving. When we pray in this way, time is no more. At once, we are in Jerusalem on the night before he died, and on the mountain of his crucifixion, and with him in paradise at the eternal banquet."

"How is it possible?" I ask, keeping a tone of cordial respect in my voice. "How is it possible to be four places at once?"

Neither Binyamin nor Aharon answer me, though their eyes are full of thoughts. Of course, logic is not a major faculty of simple people such as these. Still, I see that they believe what they tell me; they are surely sincere.

"And what is the cook fire for? There is nothing unusual about it. Why do you hold it as sacred?"

"Here Yeshua made a breakfast for my father and his companions."

Shimon plays along the shore, skipping and laughing, chasing the birds. He falls into the water and soaks himself but jumps up quickly and keeps running here and there, drying off in the sun. We smile as we watch his antics, then sit down beside the fire place. Binyamin grows serious again and continues his story.

He points out to the lake and says, "Just offshore, just there, my father and his friends Yochanan and Teoma, also Nathanael a man from Cana, and other disciples, had fished throughout one night and caught nothing. They were very tired and low in heart. Just after daybreak, they saw a man by a fire onshore—this very place where we now are. The man called to them and said, 'Children, have you caught anything?' They answered, 'Nothing!'

" 'Cast your net out to the other side,' he suggested, 'and you will find something.' So they made a cast and took in so many fish that they could not haul the catch on board.

"Then Yochanan cried out, 'It is the Lord!'

"My father was wearing next to nothing, so he threw on his clothes and jumped into the water and waded ashore. The others brought the boat in by oar, dragging the net behind them. There were one hundred and fifty-three fish, and the net was not torn. Not once in their lives had they made a catch like that. When they had all come to Yeshua, they saw a fish cooking on charcoal and bread laid out for them.

" 'Come and eat your breakfast', Yeshua said, and he gave them the food, and they ate it."

"That is a good memory", I say. "An excellent way to remember the man."

Binyamin and Aharon look at me unfathomably. There is silence for a while, and both look away from me, gazing out over the water. Then Binyamin says in a quiet voice:

"Here too another important thing happened. Three times did Yeshua ask my father if my father loved him. And three times my father replied that he did. And after each reply, Yeshua said, 'Feed my sheep.' This was because in Jerusalem my father had three times claimed he did not know Yeshua, after the Lord was arrested. But here he was given the words of atonement, to replace the denials, to heal his heart and memory of them."

"Neither your father nor Yeshua was a shepherd", I say. "What did he mean by it?"

"He foresaw everything that was to come. All mankind is his flock, and my father must feed them."

"Still, I do not understand. Was this before or after his trial?"

"It was after."

Now I realize that we have entered the realm of their mythology. Seeing my puzzlement and unbelief, Binyamin nods once and gets to his feet. He calls the boy to him, and then we all wade out to the boat and depart for Capernaum.

On the way back to town, little Shimon falls asleep. Binyamin holds the boy close under an arm, keeping a hand firmly on the tiller.

As we near our destination, he says a final thing:

"When Yeshua gave the fish to them, they saw holes in his hands and his feet. He opened his robe to his waist, and then they saw a hole in his side, next to his heart."

*

It is now night, and I am writing by lamplight in my room in the house of Binyamin Bar Shimon. Tomorrow, Aharon and I set out on our journey to Jerusalem. It will be a long route through the valley of the Jordan River, which drains the Sea of Galilee at its southern end. We will first go by boat down the lake and connect with the road at the outflow where the river begins. My guide tells me that going by water will save us three days of walking. From there onward we must proceed on foot. Aharon estimates we will be six to eight days on the road. There are numerous villages along the river, and at one of them he hopes to rent or borrow a donkey for me to ride.

I have been walking a great deal here in the north. My lungs and my limbs feel stronger than they have in decades. Once or twice I have tried to trot as I once did in my youth. I could not long sustain it. My heart is still good, but I lack the energy required for running in the thick humidity. Without the lake winds, the region would be unbearable.

We will pass first through the region of the Decapolis, where apparently there are Hellenic cities. Perhaps along the way I will meet some Greeks. After the Decapolis we will enter Peraea and cross the river near Jericho. From there we will continue westward and climb into the mountains to the city where Yeshua was executed.

An inn at Pella

It is a good feeling to enter a city that shares the same name as the city in Macedonia!

As we left behind the forests ringing the southern part of the lake, we entered the hills and verdant lowlands of the Decapolis, named for the ten cities built by Greek settlers who flooded into Judaea after the conquests. The Greeks now enjoy a measure of independence not enjoyed by the Jewish communities, but as is the case throughout the world, they are ever aware of who really rules over them. This northern part of the valley is densely populated due to its fertile bottomland and the high shield of the eastern mountains, which guards them from the winter winds. There is more rainfall here. A number of rivulets, fed by natural springs, run down from the heights. The Jordan's bed meanders in winding loops, the clear water flowing ever southward. The well-maintained road follows it in a straighter course.

So far, the journey has not been arduous. We sleep at inns or humble homes along the route. My numerous encounters with a variety of people could too easily fill these pages. Some of them merely retell what is to be found in Loukas' chronicle. In the satchel strapped across his chest, Aharon carries a manuscript written by one of the first *apostoloi*, a man named Mattityahu—Matthaios in Greek. He reads a little of it to me whenever we stop for our night's rest. I hear of matters not included in Loukas' version: Eastern kings visited Yeshua at his birth. Yeshua walked on water—even Shimon walked on water.

My doubts increase. Mythology, mythology, the curse of the human imagination! A good deal of what I am hearing surely has a base in fact, but men's minds are unstable. They must take a mystery and turn it into a marvel, forgetting in the process that they are its creators.

I write briefly tonight since I am lured to a mattressed bed, which will be a relief from the straw mats on the floors of my previous hosts. In the dining room of this inn, I also enjoyed discussion with men of my ancestry—a dramatist, a philosopher, and a merchant. All three displayed amusement regarding the legends of the Jews, and all three exercised considerable skepticism about the Yeshua stories. Fortunately, Aharon did not hear it because he had gone off somewhere to sleep in a tent, scandalized by a statue of Aphrodite, which stands at the entryway, welcoming lodgers.

I must not omit mentioning this exceptional work of art. Imported from Athens, life-sized, made with the highest skill, it surpasses anything I have seen in Crete. I was deeply stirred, held in wonder before it. How I have missed the embodiment of beauty! And how sad that the Jews deprive themselves of this kind of worship. It is sadder still that they do not know the pleasures of philosophical dialogue. What comparable consolations did Aharon find tonight? In any event, it was truly a consolation for me to converse without restraint, breathing more easily in a cultured atmosphere of reason. However, it was soon over, and doubtless tomorrow the mythologizing will resume.

An inn at Jericho

Our last night on the road. We sleep at an inn just beyond the city of Jericho, on the main route to Jerusalem. Aharon tells me that this region was once a wasteland until a prophet named Elisha poured salt into a bitter spring and the spring began to flow in great abundance and purity. This strikes me as unlikely, since salt renders water unusable for drinking or for watering plants of any kind. It cannot be doubted, however, that this part of the valley is irrigated by more than the Jordan, which flows a good deal farther to the east. All about the city and for a distance north and south, farther than the eye can see, are vineyards, garden plots, and groves of different kinds of dates. Orchards of other fruits also produce abundantly.

I am pleased to find stands of balsam trees here as well and am able to purchase a vial of their exceedingly fine sap, which Jericho merchants call "the balm of Gilead". It is useful for curing headaches and has a positive effect on cataracts of the eye. There is a variety of milkwort plant grown here that is also useful as medicine. The combination of water, rich soil, and an intense, near-suffocating heat create an oven in which all plants thrive as nowhere else. The vineyards produce grapes that are larger than any I have ever seen—the size of hen eggs, meaty and gushing with syrup, very sweet on the tongue— and every sprig groaning under the weight of them.

The modern city was built upon the ruins of ancient pagan Jericho, which was destroyed by the Israelites, who fled slavery in Egypt. According to legend, the walls were collapsed by mighty trumpet blasts, under the command of another prophet, Yehoshua by name. These Hebrew names! How can I keep track of them—most seem to have references to their god in them!

Tomorrow we will spend the final day of our journey climbing into the mountains to the west. If we depart before dawn, we may, with good fortune, arrive in Jerusalem just after nightfall. The view from my window is not appealing. The heights are stark, barren, foreboding.

Jerusalem

Now we are here. One day by water and seven days on foot. No donkey was hired because I had urged Aharon to let me walk. With full waterskins and an ample river beside us for most of the way, I did well enough. In fact, I arrived in the "holy city" feeling stronger than I have in years.

*

My reunion with Loukas takes place in a house belonging to friends of his in an older district called "the city of David". He hastens down the stairs to the entrance hall and throws his arms wide, his expression eager to know if I have been transformed during the time of separation. We embrace, and I realize that I am truly very pleased to see him.

He avoids probing me with difficult questions, keeping to matters of travel and health. But he cannot wipe a broad smile from his face, and I am hard put to decide if this is because he is glad to be reunited with me or if it is because he is presuming that my examinations have accomplished what he had hoped for—a physician healed by his patients. I must disappoint him, of course, but in the interim we converse congenially as he shows me through the house. He has arranged that two small bedrooms on the third floor will be ours for as long as we are in the city.

From my bedroom window, I see that I am high enough on the hill to overlook Jerusalem's mighty walls and beyond into the narrow Kidron Valley. Orchards cover the hill facing me on the far side of the valley, the paler green of olive and the darker green of various fruits, speared here and there by soaring cypress. Near this house is an ancient pool where the residents of the district get their water. The noise in the surrounding streets is a phenomenon to rival the forge of Hephaistos. All homes and tenements are crammed full to overspilling, and most of the streets are crowded from morning to nightfall. Loukas tells me that the population is now about a quarter of a million, but it soars to three or four times that amount during the Jewish holy days that are called "Passover".

When at last he asks me, in a most general and unmanipulative manner, about my experiences during the past few weeks, I simply tell him that I am learning much and need time to absorb it. This seems to satisfy him. He smiles, nods, clasps my arm, then says he must be off on an errand for one of the elders in the house.

The following day, he brings me copies of the Jews' historical books translated into Greek. He thinks it will give me a better understanding of their traditions. It is fascinating material, but I ask myself again and again as I read: What is fact, and what is myth? If everything in the text is true, no other race in the history of mankind is as favored as the Jews. Why, then, have they been smashed down again and again? And *why* are they so fractious and loud? Loukas informs me that Hebrew and Greek are the dominant languages among rich and learned Jews, but there is plenty of Aramaic as well. The latter is a more supple and developed language, the universal common speech of the land.

I sleep deeply each night and wake well rested. We eat our breakfasts and suppers in common with the dozen or so people who live permanently in the building. A greater number come and go at all hours, though silence seems to rule the house throughout the night. Loukas and I go out to visit famous sites during the day. Aharon is absent for the most part, visiting relatives, but comes by from time to time to see if I need anything. I am touched by his concern. I have grown fond of him and now regret my occasional lack of courtesy during our travels. Their religion breeds a kind of goodness that is rare in the world. Though deluded, these people are quite admirable, I must admit.

The city is a marvel, like none other I have visited in my life. It is very ancient, history embedded in every stone, announced at every corner. No public place lacks its swarms of visitors gawking and babbling in all the tongues of man. Their chief temple is immense and dominates the city, as does the Roman fortress, which broods over everything. God and Caesar are uneasy in each other's company here, but thus far I have seen no civic disturbances.

Tomorrow I continue my examinations.

Jerusalem
Reut

Loukas tells me that this house once belonged to a wealthy woman, an early disciple of Yeshua who is now deceased. She bequeathed it to elders of the community, to be held in perpetuity as a legacy for the believers who would be born in times thereafter. The man in charge of it now is Shimeyon Bar Clopas, the chief elder of the followers of Yeshua in Jerusalem.

On the top floor is the very place where Yeshua dined with his disciples on the eve of his crucifixion. I have spent some hours in the room, trying to imagine what happened that night. It is large enough for dozens of people to gather. The tables and reclining seats from that original meal are kept as they were thirty years ago. There is also a table of sacrifice, similar in form to the one I saw on the shore of the lake. This one is made of polished cedar wood. The wood of the gods.

Reut has come here to pray in the room and later will participate in the community's memorial meal, which they call the *Eucharist*. I am not permitted to partake of that, since I am not a believer. Whenever people gather above me, the walls seem to shake with their singing. It is a very beautiful sound—and deeply disturbing. I remind myself that beauty is dangerous—highly infectious.

Reut is about forty years of age, married, and the mother of eight, a weaver of flax-linen cloth that is sold in the marketplaces throughout the city. Her husband owns a shop in the Street of Textiles on the other side of the Temple Mount. She and her family live in rooms above the shop.

Today, Loukas translates. The woman says:

My name is Reut. In the waters of baptism I am Mahalah, which in our language means "lyre", because I have a good singing voice. At my baptism I was named Lyre of the Holy Spirit because of this. I never learned to play the lyre. It is my voice alone, you understand. There is another reason I was named this: In our language *mahlah* means "weak" or "sickly", and thus I was until he changed me, and then did this *mahlah* become *mahalah*.

I remember very clearly the day Yeshua came into Jerusalem riding on a white donkey. Tens of thousands were there to greet him as the *mashiach*. Indeed, he was the *mashiach*, but most did not understand what this truly meant. [Loukas interrupts to explain that though Reut is speaking Aramaic, she is using the Hebrew word for "anointed".]

My family was among the crowds, including my mother and father, my brothers and sisters, and several others of our kin, with me carried on my father's shoulders, for I had difficulty walking in those days. I was ill with one thing after another, could eat little, and was very thin. My skin was pale and my eyes without shine. I cried often from weariness. No physicians could help me, and I was growing worse. I was in no danger of death, but year after year I became weaker.

Multitudes had then arrived for the high holy days, the feast of unleavened bread, which we have celebrated every year from the time of Mosheh until the present day. It seemed that everyone throughout Judaea and Peraea and Galilee had come up to the city for the feast. It was impossible to move through the streets except a little at a time, so crowded was every step of the way. The noise was terrible.

It seemed like the entire people was out to meet him at the Gate of Gold, waving palm branches and declaring him king. The chief priests and elders from the Temple tried to silence us for fear of the Romans and also because of their dislike of the man himself, as he had borne witness against their evil. But nothing would silence the crowd. Indeed, it seemed to us that King David had returned and that the restoration of Jerusalem was now at hand.

I had never before seen such happiness in the faces of my parents. My father shouted the old prophecies about the *mashiach*, and my mother wept with joy. They put a little palm branch into my hands, but I could not hold it well, and I dropped it. It fell among the feet, and I never saw it again. It made me cry, a big girl like me on such a happy day, because I had lost a little bit of useless palm.

A week later, on the day of the Passover, our king was taken out through the Ephraim Gate, the gate of shame, it is called, to a hill we call Golgottha, the place of the skull, where criminals are executed. There they put him to death.

On that day too our family was with the crowds. We had gone to Gabbattha, the judgment place, because my parents were sure that there our *mashiach* would throw off his chains and destroy the Romans. But it did not happen like that. When my parents saw the soldiers bringing him out, beaten and bloody, dragging his cross, their hopes turned to disappointment and swiftly to anger. They cried out that he had deceived them and deserved to die for it. Their hopes had been lifted high only to be dashed low.

There were thousands of people all about us, and I grew afraid of so many shouting and throwing stones and spitting at the poor man. I felt that no matter what he had done, he did not deserve this. It was all feelings for me since I did not understand anything about what was happening before my eyes. But scripture passages about David came to my thoughts. Saul has killed his thousands, but David has killed his tens of thousands. I do not know why I thought it—maybe because my mind was unwell and the tens of thousands who had praised him were now the thousands who mocked him. It seemed to me, young as I was, that the story had been turned upside down. Where were the missing thousands who had praised him? They were hiding in their homes or going about their business as if nothing was wrong.

My parents and kin shouted with anger as he went by, but I could only droop my head. My grandmother—my mother's mother—was carrying me. She did not shout. Her eyes were sad. When I asked her why the soldiers and the people were doing this, she answered that she did not know why. Yeshua was a good man, she said, and it was wrong to treat him this way. But we were swept along by the crowd and out through the gate of shame.

I begged her to take me home. We tried to go back into the city, but the force of the crowd was so great that we could not make headway, and lest we be trampled under we let ourselves be pushed along farther, and then we were swept up the trail to the place of the skull. As we neared the top, the sea of people was parted by chief priests and officials of the Temple pushing through on horseback. Then Grandmother and I were forced in after them by those pressing us from behind. And so we were brought very near to the place of execution. There were three men put to death that day. Two thieves and Yeshua.

It was the first crucifixion I had ever seen. I cannot describe to you what such a sight would do to the heart of a child— would do to anyone who saw it. They stripped him naked, and hundreds mocked and laughed with their evil tongues. It was a shock to me, this shaming, yet the greater shame was in what they had done to him by beatings and other tortures. The thieves were not badly harmed, but Yeshua stood between them as a pillar of blood; every part of him had been cut. My grandmother put a hand over my eyes and pulled me back. She began to wail, a sound I had never heard from her before, and it greatly added to my fright.

"We must go from this evil place", she cried into my ear, and we sought for a way back down, searching for a gap in the wall of people. We found one and tried to squeeze our way down the hill, and then I saw the bloody footprints that he had left on the stones during his ascent. Though my grandmother tried to hold me up, my bare feet skidded, and I fell down on my face in the blood.

I screamed because the feet of others were trampling all around us, none of the people seeing that a child had fallen. I remember it very clearly, as if it happened just now. It will always be present to me, those few seconds. I can hear the roar of the crowd—like a beast it was. And the smell of the blood. Time slowed nearly to a stop, and as I lay there I saw sandals and boots and bare feet stamping unheeding in his blood.

Then my grandmother pulled me up and we struggled down toward the valley bottom, and the crowd began to thin. From there we made our way home, my grandmother wailing all the way. I still hear that sound, so frightening it was to me. I think her soul was crying out.

It was Passover, and I had been defiled by blood. So we washed ourselves and prayed the atonement prayers and wept as we waited for my parents to return. And then the sky darkened and an earthquake shook our building, dishes fell from the shelves, roof tiles cracked and pitched to the street below, but after this there was no more damage to our house. The wind howled so loudly outside the window that my grandmother's wails were drowned. We sat in the darkness for an hour clinging to each other, and then the trembling of the earth subsided and the light of the sun returned.

I can recall nothing more from that day. I fell into a deep sleep, and I was kept in my bed for the following two days. Later, people in the streets began to talk about what the whole world now knows—that he came back from the dead.

And then we noticed that I no longer needed others to hold me upright when I walked, nor did I want them to carry me anymore. I was hungry as I had never been hungry before. I did not feel the weariness I had felt since my earliest childhood. Color came into my face. I felt no urge to weep. For the first time in my life I was extremely happy, despite all the horror I had seen on the hill of the skull. Whenever I thought of it I felt sad, and shed tears, but they were not dark.

Seven weeks after Passover, our family was together under our roof—my parents, my grandmother, my brothers and sisters, as well as other kin who had come into the city for the feast of Shavuot, which our Greek brothers now call Pentecost. We went in one body up to the Temple. On our way there, we came upon a large crowd of people from many nations and races, their faces struck with amazement. There in their midst stood Kepha crying aloud wondrous things, and the followers of Yeshua who had been with him in Galilee were also proclaiming loudly. Thousands of people gathered to hear them, men of many different nations and races, and each heard Kepha and the others in his own tongue.

Kepha told them about the resurrection of Yeshua the Son of Man, the Son of God who was once dead and now is alive! And the people were cut to the heart when they remembered how they had been in the crowd before Pilate and at the place of the skull and had poured out their anger on the Lamb of God. Kepha spoke of the mercy of God and begged them to come to receive it in the name of Yeshua. Three thousand were added to the number of believers that day, and on another day five thousand more were added. And so it has grown. And so it does not cease to grow.

In our ignorance, on the day of the Lord's death, my grandmother burned the clothing I had worn when I fell in the blood of the Lamb of God and fled from it in terror. But the Lord sees all and understands all, for we are but children in his eyes—yes, all of us, young and old. Truly, he is love. He opens the door for us if we would look up from our darkness, as the angel opened it for Kepha when he was in prison under the Sadducees. All men are in prison until they know him. Yet Yeshua does not drag them from their prison. They must walk out of it and into his arms, because he wishes them to choose him in freedom. He is love, *Selah*, forever! *Selah!*

All men hate the pain of their sins but love the pleasure of their sins. This is our bondage and our test. The door is before you, Theophilos father of Loukas. In former times it was closed and locked. Now it stands open before all.

Oh, I am sorry. I did not know you had little time to spare, and now you must depart. Forgive my tongue, which never knows when to stop. I am better at singing.

Jerusalem
Shimeyon Bar Clopas

Seated on a bench in the upper room, we are three men about the same age. Shimeyon is dressed in a long-used woolen robe, frayed about the hem, a worn leather belt girding his waist, and rough sandals on his feet. Across his lap is a wooden staff such as Galilean shepherds use, the top curled into a hook. The other man wears a multicolored striped robe, a wide cloth belt, and better sandals.

Shimeyon says:

Greetings to you, father of our dear Loukas. Please accept the hospitality of my home, and of all the Lord's family here in the holy city. May you know the peace of heaven offered to men of every race and nation, through our Savior the anointed of the Most High, his only Son, Yeshua, whom your people call Iesous.

I have been the shepherd of this flock since the death three years ago of my kinsman Yaakov the Righteous, who is known to the Greeks as Iakobos. My father was the brother of Yosef, the father of Yeshua. I am related by blood also to Yochanan the baptizer, who went before the Lord to prepare the way. Yaakov is known as the Lord's brother because they were young together, and Yosef was as a father to him. From the beginning we three were united with Yeshua in family, and we were later united more surely by the coming of the Holy Spirit. Now all those who are one in him are his brothers.

I do not look for a quiet death in old age. The lights of our times, each in his turn, have poured out their lifeblood for the sake of all. First Yochanan under Herod, then Yeshua under Herod and Pilate, then Yaakov under Ananus who incited the Sadducees, for they oppressed with great cruelty all followers of Yeshua. Yaakov gave his life when Agrippa the second was king and Albinus was becoming the procurator of Judaea, though he had not yet arrived from Alexandria.

But the greatest of all lights was Yeshua. He is the light of the world. Indeed, he is the light that cannot be extinguished, for he will shine forth unto the end of the ages. Then shall the light of heaven and earth reign supreme.

May I bless you with the sign of the cross?

Yes, of course, I understand your hesitation. It is the odious sign for those who do not know what it means. He has washed it clean with his blood, and now it is the sign of light. By this sword of defeat the ancient deceiver of mankind is overcome, the serpent who is called adversary and accuser.

Yeshua is the door. See, this door opens before you. Light pours through it, yet the eyes of the flesh see only its former shame. In time you will understand. Now I see in your eyes that you fear death, and you fight it with hatred too, for hatred is the other face of fear.

Even so, a time will come when your own son will bless you with this sign. And on that day you will no longer fear.

Now I must go to my labors. Today my brothers and I will walk to Ramah, where voices are still crying, as our ancestor

Rachel wept because her children were no more. We will give witness. We will also bring healings, if the Lord wills it today.

I leave you in the company of this man. He was a close friend of the Lord.

Jerusalem
Eleazar Ben Efrayim, a man of Bethany

A quiet, thoughtful person. Though he is not educated in the classical manner, he is clearly a man of intelligence. Also, despite what he is about to tell me, there is humility here.

Eleazar says:

Yes, I was a close friend of Yeshua. My sisters and I knew him well, and he often ate with us when he came up to Jerusalem. We lived in Bethany, which is a short walk from the city. I knew him from when we were both young men. There are no family ties between us, none of the usual things that bind one to another.

It began in the Temple during my twentieth year of life. He was, I think, a year or two older than I.

I had gone up alone to pray there, asking for the deliverance of Israel from all its foes. I had made a coin offering to the treasury and given two doves for the sacrifice. As I stood in the Court of the Israelites below the altar, at first I prayed to the Lord that our present enemies would be kept from doing what Daniel had prophesied—that they would be held back from committing the abomination of the desolation. Then it came to me that my prayer was good but insufficient. And I knew I must pray that Israel be delivered from its worst foe, its sins.

As I stood there I became ashamed of my own sins as well, for a light was given to my soul to see that even the least of sins, though done in secret, does not lack its consequences. The sin of one man affects the well-being of all his people. Moreover, I understood that it was the same for a poor man and for a king. My mind said it was not so, but my heart and soul now knew that it was indeed so.

I fell to my knees and kissed the pavement stones in atonement, for though my sins were very small by human measure, I now understood that they were not small.

On my face before the altar I lay for a while, with people stepping around me and muttering about the inconvenience or worry I made for them, or the pretence of so eye-catching a gesture.

But I heeded nothing except the light of understanding that was given to me at that moment. I also prayed that the *mashiach* prophesied by Isaiah would come to us, and soon.

When at last I got to my feet, I saw a young man about my own age standing close by and looking at me. I looked back and wondered: Who is this? Do I know him?

And I did seem to know him but could not recall where we might have met. He wore a woolen garment of plain weave, a prayer cloth over his head, and the sandals of a workingman. He turned and bowed toward the Holy of Holies and said:

"The deliverance of Israel is near. Yet it will not take place as men suppose."

His words were in Hebrew; the accent was Galilean. No response arose in my mind, but I saw that he was devout and wise beyond his years. I thought he might be a country rabbi's son. He had spoken with a certain authority, as if he knew for certain the truth of what he said, but his manner was unlike that of the Pharisees and Sadducees, who were full of knowledge and glad for all to know it.

He told me his name, and I told him mine. And it seemed to me that a kinship was born in an instant, for I felt that here was a man like me.

Together we left the Temple precincts and began to walk through the city. It was not a thing decided between us; we just did it like that, and somehow both of us knew it was right.

When we had passed through the Gate of Gold I told him I must now turn east because I lived in Bethany.

"May I dine at your home?" he asked.

So unusual was this frank request that I did not think to decline, which is what I would have done in other circumstances. We had exchanged only a few words, and yet he now presumed to cross over the barriers of custom as if they did not exist.

"I would be happy to have you dine with me and my sisters", I said.

So we turned and went on toward my town. Along the way he spoke about passages from scripture that he especially loved. These were about the sufferings of the prophets. Each in his own time had been a sign of contradiction. Each had been a sign of hope for Israel, and each had been rejected.

"Israel is ever hungry for signs and wonders", he said, "and never hungry for repentance."

I agreed with him, for the very thoughts had been in my own heart when I prayed at the Temple.

I said, "Again and again we betrayed the Lord by our sins, and after each betrayal we were overwhelmed by destruction."

He nodded at this but said no more.

As we neared my home, I was faced with the question of how I would explain this unexpected guest to my sisters.

I said, "I am glad of your company, yet I am puzzled a little by our companionship. I know nothing about you."

"We know each other very well", he said.

I smiled, for I took it for a jest.

Later, when he became known throughout the land, many important things happened. You have heard what occurred in later days. He was the *mashiach*. Yet he was more than we thought the *mashiach* would be. As he said on the day of our first meeting, the deliverance of Israel would not take place as men supposed. For eight or nine years after that, his anointing was known to only a few, and none understood it fully at the time. I did not. My sisters did not.

We loved him from the first, as if he were our second brother, and he too loved us as his own. Each year when he came up to Jerusalem for the Passover, and sometimes for the Day of Atonement, he stayed with us. In our house he ate and drank, and we had many discussions about holy things, about scripture and history, about men's souls and the ways of divine providence. Zeal for the House of the Lord burned in him, and the fire within him set our hearts aflame too. Like the burning bush on Mount Horeb that Mosheh saw.

And then, during the time when he was going about preaching and healing with his disciples, I died.

I am sorry if I startled you, sir. But yes, that is what I meant: I died. I was four days in a tomb when he came and called me forth from it, and I returned to life.

This was a sign. A sign of his authority and a prefigurement of his own death and rising. The news of my rising spread throughout Israel, and the Pharisees also heard of it. That is why they tried to kill me too, because they did not want that sign, such was their unbelief. Such was the hardness of their hearts.

Now in my old age I walk toward death a second time. I do not fear it. It is no more than a gate. When my body dies I will come out into the light, and my friend will receive me into his arms again. And on the Last Day, my body too will rise.

You ask me, what was it like in the tomb?

Sir, I was truly dead. First I was severely ill, then I felt myself slipping far below. The light faded, and then it was wholly gone. My soul was not in a place of torment. I was in a place of waiting.

Then I heard his voice. He said, "Eleazar, come out!"

Jerusalem
A Pharisee

I do not learn his name, but the following dialogue between us is instructive, though the incident that occasions our meeting begins badly. I learn much in a short time about a group of people who played a major role in the death of the Christos, and I better understand the religious and political effects of his execution, which they had not anticipated and now doubtless regret.

Deep in thought, my surgeon's kit strapped over my shoulder, I am walking through the streets of Jerusalem. I am alone, trying to put a little distance between myself and Yeshua's followers. Too much of one sort of company, to the exclusion of other kinds, can influence one's judgment adversely. Loukas and his companions would be completely infectious were it not for my solid grounding in reason.

Making my way along a narrow street not far from the Temple gate, I see a heavily robed man approaching about ten paces ahead. His head is covered by a complex cap and veil; draped over his shoulders is a shawl with long tassels from knees to ankles. Strapped to his forehead is what looks like an ornately tooled leather case.

Three little boys come running along behind him and thoughtlessly collide into him, knocking him to the ground. Frightened by what they have done, they take to their heels and disappear before the man has a chance to see their faces or utter a rebuke.

Seeing that he is elderly and having trouble getting to his feet, I hasten to his aid. He mutters in Hebrew as I help him up, and then he notices my garb. Brushing the dirt from his robes, eyeing me suspiciously, he takes a step away as if my presence is an offense to him. He leans against the wall of a building, trying to catch his breath. His cheek is scraped and will probably bruise; his nose is bleeding copiously.

"*Adon*", I say. Pointing to my surgeon's kit, I continue in Greek: "I am a physician. Let me help you."

He permits me to stanch the flow of blood with a wad of cotton, and I instruct him to press it firmly to his nose with his own fingers. Apparently he understands my language, since he obeys. Still, he is winded and a little unsteady on his feet. He turns to leave but staggers and leans against the wall.

"Where do you live?" I ask. "I can escort you to your home, if you wish. You should rest there awhile."

His eyes still upon me, dark with uncertainty and anger, he nods in affirmation. I take his arm, and he turns back in the direction from which he came.

"My home is not far", he murmurs in fluent Greek with a rather stilted accent.

A few blocks along, we arrive at the gated outer court of a house. In a weak voice, the man calls through the iron bars, and a woman hastens toward us from the open doorway of the building.

Unlocking the gate, she lets us in, her eyes anxiously fixed on the man. She flutters about him, uttering sharp cries—questions, protests, fears perhaps. The woman, who I presume is his wife since she is about his age and her manner indicates familiar authority over him, helps him to sit down on a stone bench by the front steps. Then she takes a closer look at me. Alarm and distaste fill her eyes, and she begins speaking to her husband in a high-pitched, abrasive tone. Other members of the household rush out, bringing towels and a basin of water. Taking a towel and dampening it, the woman wipes the man's face and beard clean of blood. His nose is no longer bleeding, but I stand nearby to observe his condition.

The woman glances at me, then back at the man, making an abrupt gesture with her hand, indicating that he must order me to leave their home. He mutters and ignores her, rubbing his forehead as if in pain. Despite her hostility I will stay a little, and when his dizziness abates I will be most relieved to depart.

Eyeing me with something akin to loathing, the woman continues with her complaints about my presence until her husband barks at her. With a face of deep offense, she stomps up the steps and into her home, leaving me alone with the man.

Bent forward, hands clasping his knees, he continues to stare at the flagstones beneath his feet. His lips are twisted into a bitter line, his eyes brooding.

"Can you stand?" I ask. "Do you still feel faint?"

Looking up with surprise, as if he had forgotten I was there, he says, "I do not feel faint. I can stand, but I wish to sit awhile. You may go."

I turn to leave by the gate.

"Wait!" he says. Fishing in a purse at his waist, he searches with his fingers and withdraws two small coins, which he extends to me with averted eyes, as if the risk of touching my hand is one he can barely endure.

"I need no payment", I say. "You have come to no serious harm. I will now leave you to your family."

Again, I turn to go.

"Who are you?" he asks, his curiosity sparked, though his demeanor is no less guarded.

I tell him my name and where I am from and explain that I am visiting Jerusalem to write a chronicle of his people's situation. Now he looks directly at me, no longer with hostility, but retaining an inference of dislike—dislike for all foreigners, I presume.

"Our situation? What does our situation seem to you?" he murmurs irritably.

"Most difficult", I reply. Even as I say it, I am struck by the possibility that this man—clearly a priest of the Temple—could have some interesting thoughts that I might add to my examinations.

"Who will read your chronicle?" he asks.

"That is uncertain. I merely wish the truth to be set down in writing and, if possible, widely known. It seems to me that a nation suffers when its conquerors write a history of the conquered."

Now he peers at me with keen interest.

"A history of Greece might not be accurate if written by a Roman", I explain.

For my own self-clarification, I silently note that a patriotic Greek would also be capable of composing an erroneous history of Greece.

"Greeks are friends to Romans", he mutters.

"A servant in a house may become a friend of his master, yet he remains a servant. He may enjoy a certain benevolence from him but cannot claim the rights of a son or brother."

"True", says the man, stroking his beard and eyeing me sideways with a hint of grudging respect.

"Wise servants never forget this", I add.

"The truth about Israel can be known only by the House of Israel", he says, then pauses to observe my reaction.

"That is doubtless so", I reply in a thoughtful tone. "Yet one who is not of your house may learn much about you and tell others a good deal that would be helpful to you."

He averts his eyes again, frowning, weighing my words.

"Sit down," he says, gesturing to a place beside him on the bench, "if you please." He dips his head in a conciliatory gesture of courtesy until I have seated myself.

I have not brought my scroll and stylus with me today, thus memory must suffice. He begins with an account of Israel's history from ancient times until the present day. This I need not record here. My interest is in events that the man has seen with his own eyes. What follows is the best I can recall.

He says:

Then, after the Romans suppressed the Galileans by crucifying two thousand of them, the situation in the land became quiet for a time. But only for a short time. The people's anger grew hotter, sometimes flaring up, then dying down, and all the while it spread by burning beneath the ground, like smoldering roots. Then the so-called liberators of Israel began springing up again, worse than before. Whenever they appeared, more trouble followed, more suppression by the Romans, more and more spilled blood. They call themselves prophets, these liberators, but they are, in truth, our worst enemies. The foolish among our people think such men are our champions. Yes, I can tell you about "prophets". They perform signs and wonders, just as the magicians of Pharaoh in Egypt did wonders to refute Mosheh. Tricks of the devil to mislead the ignorant.

About thirty years ago the people were again on the verge of rising up to destroy the Romans. The Sanhedrin—our chief priests and elders—understood that this would bring about the destruction of the whole nation. Among the several false prophets who appeared at that time, two were especially dangerous: one named Yochanan, and the other named Yeshua, both Galileans and related to each other by blood. They must have conspired for years before they became known, and many fell into their trap due to the cleverness of their plans. At one point the people were ready to proclaim one of them king. Well, it had to be stopped. And it was stopped. Wisely, the Sanhedrin acted swiftly to show that they were false prophets, and thus the deception was revealed. Yochanan was a rabble-rouser, executed for sedition against the lawful kingship of the Herodians. Yeshua was executed by the Romans for seeking the kingship for himself and for inciting the people to overthrow the empire. There have been several like them in recent generations, and they are all of a type. Without exception, they end up destroying themselves, which is evidence of how prophetic they are.

The blindness of those who believed in them can be seen in the way some still maintain that Yeshua is not dead. Yochanan performed no signs and wonders, you see, but Yeshua, who was by far the more dangerous, performed several, and the stories are told and retold about him. After he was crucified, his followers went by night and removed his body from the tomb and buried it secretly. Even in these times they still go about telling the gullible that he has come back from the dead. No one has seen him lately, you can be sure, but there are numbers of ignorant people who continue to fall into this sect regardless of the plain facts. Their leaders do it for money, of course, and they also hope to reignite the insurrection.

Yes, I saw some of his wonder-workings. Yes, with my own eyes. But I was not fooled for an instant. As I said, magicians can perform such deeds with the power of the devil. It cannot be denied that he did very great marvels, but that is the measure of how much evil was at work. His public actions were impressive; his private life was scandalous. He was always in the company of sinners, the kind of people with whom he was most comfortable—prostitutes, tax collectors, adulterers, thieves, and all other sorts of lowlife who will not or cannot keep the law. Israel's moral lepers. What kind of prophet is that? A ritually unclean prophet is no prophet at all.

I will tell you about just one incident, and then you will understand how great was the deception:

One day, I and a group of teachers from the Temple were traveling to a nearby town, where we would give instruction on our Law, which was given to us by Mosheh our greatest prophet, who received it directly from the Most High. The priests of my group are the successors of Mosheh; we are the teachers of Israel in these times. To our surprise we came upon this Yeshua and his followers, of whom we had heard so much. There he was, looking like an ill-groomed and barely literate country rabbi, the very man whom our people were calling a great prophet and even the *mashiach*, the long-foretold anointed one who is to come for the salvation of Israel. Well, there he was before our eyes, and what did we behold? He and his followers were in someone's fields stealing wheat, and, moreover, doing it on the Sabbath day. When we confronted him with the crime, he defended himself with a clever argument. And that was when I learned how devious this man really was.

Later in the day, we entered a synagogue to give our teachings, and we found that he had gone on ahead of us and was already there. A crowd of people had come to see him, and so we were pushed aside and no one would listen to us. He began teaching his doctrine, and everyone but the learned drank it thoughtlessly to the dregs. Seeing this, and desiring to unmask the "prophet" as a Sabbath breaker, we took from the crowd a man who seemed to have a slightly deformed hand and brought him before the teacher.

"Is it lawful to work a cure on the Sabbath?" we asked.

He turned to us and said, "If one of you has a sheep that falls into a pit on the Sabbath, will you not take hold of it and pull it out? Consider how much more precious is a man than a sheep."

To the man he said, "Stretch out your hand." He stretched forth his hand and it matched the other, and he began to cry aloud that he had been healed. The crowd was in an uproar then, and no one thought to look closely or to investigate the facts, to discover how badly the hand had been withered, or whether it was thereafter truly healed. No accounts were kept, no witnesses required. It was the kind of simple trick that many a wandering magician performs. Worse than this, he had done it on the Sabbath day, proving once again his disdain for the Law.

At another place, I and my fellows happened to pass by the edges of a crowd that had gathered around him. A man possessed by evil spirits was brought before him, and the spirits left the afflicted one. Knowing that Yeshua was a fraud, it was clear to us that he could expel a demon only with the help of the prince of demons. When we made this point, hoping to awaken the people from his spell, he looked directly at us and again countered our very solid position with clever subtleties. He went further and declared that because we questioned him, we—*we*, the teachers of Israel—were blasphemers and that we would never be forgiven for it.

Now you understand the murderous insanity created by this sort of false prophet. Now you can see why my people were in grave peril from him and his kind. Madness, madness, which could end only in the destruction of the entire nation. Fortunately, the wise prevailed, and disaster was prevented. And that was the end of it.

Jerusalem
Berenike

This morning Shimeyon and Loukas bring me to the upper room, and there the elder opens a gold-covered casket that is usually kept by the community on a shelf behind the altar. Sometimes the *apostoloi* take it on their journeys to towns and cities of the land. It has traveled farther afield to Antioch and Ephesus but is always brought back here for safekeeping. It contains a cloth about the size of those used for drying hands.

The elder unrolls it and shows it to me. Loukas bows toward it, his hands folded, his eyes closed.

The cloth is badly stained by what appears to be old blood, now dried and aged to a dark brown. Varying degrees of saturation have created other tones—purple, pale rose, the rust of iron. The combined effect is shocking. As I look at it, I see a human face.

Loukas explains that it is the image of the Christos during his torturous walk from Gabbattha to Golgottha. A woman pressed this cloth to his face when he fell.

Aharon takes me to the woman's home on a side lane off the Street of Sandal Makers, two small ground-floor rooms that she shares with an unmarried sister and her aged father. The room fronting on the lane contains the old man's workshop, his bed, and the family kitchen. The woman of the cloth is Berenike, her sister is Sellene, and their father is Scopas.

In culture, the father is a Hellenized Jew of the working class. He tells me with not great sensitivity that he regrets very much the Greek influence and that if he had been wiser he would have given his daughters different names. Now a widower, he was born and raised in the city of Ascalon, which is on the coast a fair distance south of Caesarea. His two daughters were born there as well, though the family came up to live in Jerusalem when Yeshua began to preach in the holy city. His family had lived in Ascalon for generations, but it is a pagan place, he says, and Jews have always been a minority there. He and his wife were married at the age of sixteen, the both of them, and he had been eager to make his way in the world—and his world was mainly Greek at the time. Since coming to live in Jerusalem, however, he has lost many of his early habits. In the holy city he became a devout Jew and not long after, a follower of Yeshua—though he regrets that this came about only after the death of the "Kyrios".

Throughout the entire discourse, Scopas cuts leather on his lap with a sharp knife or pokes holes in it with an awl. It is a wonder that he does no harm to himself, but his hands are deft. As he talks on and on about his personal history, the history of the Herodian kings—of whom he declares he has never approved—and a myriad of other topics that run away with him, I am intrigued by the Hellenisms that creep into his speech. I have ceased transcribing and am now just listening. I will not reproduce it here. He is a good-hearted old fellow but not exactly considerate. It is his daughter, really, with whom I wish to speak. Finally, perhaps to the relief of us all, there is a knock at the door and a man comes in to buy sandals.

I am left with the two sisters. The older, Sellene, is a soft-spoken woman about fifty-five years of age, with a kindly open face not unlike her father's. She says little and seems to defer in all things to her younger sister. Berenike is about fifty, in temperament much like the other woman; there is a quiet radiance in both faces. However, suffering is evident in the lines about Berenike's mouth, and more evident in her eyes' expression. There, also, I see patience and generosity. Beneath these is a rod of fearlessness that is absent in the older woman, the kind of courage that need never abandon gentleness. I am impressed. I have no doubt that under this roof a falsehood could not take root.

In surprisingly good Greek, Berenike says:

My father is a wonderful man. He is very enthusiastic about all that has happened to our family. Sometimes he forgets himself. Thank you for your kindness in listening to him.

Yes, Ascalon was our home city before we moved to Jerusalem. It is strongly Greek in its ways, and Roman as well. The Roman soldiers at the fortress of Ascalon are more tolerant than the native people, who are a mixture of Greeks and the old Phoenicians. These are not fond of us Jews. There have been riots in recent weeks, and the wealthier of our people have been beaten and plundered. There is much anger on all sides. Young men of our people are inciting each other to take up arms and punish the Ascalonians. It is good we moved from there so many years ago.

Above all, it is good that we came here and saw Yeshua, and heard his teachings, and were present when he overcame Satan. He overcame death by death.

Here in Jerusalem the peoples of the world meet and mix among each other. Rome is like that too, I hear, and so are Antioch and Alexandria. But on Mount Zion there is a holy mixing. Even so, in this place evil ever makes war against the people of the Lord because great graces have been given here from times past until now. It is the city of Melchisedek, the city of David, and the city of Yeshua our Savior. It is his by virtue of his blood, which was spilled to cleanse it. The cleansing of our sins begins in the sanctuary, as Ezekiel prophesied. From the sanctuary it spreads through the city and out unto the whole land, and from our land it flows outward to all nations and peoples. But it begins in the sanctuary. The sins of our people fell on him, and he bore them all, though he was fully innocent. He is the true sanctuary, and in him there is no darkness. Thus, the Temple—for *he* is the Temple—was bathed in his blood for the purification of all.

A little of his blood entered my life when I least expected anything like that to happen. My part is very small.

My name is Berenike, which is because my forefathers were originally friends with Macedonian immigrants to Judaea. The Attica Greeks say it as Pherenike, and both mean "bearer of victory". Among the Jews and Greeks I am Berenike, but there are Romans among the believers now, not so many but growing in numbers. The ones who have seen the cloth in the house of our shepherd Shimeyon sometimes come to visit me. They ask how the image came to be. They call me "the lady of the true image". In their language they mix the Latin and Greek and call me *vera eikon*. And of late, when our community eats together after the feast of the holy thanksgiving, they say that my name is "Veranike". So "victory" becomes "image", and "image" becomes "victory". Indeed, it is both. In this there is a hidden truth.

Our people hold that a man's life is in his name. And in this image I found my life. It would be more true to say that in my single meeting with Yeshua, at the moment when he was brought low in humiliation and defeat, I found my life. In him, I found both the victory and the true image of God.

On the day the chief priests and elders convinced the Romans to put Yeshua to death, I was hiding from the wrath that was over the city. I was in great fear. I was timid in those days, being young and a woman. But I had heard him teach in the Court of Women on the Temple Mount, and I had seen people healed. I knew he was our king, and I knew he was greater than David and all the prophets, but there were no stepping-stones in my mind to help me understand it. I only knew it in my heart—a burning, a sweet burning, a joy such as I had never felt before. Whenever he was there and I saw him, the fire came again. I loved him, though I thought it was impossible to meet him because the crowds were always thick wherever he went.

Then when the news spread throughout the city that he was before the procurator for judgment, I fell into great terror. I became sick with grief, for it seemed the end of the world to me. The breaking of his promised kingdom was not what cast me down, for I was not one to hope for a kingdom as we had in former days. No, it seemed to me that it was the end of the promised love—a kingdom of love. It was this loss that felt like the end of the world. I had no words about it in my mind. It was all—*all* of it—in my heart.

I wanted only to hide in a corner under a bed and to weep where no one could see me. But I did not. I knelt with my sister Sellene, and we clung to each other and begged the Most High to stop the ones who were bound on destroying him. My sister cried out, pleading for an army of *angeloi*, the warriors of heaven, to come and rescue him. My father was with us, very ill on his bed, yet he pleaded too.

Even now, I do not understand why I did what I did. I jumped to my feet, threw my veil over my head, and ran out of the house. There were no thoughts in my mind, only the burning fire in me. Love was being killed, and my heart was being destroyed with it. I ran from the Street of Sandal Makers into the greater street and then down through the city to the gate of shame— faster and faster I went. It was easy to know where to go because the roaring of the crowd was like a storm battering the seacoast. It was difficult to get through all those people because Yeshua had by then passed beyond the gate and was approaching the hill we call Golgottha. This was in the valley between the fortress Antonia and Herod's palace.

I do not know how the ways of divine providence made it happen, but each time I came to a wall of people that I could see no way through—their backs were all to me, and they were wild with shouting, cursing, and throwing stones—as I ran toward them, the backs would move this way or that, and a passage would open. Again and again it happened, and each time, I went through, closer and closer—and still I was running. I reached the edge of the crowd lining the road, and there I slowed my pace because numerous soldiers were holding us back by spear and sword, and none could get near Yeshua. Then it happened again: He fell, and a soldier stepped one way and a second looked the other way, and I was through and running. I fell to my knees before Yeshua, even as rods began to strike my back. But it seemed that time slowed for us. His face was covered in blood, his eyes open and full of blood, the skin of his face torn, a helmet of thorns that they had pressed onto his head. The blood blinded him. I pulled the veil from my head and pressed it to his face so that he might see again. For an instant he looked at me. That instant held all eternity in it. And then I knew that though Love's body was being destroyed, the fire of love could never be destroyed. A soldier struck me and pushed me away with the butt of his spear, and I fell. They pulled Yeshua upright, and he went onward toward the hill. The soldiers drove me back into the crowd.

I did not go up the hill to see what they would do to him. The fire in my heart showed me that I must return to my home, to my sister and my ill father.

When I opened the cloth to show Sellene the holy blood on it, she gasped, for the face of Yeshua was printed on it. My father sat up in bed and looked at it. Then he stood and was entirely well.

I gave the cloth to Kepha afterward, months later, when the marvelous things began to happen. I never saw Yeshua after he rose from the dead, though numerous people have seen him and touched him. Their testimony is true.

It was not necessary for me to see him again. Eternity is within me. The face of Love is ever before me.

Jerusalem
A woman

Aharon and I depart from Berenike's home and are walking down the lane to the street when a woman passing by detains us. She lightly touches my sleeve. She is about forty years old, well dressed, with sharply intelligent eyes. Her expression is cordial with a small smile. Her voice is gentle, low, immensely engaging, as beautiful as her features. She inquires about our interest in Berenike, and I see no reason why we should not tell her. Doubtless the image on the cloth is not a secret.

She tells us that the image is a clever fraud. Aharon asks her why she thinks so. She replies that she was once a member of a community to which "that woman" also belonged. While she was among them, she overheard things they said about the cloth, things not known by others.

"Berenike made it. I heard her tell Yaakov the Righteous before he was killed."

"Yes," says Aharon, "she did make it—by pressing the cloth to the face of the Lord."

"No, that is not the way it happened", says the woman with a mixture of kindly regret and knowingness. "The followers of Yeshua spun the story from the thread of her account. She made the image with dye and the blood of swine that she begged from the meat shops of the Romans. Now she believes her story also—or perhaps she does not, but as it stands it is quite useful for her. People give her money."

"Go knock on her door", says Aharon evenly, upset but mastering the feeling. "Go and ask Berenike if you can enter and discuss it with her. Inside, you will see her great wealth."

The woman makes a barbed comment, which I need not record here, tosses her head, and strides away.

"Who is she?" I ask when we reach the street.

Aharon says: "It is true that she was once a member of the community, as she told us. In the beginning it seemed that she was very gifted by the Holy Spirit. Prophecies, some wisdom, good insights in her teaching. But she has a grave flaw that she would not give up to the healing power of the Lord."

"What flaw is it?"

"The one that is in all of us—pride. But she would not let go of it. Her need to rule the people around her is very great. She does it skillfully and with power. She controls by rewards and punishments. Even strong men fear her—until they begin to understand what she is doing."

"Really. I do not understand. What kind of rewards, what kind of punishments?"

"If you are approved by her, you have the pleasure of intimate friendship with a person of undoubted vitality and influence. If you fall under her disapproval, you will begin to feel pain."

"Do you mean curses? Is she a witch?"

"No", says Aharon, shaking his head. "No, she is not a witch. However, in one aspect her blindness is like that of witches, for they too seek to control. They love power."

"And the punishment?"

Aharon replies:

Whispering, whispering, whispering. Inferences, accusations behind your back, exclusion from the circle of warmth that surrounds her. When Shimon Kepha came to visit us some years ago, she tried to charm him with her personal qualities and impress him with the gifts the Lord had given to her. He saw through it immediately, before any others had eyes to see. He took her aside privately to save her from shame and exhorted her to seek the ways of humility, to strive earnestly to master her tongue, and above all to ask the Lord to reveal to her the ways in which she is driven by old habits.

She pretended docility, but in secret her pride was sorely grieved. She began to undermine his authority, and that of Yaakov, and also Shimeyon. Quietly, quietly, she split the flock of the Lord, pulled some to her side, and made it difficult for those who would not succumb to her influence. If a person would not come over to her side, or agree with her on this or that small thing, he felt her anger. She was always subtle in this, never insulting. But in the underwaters of men's hearts, there is vulnerability. And upon this vulnerability her power played, and dissension grew among us. She created quarrels among others, almost invisibly, then blamed them for quarreling. She created factions, then blamed one side of the faction for creating division. According to her, whoever agreed with her on matters great and small was submissive to the Spirit. Whoever disagreed with her was offending the Spirit, or so she said.

When Kepha next came to Jerusalem, he called an assembly and asked for an explanation of the quarrels that had grown among us like weeds in a field of wheat. Then did this woman reveal the spirit that drives her. She rose up in the assembly and made war against Kepha, at first with calm and reasonable tones. But when he stood firm, her wrath grew, and little by little she turned from argument to accusation. Still, Kepha stood firm. He was loving in manner and did not let himself be provoked.

At last she cried out for all to hear: "But why should we listen to you? You cannot read in any language, and your speech is fumbling when the Spirit is not upon you. And where is the Spirit now—why does he not give you the power of speech to answer properly my questions? It is because what I say is right and you cannot refute it. Beware, Kepha; you are dividing the flock of the Lord!"

Even then, Kepha did not let himself be provoked.

"Daughter," he said, "it is you who are dividing the flock of the Lord."

"Ha!" she laughed. "How can you say this? How can you presume to govern this flock? You who betrayed the Lord three times!"

These words were a terrible blow to Kepha. His heart was sorely wounded, and all could see it. He lowered his eyes and bowed his head.

"Yes, daughter", he said at last, looking up at her. Now his voice was steady and full of the Holy Spirit. "I denied knowing the Lord—three times I denied him. And I repented three times. And three times did he give me mercy. And three times did he command me to feed his flock."

Kepha took his wooden shepherd's staff and thumped its base on the floor.

"Now do I call *you* to repentance", he declared, and though his voice was very quiet the walls seemed to shake with the force if it.

Then the woman glared at him and stormed from the room. A few of the community went with her. No one drove her from our midst, though she tells others that she was cast out. She cast herself out. And now she slanders the brethren wherever and whenever she can.

The tongue, the tongue, proceeding from all manner of darkness in the heart.

The tongue—I fear it far more than the sword and the lion.

Jerusalem
Philetos of Alexandria

Loukas has arranged a meeting with a learned Jew for the sake of a mutual exchange about the history of Israel and its prospects under the Roman *imperium*. We are to see this eminent man at a private home in a wealthier section of Jerusalem. As we make our way to the villa in the upper city, Loukas gives me some of his history. He is one of the great intellects of the age, has written many books, and has traveled widely throughout the world. He is a native of the large *diaspora* community in Alexandria, educated in the Greek tradition, a philosopher and historian, conversant in six or seven languages, a master of Latin rhetoric, and intimate with famous Jews, Romans, Greeks, and lately the elders of the Yeshua communities. During a recent visit to Rome he met Shimon Kepha, whom the Gentile believers call Petrus, a derivative of our Greek word for "rock" or "stone". Philetos believes that Yeshua was the *meshiha*, but he has not yet been baptized.

During the reign of Gaius Caligula, when the emperor was committing sacrileges against the synagogues in Egypt and elsewhere, and in Alexandria the Greeks were provoking clashes with the Jewish colony, Philetos was the chief arbiter for the latter before the judgment seat of Gaius. So eloquently and forcefully did he argue against the outrages that the emperor grew infuriated with him and looked fit to have him killed but instead ordered him out. Greatly insulted, Philetos walked out. He reassured his anxious fellow delegates not to worry, arguing that because Gaius was so bent on evil, he was making war against God without knowing it. And that, said Philetos, would bring about this vile emperor's end, since no one could long sustain a war against God.

When Claudius came to the throne, the new emperor invited Philetos back to Rome and hosted a gathering of the entire Senate for the purpose of hearing Philetos' brilliant analysis and condemnation of Caligula's reign.

Loukas is in the midst of an ongoing list of the man's accomplishments when we arrive at the villa. It is owned by a very wealthy Graecophile Jew named Avner Ben Eliachim, a trader in oriental luxuries who owns commercial enterprises throughout Asia, Africa, and Persia. The merchant is presently away on business in Antioch, but his houseguest remains here for another two weeks, waiting for a ship to take him to Athens. Loukas has just enough time to murmur these details to me as a servant brings us through a bronze gate and into the tiled forecourt. From there we are led up a stone staircase to a fourth-floor roofed promenade and into a reception room larger than my home in Gortyna. The entire floor is covered with red and purple rugs. The few pieces of furniture are gilded seats and couches covered with plump cushions. In the center of the room, a small marble fountain erupts like a volcano, sending fine spumes of mist into the atmosphere. There are no visible pipes, so I presume they are beneath the floor and fed by the city aqueduct constructed thirty years ago by the procurator Pontius Pilatus, which he funded with money seized from the Temple treasury. The high white ceiling is unadorned, and there are no paintings or statues anywhere in sight. One entire wall is a library filled with hundreds of scrolls. The merchant is educated, it seems, or perhaps he is a collector of valuable manuscripts.

Then I take closer notice of a figure standing before the library wall—a man whom I at first thought to be a household servant.

He turns and I see he was reading a scroll, which he unhurriedly puts away. Then he walks toward us, where we stand waiting at the pillared doorway.

Without doubt, this is Philetos. He is about my age, in his mid-sixties. His garment is a simple ankle-length linen tunic, girded about the waist with a black sash. His hair is cropped short, yet he is bearded. The skin of his face is dark brown, the firm mouth accustomed to issuing commands and orations. There is a great pride here—or is it confidence? This, and the expression of habitual relentless honesty, indicate a most forceful personality. The eyes—above all the eyes—are disturbingly intelligent, analytical, penetrating, but without offensiveness. Doubtless he has already assessed me with perfect accuracy.

Loukas makes the introductions.

Clasping my hand in greeting, Philetos says in Attic Greek, "Theophilos Aristonides, I am very pleased to meet you at last, for your son has told me much about you. And you know my city well, I hear."

"Yes, I studied there for two years when I was young. I was loath to depart from its great library."

"Ah, the library", he smiles. "Men enter its wide-open portals intending to consume what is within and find themselves devoured instead."

He smiles. Loukas and I laugh.

"True enough", I say. "I barely escaped."

His smile broadens, and then he leads us to a cluster of chairs beside the fountain. We sit down facing each other, and a servant brings us cooled wine in silver goblets.

Though he opens the conversation with pleasantries and questions about my opinion of travel and the Judaean weather, clearly he is not greatly interested in my replies as such, for these exchanges are likely no more than preliminaries. And all the while his eyes are fixed on me, observing and pondering.

What kind of man is this? I wonder to myself. Is he political? If, as Loukas says, he is so well connected with powerful figures of major races that are at variance with each other, his skills with people and his strategic gifts must be considerable. Does his presence command respect wherever he goes, or does he pass through barriers because of his reputation? Perhaps he thinks not overmuch on that level and his interests are of a higher order. This is probably closer to the mark: He is ever curious to know what is in the depths of men's minds, and how it has come to be there.

Loukas finishes his drink and stands. With apologies to Philetos, he pleads an appointment elsewhere and bids us speak together in mutual trust. Philetos conducts him to the door and then returns to me. We sip our wine. I wonder what next to say.

Philetos is silent for a time, as if diverted by some private thought of his own. Looking up, he says:

"Trust is a precious commodity."

"Indeed it is", I reply.

"It is rare between men but newly met."

I nod in agreement.

"The world is a dangerous place", he goes on. "And the danger increases the higher one rises."

"That is certainly true."

"It is a consolation to recall a simpler period of my life, and above all to speak with one who is amply endowed with virtues yet has no ambitions. I am glad you have spared a little time for me."

"It is my pleasure to do so. But I hardly think of myself as endowed with virtues."

"That is a virtue in itself. However, I speak in the broadest sense of the word."

"Besides," I say with a smile, "it is Loukas who requested this meeting between us."

"Your Loukas is a man of uncommon good sense." He pauses. "That is why I agreed to meet you. He was careful to suggest that you are traveling in these lands in the interest of making historical records."

"Yes, that is accurate."

"You are also his adoptive father, and I would guess that your interests here have layers of purpose. I think you worry about him."

"I do. As you know, he is Greek, not Jewish. He is a man of medicine and philosophy. I am concerned that his great gifts are falling away as he takes a side path into unknown regions, uncharted and perilous."

"Perilous they surely are. But not unknown and not uncharted. I too am a father. I too know what it is to feel anguish and helplessness over a child. Moreover, I have spent most of my life defending my people from their adversaries, who are numerous, powerful, and often hostile. So I understand your worry."

Does he? If, as Loukas said, the man is convinced that Yeshua was the *mashiach* (*meshiha, christos*), then he could not possibly understand my worry. I do not voice this objection.

Philetos continues:

"The situation here is extremely inflammable, as I am sure you have learned. The new procurator, Gessius Florus, has governed for a year, and in that short time he has made his predecessor Albinus seem almost a benefactor by comparison. Florus is absolutely corrupt, ruthlessly and repeatedly committing outrages, plundering the estates of numerous citizens, whom he destroys through unjust imprisonment and executions. He also flouts his authority by greatly expanding the numbers of crucifixions. He provokes minor insurrections, then crushes them brutally—mainly for the purpose of enhancing his political esteem among his fellow Romans. He is a murderer and a thief and goes on with it because he knows that his position is secure. His wife is a close friend of Nero's wife, Poppaea, which is how Florus secured his position."

This is dangerous talk. But no one else is present, and Loukas has encouraged me to trust the man.

"Florus emulates his master", I say in a low voice.

"And like his master, he believes that none can stop him. And therein lies our greatest peril, for our people can endure much, but the one thing they will not suffer is desecration of the Temple."

"Has he desecrated it?"

"Indirectly, by robbing its treasury. However, such men know no bounds, and I feel sure he will move to the next stage by violation of the sanctuary—merely to prove his power over us. He will perhaps try to erect an idol, probably a statue of the emperor, his only remaining deity. This is an abiding habit of invaders. Defilement of the Temple was committed by Antiochus Epiphanes splattering the sanctuary with swine's blood, by Pompey entering the Holy of Holies, by Pilatus and others erecting statues. Even the emperor Gaius attempted to do so, though he was dissuaded at the last by tens of thousands of Jews gathering to offer their lives as a sacrificial offering. They lay down on the ground and exposed their throats, pleading with the Roman general to kill them so that they might not live to see the sacrilege. Ordinarily, such protests would not move an emperor to change his mind. It was only through a very clever intervention by Herod that war was avoided—a dinner party for the emperor that the king hosted in Rome. That is the world we now live in: A nation's survival hangs upon how lavish is the menu."

"Regardless of religious beliefs, surely common sense alone dictates that Florus avoid such actions?"

"One would think so. But Florus relishes blasphemous provocations because it serves him in a number of ways—increased power and wealth, and the pleasure he takes in the unjust shedding of blood. He does not believe in God, and thus he thinks himself safe from divine punishment. That kind of man becomes the slave of devils and does not know it."

"I can see that a statue in your temple would be offensive to your people. But why do you call it your greatest peril?"

"Desecration of the Temple always results in revolt and mass slaughter. Theophilos, you would need a profound understanding of my people in order fully to grasp the situation. Our *psychologia* is like that of no other race on earth. We believe there is no other God, for he is One. To violate his Temple is to make total war against the Creator of the universe. For all our faults— and our faults are many—we are his chosen people. To violate the Temple is to violate every Jew alive in the most absolute way. More than this, it is to attack the foundations of the world itself."

I reply: "In my observations, which one might call a science of mind and behavior, I have come to understand the power of symbols. They are the cornerstones of a psychological *kosmos*. A nation or a race stands at the precise center of its own *kosmos*, as does each man. And this is the case with the myths of all peoples."

"You raise an interesting point. What are myths, really? Are they intuitions in the soul about reality? I think we would agree that to some degree they are manifestations of a spiritual sense, would we not?"

"It would depend on the degree", I counter. "Such intuitions can take many forms in the imaginations of various peoples. Many of these symbolic figures and events are at odds with each other, and this indicates that they are not about realities but are rather reflections of man's emotions. Have you read the works of the Roman poet Vergilius?"

"Yes, and with great interest", he says. "Why do you ask?"

"I am thinking of his *Eclogues*, especially the fourth. It is a hymn to a soon-to-be-born baby who will kill a serpent."

"I know the passage", says Philetos, sitting straighter, leaning forward. He recites in Latin:

"'Under thy guidance, the traces that remain of our old wickedness, once banished, shall free the earth from never-ceasing fear. He shall receive the life of the gods, and himself be one of them, and with his father's worth reign over a world at peace.'"

"So, you see my meaning."

"I see the intuition in the poet's words. Yet it does not resolve our question. Is the child in the poem a variation of a universal type? Or does he portend the coming of a true and living child who will overcome the ancient enemy of mankind?"

"He may represent no more than the ever-renewed forces of nature, birth after birth followed by inevitable death, generation after generation. Death's insatiable appetite is merely fed until the end, yet man ever lifts hope on high to shield his eyes from terror of the void."

"The 'void', you call it. Is your concept not an interpretation of reality? Could it be that belief in the void, belief in death's victory, is a shielding of the eyes, is itself a form of faith, though one darker and more terrible than mine? How do you know for certain there is nothing beyond death?"

"No one has returned to us from beyond death."

Philetos looks into my eyes, searching.

"That is no longer so", he says quietly.

"But that is your myth."

"Is my faith one of many equals on a field of myths without horizons, or is it the fulfillment *in the real* of all those prefiguring and incomplete myths?"

"Your question is, in itself, a corollary of myth. How can it be answered? How can a man know the true answer? It is, after all, the realm of faith, not certitude. Have you read Plato's writings on the ideal Forms?"

"Yes, I have, and with close attention", Philetos nods emphatically. "Plato's intuitions, and those of Aristotle and others, Cicero among them, and also Erasistratus."

"Erasistratus! You know him?"

"How could an Alexandrian not know him?"

For a time we leave aside the question of Israel's myths and plunge together into the thought of my favorite physician-philosopher. Philetos' knowledge of Erisistratus' ideas is impressive, I might say overwhelming. And in the ensuing dialogue, he shows me how prescient was my mentor. In the end I cannot refute the points to which Philetos is so relentlessly leading me. It is a disturbing sensation: I cannot refute him, yet I cannot agree with him because the conclusions to which it would lead would be the overturning of my world. And that, to put it simply, cannot be right.

Even so, the subtle tension of strangers is now entirely gone, and I feel a companionship between myself and this very strange Jew.

I make a few more references to certain passages in Plato's dialogues, and he offers a few in return—not counterpoints, merely agreements with my position—and I realize that he has left off the storming of my psyche and is exercising a certain mercy toward me. Yet I also understand that he presumes a higher position—that while we may agree on certain points, for him they are only prefiguring points. He stands firm on what he has called *the real*.

"It seems to me that your religion has developed no philosophy", I suggest. "Is it possible that the faith of the Israelites is based on religious passions without the corrective guidance of reason?"

He smiles. "By your polite term 'religious passions', I think you mean superstitions. But our passions are adamantly opposed to superstition. Our passions derive from experience. God has acted with us, and through us, in a way that he has done with no other people."

"But that is your myth about yourselves."

"Is it?" says Philetos with a faint show of irony. "But when myth becomes reality, what then? Man's reason is confounded by it, and he is forced to a choice. Will he admit the truth of what he has seen and act accordingly, or will he deny what he has seen and cling to his reasoning, which tells him that the evidence is impossible?"

"Or his reason may tell him that there are other explanations for what he has seen. Natural explanations."

"Theophilos, the light of reason that we both reverence is not a god. Neither does the highest development of the human mind confer divinity upon us. We may quote Aristotle one moment and in the next find ourselves betraying our wives and children—for the sake of *passion*, in the name of *love*— and not know how we arrived at that lamentable state. Reason is a gift of God but of itself cannot ennoble a man."

"Well, I agree with you that reason alone cannot ennoble a man. To believe that it could is like believing that a vast knowledge of medicine ensures health of the body."

"Most people take refuge in theory and think they will become good in this way."

"Rather like some of my patients who listen attentively to me but do none of the things I tell them to do."

"Indeed", he smiles again. "That is well put. Of course, you must have read the *Ethics*. But let us return to your earlier comment that my religion has developed no philosophy. You will find our philosophy, including ethics, embedded in our history and poetry, our wisdom literature and our prophets.

Though stripped of the name *Philosophia*, you will find *Sophia* herself living among us."

"Living?"

"That is how our lovers of wisdom have personified her—because wisdom is a life giver, like a mother or a wife. A man thrives if he does what she asks of him."

"My own wife told me much the same thing."

We indulge in a conspiratorial masculine chuckle.

"Women sense things that often escape us men", he continues. "Thus, wisdom as a feminine being. There is a deep intelligence in the personification, would you not say?"

"It seems so. I must read more of your people's writings."

Now we both fall silent. He refills my goblet with the deliciously cool wine, and we speak no more for a time, sipping and musing.

"Regarding Yeshua Ben Yosef", I say at last. "If your God is One, where would you place him in the ranks of creatures?"

"He is not within the ranks of creatures."

"This makes no sense to me. He walked in this city as a man."

"He is both man and God."

"Was it not foretold that the *mashiach* would be a man?"

"Yes, and he was a man—*is* a man. But he is more than a man and is unlike all other men born of woman. It was also prophesied, in terms that have now become comprehensible, that he would be the Son of Man and the Son of God."

"The 'son of man'? That seems to prove my point, not yours."

"The name has a precise meaning for us. It enraged the Pharisees when they heard it used in reference to Yeshua. It is based on a vision of our prophets, who foresaw one whom they called the Son of Man receiving full power and glory and kingship, an eternal authority over creation that the Father bestows on his only Son. Have you read the prophet Daniel? No? I suggest you ask Loukas to give you a copy of the book."

"He has already given me certain texts in Greek translation. There is a Daniel among them, if I recall correctly. I will read it."

"You will find that in Yeshua this word of prophecy has become flesh. Moreover, he several times spoke of himself, with astounding boldness, in terms of the divine. He declared to the Pharisees, 'Before Abraham ever was, I am.' This too has a precise meaning for us, because *I Am* is God's name for himself. The Pharisees understood exactly what he meant, and from then on they sought to destroy him."

"To claim divinity in such terms, it seems to me, might be something a madman or one possessed by an evil *daemon* would say."

Philetos flinches. With his eyes gravely examining mine, he replies:

"What Yeshua said of himself could derive from one of three causes: either he was a madman, or he was possessed by a *daemon*, or he was what he said he was. Moreover, God never—I emphasize *never*—suspends the laws of creation at the bidding of madmen and demons."

Now we are at an impasse. For the sake of politeness, I do not ask Philetos if he has witnessed any suspensions of the laws of creation. Perhaps anticipating my objection, he says:

"I have seen miracles among the followers here in Jerusalem. And other miracles in Alexandria. In Rome as well. In the beginning my doubts were more severe than yours. My hostility was profound and complex, though without fatal consequences to others. Let these people be, I said to myself; let them be and they will disband as swiftly as the many other factions before them. I had come to Jerusalem for studies under Gamaliel, a famous and wise man who was called 'the teacher of all Israel'. It was Gamaliel who said that we must not hinder the work of Yeshua's followers, for we might find ourselves fighting against God himself. And if the new beliefs were not of God, he said, they would fade away to nothing of their own accord. And so I concurred. But a young Pharisee named Saul of Tarsus, whom we now call Paulus, did not agree with our opinion. Do you know Loukas' friend Paulus?"

"I have not met him."

"I met him once when he was Saul. At the time, I believed as he did, but I did not like the man at all. His hostility against the followers of Yeshua was so intense, so enflamed by all that is blind and pride-infested in our people that I feared he would drag many innocents into his net. Indeed, he did. In his zeal for the House of the Lord, he destroyed children of the household. He was responsible for numerous imprisonments and deaths. Years later I met him again in Corinth, by chance it would seem, and there I beheld a very different man. He was forceful still, but quieter, humbled, suffering. I shudder to think what he recalls of his early years. He was responsible for the deaths of those who are now dearest to him. Can you imagine what it must be like to live with that?"

"I cannot. A terrible burden it must be."

"Yes. And who could live with such a weight, such a pain? Only the healing power of God could make it possible."

Philetos then turns the conversation to a different subject. He asks if I have met or heard of an *apostolos* by the name of Mark. When I admit that I have not, he encourages me to consider a journey to Alexandria because Mark now resides there as the founder and chief shepherd of its community of believers. There too I would see many examples of the "sincerity and the great fruitfulness" of believers, as well as numerous signs from God of their authenticity.

"Do you know Lake Mareotis?" he asks. I tell him that I know it well and once bathed in this lake, which is attached to the city's south side.

"Throughout the world, the believers sell their possessions and own all things in common, living in great simplicity. But at Mareotis there is a community that does more. On a hill nearby the water, there is a large house where people live in much prayer and self-denial, opening their doors to all who seek healing of body and soul. People call them *Therapeutae*. In Egypt they have established other houses in solitary places where they can pray and offer in peace the holy sacrifices of the new covenant."

I now recall a large house on a hillside near the lake. In my youth I had sometimes wondered who lived there.

"These wondrous signs of confirmation you speak of", I say. "Have you seen them?"

"Yes, with my own eyes. In most cases no natural explanation was remotely possible."

Again he pauses to consider, his expression reflective, perhaps saddened by the critical doubts implicit in my question.

"I was once as skeptical as you are now", he says. "My heart was very hard, for I did not want to believe."

Without abandoning courtesy, he is subtly implying that my heart is hard. I do not respond. To deflect the discussion onto less sensitive matters, Philetos asks me what title I give to the book I am writing.

"I am undecided", I tell him. "Perhaps I will call it *Examinations*."

For the first time, he laughs, a quiet chuckle of appreciation.

"A suitable name", he says. "One worthy of a *Therapeuta*."

I am considering this remark with some discomfort when a servant enters to announce that visitors have arrived at the gate, asking to see Philetos of Alexandria. Should they be admitted?

"Who are they?" asks Philetos.

"Sir, one is an older man of great importance in the city. He is Ananus Ben Yochanan. The other is Yosef Ben Matthias."

"The scholar?"

"It is said he is such."

"Well, then, let them in. I will go down to greet them in a moment."

Turning to me, Philetos says, "If you wish to be completely discreet in your examinations, you may wish to leave by another door. However, I think a meeting with these two would lead to no harm and could be informative."

"I will meet them, if you think it beneficial to my book."

"Then meet them you will. I will introduce you as a man composing a chronicle of our people's current history, which you are. I will tell them that you are sympathetic to our problems, which I think you also are. But do not mention your connection to Loukas, since his name may be known to them, and it would make them suspicious of you."

And so we go down to the forecourt, and there I observe another facet of Philetos of Alexandria—the devout Jew who garners respect from every faction simply by force of character.

As a result of the brief introductions, three meetings come about.

Jerusalem
Ananus Ben Yochanan

Ananus Ben Yochanan is a priest of the Temple. Before my meeting with the man, Aharon informs me that in Jerusalem there are a number of influential people named Ananus, Ananias, and Anas, many of them priests, and I should take care

294

in my accounts not to confuse them. There is also a well-known disciple of Yeshua named Ananias who lives in Damascus, a friend of Paulus. Should these names arise in conversations, I must note their father's names and their positions, if any, in order to keep an accurate account.

This Ananus is connected to a powerful priestly family from which high priests have been appointed in recent times. He is related to Anas, the father-in-law of Caiaphas, who was instrumental in the condemnation of Yeshua. Ananus loves Israel, grieves over the Roman occupation and the Greek influences in the land, and regards the followers of Yeshua Ben Yosef as promoters of a dangerous aberration.

Aharon says that Ananus has agreed to meet me as a favor to Philetos, because he knows how influential Philetos has been with Romans in times past. Though Philetos does not presently enjoy Nero's good opinion, by the same token Nero is despised by many high Romans and may go the way of Gaius Caligula. The situation is complex in Syria and in Rome, but Ananus is a master of complexities, as were his forefathers, and thinks that Philetos may be of some use, perhaps after the end of Nero's reign.

Aharon is not my interpreter today, since there is concern that his face and name may be known to the Temple officials. Instead, an educated servant of Philetos performs this service.

The meeting takes place in a small room off the forecourt of Ananus' house, which is in a street where the prosperous reside, below the Temple Mount. The priest and I are seated on two wooden chairs facing each other. He is a man in his late forties, black-haired, somber, and proud of countenance, heavily robed in costly cloth, the crown of his head covered with an elaborate cap and veil. Standing behind him are two other priests, one young, one old. Neither of them is introduced to me.

Ananus says:

My dear friend Philetos has spoken well of you. I welcome
you to Jerusalem, the holy city, for I have heard about your
interest in my people and that you wish to make an accurate
account of the troubles and the times. Not all accounts can
be trusted. Many historians defame us, and many record what
they wish to see and ignore what they do not wish to see.
But I am assured that you are a man who will record and
pass down the truth about us, and thus you will take your
part in a more just treatment of our people, even now perhaps, or by peoples yet unborn. Such is the role of a good
historian.

An evil unsurpassed has come upon us in our time. We
esteem with great respect the noble emperor Nero, but the
man who has recently become procurator here, Gessius Florus, surpasses in evil all former rulers. The governor of Syria,
Cestius Gallus, is far away in Antioch, but Florus is near in
Caesarea and does what he wills. Though embassies have been
sent to Gallus with complaints about the looting and murders,
the governor does not respond, for Florus counters all accusations with abundant lies and false witnesses. When Gallus
and Florus visited Jerusalem at Passover this year, hundreds of
thousands gathered before the Roman palace and pleaded with
the governor to remove Florus. So angry were our people
that insults against Rome were hurled, and riots broke out.
Standing beside Gallus, Florus laughed and laughed, for our
hotheads played right into his hands. But Gallus quieted the
crowd by promising to restrain Florus' excesses, and then the
procurator's laughter died in his mouth, and the crowd was
calmed. But something happened afterward to change the wind.
We do not know for certain what it was. Florus and Gallus
returned to Caesarea together, and I think the procurator worked

on the governor's mind. Gallus went on to Antioch, and ever since then Florus has not restrained himself.

It is my belief that he wants continued strife because he hopes for a general insurrection, so that in the suppression of it he might plunder the entire nation for his own pockets. War cloaks many lesser evils, and during his short time with us he has already proven his will to foster such ways. He desires our blood, but he desires our gold more. If war breaks out, his present crimes will seem smaller, and then Nero would not remove him from office, since a hard procurator would seem best for the situation.

And so, to ensure a nationwide revolt, Florus daily provokes the general distress. He covers his evils with lies. He commits outrages, then punishes us for our protests, calling them uprisings against Rome. No ruler in former times has been as evil as he. And now he works toward the greatest evil of all.

Write about this. Write that the people of Israel want peace. Write many letters and make copies of your history and put them into powerful hands.

Jerusalem
Yosef Ben Matthias

On the day I met him in Philetos' courtyard, Yosef Ben Matthias had been robed like Ananus. They both are priests, and both are natives of Jerusalem, but now I find they are very different kinds of men. Aharon prepares me for my encounter with Ben Matthias by giving me some history of the man. He is twenty-eight years old, by birth a member of the priestly class, and a descendant of pre-Herodian kings on his mother's side. At the age of fourteen, his intellectual precocity so impressed learned men in this city that he stepped upward from level to level in the world of Jewish scholars. He has dabbled with the religious philosophies of the Pharisees, the Sadducees, and a mystical sect called the *Essanoi* but never lets himself be identified with any of them. They all would like to claim him as one of their own, since his qualities of intellect and personality are remarkable—an exemplary *eikon* of the Israelite prince. He is not a prince but is often treated as one. Last year he was in Rome as a prominent member of a delegation sent by the Jewish hierarchy to present petitions to the imperial government. The Romans were impressed by him, and the Jewish authorities were well pleased by what he accomplished.

Again, Philetos' servant is to be my interpreter. We will meet Yosef Ben Matthias at his home, a villa on the Mount of Olives. Arriving there, we see a residence that one might describe as modestly opulent. The outer walls surrounding the grounds are twice a man's height and made of heavy stone blocks. The walls of the house are white marble, its roof red tiles. The windows are glassed—an extraordinary luxury for this part of the world. A servant conducts us into an atrium-like entrance and informs me that an interpreter will not be needed because the master of the house is fluent in Greek. Philetos' servant departs, and I am led through a colonnaded passage into a garden behind the house. It is full of orange and pomegranate trees, drooping under the weight of fruit and divided into twelve sections by white gravel pathways.

Yosef Ben Matthias is waiting for me at the back of the garden, seated on a low dais before an ornamental peristyle open on the side facing the house. He stands up as I walk toward him between beds of rosebushes. We meet on the steps of the peristyle. He offers his hand and greets me in my native tongue. We sit down on marble benches in the shade.

The garden is as luxurious as a Greek or Roman one, but there is not a statue anywhere in sight, and the only symbol I see is inscribed in the marble wall behind my host: a seven-branched candelabrum.

At home, he wears simple apparel. His garment today is a white linen tunic, like Philetos', bound by a golden cloth sash. His feet are shod in fine-webbed sandals. His head is uncovered.

As we exchange opening remarks of a social nature, I make my examination of this man's character. I wish that Xanthippos were here to listen to the deep voice that is speaking so graciously to me, to plumb the underground river within the voice. Yosef is very tall for a Jew, and fair-skinned. Most remarkably, his eyes are green. His black hair is long, braided tightly, and bunched at the nape of the neck. His beard, it would seem, has never been cut. He is exceedingly handsome, yet without the surfeit of masculine vanity one often finds in men so well favored. He has no need to put forward his strength. Indeed, he seems completely contained, needing nothing from others. The shoulders are broad, the body posture implying tremendous physical vitality—and vitality of will besides. His mastery of alien vocabulary and accent, his facial expressions, and his unusual eyes indicate a man as intelligent as Philetos, though not as sagacious in the affairs of the world. Yet he has seen Rome and, in a sense, conquered it.

Here is the sort of man who would stand foremost in any venture he put his hand to. Here is the material of greatness, and it would act greatly in whatever form it chose to express itself: a scholar, a priest, a general, and perhaps, if the times were different, a king. I am impressed. And cautious. This is simply too much blessing for one man to embody without succumbing to deadly pride.

Thus far I have seen no evidence of arrogance. Rather, there is a kind of anti-hubris at work, as if he must struggle daily to suppress within himself the fatal tendencies of the great. Yet his humility has not, I think, been conferred on him by life's humbling experiences nor through formal submission. His humility, disturbingly, has been bestowed upon him by himself. Rarely in my life have I encountered this, yet I seem to recognize what it is. It is admirable—and dangerous.

Yosef Ben Matthias says:

It is of interest to me, and a cause for gratitude, that you seek to write an accurate account of our people's history. I would appreciate it greatly if you were to send me a copy when you have completed it. Too often, historical records are assembled in fragments gathered from here and there, and most often these composite works reflect the political loyalties of their authors. Ambition or fear color men's understandings of the events of their times. Hatred too is a poison—even when there is much cause for hatred. But our friend Philetos assures me that you approach your subject with a mind open to the truth of the matter—in the Greek way, which is by the light of reason.

Yes, I have studied your philosophers, and I admire their thoughts. If your people had been the chosen, I have no doubt that the entire world would now be Greek and that Athens would be its capital. But the Lord of the universe chose otherwise.

[He pauses and smiles.] Long past are the days of Demosthenes and Pericles. Long in his tomb is Alexander. Now you conquer through culture. And successful warfare it is!

I too have sought to write of certain events concerning Israel's role in mankind's history. Is man's track through time determined, or is it providential? Is it a mixture of both? Is it a dialogue between the individual will and the surrounding powers and principalities? Are we slaves, or are we obedient sons of the housemaster? On such questions, and on our responses, the resolutions of historical crises depend.

Greeks call it fate, and we call it ordination, for my people are chosen by the Most High God. I am not certain what the Romans call it, but I suspect that if they think about it at all, it is in borrowed terms—borrowed from you. They have their gods, of course, and they have their relentless hunger for control of the world, for they believe it will give them security and wealth. Doubtless, they consider themselves to be chosen—chosen by gods that do not exist. Like all other nations that have closed their jaws on Israel, the Romans will, in time, break their teeth.

Can you understand us? The Jewish people do not seek to rule the world. If such sovereignty is in our role, it will be conferred from above. We cannot seek it for ourselves with the sword. Yet we may defend ourselves with the sword. We have confounded all conquerors in the past. And we always will. Yet terrible is the cost of this mysterious pattern of victory over powers greater than our own. Our strength is not in numbers, for we are small in land and people. Our strength is not in gold, though many nations have lusted for our gold. No, our strength is in fidelity to the covenant, and this devotion is ever rekindled by knowledge that we are the chosen. The Lord Most High has acted mightily in the past, bringing down nation after nation, empire after empire that sought to devour us. And if in our times he pauses, it is because he desires us to recollect, to remember our proper kingship. The Herodians will soon be gone because they are not true kings of Israel. A true king will arise among us, to rule over us and all mankind, so say our prophets. Yet of times and places we cannot now know.

I am currently studying the records written by Nicolaos of Damascus on the reigns of Herod the Great to Archelaus. Have you read them? No? I recommend them to you. There you will learn a good deal about the adverse effects of appeasement and puppet kings.

At this moment in history, however, a prudent strategy is needed. We must compromise on matters that are not essential to our faith. We must bid for time. And we must guard against too-strong reaction. Our own factions are our worst enemies. Despite their faults, the Romans respect civil order and have permitted us certain liberties not enjoyed by their other subject peoples. They have done so not because we are a threat to the empire and should be placated. No, Rome does not placate. However, its rulers have recognized the distinctive character of our race, and they understand that needless conflicts would result if they were to impose upon our sacred places. They are astute enough to know that it is in their own interest to avoid provoking wars over religious convictions. Our convictions are peculiar to us alone, and more firm than any others in the world. And truly we *would* wage war if the Romans on a whim were to impose themselves on our holy places. Such a war would be a very costly one for them, with no profit for them. They understand that a little leniency in this preserves a prosperous peace.

The behavior of Gessius Florus is a serious matter, but this is more a problem of a corrupt official than the folly of an imperial policy. In the course of little more than a year, Florus has committed great evils throughout the land, and he seems intent on doing more. Our people work through a number of routes to bring about his removal—new embassies to Antioch and Rome, as well as less visible channels. As we wait for the resolution, our greater difficulty is to restrain our own parties, who are ever ready to push the entire nation to precipitous events. The advocates of revolution have little patience, and less wisdom.

They do not understand that everyone who wages war relies on either divine or human help. But when both are denied—as is probable in our case, at this time—the result is to bring destruction upon oneself. While it is true that we could organize two or three hundred thousand fit warriors into an army far outnumbering the legions presently in Syria, Rome's reach is longer than it seems, and many times our number would soon pour into this land. Besides, we have few weapons and no battle engines. The days when sling and arrow could win a war are gone forever.

[I ask Ben Matthias what he would do if war were to break out. For an instant his calm eyes lose their focus. He looks away from me toward a solitary fig tree in the center of the garden, as if to anchor his attention while deeper thoughts are under way. Slowly, with his eyes troubled, but in a manner no less resolved, he returns his gaze to me and says:]

That tree was planted by my grandfather. As a boy, my father ate of its fruit, and from childhood onward, I too ate of its fruit. This year, for no reason that anyone can discern, it put forth many flowers but did not produce fruit. For the first time in its life, the tree was barren. The superstitious in my household say that the tree is condemned.

My grandfather called it "the tree of Israel". That was his own name for it, this particular tree. It was only a musing, but my family has always called it that. What does it mean, this barrenness, if it means anything? The leaves are full and many, for my gardeners tend it carefully. The root and trunk and branches are healthy, the flowers abundant. Thus, I ask myself, why is there no fruit?

You ask me what I would do if a general insurrection were to break out. I do not know what my role would be. For the present, I put all my wit and energy into preventing such a disaster. But if it comes to war, I will defend my nation.

[I inquire about the factions. How many are there? Who are they? What are their objectives? His eyes grow cool, and I sense anew my alien status, my Greekness, and the fact that he hardly knows me. I detect sudden mistrust in his expression, though it is extremely subtle and immediately masked. The tone of his reply deliberately communicates that he believes I am wholly reliable and not one who would betray confidential information to the Roman authorities. Nevertheless, he is careful to tell me only what is already widely known. He says:]

The factions are many, and it is impossible to keep an account of them all. In the main there are the Sicarii, who attack Roman garrisons by surprise in order to steal weapons. There are the Idumaeans as well, who seek to raise an army for the purpose of seizing supreme power and declaring full war against the Romans. Whenever they are beaten down, they spring up again stronger than before. In Galilee, there are other insurgent groups, and Florus concentrates suppression there at this time, since the region is ideally suited for clandestine movement and for fomenting rebellion. Zealot groups of varying degrees of religious fervor are active, and all are militant. To confuse matters even more, certain prophets arise from time to time—false ones, you can be sure—who rally the people from their sufferings in the name of the crown of David. You must have heard about the seer who, some years ago, attempted an insurrection and entered Jerusalem but was overcome by the troops of Felix with the general population supporting the procurator. So you see how it is with us? One day the people support the procurator; the next day they may be entirely against him. Now one way, then another, and who can foresee which way the people will go? The country is a pot sitting on a fire, and if saner measures do not prevail, it may soon boil over. Again and again, patriots and madmen rise up and are cast down. Their numbers grow, and who knows where it will end?

[He sighs. Gesturing to a servant who stands near the peristyle ready to do his master's bidding, Ben Matthias calls out in Hebrew. The servant enters the house, then returns a few minutes later bearing a long bundle wrapped in red cloth woven with strands of gold thread. Ben Matthias unwraps it. It contains a bow of dark wood inlaid with bronze, a very costly weapon by the looks of it. Without explanation he strings it and plucks the cord until it hums. There is also an ivory quiver as long as a man's arm, incised with Hebrew letters and a decorative motif. Within it are three shafts tipped with sharp iron heads, their hilts feathered blue.

He stands and fits an arrow to the cord, cocks it, and lets fly a shot that the eye cannot follow. On the far side of the garden, a pomegranate drops from a tree. Ben Matthias unstrings the bow, wraps it and the quiver in the red cloth, and hands it to the servant, who takes it away. My host returns to his seat, still not looking at me.

What should I say? Does he expect a response? Words of admiration? An exegesis of symbolic meaning in the act? Or respectful silence? The silence between us stretches uncomfortably. I mention in a disinterested tone that I have heard about a group of people who follow a prophet named Yeshua Ben Yosef. Are they dangerous? With a frown and a dismissive wave of his hand, Ben Matthias says:]

Their prophet was but one of many. He was executed thirty years ago by the procurator at the time. But that was before my birth. I have met some who still cling to his memory, but I do not think they are a factor in the situation. Like other religious parties, they will fade away in time.

If you wish to have a taste of our real situation, I will introduce you to a man who is representative of all violent aspirations. He is one of the Zealots. In him you will see an *eikon* of our worst and best.

[To my surprise, Ben Matthias has used the word *eikon*, the most precise term for image. He now stands and offers me his hand in farewell, and wishes me good health and success in my writing. He does not conduct me to the door. The servant leads me away, and as I leave the garden I notice the bleeding pomegranate impaled on the ground by the arrow.]

Jerusalem
A Zealot

The man whose words I will now record proves true to the description by Ben Matthias. However, it seems to me an odd thing that the latter knows him and has access to him and that the Zealot agrees to a meeting with me on the strength of Ben Matthias' recommendation. I do not understand the relationship nor its implications. However, I record it here for what it may be worth.

I meet him at a rather dirty tavern on the road to Jericho, in a village a half hour's walk from the Jerusalem city gate. To arrive thus far I have been passed from hand to hand through three men whose names I do not learn. The last one remains with me as my guide and interpreter. The languages used will be Greek and Aramaic.

I am led through a public room where a half dozen people look up from their cups and eye my clothing and the length of my hair, then return to their mumbled conversations. The interpreter takes me down a narrow passageway and into a small room at the back of the house. There I find a man in his early forties, short and fierce of face, indistinguishable from the multitudes of Judaeans. He makes no gesture of welcome and speaks only in a low voice to the interpreter, who answers back in a similar tone. I sense fear and hostility in both men. The door of a separate entrance is open, with a view onto a weedy slope.

We are not introduced by name. Nor is there any shaking of hands or other basic courtesies. Neither is there insult, but I can see that I am here on sufferance. The Zealot sits down first and points to a bench facing him. I sit and open my writing tablet. He puts his hand to the hilt of a dagger at his belt, exhales through his nostrils, and fixes a piercing look on me.

"I am grateful for your generosity", I begin. "It is my whole desire to make an accurate account of the difficulties now facing your people under the procurator Gessius Florus."

He starts at the name of Florus, then relaxes a little as the interpreter translates.

"I cannot promise you that my accounts will greatly affect the situation for the better", I continue. "Yet be assured that I will do what I can. I have association with a man of authority in a Greek land under Roman government. It may be possible through him to bring Judaea's situation to the notice of the emperor."

He stares at me warily. I calm my breathing and wait for his reply. Time stretches on uncomfortably. Is he measuring my words, my honesty, my discretion? Or is my life being weighed in his hands?

I hold my stylus poised over the wax sheet. He stares at the stylus and the tablet, then back to my face. I am not using my papyrus scroll today since the pages have been dwindling too quickly. Later, I will transcribe the essentials of this meeting into the scroll—in condensed form, if need be.

He exhales again, anger in his eyes, his mouth tightened to a slit. Then he speaks:

Nero will not listen. Gallus will not listen. Our embassies speak in the high languages of Hebrew and Greek and Latin. They talk and they plead, and nothing comes of it. The language Nero understands is gold. Gold and fire and blood. He burns his own people in the imperial city. He crucifies at will. In Galilee, Florus has crucified women and children as well as men, and this is a thing unheard of in Roman ways, so I am told. Yet Florus remains in power over us. Why is this?

I will tell you why. I will tell you in the language of simple men, men without books, men with few words and much courage. I have heard the screams of my own sons crying out to me from their crosses. I have heard the screams of my brothers and my friends. I have seen the face of Roman justice. Gold and silver are their gods, and the peoples they rule are the sacrifice they offer to their gods.

It must cease.

I say it again: It must cease. Yet Israel is divided and confused under the yoke of oppression. Israel no longer has the vision to throw off the yoke. Israel no longer hears that the Lord our God is One. The words are on our lips but not in our hearts. The words are on our doorposts and tied to our foreheads but not engraved in our will.

Even so, it will be as it was on the day when David defeated the Philistines with a sling. It will be as it was when Gideon routed the Midianite army with three hundred Israelites. It will be as it was in the days of bondage in Egypt, as it was in the days of captivity in Babylon, as it was when the Syrians defiled the Temple and the menorah burned brightly for eight days with oil enough for only one. As it was in those days, it shall be again. Egypt and Babylon and Syria are upon us once more, and their feet are clay. The feet will shatter. But who will shatter those feet?

I say Israel will shatter those feet, and then the empire of Satan the adversary will fall into pieces and will be buried by the desert and will be no more.

First, the sword must strike the feet. It must be done. And when the idol falls and breaks into pieces, many in Israel shall be struck down by the falling pieces, for this is the way of the Most High with us. As he did for Abraham, so he will do again. The Eternal One, *El Olam*, will provide for us on the mountain of sacrifice. We shall climb again to the height of Moriah in Jerusalem, and there we will prepare another altar, and the Lord will spare us at last, as he spared Isaac. It is not our task to ask who will be saved and who will perish. It is the nation that must be saved. For the nation is the promise, and the nation is destined to rule every race and every other nation, for a king of righteousness will rise up over all the world, and his reign will be everlasting.

[He is still speaking when a man hurriedly enters the room through the open doorway. He bends to the Zealot's ear and murmurs something in Aramaic. The three swiftly go out the back door without a word of parting. I am alone. I close my case and make my way through the main tavern room and out onto the village street. A century of Roman soldiers is marching along the road, a half block away, apparently on routine patrol. There are no incidents.

How can I possibly present this to Gaius Varus, for conveying to Rome? Little in the text would help the Jewish cause, and much in it would throw oil on the flames of Roman wrath.

When the watchman entered the room to murmur his warning, I heard him first address the Zealot by name. I will not risk writing it here. Who can foretell the consequences if this is read by unfavorable eyes, and I have given my word on trust. My word is my life. I will not break it.]

*

Jerusalem
The voices

Four of us are walking toward the Temple: me, Loukas, Aharon, and the latter's nephew, a youth named Judah. Judah is a faithful Jew but not a follower of the Christos. His uncle is his legal guardian. However, it appears to me that the boy wants to be the guardian of us all, for we three are weaponless, while he carries a belted dagger hidden beneath his outer robe.

He explains that the Sicarii have been more active lately, especially in the open Temple areas, where large crowds fill nearly every space. These brigands and murderers, named for the deadly dagger they carry concealed in their clothing, have as their primary goal a revolt against the Romans. They kill anyone, often their own countrymen, whenever and wherever it will gain them money, weapons, or food. One of their tactics is to merge with the multitudes of distracted worshippers, plunge the knife into the breast of a victim, swiftly plunder his purse and any other valuables, then melt away into the crowd.

Judah shows us his weapon in an alley, just before we go up the final section of a street leading to the Temple gate. He scowls and says that we need not worry; he knows how to use it, and if any Sicarii try to harm us, they will learn what a blade between the ribs feels like.

Aharon shakes his head in disapproval. "He who lives by the sword will die by it", he admonishes.

"Uncle," says Judah with a tightening of his lips and resolution in his eyes, "the thousands slain in this city and throughout the land had no swords in their hands. Those who live by the sword—and the dagger—are alive!"

"Go home", says Aharon severely. "Go home, now."

"No, I will follow you, and you will thank me for it before the sun's setting."

We older men turn on our heels, hoping he will leave us, but he keeps following a few paces behind.

I will save a long story by saying that we met with no violence to ourselves that day, nor on any day thereafter during my stay in Jerusalem, though we witnessed a good deal of it. More and more I am seeing evidence of ongoing civil unrest, the brutality of soldiers suppressing disorderly groups: political and religious zealots, street-corner rhetoricians, and rabble rousers, most of them weaponless young men. I see a few beatings and two deaths in the midst of such small riots, the survivors hauled away by Jewish Temple guards or Roman legionaries to courts somewhere else in the city.

I am beginning to understand that this country is, as Ben Matthias said, a seething cauldron of rage. Hatred brews here, mixed with the elixirs of national pride and political ambitions. I am surprised at how little attention I have paid to it until now.

On this day, however, we enter the Temple precincts and soon find ourselves swallowed by a large crowd in the wide-open square called the Court of the Gentiles. Loukas and I will not be permitted to go any farther. It is most informative to read a stone tablet affixed to the yellow limestone wall separating this outer court from successive inner courts. Posted by Herod Agrippa, the stone is painted blood-red and inscribed in Latin, Greek, and Hebrew, declaring:

NO NON-JEW IS PERMITTED TO PASS BEYOND THIS BOUNDARY
HE WHO DOES SO WILL BE LIABLE TO THE DEATH PENALTY

It is an understatement to say that these people take their religion with utmost seriousness. From where we stand, it is plain to see that the entire complex is surely the glory of the nation and one of the wonders of the world. The stone is predominantly limestone, though plenty of white marble has been used. The whole dazzles the eyes, and when the sun strikes the mount in the morning or evening, it glows as luminous gold. Loukas explains that Herod the Great began its construction more than ninety years ago. It was completed only a year or so ago.

Aharon is describing the central role of sacrifice in the rituals of the Jews, which is easy to understand since it is common to all religions. He emphasizes that the sacrifice of animals and birds was a "prefigurement" belonging to what he calls the "old covenant". Yeshua is the new covenant between God and man, and he is also, in his own person, the ultimate sacrifice. Aharon is explaining lamb symbolism to me, and I am struggling to understand the connecting themes when suddenly a great tumult of yelling and physical struggle breaks out nearby. The crowd pushes forward around the inner zone of the trouble. Eight Temple guards are breaking their way through the mass of people, heading toward some steps that lead to the Antonia, the Roman fortress that is situated beside a corner of the Temple grounds.

As they push past us, I see that they have a man in custody. Barefoot, wearing rags of sackcloth, blood streaming from wounds in his head, he seems to be in his early twenties. The guards and their prisoner pass us, and the tumult subsides. The people turn away and go about their business.

I notice that Loukas and Aharon are standing very still, their lips moving silently, their hands raised toward the backs of the guards and their prisoner. Judah stares after them too, but with fists clenched and eyes fierce with anger.

"What is that about?" I ask. "Is he one of the Sicarii?"

"No", replies Aharon. "He is the farthest one can be from the spirit of the Sicarii. He is a voice of prophecy."

"What do you mean? Who is he?"

Loukas and Aharon look very sorrowful. "We call him Yoachim", says the latter. "In our language the name means 'God raises up' or 'God prepares'. No one knows his real name. The people call him that because whenever he is brought before the magistrates and they demand to know his name and where he is from, he merely says, 'God raises up!' Some think he is saying 'God prepares!'"

"But what has he done?"

"He stands in the Court of the Israelites before the altar of sacrifice and cries out a message of warning. 'Woe! Woe!' he says again and again. And also, 'The bride did not recognize the bridegroom!' He will explain nothing about what he means or why he is saying it."

"It sounds much like the message of the man you describe in your chronicle, Loukas. The one who washed people with water."

"Similar. But Yochanan the baptizer was like no other."

"Yochanan had a singular mission", says Aharon. "He too was a voice crying out. But that was only part of his role."

"'Flee from the wrath to come!'" quotes Loukas. "'Bear the fruits of repentance, for the axe is laid to the root of the tree!'"

Aharon continues: "Yochanan's voice was heeded by many—and hated by many. He proclaimed that he himself was not the *meshiha*, and that he baptized with water, but one to come would baptize with the Holy Spirit and with fire."

"Yeshua", I say.

Aharon and Loukas bow their heads reverently at the name. "Yeshua", they reply as one.

"Iesous Christos", whispers Loukas.

"This Yoachim we saw today is not the only one", says Aharon. "Three years ago, when the whole land—despite its troubles, which are ever with us—seemed to be enjoying a time of unusual peace and prosperity, another such voice arose in our midst. I should say that the city mainly was at peace, for there were, as always, outbreaks of small revolt and suppression here and there in the outlying regions. On the Feast of Tabernacles, a young man named Yeshua Ben Ananias came up from the countryside and stood in the Temple and began to shout: 'A voice from the east, a voice from the west, a voice from the four winds, a voice against Jerusalem and the sanctuary, a voice against bridegrooms and brides, a voice against the whole people!' Day and night he uttered this as he went through the streets. Some prominent citizens grew annoyed at these ominous words and had him seized. He was beaten severely and let go with warnings to keep his mouth shut. But he returned to his behavior immediately, day after day, month after month, with no word of explanation. He was most visible at the times of holy feast days.

"Finally, the Sanhedrin dragged him before the procurator, who was then Albinus. Yeshua Ben Ananias would answer none of his questions, and the procurator had him scourged. His flesh hung in ribbons, yet he neither begged for mercy nor wept, but at each blow he cried out, 'Woe to Jerusalem!' Finally, Albinus judged that he was a madman and released him. To this day he continues to walk the streets and shout his warnings. But he is no longer admitted to the Temple grounds because all the guards know his face. In recent months this new voice, Yoachim, has appeared in the Temple, doing what Yeshua Ben Ananias has done. There are others too, but most people in the city consider them to be madmen."

"Do you consider this Yoachim a madman?" I ask Aharon.

"He is a voice crying out. I do not know if he is a follower of our Yeshua. There are tens of thousands of us in Jerusalem now and many more throughout the world. And so it may be that these voices find shelter somewhere among us. I know that we give them bread and drink whenever we meet them in the streets and sometimes heal their wounds by ordinary means. It seems that they bear their wounds as part of their message. But why they do what they do is hidden from the eyes of all, even from our elders in the community. Even so, we believe that these voices are within the mystery of the Father's will. These men are sent by God, each in his own way."

*

Loukas invites me to dine with him this evening at an inn in the upper city. It is a refined establishment not open to the general public, owned by a wealthy Jewish man, a friend of Philetos. Though Loukas and I are to dine alone, it is the vastly connected, multifaceted Philetos who has arranged for our meal at his own expense.

"He regards you highly", Loukas explains. "Your conversations provoked much thought in him. Like you, he is an admirer of the works of Plato. Moreover, I think he is glad to have met an intelligent Greek who neither dismisses the stories of Iesous out of hand nor accepts them unquestioningly."

"A category to which you no longer belong?"

"That is correct. However, there are questions that open gates and questions that shut them."

"And yours are for opening?"

"Yes, I believe they are. Would it seem disrespectful to you, Theophilos, if I were to caution against locking gates before one sees what is beyond them?"

"Such a warning would not be disrespectful. I do wonder, however, why you seem so certain that I need such a warning."

A swift glance from him conveys his answer—more worry than certainty.

"Well," he says in a subdued tone, "one thing we know is that you now stand at a gate."

As the sun lowers over Jerusalem, we set out for the inn, which is in the district called the upper city. We are accompanied by three men with wooden staffs, members of the community. Loukas explains to me that while the followers of the Christos do not approve of violence, they believe that it is moral to defend oneself if attacked. The highest way, he says, is to bear violence without resistance, as Iesous did. The next is simply to run from evil. The third way, a kind of passive defense, can be used only if it does no grave harm to the attackers. One hopes merely to drive them off. This seems rather facile to me. Regardless of the moral problems involved, I am grateful for the bodyguards. Especially because there is a hooded figure following us, who skulks and darts along behind us, a half a block in the rear. When I point him out to Loukas, he shakes his head and says:

"That is our dear Judah, who wishes to rescue us from all evils. Should I tell him to leave us be?"

"No, he is young and needs his role. Besides, his lack of moral dilemmas could save our skins."

"All right, Theophilos, we'll let him have his drama. But I worry about him. This boy might fend off a thief, but, lacking wisdom, his kind could bring down an army of destruction upon us all."

The inn is a four-story building on a rise of land halfway between the Temple Mount and the height on which Herod's palace faces west over the Hinnom Valley. Here the homes and palaces are of exceedingly good quality, with much marble and well-fitted multicolored stone. As is the case elsewhere in Jerusalem, there are none of the statues or carved decorations of animate things that one finds in all other cities throughout the world.

Our three guards leave us at the inn's door with a promise to return in a few hours to escort us home. Inside the building, we are led by a servant up a wide stone staircase hung with tapestries and into a third-floor private dining room. It is decorated in the Greek style, with plastered walls painted olive green to waist height and warmest vermilion from waist to ceiling, all fronted by colonnades of slender Corinthian pillars alternating with Doric. Standing on pedestals in four alcoves are red and ocher vases on which pastoral themes are painted in black-figure: maidens playing flutes, shepherds with flocks, and forest beasts and birds. A white ceiling frieze portrays galloping horses, antlered stags, and gazelles in marvelous symmetry. The floor is a mosaic of turquoise in which numerous sea creatures cavort. I notice an octopus and a dolphin. There are no gods or goddesses present, and from this I surmise that even an irreligious house respects the more rigid customs of the land. The animals and birds are a compromise, so it may be that no Jews ever dine in this room.

A wide double door of cedar wood and flanking windows open onto a balcony, and through them the golden light of sunset pours. The room is glorious, and it makes me smile with happiness to be in such a place after months of austerity. In the center of the room is a low oval table covered with a linen cloth, on which are glass vials of flowers, finger bowls for washing, two silver cups and a wine flagon. The whole is surrounded by ebony couches, made comfortable with indigo blue cushions embroidered in a leaf pattern.

The servant fills our cups with wine and bids us seat ourselves. He departs, closing the door behind him. Loukas and I recline side by side, facing the balcony, cooled by an evening breeze blowing through.

"It is not unlike home", I say.

"We were never like this", he replies in a reflective tone.

"If I had been richer . . ."

"I am grateful that you were not."

The oddness of this response seems out of place, but I do not pursue his line of thought. We sip our wine and rest in the tranquillity of order.

Food is brought in: salvers of meats in spiced sauces, salads sprinkled with olive and garlic oils, baskets of hot bread fried in butter, bowls of yogurt, plates of cheese, smoked fish, pastries, baskets containing the largest black grapes I have ever seen, and numerous other kinds of fruit. The best of all is a cake of ground almond paste and dates, cut into thin slices and served on yellow ewe's cheese. It is wholesome fare, and I am very hungry, not having eaten since the humble breakfast at Shimeyon's house.

Loukas bows his head and prays silently before we eat. Then we begin our feast and talk most companionably throughout. Our conversation is as follows:

"These 'voices', as you call them, have a distinct role in the history of Israel. But it seems to me that the prophets I read about in the texts you gave me were not like these young men."

"That is true. Yet in essence their missions are much alike."

"Alike but not the same? What doubt do you have about it?"

"No doubt about their legitimacy, Theophilos. Rather, it is as yet unclear to me what part these later voices play in God's unfolding plans."

"Theirs is a terrible lot. Would any man—other than a madman or one possessed by an ill *daemon*—choose it for himself?"

"No man would choose such suffering for himself, yet some would accept an invitation to the mission, including its sufferings."

"Why would they?"

"Why did men stand firm at Thermopylae?"

"You make a good point. Still, these late prophets do not dress themselves as gods and arm themselves mightily."

"They are poor and clothe themselves as befits their task. Their garment is faith. Their armor is obedience. Their weapons are the words that are given to them."

"Given by whom? That is the real question: given by whom?"

"Given from above. There is no pride in them. Nothing that strives for pleasure or gain or renown. Neither do they incite rebellion. They simply warn. That is their role. They are like the watching tree."

"So you are saying they have no motive other than faithfulness to an invisible command—from above?"

"Yes, and the command, I believe, comes from God. I should say that it is not so much a command as it is a labor God asks of these men, for he does not force or possess. He is love. But the way of love that was offered to the Jews in Iesous was, for the most part, rejected by the people. He was the great grace, and his followers continue to be a sign of the new grace, the new covenant. Yet we too are rejected. Even now, however, the Father does not abandon his chosen people. And so, this remnant of the old covenant prophets give their warnings. Though Israel would not heed its own *mashiach*, it might hearken to a final voice."

"The logic of that is slim."

"Yes, but God well knows that men's hearts are rarely logical. Love continues to speak love, even as the beloved crucify him. If they reject him utterly now, he will not force them to submit. That would not be love. But they are given a final choice."

"You say 'final'. Then you believe the warnings?"

Loukas turns his sober eyes upon me and nods.

"Theophilos, do you remember the passages in my chronicle where I recounted the Lord's warnings to Jerusalem?"

"There was rather a lot in your book, and much of it astounding. If I recall correctly, he wept over the city."

"Yes, just before he entered it as a king, knowing that soon he would be put to death, jeered by the crowds that for a moment praised him. He said, 'If only you knew today the path that makes for peace! But now it is hidden from your eyes. For the days will come upon you when your enemies will encircle you with a rampart, hem you in on every side, and dash you to the ground, you and your children within you, and they will leave not one stone upon another in you, because you failed to recognize the time of your visitation.' "

"Not one stone upon another. It is difficult to comprehend. Who could destroy a city as mighty as this?"

"Think of the power of Rome."

"Even so, this immense prize would be overcome and treasured, not brought to utter ruin."

"We may not see it with our eyes, but we will know of it", says Loukas in a low voice, with some undefined grief. "This city will be no more—and its ruination will be soon."

"I do not think it likely."

"These times are abundantly full of unlikely events. The good news of the Lord is changing the world, little by little, step by step. And it is happening because a small group of people dared to believe in the unlikely—I should say, the impossible."

"Indeed, what you and others have described seems quite impossible."

"Yes, of course it does. Impossible in human terms, by human strength. But it is precisely the impossible to which we are called."

"Loukas, Loukas, 'impossible' is a word that, by its very definition, means a thing cannot happen."

"Yet the thing that none dreamed of happening has, in fact, happened."

"So say the sources of your chronicle, if they can be believed."

Loukas nods. "So say the sources of my chronicle, Theophilos. And so say my eyes and the evidence of my other senses and my mind. So say all people, the great and the small, who knew Iesous truly. He is the master of the impossible. His birth, death, and resurrection were the impossible surprise in history. And there are more surprises to come."

"This land, these people," I say, "their entire life is saturated in religious passion. Everything is sucked into it, as air itself is sucked into a fire, leaving only ashes in its wake."

"If it were merely a matter of a national culture or psychology ensnared in frenzied imaginings but with no evidence of divine intervention, I would think as you do. I would say to myself that their visions were follies produced by the dreaming mind, which holds hope on high when all true hope has been lost. And because their entire history has been one of lost and regained hopes, I would too readily dismiss their visions as phantasms."

"Clearly, you do not."

"I do not."

At the same moment, we both realize that we have come full circle and have progressed no farther than when we began. As he studies my face, with a reflective mood upon his own features, I realize that the discussion has taken much the same track as our disagreeable conversation in Caesarea.

He refills my wine cup and his own. The sun has now set, and the breeze has died down to nothing. We stand and go out onto the balcony. The noise in the streets is declining, and many lights shine in the prosperous homes crowning the hills about us. Almost a stone's throw away, it seems, the thousand windows of Herod's palace are ablaze with lamplight, and in its gardens one can see the sparks of torches. I hear the music of stringed instruments, flutes, and dancing drums coming from there.

Above us the first stars have appeared in the indigo sky. To the west the overarching dome is dark green with a slash of red on the horizon.

Loukas says: "During the past year, false prophets have appeared in the city, proclaiming a coming liberation. Some of them declare that it will be a divine intervention by the power of God; others say that God will work through Israel's leaders and warriors. The overthrow of every enemy approaches, so they say, and the restoration of the kingdom. They are all at variance with each other about how it will happen, and yet they all claim direct inspiration from God."

"More voices", I say with a tone of subtle irony.

"There are voices, and there are voices", Loukas replies, without taking offense. "False prophets always reveal themselves for what they are, given enough time. In their various ways, each clings to power, in whatever form he values it."

"And the true prophet?"

"The true prophet clings to weakness and trust in God."

"Like the woeful Yoachim whom we saw this morning?"

"Yes, like him. And there are more than prophets speaking. Even the heavens cry out. In recent months a great star appeared over the city, shaped like a broadsword. And before that, a comet that remained visible a whole year. And at the Passover, in the middle of the night, a great light shone around the altar and the sanctuary for half an hour."

"The glow of many torches?"

"It was not caused by torches. It was so bright it might have been midday. I was praying in the Court of the Gentiles when it happened, and I saw it with my own eyes. Then the East Gate of the inner sanctuary opened of its own accord—bronze doors so heavy that it takes twenty strong men to move one. Aharon and others of our community were present in the inner court and saw it. No human hand was near; no human hand opened that door. A voice like thunder came from the air, saying, 'Let us depart from here!' Then, a few days after the Passover, just before sunset, there were seen apparitions in the heavens over the whole country, sky chariots and legions of armed soldiers encircling cities in the clouds. Countless people witnessed it—with their own eyes. There is more I could tell you, but . . ."

"*But* I mistrust anything I have not seen with my own eyes? Is that what you mean to say?"

"Yes. You trust your own eyes more than you trust the word of your son."

I am hurt by this, but what he says is true enough.

We linger in silence for a time, looking out over the city. At last he says:

"I am sorry. I should realize how difficult it is for you."

"Do not be concerned about me, Loukas. You know I seek the truth. This, if nothing else, should reassure you."

He ponders, then replies: "I should be more trusting. This great quality in you, Theophilos, will lead you rightly. It always has."

A servant enters the room to announce that our escorts have arrived. It is time to go.

*

The men with staffs meet us in the inn's forecourt, one carrying a small torch to light our way. Loukas and I resume our discussion as we pass through the dimly lit streets and turn right into the depression called the Tyropoeon Valley between the Temple Mount and the upper city. It will lead us lower in the *metropolis* to the older district where I have been living, Shimeyon's house in the city of David.

As we walk along side by side, Loukas again takes up the subject: He speaks about the evil effects of false prophets. In times of adversity, he says, such men increase in influence because human judgment is then at its most unreliable:

"Too easily is man influenced by anyone who offers him deliverance from extreme peril, and thus he becomes the slave of groundless hopes. False prophets have easy access to his mind, beguiling him with flattering or reassuring interpretations. They declare that the spectral armies in the heavens are his own and that the besieged city is his enemy's. They say it is a sign of his approaching victory when in truth it foretells his coming desolation. Portents, foreshadowings, and warnings are interpreted according to the aim of the speaker and the need of the hearer. If his heart is not pure, he will bend it and even turn it on its head."

"But what is the good of such warnings", I ask, "if their purpose is distorted by those to whom they are sent?"

"Those who listen with honest ears will hear. Those who look with clear eyes will see. A genuine prophecy is an aid to man, yet it is also a test of the rightness of his heart. But a false prophecy is *only* a test, and a dark one at that! When a true prophet comes among the people and shouts 'Woe!' some will understand that woes are coming upon them. Others will tell themselves that he cries woe unto their enemies. Or a prophet cries, 'Flee from the wrath to come!' and the true of heart will flee; the others are already preparing to chase their adversaries in full wrath."

I agree with Loukas about this tendency in human nature but argue that the coin has two faces:

"Could it be that both true and false prophets, as you call them, project their visions as effluence from the deepest wells of the mind? Hope and dread alike reside there, and the upper portion of the mind materializes these humors in comprehensible figures. It is catharsis in a religious form."

"That may be true with some natural forms of prophecy, which are no more than intuitions about the shape of the *kosmos* and all that goes on within it. But false prophecy originates from an inner reservoir polluted by sin—and perhaps the water is also tainted by evil spirits. In the case of true prophecy, a man's inner spring is not itself the source. It is fed by higher springs—in fact, the living waters from above. They flow *through* him but are not *from* him."

"But how is one to know whether his is a polluted spring or a clean one?"

"There are weights and measures."

"And what are those?"

Loukas does not have a chance to reply because we hear footsteps running along the narrow street toward us. The man with the torch lifts it higher, and the two others step forward with their staffs at the ready. A shadow appears before us, gasping for breath. At his approach, he throws back his hood. It is Judah.

"Come with me!" he cries, then turns on his heels and runs back the way he came. Two blocks farther along, we arrive at a deserted square in the center of which is a water pool named Siloam. A naked human form lies beside it, as if floating in its own pool of blood.

"It is Yoachim the woe-sayer", Judah cries. "You are physicians!" he pleads. "Do something!"

Instinctively, Loukas and I kneel beside the body. Loukas puts a finger to the pulse in Yoachim's neck.

"It is weak," he tells me, "and the flesh is shaking. His end is near unless we can move him."

Swiftly, I take off my *himation* and spread it on the cobbles. The guards lift the young man by his ankles and arms and lay him onto it; then, using the cloth as a litter, they carry him to the city of David.

We make a temporary surgery in a ground-floor room of Shimeyon's house. Numerous lamps are lit, and a large one hangs from a chain over the cot on which we have laid Yoachim. One of the guards runs upstairs to inform a group of people praying in the upper room. Judah stands by the door, his face mobile with anger, anxiety, and other confused emotions. There are large water jugs here, so we wash Yoachim's body and try to locate the veins that are losing the most blood. His flesh is entirely lacerated with cuts. A flap of flesh hangs loose from one side, exposing rib bones. Lifting his eyelids, I note that the whites are showing.

I glance at Judah, who is clenching his teeth in suppressed rage, a fist on the hilt of his dagger.

"Judah," I say, "go find Aharon and bring him here." Why I say this, I cannot explain to myself. It may be that something in my mind's deepest waters has made a connection between this foolish prophet of woe and the man who knows something about him. From my carry satchel, I remove a roll of papyrus that was to have become part of my journal and find an empty page. I tear it from the roll and curl it into a funnel. Loukas sees my intention and lifts Yoachim's upper body onto cushions, then opens the man's mouth with his fingers. I insert the funnel and pour the water down his throat.

People from the upper room have arrived and are gathering about us. They kneel and raise their arms in a gesture of beseeching. Loukas goes out and returns shortly with our surgeon's kits. We sew up the torn section over the ribs and then turn our attention to similar wounds. We work with knowing hands, without hesitation or haste. Others take over the water feeding. Slowly, slowly, the bleeding declines over all Yoachim's body. The rapid, shallow breathing deepens. A little color returns to his face. He groans. The eyewhites show me that he is not conscious but is rising from the pit in which only moments before it seemed he was destined to die.

As the prayers go on, our work continues. We turn him over onto his face and find that the greater damage has been done to this side. We cleanse and sew and administer healing unguents, and finally we bind up the major wounds with linen bandages. The countless lesser wounds are now clotted and are best left to the open air. How long does all this take? Hours perhaps, but I do not feel the passing of time. As Loukas and I labor side by side, the years when we worked together in the Gortyna surgery return to us, and we are as one mind. Word-lessly, we do what is needed.

Shimeyon enters the room, accompanied by Aharon. Both begin to pray as the others do, though the elder invokes aloud a miracle of life for Yoachim. When at last Loukas and I can do no more, towels and bowls of water are brought to us. While we wash ourselves, Shimeyon and Aharon kneel beside the bed and lay their hands on Yoachim, the old man with his hands on Yoachim's head, the younger with his hands over Yoachim's heart. The others sing. It is the eerily beautiful sing-ing I once heard in Caesarea and have at times heard faintly coming from the upper room. It is in an unknown tongue— rather, it seems a blending of many tongues, an outpouring of some kind of unplanned harmonics. It is beautiful and dis-turbing to me, yet there is a strange peace in it. I feel myself drowning in a pool of mystery. No, I feel myself floating on a sea of mysteries.

Hours later, Yoachim is still alive. There has been no mirac-ulous healing, no stunning restoration, yet he has been pulled back from the path of the dead. His breathing is near normal, the pulse improved, and his unconsciousness more like sleep. It is now the middle of the night, and most of the people depart. Aharon leads Judah away to their home, wherever that may be. Shimeyon goes upstairs to bed. Only Loukas and I keep vigil, as well as a third, a solitary young woman who kneels praying in a corner of the room. How long has she remained in that uncomfortable position? She is motionless, upright, her hands clasped before her breast, eyes closed, lips moving silently. Why is she doing it? Does she personally know this poor man?

Man? Now that Yoachim's face is washed and his slender form is no longer clothed in a welter of blood, I see that he is in fact a youth, no more than seventeen or eighteen years old.

The gray light of dawn is showing in the window. The woman lies down on a mat, pulls her head veil over her face, and sleeps, yet her hands are still clasped as if her body prays, though her mind is no longer awake.

Throughout, Loukas has remained seated on the floor by Yoachim's head.

"You should sleep, Theophilos", he whispers.

"I cannot sleep", I reply, and with these words a flood of bitterness enters me. No longer a detached physician, I am once again an ordinary man, appalled by the degraded body, the terrible wounds, and the gauntness of the form lying before us.

"Is this how your God treats his servants?" I ask.

"No, this is how man treats God's servants", Loukas replies.

*

During the week that follows, Loukas tends the body of Yoachim night and day. I urge him from time to time to go upstairs to sleep for a few hours, and if I insist with severity, he obeys. Occasionally we work together, cleansing the seeping wounds, changing bandages, pouring water into Yoachim's open mouth, hoping that it fills the deep well within him.

Now, at my direction, the women of the household bring food, corn mash, and other grains boiled to a soft gruel, thinned by water and wine, and milk sweetened with a little honey. Down it goes. During the second week after the scourging, Yoachim's consciousness returns. His eyes observe us yet also seem to be staring upward a good deal of the time. He answers no questions. He speaks not at all. Whenever we must turn his body to tend to the wounds on his back, he does not cry out, yet his eyes bulge with the strain of suppressed pain, and his whole frame trembles. He is in agony still but makes no complaint.

Now he can rise on the cushions and swallow without the aid of the tube. The liquefied food goes down as well. He asks for nothing yet accepts everything we offer. I increase the quantity of food, and again he accepts it all. Once—once only—he gives me a look that may contain gratitude or perhaps wonder, or he is merely trying to assess what kind of man I am.

In my turn I look back, trying to assess what kind of man he is. Are those fathomless dark eyes the portals of madness or the gates of a temple? What is in this mind? Profound thought? Or nothing? Is he an empty broken pot cast aside by his God? Or is he God's friend, and they keep counsel together that no other man may comprehend?

From time to time, the elders of the community enter the room and stand over him or kneel close by and pray for him. Often the young woman who kept vigil the first night returns and stays awhile, silent and prayerful. She does not approach or speak to Yoachim, though I hear her conversing with others in her gentle voice.

Who is she? She is about thirty years of age, very beautiful, graceful, and quietly radiating her virtues. I note with interest that she does not look at Loukas, yet she will glance at me occasionally. Loukas, for his part, never indicates that he is aware of her presence. And then I see a pattern in his behavior. Whenever she enters, he busies himself adjusting a bandage or wiping an unbound smaller wound. His eyes do not turn in her direction, and now I note that he always lowers his glance when she enters or leaves. Not a word has passed between them, though he speaks with other men and women who come and go. And at last I understand.

*

Now Yoachim is sleeping. Loukas and I are alone in the room with him. It is long past nightfall, and we are both very weary. As we eat from a dish of lentils and dip bread into cups of curdled milk, we realize how little we have spoken with each other during the past two weeks.

"Theophilos," he says, "have you continued your examinations?"

"My examinations? Ah, you mean my interviews with those who knew your Yeshua. Well, only a little since Yoachim came. There is no time to write."

"Doubtless you keep it in your mind."

"I do. Some of what I am told is dramatic, some is quite ordinary, and strangely it all seems to have a life of its own in my memory."

"Yes, accounts of the good news are like that—both the spoken and the written. They are not a dead letter. Rather, they are a true living *word*."

"Good news", I sigh and shake my head. "You see disaster and call it good. We are surrounded by people preoccupied by strife and death, and you call it life."

"You see a part and make it the whole in your mind. The reality here is that our faith conquers death. Faith is life rising in the midst of death's seeming victory."

"Seeming?" I murmur.

Loukas glances at Yoachim.

"That life", I say coolly, "is the fruit of our labor, not a miraculous resurrection—speaking of parts and wholes."

He nods. "It is both part *and* whole. You might ask yourself, Theophilos, who gave us our knowledge and skills?"

That, of course, is a precipitate step into the realm of theology. I decline to respond. Pleading fatigue, I excuse myself and lie down on the floor with a cushion under my head. I will take a little nap, which he can hardly deny an elderly gentleman. I drift into a light doze and later awake to hear voices speaking quietly. I do not stir, but opening my eyes, I see Loukas kneeling beside Yoachim's cot. His arm is extended over the boy's head, the palm of his hand on Yoachim's forehead. I can see Loukas' face, but the sleeve of his robe hides the other's.

Then I am startled, for I see in Loukas' eyes that mysterious thing I noticed so many years ago when we worked together in Gortyna, the night we saved a disgusting specimen of humanity named Balbus.

A shameless ape, I had called him, for the man had embodied the worst sort of slavery to sensual appetites. Loukas had stared at me blankly when I uttered my loathing and, taking the hand of Balbus in one of his own, put the palm of his other on the man's forehead and stroked it gently. He had looked at the absolutely unlovable with—with love. And then I had realized that in the depths of Loukas' soul were reservoirs that I had not known were there. Was it his capacity for pity or for empathy? Yes, but it seemed to be more than that. What it was, I did not know.

Now, all these years later, I see the phenomenon again. And still I do not know what it is.

As I continue to listen, I hear my son whispering in Greek and then Hebrew. The part I can understand is about the

331

sufferings of Yeshua on the cross. He asks Yoachim if he knows about Yeshua. There is no answer.

More is said about faith in the Christos, about life and death, about missions and obediences. To all of it there is no reply.

Quietly I get to my feet and move closer. Now I can see Yoachim's face. His expression is reposed, the eyes open, listening, reflective, without fear—yet his mouth is still completely silent.

Loukas traces the sign of a cross on the other's forehead and speaks in Hebrew, a few words with the name Yeshua embedded in them. A great sigh comes from the boy, and he breathes a word:

"*Hatan.*"

Loukas asks a question in Hebrew. The boy whispers a reply, which I hear as "Yoachim". There are a few more words; then he closes his eyes and returns to his sleep.

Loukas rises and notices me standing near.

"He is recovering", he says.

"Yes, but what will happen to him?"

"I do not know. But now I am certain that he is within the firm hands of God's will. And I have learned more about him. His name is Mattan, and he is from Bethlehem, a village near Jerusalem."

"Then his name is not Yoachim?"

"No. *Yoachim* is part of his message—'*God prepares.*' And perhaps it is also an explanation of his mission."

"His first word was *hatan*. What does it mean?"

"Bridegroom. When I made the sign of the cross over him and prayed the name of Yeshua, he said, 'The Bridegroom.'"

*

Loukas and I are really quite exhausted after three or four weeks of tending the stricken prophet. Now other members of the community stay awake and watch over Mattan and insist that we return to normal night-sleep. Gratefully we comply. We come by the room to check on him several times a day. He is beyond mortal danger and is sitting up more often, and standing as well. Intent on regaining his walking strength, he goes back and forth across the room with a sheet wrapped about his spindly frame, then onto the cot for a rest. Each attempt to walk opens some minor wound or other, and thus the sheet is usually spotted with red regardless of how often it is washed. Yet he is healing rapidly and putting on a little weight besides. I emphasize the word "little".

"This tragic soul is skin and bones", I comment one day.

"This anointed soul fasts continually", Loukas replies.

"Well, it may be to his benefit that the Romans scourged him. At last he can give himself permission to eat."

Loukas offers no reply.

People in the household have tried to give Mattan articles of clothing. He will not agree to wear any—vigorous shakes of his head convey his refusal. He clings tightly to his blood-stained sheet. Once again I wonder if he is seriously deranged. The nights have a chill in them now, since the city is high in the mountains and the winter approaches. There have been a few brief rainstorms, cooling the earth and the human brow, and one torrential downpour that drove everyone indoors, turning the streets into brooks, filling wells, and washing everything clean. Cleansing the blood-stained cobbles as well, I presume. Mattan sleeps better these days and is not in so much pain. I have given him my old wool *himation* to use as a blanket.

One morning, he stands up in the room and hobbles back and forth in front of a few of us who have gathered there, my *himation* wrapped closely around him. Still he will accept no gifts of clothing. He gestures with sufficient meaning, and we realize that he is asking for his rags. Where are his rags? No one knows. Aharon tells him they are probably gone forever.

Loukas suggests to the others that the tatters of cloth may have been part of Mattan's mission. "A word in themselves", he says. This is beyond my understanding, but I step forward and ask Mattan if he will accept my cloak as a gift, to cover his nakedness. Aharon translates. I further plead the case, pointing to the frayed hem, the patches my wife sewed over moth holes, the stains that will not wash out. Mattan is undecided.

The young woman who kept such valiant watch during the first week now steps forward and speaks to him in Aramaic. He stares at the floor as he listens, then finally nods in assent to whatever she has said. She and the other women leave the room. Mattan takes off the cloak, hands it to Aharon, and lies down on the cot with his face to the wall.

Later, Aharon returns with the cloak and draws Mattan to his feet. Over his wretched body it goes, but it no longer resembles my dear old *himation* that stood me in good stead through many trials and much inclement weather. It has been sewn up into a tunic that drops over the head like a sack, with armholes and neckhole hemmed with yarn. The garment hangs loosely from the shoulders. Next, a length of old rope for a belt. Mattan looks down at himself, somewhat saddened by this luxurious apparel but not entirely displeased. The others in the room break into smiles and exclamations of approval. Then a song in Hebrew with raised hands.

Mattan opens his lips and sings with them soundlessly, though as always there is something about him that stands apart. At the end of it, as people are leaving the room, one of the men offers him sandals, but Mattan firmly shakes his head. He lies down on the cot and falls asleep.

Loukas takes me by the arm and says, "Come up to the roof with me. There is something I must tell you."

The flat roof is above the fourth floor and walled to waist height by brickwork. The surface underfoot is smoothly mortared and inclined a few degrees to permit rainwater to run off to drain holes that feed a cistern in the cellar. The sky is clearing and the sun appears, warming us, turning the dampness into a fine mist. A striped cotton awning covers half the space, held up by wooden poles mortared into sockets. Here and there, flowering shrubs are blooming in large clay pots.

Loukas and I gaze out over the city for a time. It is noisy, bustling like a hill of ants. I wonder if Rome is like this. It is said that the four greatest cities in the world are Rome, Alexandria, Antioch, and Jerusalem. Compared to any of them, Gortyna is a village.

"Theophilos, I have received news that changes my plans", he begins. "Today, word reached me that my friend Paul will soon face his second trial. He asks that I come to him swiftly. The Roman law basilicas are clogged, but their justice creeps onward, and he foresees that within two or three months he will be brought before the magistrate."

"Could not someone else go?"

"He asks for me. Moreover, our shepherd Shimon Kepha also asks me to come. Both men now minister in Rome, and both want my presence at what approaches."

"Surely there are plenty of physicians in so great a city."

"They do not need me as a physician. I go as a brother and son. I go also as one who keeps an account of what comes to pass in their lives. Mainly Paul, but Shimon too. You have not yet read my second chronicle. I will send it to you when I complete it."

"When will that be?"

"I do not know. For now, I must leave for Caesarea in the morning. I will try to find a ship that will take me directly to Ostia."

"After the trial, will you return to live in Gortyna?"

"No, Theophilos, I cannot. After the trial, whatever its outcome, I will return to Antioch. And there I must remain."

I stare at him indignantly.

"And who commands this of you?"

"Our Lord asks this of me."

"Your Lord—Yeshua?"

He nods and lowers his eyes—whether in embarrassment or reverence, I cannot tell.

I am feeling very angry. This cult has indeed ensnared him. They command, and he obeys! Without question, without heed for those who love him, he simply obeys!

"That is the rhetoric of slavery", I say irritably.

"That is the dialogue of love", he answers.

"Love!" I snort. "This blood and death at every turn. Is this love?"

"Theophilos", he says, placing a hand on my arm. "Theophilos, you have been immersed in blood and fought death all your life, and you say this?"

"It was my labor in the world."

"It was your labor and your love."

We would say more, but we hear steps running up the staircase from the floor below. We turn to the sound and see the young woman who has shared so many of our vigils. She comes to us in haste, with worry in her face.

"Mattan has gone", she says.

"Gone?" Loukas exclaims.

"I went into the room just now, to bring him a meal, and it was empty. A man at the door told me that Mattan went out into the street and disappeared into the crowd."

Jerusalem
Supper on the shore of destruction

The afternoon grows warmer. We walk the streets looking for our lost prophet, but all searchers return to the house by sunset with nothing to report. He has merged into the vast populace and doubtless will emerge at some point, in some public place, crying out his warnings.

Several of the community gather on the roof for a meal in common, Loukas and I among them. A cool breeze riffles the awning. Lamps are lit. Long tables are brought up from below, rugs and cushions spread about. Women and men bring pots and baskets of food from the kitchen on the ground floor. Shimeyon prays a blessing over the meal in Hebrew, Aharon prays another in Aramaic, and Loukas in Greek. The Father, the Son, and the Holy Spirit.

Abba, Parakletos, Yeshua, Iesous, Kyrios, Christos, Meshiha! *Mashiach*! Names, names, names! Words upon words!

I am still nursing my anger, yet it is mostly sadness now, a helpless grief. To whom do I pray? This absence within me, this lack of focus, momentarily yawns before my eyes like an abyss, but I turn my thoughts from it. I remind myself that I have my life, my skills, my ethics, my studies, and those whom I love and who love me. Is that not enough for a man? Do I need a god? No, I do not. Especially I do not need a god whom I cannot force myself to believe in.

I keep my thoughts to myself, and as we eat our meal I listen to the quiet conversation of the others. Loukas translates some it for me. There is discussion about Paul and Shimon, about a Yaakov who is traveling in Spain, and Yochanan in Ephesus. There is a good deal about Nero's persecution and the execution of some of their friends here and there in the Roman world. It reinforces my dismay over their beliefs and their way of life, and with dread I sense that Loukas may one day suffer the fate of the others.

Later, most of them go below to the large room where Yeshua had his last supper in this world. I hear many voices, so it seems that numerous people who live elsewhere have arrived. Loukas and I remain seated at the table. When the singing begins, rising through the open stairwell, we find ourselves alone.

"Do you not want to join them?" I ask.

"I will pray later", he says. I look up and see that he is regarding me with some concern.

"Will you remain here in Jerusalem, Theophilos? You need not go merely because I am departing. Shimeyon would welcome you to stay on as our guest. There are others you should meet, so that you can continue your examinations."

"No. I am finished with them. I will return to Crete."

"I see", he nods. "As you wish, then. But I regret you won't stay a while longer, for there is more you should know."

"I have seen enough."

He smiles reflectively. "There is no end to what may be learned about him. There is no end to the new realm that is growing all around us. We are at its beginning."

"Your new world grows ever more confusing, Loukas, with myriad mysteries and contradictions. You invite me to a breakfast on the shore of eternity, and it turns out to be a supper on the brink of catastrophe. You heal a poor fellow like Mattan and call him a prophet—a *true* prophet, mind you—yet he speaks only of destruction, woes, a cataclysmic end."

"He speaks of the ending of the old world. That ending is the labor pain of what is being born. Iesous foretold it all. It is written in my chronicle. Do you not remember?"

"No, I do not remember. Living word or dead word, whatever it may be, I do not remember it."

My curtness silences him. He looks away over the city and says:

"When Iesous approached Jerusalem, he wept over it. He told his followers that the city would be utterly destroyed. When he came the last time into Jerusalem, he taught in the Temple before his arrest, and there he spoke his final warnings. He told them that when they saw the city encircled by armies, they would know that its devastation was near. Those in Judaea at the time must flee to the mountains, he said, and those in the heart of the city must escape it, and those in the countryside must not return to it."

"Escape it? But I can see that if the gates were closed, it would be one of the mightiest fortresses in the world!"

"Yes, and that would bring about the demise of the whole people. Do you understand what will happen in this land? A revolt will break out, battles between Jews and Romans here and there, and perhaps the Jews will win some. And then the whole people will come into peril because of it. You can be sure that the *imperium* will not tolerate it for long. Greater Roman armies will be sent to crush the rebellion. And then all the people of the land will flee for refuge into the city, thinking themselves safest here."

"And Iesous advised the opposite course. To scatter away from it."

"Yes. Once the siege is broken, the rage of Rome will fall full force upon the city. And when that comes, he said, not one stone will remain standing upon another."

"Like Troy, I suppose."

"A thousand times worse than the fall of Troy. And it *will* come. Indeed, it is near."

"How near?"

"Within a year or two, a war will begin. In recent months, our prophets in the Holy Spirit have warned that we must soon go away. To the hill country, and to south and east, to

Asia Minor, to other cities such as Antioch and Tarsus and Alexandria, where our communities are growing. Many will go to Pella in the Decapolis."

"Pella?" I say. "Why there?"

"Because the Decapolis is mainly Greek and will not participate overmuch in the revolt. And thus the Romans will pass us by, concentrating on the regions where the Jews are strongest. Pella has a large community of our faith. Even now, preparations are being made to receive as many as possible. There, if the Lord wills it, we will wait out the storm."

"*We*, you say. I thought you were going to Rome."

"By *we*, I mean the body of believers, the *koinonia*."

"Did Iesous speak of what comes after?"

"Yes, he did. He said that the distress in the land and the wrath against this people will be great. They will fall before the sword, and those who remain will be led captive in the midst of the Gentiles. Jerusalem will be trampled by the Gentiles until the times of the Gentiles are fulfilled."

"The times of the Gentiles? What does this mean?"

In answer Loukas crouches down and with his forefinger traces a line across the mortared roof.

"This is how men see *kronos*. They understand time as a line along which they travel from the past into the future, bound to it inescapably while they are alive."

"A perception that is quite true", I say.

"Only in one dimension. When the voice of God speaks of a mystery that is both within time and yet beyond the immediate time, and even eternal in significance, men cannot help but misinterpret what is said. In their thoughts they turn a sphere into a line. Unless they have eyes to see."

"I confess that I fail to see what you mean, and what he meant."

"The end of the age is upon us, Theophilos, and a new time has begun for mankind. A new world and a new

340

unfolding of the plans of God. Until now we have been blind. Now we are given eyes to see, if we accept them. Iesous spoke with an eternal voice that sees both the present and the future. He said, 'The present generation will not pass away until all this takes place. The heavens and earth will pass away, but my words will not pass away.' He was speaking about the coming destruction of Jerusalem and about a time in an *aeon* to come when he would return again in glory, at the end of the age of the Gentiles."

"Again, the age of the Gentiles. But what is the meaning of it?"

"The revelation of God came first to the Jews. Now, through the Christos, the fuller revelation spreads ever outward to the whole word, to all races and nations—the Gentiles. Even so, the age now beginning will come to its end as well. Iesous is speaking simultaneously of the immediate end, which is very near, and of an ultimate end far beyond our knowledge. Paul speaks about this too. In the visions and inspirations of the Holy Spirit, he sees deeply into the coming times. The world will accept the good news of Iesous, the new covenant between God and man, but toward the latter end of time the people of that age will grow weary and dissolute and cold of heart. They will reject the great gift that God has given to them in Iesous and will worship other gods. Satan the *diabolos* will be unleashed as never before and will blind mankind again, seducing most. And the suffering of that people will be more terrible than what is soon to happen in our times, for they will have known Iesous and abandoned him. Then the end will come."

"So you speak of two endings."

"The immediate and the distant. The destruction of Jerusalem will be a sign, a warning for those who are born in the future. The purification of the world begins in the sanctuary of the household of God."

"It seems a hopeless religion if everything must end in destruction."

"It is the most hopeful religion of all. For it is the foundation of the heavens and the earth. You fear catastrophe, Theophilos, as do we all. You fear pain and death. But you must try to understand that the end of evil will not be a catastrophe for mankind, though we must pass through many evils until then. Sin and the reign of the *diabolos* are the catastrophe. The new heavens and new earth will come. Then will all those who are saved rejoice. Our task is to live in this present era and spread the good news. Now we must work and we must suffer so that many will be saved."

The singing in the room below ends, and footsteps rise toward us from the stairwell.

Two women in shadows approach us. One carries a small lamp, its wick flickering in the breeze.

They bow to us, and one says, "Theophilos, Loukas, the *Eucharist* is ended. Shimeyon invites you both to join us, if you wish."

"Thank you", says Loukas. "I do not think you have met my father, though I see you know his name."

The women step closer, smiling, and introduce themselves: The one who had spoken is a very dignified old lady named Constanta. The other is the silent young beauty who kept vigil with Mattan. Her name is Elisheva.

Elisheva, a woman of the Jerusalem community

As is his unbroken custom, Loukas does not meet the eyes of the young woman; nor does she look to his. Yet they seem to know each other, considering their familiarity with names.

We go downstairs into the upper room and join a group of about forty people. The fragrance of incense and candle smoke is in the air. Dozens of hanging lamps flicker above our heads. Their rituals completed, people stand about talking informally, though here and there some remain kneeling in prayer or reading quietly from scrolls.

Loukas turns aside to talk with a man, leaving me with Constanta and Elisheva. The older woman takes my hand and thanks me for giving my cloak to Mattan. I ask if anyone has heard news about him. No, none have. Constanta reassures me that the followers of Yeshua in the city all know about him now and will keep their eyes open. They are praying for his mission, she says, and will offer food and refuge if they happen to come upon him.

I ask her how his mission differs from that of their own prophets.

Though silently deferring to the older woman until now, Elisheva answers:

"Mattan's labor is as a lamb of sacrifice. He is a voice that cries out, a voice that will be heard by the few, a voice that will be rejected by the many. The Lord Most High can raise up prophets from the stones, yet he has chosen a man of humble station to speak. He sends a messenger to those who do not know his Son, for the people of the old covenant are the firstborn and he will love them eternally. So too, the prophets of the new covenant are speaking. So too, the lambs of the new covenant are being sacrificed for the sake of the revelation. Throughout the world, we are offered up."

"Do you expect to die?" I ask.

"We do not seek it. If it comes, we accept it."

"I mean do *you*, in your person, foresee that you will be put to death?"

Her face grows solemn yet retains its composure.

"Of this the Holy Spirit does not speak to me. I entrust myself to him and leave all things in his hands."

"Why? Why do you place yourselves in such peril?"

She considers this, then says: "We put our feet onto the path of life. If we are hated by the spirit of murder, and if the adversary strikes us down, then more is our victory, for he loses ground even as he thinks he gains. If it is the will of the Lord that this one or that one die for the sake of his holy name, then we know we are on the cross with him."

Involuntarily, I shudder with horror at the thought. It is unbearable to imagine what a woman like this would suffer at the hands of Roman torturers. If she were to undergo such an ordeal, her death would be a blessed relief.

"If the political situation grows worse, will you flee? Will you flee from the wrath to come?" I ask, quoting their Yochanan the baptizer.

"The Lord has already exhorted us to go forth into the world. Some have gone already. Some are departing soon. Others will remain until Jerusalem begins to be encircled by armies."

"And God has informed you of all this?"

Constanta and Elisheva both nod in affirmation. I see no flicker of doubt in their eyes. For them, this is absolute certainty. Terrifying as it is, they do not appear to fear it.

"Well, it seems a troubled city", I murmur in a reasonable tone. "It might well be wise to find a quieter place to live."

They are looking back guilelessly into my eyes, saying nothing, when a loud exclamation comes from the corner of the room where three people are kneeling on the floor before the altar of sacrifice. Two men and a young woman. One of them, a bearded man about forty years old, is speaking aloud in a language I do not recognize. Shimeyon, Aharon, other elders, and the remaining people in the room go to them and kneel around. They raise their arms in supplication and

344

begin murmuring prayers. There are a number of Gentiles present, and thus the prayers are in several languages. Loukas takes my arm and gently guides me near to the group, but I hold back.

"No", I whisper to him. "I do not wish to be part of your rites."

He accepts this and kneels with the others, leaving me standing apart, observing.

The man who had first spoken cries out again. It sounds like Hebrew. He is not so much speaking as he is singing—a mellifluous outpouring of speech that flows in an elusive, yet strong, harmonic course. He ceases singing, and silence follows.

Elisheva now raises her hands and sings a few words in Hebrew. Then she speaks in her normal voice. What she says, I do not know. Another person raises his arms and says in Greek:

"Set Theophilos before me and I will bless him."

This is too much! I am at first frightened and then irritated. Surely they have conspired this, seeking to pull me in. I remain firmly planted where I stand. Loukas looks up from his silent prayer and glances at me. I stare back at him and cross my arms. No one says any more; no one tries to convince me or coerce me to do as they do. They simply pray and wait.

Finally, I realize that this is going on too long. These are Loukas' friends, I remind myself. They have been hospitable to me. Am I making them uncomfortable? What harm would come of it if I were to pretend compliance? Courtesy alone asks it of me. With an inaudible groan, I kneel down at the outer edge of the ring.

All right, I say to myself. I have set myself before them. Now, doubtless, one of them will say something that they hope will turn my mind.

To my great astonishment, none of those whom I know says a word. Instead, a little boy about eight years of age, who has until now been lying half-asleep near the wall, sits up and rubs his eyes. In a completely normal child's voice he says:

"Set Theophilos before me and I will bless him."

Loukas catches my eye and smiles a reassurance to me. The others turn the palms of their hands toward me, their lips moving in prayer. Elisheva and another young woman are kneeling a few feet away, facing me, eyes closed, arms raised. Elisheva sings a few lines in a voice like a silver tong striking on finest glass. I do not recognize the language. She falls silent, and the other young woman speaks:

"Hear me now, O my son, my Theophilos", she begins. "Though you do not know me, I say to you that I know you. On all your journeys have I been with you, and am with you in the journeys that lie ahead. You do not know where I am taking you, yet in the end you will understand. Fear nothing."

I am shaken, even moved, but immediately I understand the intention and the consequences of this semblance of oracular utterance. They wish to bring down my resistance to their faith. They wish to tell me that God is speaking to me so that I will be constrained to think as they do.

Now I am filled with cold anger. I have always hated the ways of manipulation, the enforcement of one will upon another. And while I admit that these people are not forcing me through the usual methods, I know they are seeking power over me. I am preparing to stand and leave the room abruptly when the little boy speaks again:

"Did you not cry out to me when you buried the ashes of your sister? Did you not cry out to me on the ship that bore you away from the city of plague? Did you not cry out to me when the eight died on the cross? Did you not cry out to me over the many who died in your hands as you sought to save them, though you did not know my name?"

Now I am shocked, for some of this Loukas does not know, and could not have told them. What spirits are in the air, what geniuses and muses, they who alone can cross the barriers that separate human minds one from another, and can impart knowledge by means beyond the languages of men!

My hands are trembling, my mind struggling to assert reason over religious passion—so dangerous and misleading, these passions, this fire of the Spirit, as they call it. It would burn up all that the rational mind has struggled to create throughout millennia. It would burn up the nations, leaving ashes in its wake. Oracles, oracles, ever speaking and omnipresent in the world—giving a token that aids us, even as they plunder our powers of logic. Yes, I have seen more than enough witches and fortune-tellers in trances, and I know they are instruments of evil. But this boy! How strange that his demeanor is not like that. He speaks as a child would speak when commenting on the sun in the sky or the little dramas of his play. A face and a voice full of wholesome joy.

"Hear me now, I speak to you once more, Theophilos," the boy continues, "for you are my son, though you do not know it."

I suppose my mouth is gaping in astonishment. My reasoning prompts me to vocally contradict the child. Yet I know it would be absurd to do so.

"This is my word to you", he continues. "It is for your strengthening and for your fruitfulness. Death is not the victor, and though death will claim your body, you shall rise if you come to me, even though you told Xanthippos that you would sink to the regions below. I am calling you forth from death's realm. I am calling you into the desert of this age, and you will find me if you seek me. Know that you will be tested by fire, but I am with you always."

347

With that, the boy sighs, smiles, lies down on the floor again, and returns to his sleep. The others burst into song, Loukas among them. Hastily, I stride out on shaking legs and go to my room. There I sit down on the bed, put my face in my hands, and can no longer make sense of anything.

Caesarea

Before dawn, Loukas shakes my shoulder and quietly says it is time to go. At some point during the night I must have fallen into a deep sleep, for I had not heard him come to bed. In other times and places I would have lain awake all night wrestling with strong emotions and stronger questions. But my exhaustion had not permitted it.

We eat a simple breakfast in the ground-floor kitchen, joined by Aharon and two other men. These latter will accompany Loukas and me to Caesarea. I thank my translator for his months of service, and though I bid him well and offer the hospitality of my home if he should ever come to Crete, my mind and heart are elsewhere. The incidents of the night before rise up fresh in my mind, and with them returns my anguish, which I hide from the others' eyes with a screen of courtesies.

Shimeyon and several people, including Elisheva and Constanta, come with us to the street door. When Shimeyon makes the sign of the cross over the travelers, I look away, flinching. With that, we depart.

I say little on the journey, for I do not trust my mind, nor what words might spring from it. Confusion of thought and angry emotions fight for mastery, but I make an effort to distract myself from them, as much as I am able, by concentration on the physical labor of the journey. My health has very greatly improved during my time in Judaea and Galilee, my legs now as sturdy as they were in my youth, my breath full and clear. Though my body is old, I no longer feel that it is. It is my soul, rather, that seems wearied by age.

But the weather is good, and the traffic of men and beasts and vehicles is constant, with soldiers coming to and from the capital of Judaea as well as Greeks and Jews afoot on private purposes, and other races bringing wares to sell in Jerusalem or passing on ahead of us, bound for the port. The road goes ever downward and does not tax our strength. We stop from time to time to eat a little. We stay the night at an inn. No one troubles us.

On the second day, perhaps concerned about my silence, Loukas begins to probe with his surgeon's instruments.

"The evening before our departure was a time of grace for you," he says, "was it not?"

I make no reply, which I hope will shield what clearly he desires to examine. But he is not so easily dissuaded.

"Did you hear the voice of the Lord speaking to you?" he presses in gentlest tones.

"I heard human mouths speaking to me", I mutter.

He is about to say something more, and so I throw a distraction across the path:

"I can see well enough that you love that woman."

"What woman?" he says with a note of gravity.

"Elisheva, the one who kept vigil with us."

Now it is his turn to delay response.

"Moreover," I add, "I can see that she loves you."

He tilts his head in the very manner he used as a youth whenever he wanted to weigh a matter without speaking and at the same time deflect any further inquiry into his most private thoughts. It makes me smile to see it again.

"Are you sick with love, Loukas?"

He shoots a glance at me, which I anticipated, feeling sure it would be one of censure. But it is not. There is understanding in it. It seems that he simultaneously reads my motives and his own heart better than I had supposed.

"I love her very much," he says, "for she is the most lovable of all other souls I have known. I do not know if she cares for me in the same way, and it is not my part to know for certain."

"Really!" I protest. "That is most unnatural."

"Is it? No, Theophilos, I think it is not. You fail to plumb the waters, high and deep, of love itself."

"I fail to know what you mean at all."

"I have put my feet on a path that leads to other forms of love. I will live unmarried for the sake of love. Can you understand this?"

"No, I cannot", I shake my head. "There is something very wrong in it. You do yourself harm by going against man's nature."

"Consider man's nature, Theophilos: Is it not the truest and best of our nature to love the highest good? And is not the love of God our highest good?"

"If God exists, then what you say would be true. But why would love for him prevent you from loving a woman? Would not the delights of human love be a means of sensing the delights of love's creator?"

"Indeed they would. Yet if one were given the delights of love's creator without the sensual delights, would marriage be an absolute necessity?"

"But *your* path to delight, it strikes me, offers you much suffering."

"Is there no suffering in married life?"

I fall silent. How can I argue against this point? The only flaw I can see in it is that it stands entirely on the belief that this highest good is real. How can he be so sure that it is not merely a lofty dream or a kind of poetics?

"The love of man for woman in the heart and flesh is a holy gift", he continues. "Yet there is another way, in which love bridges all aspects of our being."

"What way?"

"A man may love another soul with great power and passion, yet this kind of love does not die if it is absorbed into a greater love, as a brook becomes part of a river, wide and deep. It finds no fulfillment in the body, yet in the soul it grows and grows. In a manner of speaking, it becomes the river without losing itself."

"But why not let body and soul unite? Why not have all of man's gifts in one?"

"For most people, that is indeed the path, for marriage is holy. If God had called me to the path of marriage, I can think of no other woman with whom I would happily spend my life. In truth, it would be a taste of paradise for me."

"Then why not seek it? I can testify that you would find a willing response in her heart."

"Can you? How would you know such a thing?"

"I may not be wise in the way your fellows think you are wise, but I know a few things."

He chuckles suddenly and says, "This is true", and claps me affectionately on the shoulder.

We walk on a league or two before he speaks again:

"Theophilos, we have two ways of knowing a thing: the *gnosis* we can obtain through what others tell us and also that which we can acquire for ourselves. By the first means, we grasp it through words. I can attempt to describe to you the higher dimensions of love, and even if you were to accept what I say, it would remain as a thought in your mind, without images or solid form to lay hold of. The direct experience of an object, on the other hand, means encountering it as a living, breathing phenomenon that has its own life and identity. In this second sort of knowledge, the form of the object communes with the soul and awakens its desire like a foretaste, in proper relationship to its beauty."

"But that is Plato's idea. Are the followers of Yeshua becoming Platonists?"

"No. Though the Greek light can inform us, providing words for certain mysteries, it is not the whole thing."

"What do you mean, the Greek light can inform *us*? Are you no longer Greek?"

"In Christos there is neither Jew nor Greek, neither slave nor freeman. All are of equal worth to him."

"So you abandon the philosophical powers of reason?"

"Now reason finds its proper role. Indeed, it is a pale shadow of what has become flesh. Yes, Theophilos, the Word of Love himself has become flesh, and this is the transforming of the world we once knew. This is the birth of a new world that is without end."

"The birth looks difficult," I say, "and more likely is the death of child and mother."

"No", he shakes his head. "This child will not die. It will grow to full maturity. However, you are right when you say that the birth is difficult."

"Then why not choose a little happiness along the way?"

"I am already very happy."

"You say you are happy? You think you are happy even without this great love that stands no more than a few paces away from you and so silently waits for you?"

"You misunderstand. She does not pine for me, though it may be that she feels much for me. Her heart is happy too and seeks the things that are above. She is consecrated to a life outside the marriage bond. Our Lord asked it of her, and she accepted and has made a vow. We both love our Savior. How can you understand the beauty of his love? My words cannot explain it to you. Only if you meet him will you know what I am speaking about."

"Meet him? How would that be possible? Loukas, you speak of loving your savior, but many people love the old gods too. It seems to me that they love the forms that artists carve for them, and in fact they are loving only themselves perfected in a mirror. But it is a lie. It is not their true selves."

"Yes," Loukas nods, "Plato says as much."

"Could it be that you are doing the same?"

"We do not worship statues. When the Lord embraces us through heart and soul and mind, we do not feel stone arms around us, for the beauty made by human hands is cold and has no life. Often the demons have used such forms to beguile man into false worship. And even when a statue is the medium of no evil, too easily do we fall into worshipping ourselves instead, without knowing it. Whatever warmth we may sense from it is the warmth within ourselves reflected back to us. But in Iesous the living God, true warmth is given to us by him."

"That is your belief", I say coolly.

"That is my experience."

"And so he gives you an embrace and then bids you deny yourself all other embraces? That is cruel."

Again he smiles.

"You would have to know the embrace before rendering judgment about it. Besides, this self-denial is only for a few."

"But what is its purpose?"

"That we who are called to it might serve all others with greater focus and dedication. That we might bring forth ever more love through this life path."

"There are vestal virgins in Rome", I argue. "Do they too serve your God by their virginity?"

"They serve false gods through a sacrifice that is but a mimicry of the true thing. They have nothing to offer their people other than a *sign* of sacrifice, but it is a dead one. They are proud, willful, and at times cruel and capricious. That is not love."

"So you speak instead of a Jewish custom."

"It is not a Jewish custom, for the Jews are very fruitful, and rare are those who do not marry and give birth to many. In this you may see yet another way in which the new covenant differs from the old. In former times it was a *logos*, a word, that taught men. Now begins the new era, since the Christos has come in person, the eternal *Logos*, he who is both man and God, and all things are changed by this."

"The world will not change overmuch, I would wager. Marvels spring up in history and capture our attention for a time, then fade away. If remembered at all, they become a legend recounted about times long past. But in every generation the world remains the same. The cities may be larger, the inventions more clever, but man's heart does not change from age to age."

"You discount that some things are coming into the world that have never before been seen. In former times, if philosophy, ethics, and all that is best in human nature had been enough to lead man to his destiny, the coming of the living word among us would not have been necessary. Consider the *apostoloi*, our fathers in the faith. The Jewish Law could not save them. The Law did not enflame their hearts with love. Then they met Love incarnate, heard his words, and witnessed his miracles and all that he suffered for mankind's sake. They saw him die and rise again and return to paradise."

"Yet they fled from him at his greatest trial, or denied him or betrayed him. Why do you have any confidence in men like that?"

"Because we are all men like that, and because they were afterward greatly changed."

"How so?"

"They had shared the life of Iesous and seen astounding things, yet in themselves they manifested nothing new or truly spiritual until they had been baptized by the Holy Spirit. Only then was the true fire kindled within them and, through them, kindled in others."

"And so you deny yourself all human love."

"No, no, still you do not see it, Theophilos. What you fail to understand is that for me and those like me, all human loves are given to us in another form, in great fullness and joy, though not without suffering. That is how our Lord lived, and that is what he foretold would be the task for some of us, though none who followed him understood his meaning at the time."

"And that is why you turn your eyes away from Elisheva."

"But not my heart and my soul, and above all not my prayers. And perhaps it is the same for her. I do not cling to her, for then we two might seize a human happiness for a time and leave our true fruitfulness undone. And what we might have called love in the beginning would turn to barrenness."

I shake my head, saddened, more alienated from their religion than ever.

He tells me that Elisheva is the daughter of a man named Philip, one of the *apostoloi*. She and her sisters are prophetesses.

"The elderly woman, Constanta," I ask, "is she her older sister? Or perhaps she is her mother?"

"She is neither. She is the spiritual mother of a household where Elisheva lives. There they minister to women in the city who have been cast out or condemned or who are with child but lack husbands, and prostitutes whom they have rescued from that sin."

"This surprises me", I exclaim. "Such a dignified matron. Hers is a distasteful task. Why would any woman accept to do it?"

"Constanta was once one of them. When she was young, Iesous himself saved her from death, for she was caught in the act of adultery and was dragged in humiliation before him by the Pharisees and scribes of the Temple. They wished to test him and would have stoned her. But the eyes of Iesous glanced at them, and with a few words he probed their own consciences, for all of us are sinners, each in his own way. Thus he brought her back from the brink of death. And she who was once in great darkness is now a great light to many."

"Is this also the story of the one you love?"

"No. Elisheva is a consecrated virgin. The beauty of her holiness far surpasses the beauty of her countenance."

"A great loss", I murmur.

"A great gain", Loukas replies. He pauses a moment, then says, "Soon they depart for the city of Hierapolis in Asia and will remain there."

Now I understood the measure of his sacrifice. He is bound for Rome and then to Antioch. He will never see her again. They exchanged no word at parting, nor did their eyes meet, nor did they give indication that they knew each other. Yet I know with certainty that he loves her as he has never loved another.

Here the conversation ends.

What sense can be made of this very strange religion?

*

Two days later we have crossed the Plain of Sharon and are following the Roman road along the coast, approaching Caesarea from the south. I feel relief when we first sight its numerous Greek and Roman buildings rising high above the flat land. Strato's Tower is the gateway to my home in the west. The surf is audible now and beckons me:

Thalassa, thalassa, the sea, the sea! O my beloved sunlit sea!

Before reaching the outskirts, however, we turn off onto a lesser road that veers away from the shore and circles around the massive amphitheater. Thus we avoid entering the city altogether and continue on this well-trodden route through several outcroppings of habitation and sprawling orchards, arriving in the evening at a village a stone's throw from the northernmost suburb. There we come to the gate of a moderately large villa beside the water. The main building is Roman architecture, the surrounding property walled on three sides, with the sea as the fourth.

"What house is this?" I ask Loukas. "I thought we were going to the Street of Silversmiths."

"This is the home of Shimon Kepha's friend Cornelius. He has now gone to his reward, but his heir and family still live within. They know of our coming and will welcome us. Here we will stay until we find our ships."

Through the iron bars of the gate I see fruit trees and rows of grapevines within. A young man and woman are standing nearby, pruning a tree. On a blanket beyond the green canopy of its branches, a baby is sleeping. Loukas calls:

"Eutychus! Hermione! Here we are!"

The woman turns toward us first and, breaking into smiles, runs forward to unlock the gate. The young man scoops up the child in his arms and approaches behind her. He too is smiling broadly.

"Loukas, Loukas!" they cry joyfully, letting us in. Embraces and kisses follow, the couple patting Loukas' arms and shoulders as if he were a boy. Then they turn to the two who have accompanied us from Jerusalem and greet them warmly.

The baby stirs in the father's arms and opens a drowsy eye. Loukas kisses its round red cheeks and murmurs babyish sounds, making everyone laugh. Now I am introduced, and the young man steps forward to clasp the hand of Loukas' father—as if I am the one who brought him into their lives. He greets me with beaming face and heartfelt words of gratitude that I have come under his roof. He is so open, so genuine, that I am at a loss for how to respond. Add to this his religious utterances of thanks for our safe arrival, and my paralysis is complete. Loukas steps in to rescue me, and then we all turn and make our way toward the main entrance of the house on a grassy slope that feels mercifully cool beneath our tired feet.

As the animated conversation of these reunited people continues, I learn that the couple are man and wife. They reside here in some unknown arrangement. I wonder if they are servants, though employing servants does not seem to be the usual custom among Yeshua's people. Owning slaves, I have heard, is extremely rare for them.

We go inside, and in the entry hall Eutychus gives the baby to its mother and busies himself taking our staffs and cloaks from us and depositing them in a corner. People come forward from nearby rooms and from other regions of the house. Numerous introductions follow. I cannot record it all here. Everyone is very kind, but I am too weary.

I must sleep now.

*

The following morning, after breakfast, Loukas and I are seated on the grass beneath a fig tree that is heavy with fruit, in a garden entirely enclosed by the four wings of the building. I learn more about the place. Twenty people are in residence here, several of whom minister to the sick and dying, who are cared for in one of the wings.

The son of Cornelius is the titular owner of the property under civil law, though long ago his father gave it by solemn word to the community of believers in Caesarea. The son too has renewed the gift. His name is Decius Ciprianus, and he is a physician. He works mainly with the sick who come here, but today he is away in the city, where he has other patients. He has good connections with the Roman and Greek communities and will try to arrange passage for us on ships bound for Ostia and Crete.

I ask Loukas why physicians are needed in this new religion. Why does his Lord heal some but not others? He replies that it is a mystery connected to the unfolding of a purpose in the life of each soul—a purpose known by God but largely incomprehensible to our minds.

"Come, come", I say. "Surely with these miracles abounding all about you, you must have given it some thought."

"I do not know the answer for certain, but Paul has spoken much about this mystery. He believes that the Lord has fulfilled the act of redemption completely through his sacrifice of suffering and death. Yet he did not choose it to be a gift bestowed entirely from above. He asks each of us to take a part in the sacrifice, in a manner that is particular to one's soul. Thus, while man cannot redeem himself, he may participate in his own redemption. We can offer our sufferings to God through the cross of Iesous and invoke grace for ourselves and others. Some carry small crosses, some carry large ones. Some are healed in totality, others a little, some not at all—and who can judge which is the greater part? Even so, he is the Lord of life, and thus we work to foster life in whatever ways we can. If we fail after all effort, we accept it, and God brings from the suffering another good."

Eutychus comes out a door of the medical wing, and Loukas calls to him, urging him to join us. The young man sits down beside me, as if he is an equal. Today he wears a short tunic, for the day promises to be warm, despite the onset of winter. For the first time I notice scars of major bone fractures on his legs and arms and a web of heavy scars across the back of his short-cropped head. It looks very much like the skull was once shattered. I am amazed that he is alive.

"We were discussing the question of why the Lord heals some and not others", Loukas explains to Eutychus.

There is a transformation in the young man's face. The guileless, unguarded, nearly childish expression I beheld the day before is no less glowing. It has retained its innocence beyond his years, yet now I see a measure of thought within. The eyes become reflective.

"Ah, yes," he says in his clear Greek dialect, "but the Lord knows what is good for us even when we do not. Faith is required, yet faith does not guarantee healing—indeed, not even great faith in the name of Iesous assures it. But peace is given to all who ask."

Loukas nods, but I am unsatisfied.

"You have suffered", I say, pointing to a ridge of scar tissue on his shin.

He nods and smiles.

"When you were suffering," I press on, "when you were in the most terrible pain, did you think that your God was bringing good from it?"

"I did not think at all, sir, for I was dead."

"You were ... dead?" I murmur, my face falling.

"I was there that night", says Loukas. "Indeed, our Eutychus was dead."

"Maybe you only thought he was dead. What happened?"

Eutychus answers:

"The city of Troas was my home, Greece the land of my birth, and there I lived all my life until I came here with Loukas and Timotheos to work for the sick. Paul and his companions had arrived in Troas from Macedonia, and after the breaking of the bread one night, he preached to us. I was very young at the time, just a lad, and I did not understand everything he spoke about.

But my parents were strong in the faith and had brought me along to receive the holy *Eucharist*.

"Paul talked on and on, with all eyes upon him. But the hours stretched long for me, and I grew drowsier. The night was hot, and we were in an upstairs room, the third story above the street. I sat on the window sill and tried to stay awake. It was pleasant there, for a little breeze cooled me. Around the middle of the night, my eyes closed, and I fell asleep. Then I toppled out the window and hit the pavement below.

"People ran downstairs, everyone, including my parents and the *apostoloi* and others. The first to reach me picked me up, for they saw that my bones were broken and that I was dead."

"Is it certain you were dead?" I ask. "Maybe you were unconscious."

"Theophilos, I was there", Loukas interjects. "The boy was dead. The blood had ceased pouring, there was no pulse, the breath of life was no longer in him."

"Did you see anything after you ... died?" I ask Eutychus.

"I had been baptized and had confessed my sins by then. My soul was clean, and so the evil one had no claim over me. I remember sinking and sinking into quietness beyond all feeling, and then someone's arms caught me like a bird in a nest. I felt a warm hand on my head. I know it was the Lord because the hand had a hole in it, though it touched me most gently. It was a very peaceful feeling. But it was strange too. I do not understand it even now: I was no longer in my body of flesh, but I had a body still. My body of flesh was broken, my head cracked into pieces. Then the Lord gave me to another man who held me; I heard that man speak, but not with his lips, and then I came back into my body of flesh. I remember nothing about what happened after that."

"It was Paul who held him", says Loukas. "He had come rushing down the stairs behind the rest of us, and when he saw what had happened he ran forward and took Eutychus in his arms and held him tightly to himself. Then he told us that the soul was still in the boy and that he would live. The family took Eutychus away to his home, alive. His bones later mended in the normal way."

"There were others", Eutychus says. "Paul has brought back others from the dead, but he does not like to draw attention to himself when it happens. Shimon Kepha also has brought people to life again—always in the name of Iesous. Greek, Roman, Jew—they speak the name of our Savior, and people beyond all hope return to us."

More people risen from the dead! I think to myself. How true is this? It cannot be! Do they really believe it? Where will it end?

I plead the need for rest, stand, and go to my room. I lie down but cannot sleep. Now anxiety consumes me, for I see that my son is lost to them. The power of their delusions is immense. No one—no one—returns from real death. No matter what they think about it, the boy was not dead. Their inability to grasp reality is the worst symptom of their disease.

I get up and record these most recent encounters in my examinations. They are hardly science and hardly *gnosis*. Scattered things they are, inconclusive, the stories of prejudging minds that translate fragments of reality into what they desire to see.

*

The following morning, as Loukas and I walk together in the garden, I boldly confront the illusion. I ask him if he personally has raised people from the dead. He says that he has not, though he has witnessed it several times. I then ask if other kinds of miracles occur when he prays over people. He gazes at me thoughtfully and says, "Yes. Sometimes there are healings."

"I would like to see one", I say. "Let us go now to the ward of the sick, and you could pray over them."

"I and others have already prayed over them. Their souls are well, their bodies ailing."

"So there will be no miracles that I may see with my own eyes."

He casts a look of sadness upon me.

"Why not do it?" I go on. "Surely a miracle would bring down the walls of my unbelief."

"Theophilos, how little you understand yourself. It is not miracles you need but faith. During the Lord's time on this earth, the Pharisees and their scribes demanded that he work wonders for them, but he would not. Sometimes they saw his great healings, but that was only because they happened to be there among the crowds. Even so, they denied what they had seen—with their own eyes."

"Are you saying that I am like them?"

"We are all like them to some degree, until the heart is purified. As is the case with the eye's vision, it is the nature of blindness not to *see* the blindness."

"A pretty wordplay", I reply. "But I think you have not really answered my point."

"I have answered it clearly, but it seems you do not see it. You want a sign that you may accept or refute. You wish to be master over the meaning of the sign. You would be judge over it, and that would not bring you any closer to the truth. Iesous told the Pharisees as much. They too demanded a sign. He replied only this:

"'An evil and adulterous generation craves for a sign; and yet no sign shall be given to it but the sign of Jonas the prophet: for just as Jonas was three days and three nights in the belly of the sea monster, so shall the Son of Man be three days and three nights in the depths of the earth.'"

363

Evil and adulterous? These are hard words. Instinctively I feel hurt.

"You are a man of goodwill", he continues. "You are faithful to your family and your word, and this is good. Yet it is not enough. It is the soil prepared for planting, but it is not the harvest. The harvest is what I desire most for you."

I am too disturbed to reply. He waits for me to answer. I murmur that I have much to think about. I take my leave and go for a walk along the shore.

*

This evening the residents and guests eat in common, about thirty or more of us. We are served simple fare—fish, bread, fruit—in a large room that was once the atrium of the house. Though there is blessing prayer beforehand, this meal is not a ritual. Loukas is engaged in discussion at the other end of a long table. I am seated beside the physician Decius, the son of Cornelius.

He is about forty years old, clean-shaven, wearing a Roman *tunica*. He is fluent in three languages, but we are comfortable with his native tongue and speak in Latin throughout our conversation. He is an intelligent man, trained in Alexandria, just as I was. Though he is obviously a member of this community, he is considerate enough to keep to topics mutually congenial: memories of the great city and its library, names of persons who might or might not be known to us both. To my pleasure I learn that he corresponds with an Alexandrian Greek who was once my classmate and is now a teacher of surgery.

After the meal, most people leave the room. Decius and I remain seated and resume with a discussion about medical developments. I further warm to the man when he mentions that he does not approve of bloodletting. I ask him if he was influenced by Erasistratus. He has read some of the teacher's writings, but not all of them, he says. No, it was in prayer that he came to the knowledge that bloodletting is superstition. This effectively dampens the conversation.

Not long after, I hear faint music coming from another part of the house—the hauntingly beautiful singing of their worship. He stands and shakes my hand. He must go to pray, he explains. Before leaving, however, he gives me the news that he has found a berth for me on a ship bound for Carthage that will harbor midvoyage at Crete. Its name is the *Hesperos*, and it departs from the port of Caesarea two days from now. He has also found a berth for Loukas on a trade ship bound directly for Ostia, leaving tomorrow morning.

Later, Loukas taps on my bedroom door and comes in. He looks unusually happy. He has prayed with the others, he says, and he has asked a favor of the Lord. The Holy Spirit desires that when he has completed his task in Rome he should go to Antioch. But he is free to come by way of Crete to visit his beloved family.

"Oh, that is good", I say. But I do not believe it will happen. All promises given by this religion are to be fulfilled in a mythic future, beyond the span of living men. I do not give voice to this.

We bid each other good night.

*

And so in the predawn, several people gather in the lamp-lit forecourt. All but I kneel while prayers are offered for the voyagers. That I remain standing does not seem to bother them. After that, there are tears and kisses and many embraces, as well as verbal and written messages that Loukas is to deliver to Paul and Shimon Kepha.

Loukas and I, Decius, Eutychus, and three others walk into the city and arrive at the port as the sun is rising over the hills east of the Plain of Sharon. We pass through much evidence of Roman military activity, and I find that several warships are anchored within the harbor, and more of them are anchored out at sea beyond the harbor walls. The winter winds are not the best for sailing, and dark clouds are coming in from the west.

We find the Ostia vessel soon enough, rising and falling on the south arm of the quay. It is a commercial ship, fairly large but with a deck closer to the water than the triremes.

Loukas' friends embrace him again, then step back a few paces, leaving us alone. As we stand side by side, waiting for the signal that will allow passengers to board, he turns to me and says:

"You believe in fate, Theophilos, but the tyranny of the fates over the mind can extinguish hope."

"I am not without hope", I say.

"Fate does not govern our lives. The hand of God working through his providence guides us and goes ahead of us to prepare the way. 'God prepares', our Yoachim said."

"Then misery and death are God's will for us."

"In this age they are part of our existence but not the whole, and they will not last."

"That is your faith and your hope, but it is not mine."

"It is yours for the asking, if you open your hands to receive it."

I open the palms of my hands toward him and say:

"These hands hold back misery and death for others. Yet they cannot keep it back forever. Armored only with the skill of these hands, I have labored, and always without a god to assist me. And now, my son, I am to become more alone than ever."

"Though you feel alone, Theophilos, you are not alone. You do not need armor. You need hope. Providence has a

366

human face and a human heart. One day you may come to love him as he loves you, for he has given his life for you." Now Loukas opens his own palms toward me. "The hands of Iesous healed men from misery and death. His hands were pierced, and they bled. Through his dying he conquered death, and in his rising he gave us the sign and promise that one day his victory will be for all men."

"Loukas, Loukas", I whisper. "I have had enough of words."

A sailor at the boarding plank blows a small trumpet, and people push forward around us.

He embraces me and says, "My father."

Then he goes into the boat. I turn away, certain that never again in this world will I see him.

MORPHAEON

And so I depart the next day.

My hosts accompany me to the port to see me safely off. If they pray for me, it is hidden from my eyes. They are very kind and treat me fondly at farewell, with gifts to ease my journey. Eutychus, like a child, embraces me as one of his own kin and gives me a small sack to take with me. Later, on board, I open it and find a cluster of figs within. On top of the fruit sits a rolled strip of papyrus. Written on it in childish script:

> Then the Lord said to me: What do you see, Jeremiah? "Figs", I replied. "The good ones are very good, but the bad ones are very bad, so bad they cannot be eaten." Thereupon this word of the Lord came to me: Thus says the Lord, the God of Israel: Like these good figs, even so will I regard with favor Judah's exiles whom I have sent forth from this place to the land of the Chaldaeans. My eyes will watch over them for their good, to bring them back to this land, to build them up and not break them down, to plant them and not tear them up. I will give them a heart to understand that I am the Lord.

It is a quotation from one of the Hebrew prophets, I believe. Yes, even figs become messages for those people.

The *Hesperos* passes through the harbor mouth and courses outward onto the open sea. I go forward to the bow, turn my back to the troubled land, and keep my eyes fixed on the horizon beyond which is my home.

The first night, I remain awake in my cabin. I extinguish the lamp swinging on its chain and listen to the ship speaking: the groans of the timbers and sailors' shouts, the rushing waves and howling wind, for we are heading into a storm. I slide the wooden slat from the window and observe the sky. The stars are burning above, but before long they disappear. The ship begins to heave. I close the shutter and latch it tight and lie down again in the dark.

My heart is sore, when it is not numb. I try to imagine the Yeshua who walked in that ill-fated land thirty years ago and changed so many lives. I still do not grasp his personality, though there is no denying that he was a great soul. My mind stretches as I ponder what he taught, yet I cannot understand all of it nor agree with everything, for the truths are embedded in the limitations of his religious culture. There is myth at work in his legend—moreover, I can see that I am present at the origins of a very great myth.

Is what I have written in the above lines a contradiction? How can fact be myth? Only . . . only if one understands the facts as symbolic of higher truths. Was he a god? Was he a man? It seems that he was intent on showing his people that he was very much a man. It may be that he was one in whom Plato's ideal Forms were made manifest. If this is true, it is a wondrous thing and is meant to be told throughout the world.

However, what if it is more than that? What if the human testimonies and the powers of confirmation that seem to pour from the heavens happened as I have heard them described? If that is the case, do they bear witness to a singular event in human history, the axis of the past and the future? If such be the case, it would overturn the world. Last year I wrote to Loukas that it would not, could not, overturn the world. Now I am not so certain.

No, no, no, it cannot be! I have fallen momentarily under the spell that takes an unseen truth and transforms it into human dramas, human forms, as the great sculptors take raw stone and turn it into a semblance of man—one more perfect than any human form that is found in actuality. Myron and Praxiteles present to us their gods and goddesses, and if we were to lack restraint we would fall by compulsion to our knees and worship such perfection. Yet if that beauty fell on us we would be crushed. Man—and man alone—is the creator of his own illusions, chimeras, visions, and dreams.

Yet Loukas used the concept of stone gods to refute the very case I make! "Empty idols", he called them, and I agreed with him on that. What, then, is symbolic, and what is actual? Who can rightly discern it? Our minds are unstable, metamorphosing what we see into what we want to see—and in some cases, what we fear to see. All races have their oracles of the divine, but always the word they hear is filtered, transformed into something else as it passes through the human screen into our world. Who speaks it, and what is the original intention of the speaker? And how can men be trusted to receive such words rightly when we warp everything we touch?

Prophecy and interpretation? But prophecy *is* interpretation! Regardless of how carefully the followers of Yeshua-Iesous divide the two roles, they are one and the same.

Prophecy, prophecy, the drug of the world! Is it a madness of the mind? Is it a higher form of poetry? Is it the translation of the invisible into shapes and features easily identified, forgetting that in the shaping we easily lose its meaning?

I fall asleep at last, tossed about by these unresolved questions.

*

I am recovered now. Three days I lay abed with fever, hovering between wakefulness and sleep, raving at times. The ship's cook who brought me water and gruel, forcing me to sit up to drink it, later told me that I babbled incoherently. I remember that there were troubled dreams but cannot now

373

recall what they were about. Once, I thought Loukas stood beside the cot and tended me as a physician. I felt his hand upon my sweating brow, but when I reached for it, I touched a bleeding hole in his palm and recoiled in horror. A dream or a night shade? I do not know.

*

I sleep through much of the passing days, still recovering. I eat the figs and find they are excellent.

Again and again my thoughts turn to the boy who spoke in the upper room, telling me about hidden things unknown to any but me. Loukas may have told what little he knew and come by intuition to the rest. But not all of it. How could that child have seen my deepest griefs and my prayers to an unseen God in whom I barely believed?

*

That is the nature of belief in the invisible. We live enclosed within our material senses and the small thoughts in the sphere of the skull, knowing little, understanding less. Then a light flares in the night sky or a creature surfaces for an instant from beneath the waves, then plunges again, and we ask if we have truly seen what our eyes beheld. In times of woe we cast our glance to the heavens; then the force of gravity pulls us down. Again and again, our prayers rise like fragile-feathered birds but are blown away on the storm wind.

*

I fell asleep again, and then came dreams of a kind I did not know existed:

I am walking across a slope overlooking a wide green valley bordered on all sides by hills. Above me the sky is overcast, the clouds black and purple and gray. Thunder rumbles within them. A stiff wind is blowing from the east, scattering leaves and creating spirals of dust.

Standing at a distance on the brow of a hill, a lone figure gazes out over the vistas. As I near him I see that he is a child about nine or ten years old. He is robed to the shins in rough brown cloth, with a cord cinching his waist and a white woolen cloth about his shoulders. He is standing perfectly still.

Now I am a few steps away from him, but he does not seem to notice my presence. I understand that I am within a dream but viewing a living scene. He is real. I am a visitor from another time and another place.

The wind increases, chilly and torn by wailing gusts, and his long black hair lashes about his face. His skin is light brown, his eyes large and dark, the other features unremarkable. In his expression there is a reflective mood, as if he is pondering hidden thoughts or is waiting for something. His self-composure is that of an older man who holds himself with dignity. My eyes record no significant attributes, nothing that would make him stand out. He is ordinary, and yet not ordinary. My spirit senses a power of soul within him, and above him an invisible hand hovers, protecting him, guiding his destiny. In that destiny there will be suffering, but it has not yet come.

The rain begins, a few large drops, splattering on his shoulders. Then sheets of it hit hard, and his robe is soon soaked. He does not move, does not seek shelter. His face is uplifted to the sky, bathed by its outpouring. His hair hangs down in wet strings. He raises his hands like cups and receives the water. They quickly fill, and he drinks from them.

Again he raises his face to the sky.

Lightning flashes, followed almost instantly by a crack of thunder. Flash after flash, across the valley, the rumbling of the heavens like a cavalcade of war engines besieging a city. The light grows dim beneath the blackening cloud layer. Still he looks up, his eyes closed, his hands open to receive.

I hear a voice, a woman calling:

"Yeshua."

He turns and opens his eyes. He smiles.

*

He is twelve years old, standing before several men who are seated on a balustrade in the shade of a columned portico. I recognize the Temple in Jerusalem. Beyond the pillars, crowds of people are milling about in a vast courtyard, and rising above it is the sanctuary.

I hear the voices of the elders as low rumbles, while the boy's is high and clear, but I cannot understand what they are saying. When I arrive, they have been in discussion for some time. He listens to them with attention and asks them questions. He replies to what they say in a calm and certain voice. They are amazed by the intelligence of his answers.

His robe is white and ankle-length, his feet sandaled, his long hair parted in the middle and neatly gathered into a single rope at the back of his head, secured by a brown cord. About his right forearm, cloth bands are wrapped, with a small leather case tied at the wrist.

He points to the case, then to the sanctuary, then to his heart. The men frown, look at each other, murmur among themselves. With my ears I hear what is said but cannot understand the language. Then, suddenly, I am hearing in a different way, as if the meaning of words is given to me independent of language:

"Fathers and teachers, I ponder," says the boy, "did not the Lord tell us that the word must be written in our hearts?"

Some of the old men nod in affirmation, regarding him with keen interest. Others look at him nervously or with disapproval. They do not like to be instructed or questioned in this manner.

"And if it is written in our hearts, does not the word become flesh?" he goes on.

"Little doctor of the Law", says one with a cool smile. "Do you know to whom you speak?"

"I know to whom I speak and from whom I speak", he replies.

"*From* whom you speak!" another exclaims. "What can this mean?"

The boy does not answer directly. Instead, he says:

"In paradise, glory and honor and praise is given continuously to the One who lives forever, seated upon his throne. And the elders fall down before him and worship him."

"What elders are these?" asks a middle-aged man.

"Nicodemus," says the boy, "surely you know of what elders I speak."

"How do you know my name, child?" the man asks in kindly fashion.

But another replies with subtle mockery:

"Oh, Nicodemus, how famous you are becoming that a country lad knows you so well!"

The others laugh.

Again, the boy does not reply to the question put to him. Instead, he says:

"The elders too will fall down before the Lamb of sacrifice."

At this, the old men begin to dispute with each other, and some are eyeing the boy suspiciously.

"Fall down?" says one.

"What lamb?" says another.

"Are you speaking of the prophets' visions?" asks a third.

"I speak of what I have seen", says the boy, gazing at them somberly.

Now a few of the men get to their feet with anger in their faces.

"Nonsense! Ridiculous! How can you say such a thing?"

"A child of Galilean fanatics, no doubt!"

"Wait, give the boy a minute", says a man who has until now kept silent. "These are not the eyes of a fanatic. There is learning in him and wisdom beyond his years."

"Yosef of Aramathea," says the boy, "we see what is already within ourselves, the good and the bad."

"Oho!" says one of the others. "It seems you are famous too, Yosef!"

"Let him speak", says Yosef.

The others murmur irritably but seat themselves again.

"You were telling us about a lamb", prompts Nicodemus. "Do you mean the Passover sacrifice?"

"Yes", says the boy. "In him is the Passover fulfilled."

"*Him? Him?* What are you saying?" cries an elder.

"The Son of Man is to be the Lamb."

A fractious discussion breaks out between the elders. None of them notices a poor rustic couple approaching. The boy turns to them and smiles.

The woman says, "Son, why have you done this to us? Your father and I have been searching for you in great anxiety."

The boy goes to them and takes their hands, looking up into their faces with guileless confidence. He loves them very much and is sorry they were worried. In a voice that only they can hear, he tries to explain:

"Did you not know that I must be in my Father's house?"

The man and the woman are perplexed by this. It seems to make no sense. The father puts an arm around the boy's shoulders and leads him away.

In the midst of the arguing elders, only Nicodemus and Yosef of Aramathea silently observe the father and mother and son melt into the crowd.

*

He is thirteen or fourteen years old, standing in the street before the Nazareth synagogue. He is among a company of boys his own age. Of the twenty or more gathered there, he is neither the tallest nor the shortest, yet he is the quietest. He stands with another boy who, like him, is silently facing the open doorway. The rest are nervously twitching, jostling, whispering to each other.

Men file out of the building, with prayer cloths over their heads. All the boys stand straighter and flip cloths over their own heads.

Each man goes to a boy and leads him inside the building, father with son.

Last of all, a man goes to the two remaining boys. He smiles at them, murmuring, "Yeshua, Yaakov." They step forward, one to his left and the other to his right. For an instant the man puts his hand to the shoulder of one and says:

"Yaakov, your father is with Abraham, and thus today I am your father."

The boy nods solemnly.

They move toward the synagogue.

I wish to follow them, and try to do so, but an invisible hand prevents me. It is not permitted.

The boy named Yeshua halts in the entrance and looks back at me. His eyes speak, but what he says I do not understand. He goes inside.

*

He is about fifteen years old, standing in the backyard of a shop, observing a man at work. A clay furnace is throwing off tremendous heat, its mouth open wide to reveal a heap of red and white embers. The man, about twenty years old, with bare muscled arms, and sweat dropping off his forehead, manipulates tongs to remove a bar of metal from the furnace. Swiftly he transfers it to an anvil, takes up an iron mallet, and begins to hammer. The clanging is loud but is a pleasurable sound nonetheless. The boy steps closer.

The man flattens one end of the red-hot metal, then takes an awl and bangs three holes into it. That done, he begins to beat the other end, making it turn little by little around the anvil's rounded side. When the bar has been reshaped into a hook, he thrusts it into a bucket of water. In the cloud of hissing steam, the man pauses to wipe sweat from his brow.

"You are making a pruning hook today, Asher?" says the boy. His voice is no longer a child's.

The man nods. "Yes, and I could use some help."

"I would help you gladly, but it is already made."

"There is the handle still to make. Can a carpenter's son make a handle?"

"If you give me the wood, I will make you a handle."

With a look of eager concentration the boy rolls up his sleeves and takes the pole of olive sapling that the man gives him. With a short saw he cuts it down to the desired length, slightly longer than a hand's grasp. With mallet and chisel he splits the piece carefully into two halves along its length. That done, he uses a brace and bit to bore three holes in each, measuring with his eye to make sure they are in line with the holes in the hook's handle, which is now cool and has been removed from the bucket.

Asher, with a studious frown, takes the wooden parts and fits them to the metal. The holes match perfectly.

"Good", he says.

The boy stands by and watches as the man inserts rough wooden pegs into each of the holes, then taps them until they tightly join the handle's parts together. With a smaller hammer he flattens their ends on both sides.

"Now we are done", says the boy.

The man brandishes the hook above his head as if he is pruning branches.

"This will cut air or butter," he says, "but nothing else until we sharpen it."

He takes a honing stone and scrapes along the inside of the hook.

"Here, you do it, Yeshua", he says, giving the boy the stone and hook. The boy sits down on the ground and sets to work.

As the scraping continues, the man takes up another bar, pumps the oven's bellows, and thrusts the bar into the flaring coals. Stepping back a few paces from the resurgent heat, he stands with his hands on his waist, staring at the fire, waiting for the bar to turn red.

"Asher", says the boy. "Do you remember when the prophet Daniel speaks about fire?"

"You mean the three young men in the fiery furnace? Yes, of course."

"I am thinking about another place. In one of Daniel's visions he saw the Most High, the Ancient of Days, taking his seat upon a throne, and his throne was a blaze of fire with wheels of burning fire."

"Ah, yes, I remember it now."

Scraping, scraping, with his eyes on the blade, Yeshua says: "The vision terrified the prophet, yet it is easily forgotten by men."

Asher shrugs. "That is the way we are. Always forgetting important things and remembering nothings from morn till night."

The boy continues to scrape.

"But if I were to forget my little nothings," chuckles Asher, "I would soon burn my hand or flatten my thumb. There is divine fire and there is earthly fire. But the earthly fire too has come forth from the Creator of the world and with a book of rules to manage it."

"Yes," says Yeshua, "everything is given from above."

"Here, let me test that edge", says the man, going down on one knee, sliding his thumb along the blade. "Yeshua, where is your strength? Push harder, but watch that you do not slice your fingers."

So the boy pushes harder. Sweat is now beading on his brow. He pauses to wipe his face with the back of his hand.

"Asher," he says in a musing tone as he resumes his work, "could it be that the fire of the Most High acts on us as earthly fire acts upon iron?"

"What do you mean?"

"The iron is hard and cold and often grimed with dirt and rust. When you put it into your oven, it is cleansed. It is changed into the likeness of fire itself."

"Yet it keeps its shape in there", says Asher, staring at the bar in the flames. "It does not cease to be what it was."

"Is it not more true to say that it becomes what it is?"

With a furrowed brow, Asher glances at the boy.

"*Becomes* what it *is*?"

"Becomes what it was meant to be from the beginning."

The man does not really understand. He shrugs it off. "Maybe", he mutters, and takes up the tongs to turn the bar.

"Asher," says the boy, "the Holy Spirit of the Most High is a stream of fire. That fire when it comes will warm and soften and purify a man, and then he will be transformed."

*

The night stars are blazing over the hill country. A small town is preparing for sleep beneath a quarter moon, the last lamp-lights flickering in a few open windows. I am standing at a distance beyond the edge of habitation, listening to the chanting of men's voices. It is prayer, and after prayer there is song.

Then I see a movement in the upper heights, a pale shape among the rocks and bushes, making its way slowly down toward a building that I now recognize as the synagogue of Nazareth. In an instant I am before the portico of the entrance but am keeping my eyes on the approaching shape. At first it looks like a descending cross; then I see that it is a human, carrying another in its arms.

Now they are here. Two men. The one who carries the other carefully lowers him to the ground at the back of the building. Inside, the chanting has resumed. The younger man—in fact, a youth—helps the carried one to kneel by the wall. Both remain without motion or speech, leaning with their foreheads pressed to the wall.

The chanting ceases. Shortly after, groups of men talking in low voices leave the synagogue and go their separate ways. When the last lamps of the town are extinguished, the two at the rear of the building stir themselves. The young man lifts the other into his arms and carries him up into the hills.

*

The sun is at midmorning; the day is hot. The hillside is seared by summer drought while the broad valley below is verdant green. Walking toward me along a dusty lane is the one I have come to recognize as Yeshua. He is now about sixteen or seventeen years old. The skin of his face is sunburned brown; on his chin is the sparse growth of his first beard.

He carries a tree trunk balanced on one shoulder, a beam about ten foot-lengths from end to end. Hanging on a belt strap at his waist is a short axe. He is wearing sandals on his dusty feet, and on his body a rough-weave working garment that hangs to his knees. It is soaked about the neck and arms with sweat. The weight of the tree strains every muscle. His mouth is open, panting.

Approaching the edge of the village, he stops for a rest, setting the log onto the ground beside the path. On a rise in a nearby field of weeds stands a thatched house, a conglomerate of stone and earthen bricks, with additions made of wood poles, unevenly plastered with mud. Numerous people are leaving the place, all carrying household objects, some with satisfied looks on their faces, others in quarrelsome discussion. Yeshua waits until all have departed, then regards the house for some minutes, examining its open door and the torn cloths hanging out the windows like parched tongues. He wipes his hands on his chest and then goes up to the house.

He stands for a moment at the doorway. He hears muted sobbing within. Entering the dwelling, he finds a man about forty years old sitting on the dirt floor with his face in his hands, his back to a wall.

Yeshua waits, saying nothing.

At last the man looks up with red eyes and is startled by the other's presence.

"There is nothing left", he murmurs with a choked voice. "There is nothing for you to purchase. The creditors have taken it all."

"I have not come to purchase anything", says Yeshua. "I heard your voice calling as I was walking past."

"I did not call", says the man.

"You called to me, though you did not know the one whom you called."

The man wipes his eyes on a dirty sleeve and gazes at the visitor with momentary curiosity. But he seems to have no strength to inquire further, for his troubles are too great. He hangs his head.

"Go away", he whispers.

"I wish to stay with you", says Yeshua. "I am hungry and thirsty."

"Water you may have from the skin at the door peg," says the man, "but I have nothing for you to eat."

"Is there not something in that pot?"

On the floor beside the man is his last possession, a cracked clay pot, chipped at the rim.

"No one wanted it", he says. "It is all that is left to me, and it is empty."

"A thing may appear empty and yet not be truly empty", says the visitor.

"Look inside for yourself, if you will."

Yeshua bends and peers into the pot.

"It is not empty", he says.

"If you like to eat chaff, it is not empty", retorts the man, with bitterness working in his features and tears brimming again.

"What has brought you to this?" asks Yeshua with sympathy.

"It is my sins that have brought me to this. Though I know not what they are, for they are hidden from my eyes, but they must be great indeed if the Most High punishes me and my family thus."

"The Lord Most High is not punishing you."

"Does not holy scripture tell us over and over again that he rewards the just man?"

"Does not the holy scripture say that many are the trials of the just man, but out of them all the Lord delivers him?"

Now the man looks up.

"Do I know you?" he asks. "I seem to know you. Oh yes, you are the son of the carpenter. I have seen you at the synagogue."

"And you, sir, what is your name?"

"I am Iyyov Bar Havel."

"And where is your family?"

"They could not bear to see the stripping of our home. My wife Michal is now with our twelve young ones in the valley, gleaning the fields. If they gather enough cast-off grain we may have bread for a day or two, but where we will bake it and under what roof we will sleep I do not know. We are left with nothing but ourselves."

"How has this come to pass?"

"Sickness took my ewes and lambs, a wolf seized the donkey, and the blight and worm killed the grain of our little plot and all the vegetables too. The sun burned up the rest. I borrowed and begged enough to keep us until the rains and next year's planting, but now the lenders demand their payment. The pockets of the generous are sealed against a family so large. There is no work to be found, and by nightfall the house will be taken too. Nor will the new owner let us stay a day longer. He and his men will beat me when they come, if they find me here."

Yeshua kneels before the man.

"Go away", says the latter. "Go away or they will beat you too. Besides, I have nothing to give you."

Still the visitor does not leave. He merely continues to gaze into the other's face. Iyyov lowers his eyes, then covers them with his hands.

"You say you have nothing to give me?" says Yeshua. "Look again and tell me if you have nothing to give me."

The man reaches to the pot and turns it over. Out spills a handful of chaff.

"Look again", says Yeshua.

He looks again.

"You see, there is nothing."

"Iyyov Bar Havel, look within your very self."

His face contorted with anguish, the man lowers his head and slowly puts his hands out before him, the palms trembling and open.

"Nothing", he whispers.

Then a change comes over him; his face grows quiet, and it seems as if he is now seeing something behind the screen of his closed eyelids.

"Oh, what I would have given to the Lord!" he sobs. "I would have given him true devotion and a holy life offered up for him, but I could not. I would have given him the first-fruits of my field and flock for the Temple in Jerusalem and for the house of prayer in Nazareth. I would have fed my wife and children on the good of his bounty, for he is the giver of all good things. But now they go hungry, gleaning the fields of others like sparrows and mice! I would have given abundantly the fruits of my labors to the poor as well. But now I *am* the poor! I would have raised myself up before dawn to praise him, and I would have lain myself down to sleep with praises on my lips. But now the heart is torn out of me, and I can lift my voice in prayer no more! I would have given him my children as people to love and serve him. But my children have seen with their eyes that those who follow the Lord most closely are cast out! I have failed them, for I was too small for all this need! I have failed the All-Holy One, for I was not holy! I would have gone to my old age with the Torah written in my heart and on my lips. But now I cannot think, I cannot remember his words, which were sacred to me, which I wrote on my doorpost and never failed to kiss upon entering and leaving my home. Now doorpost and home alike are taken away! Now I must go down into dust! And great my fear—great my fear—that my beloved little ones will soon lie there with me!"

I am seeing what Iyyov sees, feeling what he feels, and it is dreadful to me. I am filled with panic, struggling to awake, but I cannot.

Now the lips of the man are silent, and his heart begins to speak. I see him before a great court and a greater throne, and multitudes are listening:

"Yet will I praise his holy name, now and forever! From bounty I have praised you, O Most High, and now from the dust I praise you!

"I give you my life, which you first gave to me. I give you the love I poured out for my wife and children, whom you have given to me. I give you the strength and the knowledge and the fertile soil you gave unto me, year after year throughout all my days until now. I give you the labor of my hands, which you have filled with countless good things throughout all my life until now. I give you my hands, though they are empty. I give you my heart, though it is empty. I give you my mind, though it is empty. For all things come from you and all things must return to you, their giver.

"My Michal you gave to me, and our children you gave to me, though I was not worthy of them!"

Now, one by one, the man offers every member of his family, the eldest to the youngest, pausing over each as he sees their distinct souls, their qualities, their beauty, the love within them, the good they have done in their lives. And he thanks the Most High for the gift of each life and offers it back again. He asks for nothing. He only offers.

"Nothing have I to give you but this empty pot and handful of chaff, for it is me. Praised be your holy name, now and forever. From bounty I have praised you, and now from the dust I praise you!"

His chest heaves a great sigh. All anguish is gone from his face. Emptiness and sadness remain, but there is also peace.

Yeshua takes him by the elbow and helps him to rise to his feet.

"Sir," he says, bowing toward Iyyov, "I have heard of a man with rich fields down in the Jezreel Valley not far from here. His foreman has departed for another region, and the owner is searching for a reliable man to take his place. There is a house to live in for the one he hires. May I take you to him?"

Stunned, Iyyov does not reply, but allows the young visitor to lead him outside. With no more said, they walk through the yard to the path and make their way together to the road that goes down to Jezreel. As they are entering the valley bottom, they see a smiling woman walking toward them surrounded by several children. The oldest among them shoot their hands into the air and shout, "Abba, we have good news!"

The youngest ones, recognizing their father, run on ahead with beaming faces, laughing and leaping.

"Abba, Abba, Abba!"

*

The sky is deep blue over Nazareth, and the fields below are a lighter blue with the flax fields in full bloom. Six youths stand together in a pasture above a house where a wedding celebration is in progress. Below them, people are dancing in circles hand in hand. The music of lyres, harps, drums, and flutes is loud and joyous. The youths are watching it all, smiling. Some of them clap their hands in rhythm.

The six are robed in white garments, but each wears a different-colored belt. They are cousins to each other, related by blood or marriage. Yeshua, now eighteen, is among them.

A group of girls—young women—run forth from the dance to catch their breath on the edge of the celebration. They are flushed and animated, laughing and talking all at once, though what they say cannot be heard by the youths on the hill, who remain unnoticed by those below.

The youths gaze at them with admiration and a quickening of hearts.

"Oh, so beautiful!" breathes one named Yehudah.

"Have patience, brother", says one named Yaakov. "Three months more until your wedding day."

"And don't forget how Yaakov our forefather waited seven years for Rachel!" says one named Shimeyon.

"I would be willing to labor fourteen years if her father were Laban."

"How blessed you are that he is not."

"Still," sighs Yehudah, "this waiting of love is an eternity."

Their eyes shining with affection, all six continue to watch the maidens below.

"Waiting is the fasting of love", says Yeshua.

"How sweet and good they are," exclaims one named Yosef, "like the best of wine and finest bread."

"If woman had not been created," says Yaakov, "our hearts would become deserts."

"It seems that the Most High has made them very different from us!" exclaims Shimeyon, who is the youngest.

The others look at him and chuckle.

"Shimeyon, has your father spoken with the father of Esther?" Yosef asks.

"Not yet. He says I am too young to be betrothed. Next year perhaps."

As the discussion continues along this line, Yeshua glances at one of his cousins, a somber youth with tousled beard and of uncouth appearance who has remained silent until now. Without a word, they turn from their kin and walk up higher in the pasture.

Reaching a crest midway to the height of land, they sit down on a rock side by side.

"Yochanan, you have come a great distance to be here, and I am glad of it."

"I am glad of it too", replies the other in a voice that is rough, unaccustomed to speaking.

"In my soul I hear that soon you will go a great distance farther."

Yochanan glances at his cousin with interest.

"Why do you think this? Rather, how do you know it?"

Yeshua does not answer.

"Well, it is true that I mean to go away."

"Into the desert?"

"Yes," Yochanan nods, "into the desert."

"To Moab in the lands beyond the Jordan?"

"Yes, there. It is a place where I have been at times, alone."

"Do you have peace in that place?"

"Much peace, for among the rocks and briars I hear a voice speaking in my soul as nowhere else."

"The breath of the Holy Spirit, the still, small voice that Elijah heard."

"I believe it is so. Whenever I hear that voice, I become who I was meant to be."

"Meant to be from the beginning."

"Yes, from the beginning."

"If the Most High calls you, then you must go."

"Yeshua, though we have met but three or four times in our lives, I seem to know you better than I know any other."

"Yochanan, I know you too."

"How has it come to us, this mystery of knowing?"

"Did your mother not speak of it before her death?"

"A little. But she told me more about your mother."

Yeshua smiles. "And my mother told me about yours. You danced in her womb, she said."

Now Yochanan smiles. "It must be so, though I do not remember it, of course. She told me things about you too. But that is for a day when the Most High will reveal it. I cannot speak of it."

"Nor can I, until the appointed time. Still, in the heart of the soul, one may hear and know a thing before it has been revealed."

"Yes. And that is why I must now go into the desolate places and find a spring of water. As Mosheh brought forth water from the rock, so shall we."

"*We*? Do you mean our people? Or do you mean yourself and me?"

"Yeshua, the Lord brought forth the unexpected water for our people. For all peoples he will bring forth the unexpected living water. From our people, the Lord brought forth the unexpected birth. For all peoples he will bring forth the unexpected second birth."

"And all this he has shown you in the desert?"

"In the desert he has shown me some of what will come to pass, though not everything. I know this: My task is to obey. And in this obedience is my joy. From this obedience, and from yours, he will bring forth the long-expected salvation."

"But I think it will not be as men now commonly suppose."

"Nay, my brother, I believe you *know* it."

Yeshua nods. "The prophets also knew."

"They knew because they had been purified in the refiner's fire."

"And is it for this reason, Yochanan, that you also are called out into the desert, there to be tested by fire?"

"Yes, that is why. So that I might become a voice crying out in the desert, to prepare the way for the one who comes after."

"You quote Isaiah, who spoke of the herald to come. Thus, the prophet prophesied the prophet."

"And he in turn will be the prophet of the One", whispers Yochanan with a light in his eyes. "Yet of these two, the first is lesser and the last is greater. The lesser was born first, and the greater born after."

Yeshua regards him with solemn attention.

"I am the lesser", says Yochanan. "And great is my joy that it is so."

"I very much desire to go with you into the desert", says Yeshua with yearning.

"Is that the Father's will? O wondrous blessing it would be, were you my fellow sojourner. But it is not to be. Here you must live as other men, and here you will grow and labor and do much good until the appointed day."

"When will that day come?"

"You will know when it approaches. You will know when you need to know it."

Without further speech, as if they have come to a mutual understanding, both young men rise and remove prayer shawls from around their necks. They stand, put the cloths over their heads, raise their arms, and pray.

In unison they recite: "*Shema Yisraeil Adonai Eloheinu Adonai echad!* Hear, O Israel, the Lord is our God, the Lord is One!"

Yochanan cries out: "*Barukh sheim k'vod malkhuto l'olam va'ed!* Blessed be the name of his glorious kingdom for ever and ever!"

Yeshua's voice leaps higher, the words rising among the swallows on the wing circling above them: "*V'ahav'ta eit Adonai Elohekha b'khol l'vav'kha uv'khol naf'sh'kha uv'khol m'odekha!* And you shall love the Lord your God with all your heart and with all your soul and with all your might!"

They remain in silent prayer for a time. At last, turning to each other, they bow, and Yeshua goes back down the slope to rejoin the wedding party. Yochanan watches him descend and mingle with the crowd. He turns away and climbs to the height of the hills above Nazareth and passes over into other lands.

*

I am standing on a hill overlooking Jerusalem to the east. The sun is setting behind me, casting rose and gold over the mighty city. All about me are thousands of tents, multipatterned and multicolored, made from cloth and animal hides. The shouting-laughing voices of children running between the tents can be heard in every direction, adding to the braying of donkeys and loud conversations among adults gathering before countless cook fires.

Yosef Bar Yaakov stands nearby in a small clearing within a circle of tents. He is tethering a donkey to a stake and talking with a group of men his own age, all in their late forties. Their robes are soiled and travel-worn, their feet and bare shins dusty. They have removed their sandals and are savoring the feel of grass between their toes. The discussion is animated yet companionable. These men know each other, for some are fellow Nazareans and some are Yosef's relatives from other villages.

Yeshua is feeding a handful of grain to the donkey and stroking its back, all the while listening to the men's conversation. He does not intrude on it. He is now about twenty years of age, his beard longer and fuller, his face thoroughly a man's—all trace of the boy and youth gone from it. He listens with an inner repose, with total attention—not so much to what is being said by the others, for that is about weather and travel, but rather to their states of mind or soul. His eyes often return to his father's face, and sometimes he smiles at what the man says. The words are not amusing; it is the quality of the man himself that the son loves greatly.

He leaves the group and walks to a tent at my right hand. It is a small one made of goat hide, cut into black and white strips sewn into a ribbed pattern. The door flap is open, and a breeze billows the tent, tugging at the ground pegs. There is an awning on one side, or more exactly an extra room with one wall open to a view of the city. It is floored with mats and blankets. On these sits a woman about thirty-five years old, unpacking food from a basket.

Yeshua kneels before the woman and gives her a small wild-flower. She smells it and thanks him with a look. He sits down on the ground outside, observing her work.

He notices her glancing about the clearing and understands that she is seeking her husband with her eyes. There he is, their Yosef, bending over the donkey's legs, scraping pebbles from the insides of the hooves.

"I long for the day when he will come to me", says Yeshua in a reflective tone, his eyes shining. His mother sees how much he loves his father, yet she is puzzled.

"He is here with us, Yeshua. What do you mean?"

He looks back at her steadily. He desires to explain something, but that is not yet possible. She would not understand it with her mind, though she would understand it with her heart.

Is it the time to speak? Is it the time to reveal another coming sorrow that will be the gateway to a new joy? He is uncertain of this. For now, he merely smiles at her and asks what she is preparing for their supper.

But I know the meaning of his words, "I long for the day when he will come to me."

He longs for the day when Yosef will die so that he will come into eternal joy.

*

I am walking. I do not know where I am going, for my eyes are cast down. I see only my lower legs and my feet. I am robed but barefoot. The surface underfoot is rocky, and I can see only a little space in front of my toes. Walking, walking, walking. To where, from where, I do not know.

Now the sun sets, the light fades, and I am still walking.

The sun rises, and I have not ceased to walk. Suddenly, without warning, my toes teeter over a precipice, but I am halted and I do not fall into it—saved not by my own knowledge of an approaching peril but by something else. By what I do not know.

I hear a voice cry out:

"By the Lord are the steps of a man made firm. Though he fall, he does not lie prostrate, for the hand of the Lord sustains him."

Now I am walking again, my eyes cast down, unable to lift my face to scan the path ahead. It is the same as before, though now the ground is uneven, ever rising, and strewn with sharp stones. I am feeling deep grief over the follies of my youth. I stumble and fall from time to time. I pick myself up, but still I cannot raise my head.

Now my legs and feet are increasing their speed. My heart beats harder, my breath becomes a wind rushing in and out of my lungs. My eyes remain fixed on the ground before me, even as I begin to run.

Rising suddenly before me is a wall of fire, and my feet propel me into it at full speed. My body bursts into flames; my eyes are melting. But I am pulled back by an unseen hand.

I hear: "Not yet."

*

Yeshua is walking in the light of day's end. All about him is a high rocky land where no living thing grows. He pauses and looks down into a broad, deep valley. At its bottom is a lake receding into the distance, ringed by wastelands, guarded by barren mountains. The sun is a red ball balanced upon the teeth of a ridge on the other side of the lake.

As he gazes into the shadowed rift, he sees two cities on the plain not far from the water. They are entirely in flames, churning up billows of black smoke that rise and spread until they fill the air with noxious stench and further reduce the light of the sky.

He glances along the far shore and there beholds a tower of rock, on the top of which sits a fortress. It is ringed by armies on the valley floor. The armies are blaring trumpets, banging drums, and hurtling missiles over the fortress walls. In answer, a rain of arrows falls upon the besiegers, but they press on and begin to climb.

The fortress becomes a winepress, filling with the blood of men and women and children. When it is full, the wine spills over and runs down the slopes of the rock and spreads throughout the valley. Yet the valley is not watered by it and remains sterile.

Yeshua kneels and raises his arms to the sky.

Then I see that he is no longer alone. A shadow approaches from lower in the hills—a man whose face I cannot see. He draws nearer, comes to a stop before Yeshua, and begins to speak to him.

Yeshua seems weighed down by something invisible. He is thinner than before, and I know that he is very hungry. In his heart are feelings of horror, and in his flesh there is gnawing deprivation. He lowers his arms and covers his face with his hands.

The shadow points to rocks about his feet, then points to Yeshua's belly. Yeshua does not look at him. He replies, but what he says I cannot hear.

Again, he raises his arms to the heavens, the palms open like a beggar's cup. His head is bowed, his eyes closed. The shadow steps forward as if to put something into the open palms, but Yeshua speaks and the shadow staggers backward.

The shadow turns toward me. I too am hungry, afraid, and alone. My belly is emptier than it has ever felt before. I open my hands to the shadow, for if Yeshua will not accept what is offered, it might be good enough for me.

Now the hood of the shadow falls back and I behold the face within it. It is a noble countenance, full of all knowledge and power, and it wishes me well. I step forward to receive what it would give.

Without warning, Yeshua rises up and steps between me and the shadow, his back to the other. Into my hands he places a cracked earthen pot. I thrust my hand into it and pull out a handful of chaff. I cry out in disappointment.

"Eat", says Yeshua.

I cram the dry stubble into my mouth, choking. Then to my astonishment I taste the chaff and find that it has become bread—bread made from finest wheat.

*

My eyes are closed. I feel my body lying on soft turf with a cool breeze upon my cheek. I smell the perfume of new-growing grass, hear water running nearby. Birds are calling. I love them very much. It is because they are free to fly above the gravity that sucks mankind down to Elysion. I yearn to rise beyond death, yet I fear to do so. I would go upward if I could! But I cannot.

Now I hear the murmuring of human voices. I open my eyes and see that I am lying on a riverbank, and two men are standing near me in the water. Yeshua is knee-deep in it, and

Yochanan is beside him. Yochanan cups his hands and fills them with water, then pours it over Yeshua's head.

A white bird descends from the clouds. It hovers above Yeshua.

Then *kronos* itself becomes water, ever-flowing, rising into clouds, the clouds spilling rain, filling rivers and seas, the seas rising into clouds again, the past becoming the present and the present becoming the future, as the waters flow ever onward. Loukas is swimming in it now. He is six years old, laughing and calling to a man and woman who stand on the shore watching him—Thea and Timo. Their son is leaping and splashing about in the river Axios. The meadow birds of Macedonia are wheeling above his head.

A speck appears in the sky and slowly spirals down, then becomes a bird. Its color is radiant blue, not a reflection of the sun but glowing from within. Smaller than a sparrow, it hovers above Loukas' head, and then it grows in size and perches on his shoulder. He notices it and ceases to jump about in the water. Held in wonder, open-mouthed and smiling, he gazes at it steadily, listening to its song. Now the singing enters his heart and flows through it, and out again through his lips.

The river is rising. At first the boy is waist-deep in it; then the current is at his chest, then his neck. Swiftly it becomes a torrent that covers his head.

I cry out in alarm, "Loukas, Loukas!"

I race toward the shore and into the shallows, then leap into deeper water in hope of saving him before he drowns. But the current pulls me away from him and pushes me under. I gasp for air; my lungs fill; I am drowning.

Now I am rising again, coughing water from my lungs. I swim desperately toward the place where Loukas went down. As I reach it, he bursts upward from the depths and rises into the air. He is entirely enfolded by the bird, which is now very great in size. As they rise together, the bird becomes white. Together they disappear into the sky.

Near me stand Yeshua and Yochanan. The last drops of water trickle down from Yeshua's head, and I see that the Axios has become the Jordan.

*

Darkness. I hear a woman groaning. The light increases, and now I see her. She is kneeling alone in a desert under a lowering sky that is latent with rage. She is pregnant and in labor, crying aloud with pain. I rush forward to assist her, but a maddened wind blows between us, blurring my eyes with smoke and dust. As she continues to cry out, I stumble through thorn bushes and rubble, searching for her. At first I think she is Leto giving birth on her floating island, but then I remember that we are in a barren flatland.

I hear thunderous roaring and see darts of flame all about. The woman appears before me, surrounded by light, the child coming forth from her body and about to fall into the open jaws of a dragon.

I shout and leap forward to stop it, but the image dissolves.

Now I see a baby about one year old, crawling on all fours in the dust. He is laughing and singing little songs as he goes along. He pauses beside a small hole in the ground and sits himself upright, looking at the hole.

The head of a snake appears in the mouth of the hole; then slowly the serpent emerges, encircling the child all around. I shout in alarm, for it is a deadly viper.

I rush forward to seize it, knowing that this will cause my death. I will die, but I will fling it far away from the child. The serpent spots me and arches its neck to strike my hand as I reach for its throat.

400

Before it can sink its fangs into me, a foot stamps on its head.

I look up. It is the woman. Her heel firmly on the head of the lashing serpent, she bends and picks up the child, holds him closely to herself. When the serpent's convulsions cease, she removes her heel from its crushed head and begins to nurse the child.

I fall down on my back in the dust, unhurt but stunned.

It is nearly unbearable, this terror, this beauty, and I wake up.

*

[Journal entry, December 21, A.D. 65]
Poseideion—December

And so I awoke from my dreams. I learned from a sailor who brought me food and drink that I had fallen into delirium again. For days I had raved, he told me, but the worst was over now and I was recovering. I went to the deck on wobbling legs and clung to the rails, breathing deeply the fresh sea wind.

Moved, disturbed, perplexed, I could not assess the meaning of those dreams. Were they Homer's and Vergil's gates? Were they the horn of reality or the ivory of splendid delusion?

Four days later, when the *Hesperos* sighted the east coast of Crete, my heart quickened, for home was near. Yet it seemed to me that what I had once called my home was no longer entirely so. And what I had once called my self was no longer entirely so. Hour after hour, I walked the ship from prow to stern and wrestled with this sense of displacement. That I had been changed I could not dispute. I had looked farther into the world than my eyes had ever looked before. But what, really, had I seen? Visions and dreams? Sleeping reality or waking phantasms? Faces and scenes arose in my mind, cities and villages, power and weakness, fate and providence, old blood and new blood, rich men and poor men, the ignorant and the wise—yet in all that vast crowd of witnesses and deniers I could not find myself.

From the stern of the ship I viewed the past. From its prow I gazed ahead into the future. Both were mysterious; both were beyond my ability to comprehend.

By nightfall we were coasting parallel to the southern shore, and I began to recognize island landmarks. My yearning grew and grew for the sight of my family, for their warm embraces, their familiar arms in which I might rest, the consoling safety of the known and beloved.

I thought most of my Paeonia, of her goodness, her wisdom, her abiding care for me. Then of my daughters and their children. They lived in this one solid place in the revolving world, positioned in orbit because of my choices made so many years ago. Love had compelled us, each in his own way, to make a covenant of our lives: father and husband; wife and mother; child and parent and grandchild; sons-in-law; and a son in heart. Yes, all fused together through the heart, by love unto love in its myriad forms.

But what, really, was love? What was its source and what was its end, and what determined the route of its journey from embarkation to arrival at port?

*

The ship docked at Fair Havens the next evening in the midst of a winter storm. The sea outside the curve of the bay was a madly thrashing thing, and even by the wharf the hull lifted up and down dangerously. The passengers made it ashore without mishap, and there we found a cartman willing to take us through the dark on the road to Gortyna. It was raining heavily by then, but the cart was tented over, the canvas roped fast to its staves. Some Roman soldiers hunching inside their capes rode along on horseback beside us, which gave us protection from road thieves.

The city was asleep when we arrived at its gates. Few lights shone in windows, but my feet seemed to know the way through the deserted streets and brought me safely to our district. My heart beat faster with each step. Home, home, I thought. O my beloveds, soon I will see your faces, which are the dearest in all the world!

And now at last I had come to the gate of my home. It was locked. I pounded with my fist and shouted through the lookhole to the dark house, but no one came to answer. Finally a spark appeared near the hut at the back of the garden and approached warily.

"Who be there?" demanded an old man's voice, which at first I did not recognize. "Who is it, fool or scoundrel? Answer me, or be off before I crack your skull!"

"Tranquilatus," I laughed, "it is Theophilos! Open this door and let me in, and please do not crack my skull."

After a rattling of keys and sliding of bolts, the gate door creaked open and I pushed my way in. There stood our gardener peering at me, shielding the lamp wick from the rain with his hand, his intimidating stick stuck through his belt like a sword.

"Aye, aye, Master, it is you in truth! Well, come in now and get yourself warm and dry."

"But why are you here so late?" I asked.

"I am watching the house while the mistress is away", he said.

"Away?" I cried, my heart sinking.

"Aye, away to Phoenix, visiting Theodosia and the children. We knew not when you would return, and I wager she was sore alone for missing you and needed the company. Cleon and Mila took her there three days past, and none have yet come back."

We were now in the kitchen, where the old man busied himself lighting a fire in the oven. He made noises of disapproval, clicking his tongue and muttering senseless things to himself.

"Then none of my kin are here?" I asked.

He shook his head.

"But when will they return?"

"When the new moon turns, if the weather be good."

Soon the chill was driven from the room, and warmth began to spread through the house. I bade Tranquilatus eat with me, and he came to the table and sat himself down on the bench facing mine. I noticed that his manner was uneasy, his eyes reluctant to meet my gaze. This was new behavior, since we had often eaten together, and whenever we did, the unwritten contract between master and servant was dismissed for a time. Though he was never garrulous, he had always used such occasions to raise questions about garden plantings and repairs to the house and to impart harmless bits of neighborhood gossip. Now, however, we ate in silence, consuming bread and cheese and a cup of wine. His manner was furtive, it seemed to me, as if he knew a secret that he did not wish to divulge. From time to time he shot a look at me from the corner of his eyes, a flicker, a frown, and then he returned to the food he was consuming so studiously.

"Is my family in good health?" I asked, observing his response with close attention.

"Aye," he nodded, "they are well."

He was not lying. But why did his glance linger on me, then dart away so quickly, as if he had seen something about me, or in me, that worried him? What had come over him; what had happened in my absence? Perhaps he was merely fatigued, an old man dragged from his bed in the middle of the night and eager to return to it. Yet I sensed that more was at work in him.

"What troubles you?" I asked in a low voice.

Again the eyes darted, he inhaled sharply, and his hands trembled a little before he brought them under control.

"Nothing", he murmured.

Abruptly, I opened my arms wide, about to protest that *something* was bothering him, when my hand hit my wine cup and it flew to the floor and smashed. Tranquilatus leaped up and began to gather the clay fragments in his hands.

"A nice cup, a nice cup", he mumbled and lamented. "Oh, what a pity, such a cup."

I watched him crawl about the floor gathering large pieces and wondered over the unprecedented sight of tears in his eyes. When he began to sweep up the finer splinters with his bare hands, I felt sorrow over his subservience to my mistake.

"We have abundant cups", I remonstrated. "Let it be. And go back to bed, for I can see that you are very tired."

He stood and bowed his head to me, the perfect picture of a docile servant, and departed for the hut, leaving me alone with my empty house.

I went into the bedroom, carrying a lamp, seeking the faint scent of my absent spouse. I noticed a white stone on the table beside the bed and picked it up. It was the one I had brought back from the theater Loukas and I made above the sea by Iraklion so many years ago. With my fingertips I traced the primitive lettering of his name and wondered why Paeonia had brought it here from my surgery. Had she looked at it each night and asked where her husband and son might be? Had she kept it as a sign that a son would be brought home to her again? I had failed to bring him home, and soon she would know. Soon she would grieve over it.

I blew out the lamp and lay down on the mattress. My mind and body and spirit were now gripped with a lonely anguish of a kind that I had not felt since the worst of my losses in Macedonia, when death had swallowed my family in near entirety. Yet I was so exhausted I could not remain awake to fight it.

*

I awoke in the late morning, at the hour before midday. My joints ached and my throat was constricted with the beginnings of an infection. The window showed a pale gray light beyond the heavy curtain of rain running off the roof. I flung my arm toward the space where Paeonia habitually slept, and the reality of her absence hit me full force. To escape the resurge of anguish, I hastily got up and made my way to the kitchen. There I found that Tranquilatus had made a fresh fire in the stove, though he was nowhere to be seen. I wondered where he had gone. A pot of hot water was simmering, and I drank a cupful mulled with lemon and cloves.

Throughout that day, as I waited for the rains to abate, I wandered restlessly from room to room, picking up objects that were tokens of her presence. Her distaff and spindle lay atop a basket of raw wool. I twirled the spindle as if it were a child's toy. Her summer cloak hung on a peg by the back door, and I embraced it with yearning. In the bathroom, I thought I should wash myself, or at least shave, but when I picked up the barber's blade I had no energy for it. There would be time enough to clean my outer appearance before her return. For now, I seemed to have no motive for it—nor for any other actions.

I tried to read in the library, selecting certain volumes that had been of utmost importance to me before my journey. But the words on the page held no interest now, and my mind slipped away, wandering, wandering in a gray land soaked in unceasing rain where all landmarks and all well-loved faces had dissolved.

I think I slept a little in the afternoon, or dozed half-awake, until I heard clinking and clanking in the kitchen, and got up. My throat was somewhat better, and no serious cough had developed. Yet I was chilled, and searching for my best *himation*, I found it neatly folded where Paeonia had stored it in the wooden trunk at the foot of our bed. It warmed me, and its bright blue color cheered me a little, though my feet were nearly numb. Thinking of Mattan the prophet of doom, I walked barefoot on the floor's cold flagstones to the kitchen and there found Tranquilatus stirring a pot.

"Good day, Master", he said with a dip of the head. "Since the family went away, Calliope has gone off to her village until they all return. Now that you're back, do you still want me to sleep in the hut and tend the fire?"

"Yes", I said abruptly, for I was irritated by his manner. Though the tone of his words was as usual, his facial gestures continued in the new pattern—guarded. What was he guarding, what was he hiding?

Ah, well, I told myself, he has always been odd, and it may be that some matter concerning his own family is burdening his innermost feelings. That he gives no hint of the cause means that it is not a thing with which I can help him, or it may be something shameful. I knew that he had a son in his home village, an hour's walk east of the city. Perhaps the son had run afoul of the law. I vaguely recalled that there were some granddaughters—or were they great-granddaughters? As any father knows, girls are ever a cause of concern, for their protection demands constant vigilance.

"Is your own family well?" I asked, again carefully observing the reply.

His eyes smiled for an instant, and he nodded. "Aye, all's well with them."

"And your own health?"

He didn't smile, but he made a humorous puckering of his lips, and from this familiar expression I learned there was no change in that regard.

"We grow old, we grow old, Master. Why should I complain about things? Everyone has ailments, and many are worse than mine."

"Indeed, we might all say such, for it is true."

He nodded and nodded. Then, surprising me, he went on:

"A man may drink a cup of wine, and when it is empty, he will look into it. He will say one thing or another."

"One thing or another? What will he say?"

"He will say with a bitter heart, 'Oh, see my cup is empty again. Always my cup is empty.' Yet another man will look into his empty cup and say to himself, 'Oh, what a fine cup of wine I have just drunk. It was most delicious.' "

For Tranquilatus, this was grandiloquence, a veritable outpouring of oratory.

"Do not worry about last night's broken cup", I said. "We have many, and besides, Calliope breaks them as a habit, not to mention the hundreds the children broke."

The furtive look returned to his eyes, and he changed the subject.

"Here's soup for you, Master. I went to the shops this morning and purchased bread and other foods. I paid with money from the kitchen coin pot; I hope you do not mind. May I go now?"

"I do not mind, and I am glad for your thoughtfulness. But stay and eat with me, if you wish."

"Thank you, but I must be off to my home. I have chores to do there. I will return to sleep in the hut each night. Two men and a stout stick is best for warding off thieves."

And thus another dreary day and night ensued. I slept off and on, drank hot water and lemon juice, got up, lay down, and all the while the sense of oppression increased. It was caused by the dismal light, of course, and the ceaseless sound of rain falling on the roof tiles and splashing on the stones in the garden. Once I glanced out the window at the statue of Aesclepios, and he looked as forlorn as I felt, his head bowed in abject despondency.

I slept again and awoke sometime after nightfall. Later I heard Tranquilatus enter the house with a rattle of keys. He looked in on me to ask if I needed anything, and when I told him that I did not, he went away to his hut for the night.

By the next morning, the rain had eased to a light drizzle, with much mist. I knocked on the door of the hut, but Tranquilatus had already departed for the day—off to the world of his own home, which must surely be more real and important to him than mine, and who could blame him for it? Yet I missed his presence. Nearly any presence would have sufficed, and I wondered at myself, for solitude had always been a comfort, never an affliction. I thought of sending a message to my family in Phoenix and wrote a note to Paeonia, sealed it, and wrapped it in waxed cloth as protection from the damp weather. Then I dressed myself to go out in the chill of the morning in search of a courier.

The streets ran with trickles, and standing pools of rainwater had collected here and there among the cobbles, with oozing mud in spots that lacked pavestones. The city seemed deserted, though I knew it was not so, for chimney pots spewed black smoke, which the heavy overcast pressed back down into the maze of houses, spreading the mingled scents of cooking and poorly burned damp firewood. Near the praetorium, I found a stable where carts were usually for hire, and always a runner boy who would take a message for a coin or two. But the cartman told me that the road to Phoenix had become impassable until the sun returned—a sea of mud, he said, though it was possible that a runner could go by foot, skirting the road on higher ground. The latter way would be several days' labor and thus would cost some silver. Four denarii, in fact.

The price was pure extortion. Regardless, I determined to send my message to Paeonia by this method. The owner of the place looked over the louts lying about on straw, an ill-groomed bunch who eyed me with resentment as they chewed on sticks of licorice root and scratched their hind ends like donkeys and generally pretended they had no interest in wages. But one who eyed my purse with some interest was given the task by his master, and a handful of copper pieces, with a promise of more when he returned after delivering my letter. The cartman pocketed the rest. After repeating my instructions until I was sure he had gotten it right—the House of Leandros in the Street of Lumber Merchants in Phoenix—the boy set off under an ox-hide cape, his rough feet smacking the cobbles like hooves.

Not wanting to return to my empty house, I wandered here and there and soon was soaked by drizzle. Without my realizing it, my feet brought me to Cleon and Mila's house. Peering through the look hole, I saw shuttered windows, no smoke in the chimney, and their violent watch-goose heading straight toward the gate, raising an alarming racket. With a sigh, I walked on.

In time I found myself approaching the Villa Varus near the Lethaios. I could hear the roar of the river's swollen passage and was forced to wade through inches of water, for it had flooded its banks. Gaius' villa was on slightly higher ground than the surrounding streets, and thus I stood on bare pavement as I banged on the gate. Repeated banging brought a servant, who peered at me through the hole, then opened the door reluctantly.

I pulled back my hood to expose my face. "Is your master home?" I asked.

"He has gone," mumbled the fellow, "and when he will return, none can say."

"*Can* not say or *will* not say?"

"Can not, for he left three weeks past, as did his wife and other kin."

The servant's logic was weak, and moreover, I could see that information would have to be dug out of him pebble by pebble.

"Where has he gone?"

"The family went to Tuscia for a time, where they have an estate. That is in Italy."

"Yes, I know it is in Italy. But I asked you where your master has gone."

A guarded look crossed the servant's face—this man who at one time had welcomed me into the villa as if I were a family member.

"Is he home but does not wish to receive guests?" I probed.

"Nay, nay, sir, that is not the case. Truly, he is gone."

"Then you must tell me where he has gone."

"Must I?" he replied, putting on the mask of a confused simpleton.

"Come, you can tell me, for I am his friend. I am Theophilos of Ariston. You know me well."

He rubbed his eyes and squinted, inserted a finger in one ear, and squeaked it around.

"Ah, Master Theophilos. Yes, yes, now I know you. I have a letter for you. Gaius Varus said I should give it to you when you return from your journeys."

"Then get it, man, and make haste", I growled, losing patience.

He was back in minutes and handed me a roll of parchment, and then I turned away.

Back in my kitchen, I lit a fire and set a few burning lamps on the table to dispel the gloom of the afternoon. I sat down, cracked the wax seal of Gaius' letter, and unrolled its single page. I read:

Dies lunae IV Non. December DCCCXVIII anno Urbis conditae

> A riddle for you to read upon your return,
> If I be not here to speak it or explain it.
> I go forth upon the sea in search of octopus,
> To hunt it and perchance to slay it,
> Or, if Fortune smiles less warmly,
> I shall drive it from our shores.

I much desire to give you the clay pot from Knossos. Do you remember it? Do you remember what we discussed that day, though our words were few and yours evasive? Ask my servant for it, and he will obey my instructions. Look at its lovely shape and ponder the image that the dangerous hand of a genius painted upon it. See the riddle and understand where I have gone.

If we do not meet again in this world, know that I am your friend in time and in eternity. For friendship's sake, take a walk in the hills beyond the east gate, and as you go, think about riddles and clay.

G. P. V.

Frowning, irritated, I read it again and again. What did this bit of nonsense mean? Gaius a riddler? Gaius a slayer of sea monsters? Why had he not simply explained the reason for his departure? And why had he lacked the courtesy to address me by name and chosen to sign the message without his full name? What joke was this?

The rain had ceased. The sky was still dark and the air full of reeking mists. Yet for friendship's sake I got up and went out in it, and like a sacrificial victim trapped in the Labyrinth, I picked my way through the maze of Gortyna's streets toward the city's east gate. Passing through it I came upon the main road and the lesser roads that swing away to north and south, ringing the walls. I turned north onto the one that would bring me into the foothills of the island's central range, thinking about riddles and clay as I went. The fresh air did me good, though it was thick with dampness, and there was poor visibility save for a short way ahead of my steps. Slowly the fog began to lift, exposing the hillside to my right. I walked on for a time until, without warning, I smelled stench. The pit of the dead was near, and I now realized that I was immediately below the hill of crucifixion.

I stopped, paralyzed momentarily by that most dreadful memory, the crucifixion of the eight that had so disturbed me more than a year ago. I turned around to reverse my steps back to the city, and then I noticed that the fog had lifted higher behind me and had become a low hanging cloud above the hill. I shuddered and would have turned away, but in an instant my eyes took in a sight that could not be accounted for. The hill was covered with crosses, so many that the crest was thick with them, and this forest had begun to creep down toward the road. In a panic, I desired to run away. But I could not, for my mind refused to believe what the eyes told it, and it determined to assert reason over optic illusion.

But this was not possible, for the crosses and the bodies upon them were real. Several dozen people were dying in agony, or had died, mostly men but some women as well, and a few youths who looked to be scarcely more than children. I climbed higher toward them. At the top, three Roman soldiers leaned on their spears, complaining loudly about rain and boredom and lost wagers they had made at the games in the city's gladiator arena. They eyed me moodily as I approached but did not warn me off. Standing here and there in the thickets of crosses, clusters of people huddled, weeping quietly, lifting their arms to the executed. I heard no screams of lamentation from them, no maddened grief. About the entire scene there was a most strange silence. I noted that all the bodies had been horribly mutilated by scourging and other tortures, and I marveled that some were still alive.

Suddenly, convulsed with outrage, I felt a searing flame of hatred for the soldiers and for Rome itself. I wheeled and went back down the hill. When I passed through the city gate, I hastened my steps and tried to run but succeeded only in stumbling and groping my way back to my home. Slamming the outer gates shut behind me, locking them, I went into the kitchen and fell onto a bench, staring at the tabletop.

The late afternoon murk in the sky steadily darkened, and once again the rain resumed its monotonous drone, heavier than ever. I lit lamps throughout the house, tried to eat something but could not, then stood at the open doorway hoping that Tranquilatus would soon return. I went to my library and sat for a while in the company of my books, those monuments to human reason, to all that was best in man's nature, yet they gave me no comfort. I stared into the flame of a lamp and tried to imagine the grieving people standing about on the hill and hoped they would have sense enough to return to their homes. I hoped, as well, that the soldiers were under orders to remain on guard and would sicken and die. I hoped that the cold rain would sooth, even if only a little, the burning pains of the criminals' lacerated flesh.

Criminals? Why so many all at once? And why crucifixion? There were dozens upon dozens of crosses. Had an insurrection flared up during my absence in Syria? If so, a strange insurrection it must have been with women and children among the rebels.

Tranquilatus knocked on the door several hours later and entered, bearing a package in his arms.

"Master, a servant of Gaius Varus came to the gate as I was arriving and asked me to give you this." He handed me a bundle of cloth, tied securely with string. "Sleep well", he muttered, his eyes averted as he turned away to leave. As he went out the door into the garden, I called after him, "Tranquilatus, do you know anything about the crucifixions?" But he did not hear me, and I watched as the old man, bent and weary, carrying only a spark of lantern light, entered the hut and closed the door.

*

How long was it? How long did I sit in the library with the clay pot before me on a low table? It may have been minutes, it may have been hours, and I recall only this—that the eyes of the octopus seemed alive, staring at me, at first catching my attention, then holding it, then growing ever larger in the ill-lit room. Now I deciphered Gaius' riddle, for the riddle had become a solid metaphor.

"Yes, I understand, my friend", I whispered. "May you fare well, and may you slip a blade between the ribs of the bloated god, or slit his throat so that no longer will the poetry of hell spew from his lips."

Was it assassination Gaius planned? Or was it a strategic word or two, uttered with a smile and urbane glance, on the heights of the Palatine among the *amici Caesaris*? I hoped for both. Most of all, I hoped for the blade to do its work. And it seemed to me that once the primary blade had cut evil's throat, other blades would then come into play across the whole empire, bringing down princes and governors who turned their high seats into thrones reigning over pits of the dead. State justice, they called their most odious acts. But that was a lie, for there was no spark of *iustitia* in them. My hatred grew and grew, like ink spreading in my innermost sea, and I seethed with lust for their deaths, for I believed now that murder must be countered by murder. I hoped that the gods—the benevolent ones—would guide the hand of Gaius to the pulsing vein in the killer's neck.

How long did I remain in thrall to that dark spirit, embodied by the painted figure on an ancient piece of clay; how long did my awakened malice clash against the omnipresent malice governing the world? I do not know. But the longer I remained in that mental condition, the more the struggle increased in intensity. As I stared at the spherical jug, I knew that its form had remained unchanged for a millennium, and that the eyes of the octopus were no more than two dots of paint. Yet with my innermost eyes I was seeing on another level, for the pot began slowly to revolve, and I understood that it was the world itself.

First, I saw Crete. All about our little island spread the great middle sea, and beyond it were the lands to north and south and east and west, and the greater seas farther still. The sphere increased its rotation, slowly at first then gathering speed, and all the while it floated upon the immensity of the *kosmos*, the superterrestrial sea. I plunged down toward the waters of the sphere and found myself alighting upon a small ship.

Midway between Italy and Syria and Africa, a black octopus surfaced before the bow. It began as a dark spot that swiftly swelled, became enormous, its eight legs spreading in all directions as it coiled entirely about the sphere. The eyes in its head stared straight at me, probing me with hatred so intense that I cried out and sought to flee from it.

Inhaling sharply, I blinked my eyes and sat straighter, laughed mirthlessly, and reminded myself that I was seated in my library in my own home. I told myself that my horror over the crucifixions on the hill, and my loneliness and fatigue, had stirred a dark imagining in my soul.

But within minutes my eyes were recaptured by the gaze of the octopus, and now I struggled to pull my thoughts away from it, to get up and leave the room, or to hurl the thing to the floor where it would shatter into fragments. But I could not. Then my heart beat faster, for the monster grew at a rate that no man could outrun or outswim. It opened its mouth and began to suck my ship into it—for I was again on the little ship—and it was intent on sucking everything into itself, all waters and lands and peoples pouring into its throat, as if after first enwrapping the world, then it would devour it, and finally it would *become* the world it had devoured.

"The darkness is winning!" I screamed, though to my ears the scream was a feeble choking sound.

Then I heard the voice of Xanthippos from the past:

The light will win, he said as he lay dying on a ship that bore us away from the plague city. *The light will win, and you must not doubt it. No human eyes can foresee the ways in which the war will be won.*

"But I am dying, Xanthippos, I am dying", I pleaded.

You are not dying, Theophilos; you are being born.

In hindsight, I now think that the memory of his wise and humble voice gave me strength for a moment, just enough to gather the wrapping cloths and throw them over the pot. I shook my head to clear my thoughts, breathing noisily for some minutes until my heartbeat slowed. I wondered if in ages past a witch had put magic curses on the thing, or if the shades of dead kings still haunted it, or if the darkness had nothing whatsoever to do with this clay creation but was wholly within me. Was the pot and its decoration no more than a fixed node onto which I had cast my own inner shadows? I did not know, and for the moment did not want to know. I busied myself tying it up with string and then carried it to the kitchen, where I placed it into a kindling box by the back door.

*

I returned to the library, still trying to shed the mood induced by ill fantasy and sleepless visions. I read a few passages from Horace, wanting my emotions soothed by beautiful phrases and my mind steadied by rational concepts, but the effort this demanded was too great for me, and I let the scroll roll closed by its own weight.

I drank a little wine, and when the cup was empty, I poured another. I have ever despised drunkenness in others, for after my brief experimentation with the condition when I was a youth, I had vowed never to repeat it. But my anguish now prompted me to take more than was my custom. I did not become drunk, nor did I feel even tipsiness, though the pain of my fears eased, and my thoughts, like an unmoored boat, began to drift.

In this cup of musing there was a sweet, dark pleasure with bitterness in the dregs. I, who throughout my life had sacrificed everything to do good to others, and to avoid doing harm, obeying my philosophers and my mentors Hippocrates and Xanthippos, now saw that a foul king's blood should be spilled, for he had slain countless people for ambition's sake or for amusement. Here, then, was murder in my own heart. Yes, I nodded to myself, it was there in us, we humans. I was not shocked by the revelation. No, I approved of it, for I felt it to be most honest. I smiled at this new understanding; indeed, I gloated with pleasure over it, and pondered ways in which solicitous killing might be done. Was it not an act of surgery upon the sick body of a people? A physician must murder the tumor that is murdering the patient, and thus this vile emperor must be excised, along with all the lesser growths that sprang up around him.

Another thought led logically from the first: Killing a man, then, was not wrong in itself. In war we do it, and in the suppression of the most dangerous criminals we do it. Death ruled the world. Death always ruled. And though we called death an evil, if one were to seize the instruments of death and wield them wisely for the purpose of serving the good, where was the evil in that?

Suppose that a man of honor were to hold the scalpel and that all those who harbored ill will toward the good were denied the instruments they used for *their* purposes. Then the good men of the earth would control the unfolding of human destinies and would labor always for the highest possible goals. Was this not just? Yes, it was very just!

During this dialogue with myself, recent memories surfaced, and I saw with new clarity the follies of the people who followed the cult of Yeshua. How blind, their pathetic capitulation to the rule of evil men! How cowardly, their refusal to seize the instruments of death, disguising their timidity as mystical philosophy! Their Yeshua was quite, quite dead, and had not risen from the grave, for no man returns alive from it. Their stories, their legends, their myths about themselves grew and grew, and thus the blindness increased until these people became incapable of seeing the true source of their beliefs. Their faith had its roots in something as old and as tragic as mankind's fate, and this thing, this dark undersoil of consciousness, was the rotting corpse of our supposed divinity. They could not accept the truth of man's mortality.

They might agree with me that my heroes and gods were no more than our very selves projected upon the empty universe. Yet in the next breath, these followers of Christos projected a new god and new heavens, casting a shadow of hope where there was no hope at all, for it led them into torture chambers and onto hills forested by crosses throughout the world. We Greeks were more honest about man's nature. When we worshipped, we knew that our imagined gods killed and were killed, tricked and betrayed, punished and rewarded, loved us or despised us, for in them we observed our own dramas writ large upon a stage. But the followers of Christos were dishonest about the nature of the world. They blamed all evils on a malevolent spirit whom they declared was as real as any man, but at the same time they did not doubt the very God who apparently had made that spirit.

I laughed bitterly and sipped my wine, remembering the stories I had been told about Yeshua, and my dreams of him on the *Hesperos*, and the chronicles I had read written by his devotees, my own son among them. Yes, the story was most impressive. This Yeshua would have his effect in the world, and his life would, to a degree, accomplish some good. But in the wake of that good a greater evil would come, and then the entire world would hate him. Moreover, the entire world would hate his followers, the visible images of their unseen god. And my Loukas would be nailed to a cross along with them.

I laughed derisively at such madness, though in the laughter there were unexpected tears, a grief so deep that it would have become a shout of pain were it to be given utterance. I calmed myself and turned my thoughts to Plato and Aristotle, even to Gaius' Cicero, fragments of their dialogues swirling in my mind. They had been the true heroes, those knowers and searchers. They had fought, and fought hard, against the lies by which man blinds himself. Socrates had drunk the hemlock only because he knew that this was his final argument, his final teaching, and that he had spoken all that he could to change men's minds, to illumine their motives, and that it had done little good. His students, he hoped, would recall some of what he said and write it down, and then some future generation might read it and begin to ask questions again—the questions that elevate a man from the level of a beast.

But what of Yeshua? He too had accepted death when he might have fled or fought it. His students wrote down his teachings. Yes, but there the similarities ended. Yeshua created no dialogues, no commerce of advanced thought for the stirring of man's proper meditation on reality. And that, it seemed to me, was the core weakness of their cult. There was no discussion. For them, it was all revelation, all given from above, and they, like mute beasts, must accept it unthinkingly and carry the crushing burden of his teachings as they plodded inevitably toward various forms of violent death.

Now I tried to imagine Yeshua seated across from me, listening to my arguments, unable to refute them.

"Why did you come into this world?" I asked. "Why did you promise salvation when, as you see these many years later, nothing has been saved by your words, still less by your sacrifice?"

Of course, he did not answer.

"You died on a cross, just as those poor people are dying on the hill of Gortyna."

I imagined his face as I had seen it in my shipboard dreams—first the boy, then the youth, next the man, and finally the wreckage of human flesh pinned fast to the wood and bled near dry, uttering its final gasps. From the cross he gazed back at me, his eyes fully attentive—and fathomless. And still he made no reply.

"Nothing changes", I said to him as the blood trickled down the tree and vanished into the indifferent earth. "You have not defeated death."

Yet he continued to look at me, and I lowered my eyes, not wanting to indulge the fantasy too far, for I knew the power of the mind's theater, knew that if a sea creature had access to it, so might a supposed god.

When I looked up again, we held each other's gaze for a moment, as if across an abyss.

Then my weariness swept over me like a wave, and I emptied my cup down my throat and flashed a look at him as if to bid him good night and good-bye forever.

"You say nothing", I whispered, shaking my head in pity for his futile life. "You say nothing because you no longer have anything to say, for death has spoken the final word."

I sighed, rose to my feet, and turned toward the lampstand, preparing to blow out the flame.

And at that moment it seemed to me that I heard a voice speak.

Come to me and live.

But I knew it was no more than a night breeze, or the pause between the cessation and resumption of rain at the window. I blew out the lamp and went to bed.

*

How good it felt finally to have disposed of the Galilean myth. How pleasant it was to enfold myself in the blankets that my married love had made sacred to me. How consoling to know that within days, a week or so at the most, Paeonia would again be beside me, and then our life would return to normal. As my mind drifted down into deepest rest, I felt a moment's gratitude for what my ancestors had bequeathed in their lore, the richness of its symbols and the pageantry of its mythic dramas, and our people's greatness, the nobler aspects of our thought and history, and our abiding love of beauty.

In my sleep I dreamed of our glory, for I walked in laurel groves and flowered alpine glens in a company of philosophers. Beyond a copse of golden woods, above the pillars of ivory temples, a mountain rose before us, its peak high and white, and I knew that it was Parnassos in the north. I stopped and beheld it in wonder. Splendid to my eyes it was, and as I breathed the cool air and fragrance of the meadows, I felt exalted. The beast from the sea, the cities of destruction, the armies of death and their hills of crosses were gone.

Peace, peace, I sighed with relief.

But short-lived was this peace. From the mountain heights a great serpent coiled downward toward the valley floor. It sprouted wings and claws, and then it rose up into the air.

I looked to my philosopher companions for counsel but found that all had fled, leaving me alone to face the peril. The monster flew this way and that, searching, and I knew that it had sensed my presence and wanted me.

"*Apollo! Apollo!*" I cried, certain that the serpent slayer would not fail to protect me. But no god appeared.

From a great distance the serpent caught sight of me; then it flew toward me at lightning speed. It was now a dragon of immense size, its eyes keenly intelligent and full of hatred. It came to a halt before me, roaring and vomiting fire, its jaws as great as a city gate. And though I was sorely frightened, I did not run from it. When it saw that its terrifying aspect had little effect on me, it transformed itself. All fire and smoke and malice dissolved; the monster shrank and became a beautiful figure of light in human form.

It began to speak in a low, soothing tone, with calmest rational voice, flattering me, beguiling me, and soon I could no longer keep in mind that it was the serpent that had tried to eat Leto's children.

Little by little my eyes, heart, and mind were deceived. It spun a web of beauty and philosophy, of sensory delights and pride of intellect, and it told me through all of this that I am one who may rise and rise and become as great as he. And when I would become as great as he, the serpent promised, I would be able to defeat death, for I too would be a lord of life and death. Slowly, slowly I sank into the waters of Lethe, the river of forgetfulness. But in the deepest waters, my soul was not yet drowned and suddenly cried out:

Diabolos, diabolos!

I awoke in a state of terror, my heart hammering hard and cold sweat breaking out on my brow. But the terror did not fade as it should have in the manner of dark dreams. My fear increased, for now I sensed a presence in the room, a shadow deeper than the shadows of the eyes, darker than the pit in the field of the dead, and full of black fire that gave no light. And verily I smelled the stench. It opened wide its presence and became the mouth of hell and began to close over me. I was paralyzed and would have been consumed, but a tiny light remaining in my soul cried out, *O God!*

The shadow paused and withdrew a little, but only for a moment. And in that moment I struggled upright and fled from the room, stumbling through the house, seeking a door.

The sky in the east was growing pale as I tumbled out into the garden, gasping for breath, my heart beating wildly. I ran straight to the hut where my servant lay. The terror followed hard on my heels and was on the verge of engulfing me. I opened the door and went in, slamming it closed behind me. The terror did not enter.

Tranquilatus was already awake and in a strange position— kneeling on the floor with his back to me, clutching something in his hands that I could not see. At the sound of the door banging open and closed, he turned his head and stared. There was fright in his expression, and I wondered at it.

"M-master," he stammered, "why are you up and about so early?"

I sat down on a bench as he got up from his knees. What-ever he had been holding was now hidden inside the breast of his tunic.

Feeling humiliated by my need for company, my fear of being alone, I wiped my brow with trembling hands. And then I noticed that his hands were trembling too, clasping the hid-den thing inside his clothes.

"What is that, Tranquilatus?" I asked. "What is it you are hiding?" I thought for a fleeting moment that he had stolen something from the house and I had surprised him in the act of secreting it beneath a floorboard. But I cast off the thought, for I knew he was an honest man.

He sat down on his cot and hung his head.

"Show me", I insisted, for I felt at the moment that an exercise of authority might restore my poise.

He opened his tunic and brought forth a small piece of wood.

Repulsed, amazed, perplexed, I merely stared at it.

"A cross", I said. "Why do you have such a wicked thing?"

"Master", he whispered in a shaking voice. "O Master, do not say it is wicked."

"But it *is*", I growled, and seized it from his hands. He let me take it and closed his eyes, shaking all over now.

Scratched on the bare wood was the form of a crucified man, with holes in the hands and feet and another in the side near the heart. I held it, not knowing what to say. Together we sat for a time in silence.

At last the old man looked up at me with red eyes and said: "Will you give me to the Romans, Master? Please do not, for I am young in the faith and have not endurance nor much courage."

"What do you mean?" I demanded.

"The governor has begun to put us to death, for he wishes to please the emperor."

"Are you a follower of the Christos?"

He nodded and could not meet my eyes.

I gave the cross back to him, and he took it greedily and hid it away in his garments.

I could say no more, and do no more, for it now seemed to me that we two were adrift on a dark sea and that the waters all about us were flowing, flowing inexorably toward wide-open jaws. So great was my confusion, and so great the terror that now returned with renewed force, that I covered my face with my hands and had no strength to leave.

At last I looked up and saw him staring at me curiously.

"Take me to the place where you gather together", I said.

He swallowed and trembled and said, "I cannot."

"Please", I begged in a whisper. "Please take me to them, for I have questions to ask."

He shook his head.

I went down on my knees and took his hands in my own.

"If you do not," I pleaded, "the *diabolos* will eat me."

Then his eyes changed, and he stood and brought me to my feet and led me out into the city.

*

The feeble sun was just rising, trying to break out from between the hills and the heavily overcast sky. The air was chill and humid, making it difficult to breathe.

The house we sought was beyond the south gate, in a neighborhood of poorer homes, an overspilling of the city. Tranquilatus knocked on the solid wooden door in the walls surrounding the building's foreyard. A woman peered through the look-hole, recognized him, and let us in. We were led into a two-story house of humble construction, almost bare of furniture and decoration.

A man came forward to greet us. My servant spoke first, hurriedly and with some anxiety. He explained that I was the father of Loukas, that he thought I would not be a threat to the community, and that I had questions to ask.

"I am Tychicus", the man said. "Loukas, whom I know well, is as a brother to me. Be welcome among us."

I was choking with fear. Fear, not of these men nor of the Romans, but fear of the dark spirit that had not entered with us yet still lurked outside the gate, waiting for me. I could not speak. My hands continued trembling.

Tychicus closed his eyes, praying. Looking at me again, he said:

"Stay with us a time. Have no fear. No darkness will devour you here."

I put a hand across my eyes, blinded by tears, my mind empty save for scattered images of fire and woe, sinking ships and burning cities, of men and women nailed to crosses and torn into pieces by wild beasts as the roaring audience applauded.

I saw all my labors, my entire life poured out for others, and what had it brought me? It had shown me the futility of human effort and the pathetic weakness of human consolations. Above all, I saw the fragility of the mind. How proud I had been of my great intellect, my learning, my noble service to mankind. Yet countless lives had poured through my hands into the jaws of death, and my own life too was pouring through my hands into those jaws of death—yet more than death. Evil, I now knew, was not merely error and ill habit in human nature. It was embodied by a presence, and I saw that it was stronger—far stronger—than good. Mankind was defeated, and I was inescapably imprisoned among mankind. I was no better than the people I loathed, men like the emperor, men like the Pharisees, even men like Balbus whose dislocated shoulder I had restored but whom I could not bring to goodness and virtue.

I began to sob loudly. My dignity, my costly robes, my superior mind, my status, and my connections to men of influence were gone—it all fell away. All, all fell away. I was alone with my soul, naked and poor.

*

What do I remember now? What images of those days arise in my memory? Only a few: I was received as a guest, given a cot in small room. I was offered food and drink, but I refused it. I felt that I was dying. Indeed, I wanted to die.

A single window in my room overlooked an enclosed garden, flagged with uncut stones. Beyond the back wall, the tips of hills greened by winter rain could be seen. In the center of the garden stood a raised outdoor pool made of finer stone. I turned away and looked about the room where I would stay. Cut into the mortared wall above the door were the Greek letters ICXC, and beside these NIKA.

"Iesous Christos conquers", Tranquilatus explained.

Inscribed in simple but careful script above the window frame were others:

TITOS—shepherd-father—Crete

Tranquilatus left me, for he was intent on returning to my house, where he would keep watch until my family's return.

I was alone with my sick soul. I could not think; I could not pray. I, a demolisher of myths, had nearly been devoured by a myth that had proven to be real. Swollen with pride, I had thought I was humble. I was a killer who had not known he was a killer. I was the best of men and the worst of men. I could only suffer and hope to die, to be swiftly relieved of the terrible burden of life. I lay down on the cot and stared out the window at the roof tiles of neighboring houses, the hills, and the rain. The monster was kept at bay, the fear had receded, but what was my future? Even my past was now no longer what it had seemed: It had been a failure, an emptiness, and all my battles a prolonged defeat. Now as it approached the end, I felt that everything I had believed and labored for had been a waste.

*

On the second day, Tychicus entered my room and asked me to come down and sit with him in the garden. To escape the void within me, I got up and went with him. The rain had ceased, though there was no open sky as yet. We sat down beside each other on a wooden bench. He did not press me for conversation. He was merely present with me. I listened to children's voices out of sight. Small sparrows bathed and flittered and drank from puddles of rainwater among the stones at our feet.

"What recompense", I croaked at last, "may I pay you for your hospitality?"

"None is needed", the man replied. "You are our guest, and a brother too."

"I am not a brother", I shook my head.

He put a hand to my arm and smiled with sympathy. "You are a brother."

He said no more.

I heard the homely sounds of people busy in the house. I smelled food cooking. Later I heard the murmur of several voices reciting in unison. It came from one of the doorways opening onto the garden. Tychicus stood and went in to join them. Again I was alone. Now I noticed that despite the garden's barrenness there were plants growing here, pots of kitchen herbs, a little fig tree flush with leaves, a single large plane tree towering before the south wall. The walls were high, and there were no exits other than the doors into the house. It was a safe place.

My eyes wandered to the stone bath. Now I read letters cut into one side of it: ICHTHYS contained within a symbol of a fish.

A young woman brought me a cup of wine and a bowl of bread sprinkled with olive oil. Her smile was a sunrise as she offered it, but it did not illumine my inner night.

"Please, eat, Master Theophilos", she urged gently. "It will do you good."

Good? I asked silently. What is good?

Maternally, she put a hand on mine, still pleading with her eyes. I withdrew my hand abruptly, turned my face from her, and thought:

Let me die. I am Chiron. I am the healer who cannot heal himself.

Seeing that I would not eat or drink, she took the meal away.

A spear of sun broke through the clouds and slowly spread across the flagstones. The sparrows hopped about, and one landed on my toes. I noticed suddenly that my feet and sandals were very dirty. I had not washed since I left the ship.

Later, an old man approached bearing a bowl and jug, with a towel over his shoulder. Had he come to bathe himself? No, he knelt before me and began to unstrap my sandals.

"Why are you doing that?" I asked, jerking back my feet.

"May I wash your feet, sir?" he said in Greek tainted with the Latin accent. "It is what we do here. And I can see that you are weary and have need of it."

Unhappily, I let him perform this lowly task. As he scrubbed and rinsed, then began to wash me again, I observed his face. I felt that I knew him but could not remember when or where we might have met.

Though his posture was that of a servant, and his facial expression was absorbed in what he was doing, I could see that this was a man of substance—or once had been. His robe was a toga of fine cloth that had been cut down and reshaped into a functional garment, long used and threadbare in parts. His own feet were unshod. His hands were spotted and very wrinkled by age, but they were not those of a laborer. His body frame was large, and I could see from the folds of drooping flesh about the jowls and neck that he must have been at one time a man of immense obesity. Now he was thin.

"What is your name?" I asked.

He looked up and smiled. "Do you not remember me, Theophilos? Many years ago you cared for me, during a time when I was a prisoner of shame. My name is Sergius Balbus."

I stared at him, perplexed.

He put a hand to his shoulder. "Do you remember?"

I nodded in affirmation.

He dried my feet, stood up, and went away.

*

On the morning of my third day with them, Tranquilatus returned and found me alone in the garden.

"No word of the family, Master," he said, "but do not worry. They will be home before long."

Tychicus approached us, saying that prayers were about to begin. He asked if I would join him and the others who were gathering.

I shook my head.

"Our brother Tranquilatus told us that you have questions. Would you like to ask them now?"

"No", I murmured.

"As you wish", he said, and he and Tranquilatus went into the house. Once again I was alone in the garden.

I sat and listened to their prayers for a while. It was not loud, and I guessed that their quietness was because they feared to bring attention to themselves during this time of persecution. When they began to sing, I stood. Then, for no reason that I could apprehend, I went to the open doorway. There I saw about thirty or forty people gathered within, all kneeling with arms raised and singing softly. Once again, I was appalled by the strange contradictions in their faith, which led them to sing most beautifully yet made them abhor all weapons that might defend the singing. The entry from the garden was at the rear of the room, and so I stepped inside unnoticed. I saw at the other end their table of sacrifice, and standing upon it a wooden cross. I shuddered at the sight of it, the insanity of its presence in the room. But it seemed there was no ritual at the moment—they were merely praying.

I sat down on a chair by the doorpost and listened.

While I was there, the songs continued, along with silences sometimes and sudden words from men and women in diverse languages, which I could not comprehend. I grew drowsy and closed my eyes.

In my half-wakefulness I felt the sun's strength wax strong in the garden, for the light and heat now grew intense. Then the light flared on one side of my face, and I was startled, wondering if a fire had broken out. My eyes flew open, and I looked to the open doorway but was blinded for a moment. No others in the room seemed to notice, though near-silence had fallen all about me, with only whispered prayers.

As my sight cleared, I saw a human form standing in the great light from the garden, a child, I thought. In fact, a boy. But he was like no other boy I had ever seen, for his face shone like burnished bronze under the noonday sun, and his robe was dazzling white. He gazed at me steadily. I could not look away, not from awe of his luminous appearance, but because he looked at me with love, and in his eyes was understanding beyond all human understanding, far surpassing even the wise. He stepped into the room and held out his right hand to me. Sitting in his palm was a white stone. At first I thought it was the stone I had brought from Iraklion, the one on which Loukas had inscribed his name. Then I saw that it was not, for it was of a different shape and whiter still.

Then he spoke, and I do not know if he spoke to my ears or to my soul alone. But speak he did, and no other words that I have heard in my life were given with such authority: "Come to me and live! Remain faithful until death, and I will give you the crown of life, and you shall never be harmed by the second death. To the victor I will give the hidden manna. I will also give him a white stone upon which is inscribed a new name, to be known only by him who receives it."

*

[Journal entry, October 18, A.D. 71]

Gortyna
October

As I sit here in my library, with a lamp upon the desk before me, I take up again the unfinished journal I left aside some years ago. Can it be that so much time has passed? It is six years since that day—six full and blessed years.

Yesterday evening I noticed the scrolls tucked away on my shelves beneath Loukas' account of the travels of his fellows, Paul and Petros—both now dead. There are also two copies of his chronicle of the life of Iesous, the first written before I came to the faith, the second sent to me when I was a catechumen. The latter is a fuller version, and I am intrigued whenever I compare the changes he made to the preface:

I too have carefully traced the whole sequence of events from the beginning, and have decided to set it in writing for you, most excellent Theophilos, so that you may see how reliable is the instruction that you received.

The use of "most excellent" is an interesting honorific, for I hold no official position. It is, I think, the *paean* of a son honoring his father.

I have often reread my son's books but, strangely, have not touched my own until now. I was a different man then, blind and full of self, unsuspecting how far my Lord would take me. And so from gratitude or curiosity, I blew the dust from my old journal and, with a smile of recognition, unrolled the scrolls one more time. I reread it entirely, and marveled—as I have so often done before—over my state of mind during that period of my life.

A multitude of testimonies had been given to me during the journey, yet I had suspected them all—feared them, denied them, even as I convinced myself that I was fairly and most nobly weighing all the evidence with an unprejudiced mind. I now think that there is no greater imprisonment of the mind than the illusion that it is free and superior. The prisoner who does not see his own chains feels no need to break them. How, then, can they be broken? Again and again the witnesses showed me my bondage, but I would not admit the truth of what they revealed to me about myself.

Then came the mysterious dreams on the ship that brought me home. They portrayed fragments of the life of Iesous, some in literal fashion, some in symbolic. So real were they, I experienced them as events through which I had lived. Even now I do not know if his life was as it appeared in the theater of my dreaming mind. Perhaps it was a grace, given that I might see the meaning of certain moments of his unknown years, filtered through the imagination but in essence the truth. They were unlike any dreams I have ever had, before or since, not only in their subject but in their quantity and character. I feel certain now that they were sent as a final attempt to reach an unbelieving man. Yet, upon awaking, I had rejected them too, feared them, denied them—and again asserted my fair and noble reasoning in order to maintain my prejudice.

Then there was nothing more that God could do but permit me to see the unmasking of darkness: the darkness within me and the darkness that makes war against heaven itself. Then, and only then, did I begin to understand the nature of things, but fled in terror from it. No antique god came to my rescue; no philosopher's brilliant exercise of intellect restored my reason to its throne. No army overcame the dragon that would have devoured me.

As I read on through my journal, I shook my head in amazement over my blindness. I understood it, of course, saw how it could not have been otherwise save for an extraordinary openness to grace. But why had I been so long closed to that grace? Detail after detail showed me the man I once had been, and though I loved him and pitied him, I sorrowed that I had made my own life's journey so much harder than it might have been.

I had forgotten about the octopus pot—or I should say I had forgotten its hold on my imagination. A month after that crucial night, I went to Knossos during a break in the winter weather, and with the aid of a brother whom I had come to know by then, buried the pot deep in a grave that had been plundered by treasure hunters. We capped it with stones and covered it with soil, leaving it for future generations to find, for terror or edification. The pot was too beautiful to destroy, and I had learned in the interim that the evil was in myself.

It should be noted, as well, that Gaius returned from Italy with no blood on his hands. He had argued before the Senate in favor of a return to the just administration of law in the provinces and by implication an end to the persecution of religious minorities. His efforts had little effect, and he returned to Crete under a cloud of imperial suspicion; yet not long after, the emperor was brought down by his own hand.

Oh, *kronos, kronos!* So much has come to pass that I could not have foreseen!

Loukas has visited us more than once during the past six years. I will not write much here about those remarkable reunions, lest I begin another book that has no end. It is enough to say that they were filled to overflowing with an unprecedented joy, an unexpected happiness, as together we built upon the foundation that grace had laid. Now we must be content with his letters, for he is based in Antioch and labors mainly in the lands north and east of that city. As always, I miss him greatly, this son of my heart. It is part of the loss that is gain.

The account of the Child who came to me that day is the final entry in my journal, followed by these two blank pages—a single leaf connecting to the umbilicus rod. As leaves of papyrus stitched together into a road on which the stylus travels and leaves its marks, so is a man's journey. My account has moved from its beginning to its end, and perhaps it has left some footprints along the way. Though we pass through a land and are never seen again by those who dwell there and those who follow after, it may be that other souls are changed a little by our presence. I have contributed my memories to the great story that is spreading throughout the world. It is no more than a fragment of one man's life that intersected for a moment with lives far greater than his own.

"Life is short; Art is long", wrote Hippocrates. This truth does not vary from generation to generation, and it will remain so until the final consummation of the world. I named the final section of my journal *Morphaeon*, a time of dreams. Indeed, this book contains all manner of dreams—some drawn from the natural reservoir within, and some, I think, fed by pure streams from above. Much was nature, and much was grace.

Even so, I wonder: If this poor book be read by men yet unborn, ages and ages from now, will they comprehend the reality of what I have heard and what I have seen with my own eyes? Will they call it myth? Will they call it a dream? I do not know. But I am certain of this: As long as man prevails on this old earth, he will look up to the heavens and ask his questions, and wonder, and listen, and marvel, and hope again. And most important of all, grace will be present until the final day. My words may crumble into dust, yet His will remain forever.

*

My beloved wife is now resting in our bedroom, waiting for me. A little granddaughter is visiting us for a few days and sleeps with her grandmother's arm around her. No dark dreams trouble them. Peace is upon our whole household, and fairest peace within it. The other rooms are filled with sleeping guests who have come for prayers or a physician's skill. The persecution is over, the Church grows, the world changes and changes. And I do not cease to wonder over it.

How did I know that the boy who brought me light was Iesous? What is this knowing in the soul? It is surely given from above, for no human imagination could have produced it. The Lord visited me as a little child. One of the Hebrew prophets foretold that a little child would lead us. And so he has done. And so he will do until the end of time. But why in the form of a child? I have often asked myself. Is it because his is the heart totally innocent yet totally wise, the heart that existed from before all ages, the heart of love itself? Such is the confounding of man's pride and his assumptions about the shape of reality! A little child overcomes the dragon, and in this too our small understandings are confounded, and we learn that good is infinitely stronger than evil.

I remember what I felt during the moments immediately after he spoke to me. There was a final look from him, and then he disappeared. How can I record what I felt at that moment? How can the light of paradise be translated through the groping script of man? To say that it was both blessing and wound, loss and gain, emptiness and fullness, is an approximation that misleads. I remember it perfectly, but I cannot retell it in such a way that another would experience it as his own. In this library are more books than I care to count, containing the thoughts of intelligent minds published in several languages of man, and they too lack words for it. The eternal will not permit itself to be seized and rolled tightly into scrolls and stored away as artifact. We may ponder it and inscribe our thoughts about it, and learn from it, but we will never master it. The book of a man's life unrolls as he lives it, and we read it to the best of our limited ability. The book of eternal life unrolls with it, but is read by God alone.

On that day I was inebriated with joy, yet I felt sorrow too. In the radiance of the unexpected light, I saw exposed my secret despair, my lack of hope, my adoration of beauty, my hatred of men of power, my contempt for the morally fallen, and beneath it all, my subtle and most dangerously disguised pride—which is like a field of the dead. Then did I understand that throughout my life, my sins had been the only real waste. Yet everything had played its part in leading me to this moment, and even my evil choices might be transformed in the cleansing waters of repentance. Whatever was good in my past also would be transformed by this encounter and in time become like a tree of life planted beside a river, bearing fruit that others would eat. Moreover, I saw a multitude of rivers flowing along beside me as one great river, pouring into the ocean of God's mercy. And from that ocean a cloud of witnesses would arise and pour forth its sweet rain.

All this I saw in an instant. Then I knelt and turned toward the cross and no longer feared it.

Then my brothers came to me and prayed with me. And my life was begun.

A LETTER

Dies Saturni IV Non. November DCCCXXIV anno Urbis conditae

In aetati Domini
Gortyna

From Stephanos in the waters of Baptism,
To Loukas whom I love as a son, though he is my father,
And to all my brothers and sisters in the Church at Antioch.

May mercy, peace, and grace be yours in ever greater measure!

I write to you with mixed joy and sorrow, for our beloved Theophilos has passed fully into the hands of our master and Lord.

Loukas, grieve not too much, for your father died as he had lived, that is, resisting death. Yet in his last resistance he did a thing that is more precious than any other throughout his long years of service to mankind. He has overcome death by death, and this in the manner that our Lord Jesus set before us as our pattern and our portal into everlasting life.

Two days ago, Theophilos returned from his journey to Fair Havens, where he regularly ministers to the sick on harbored ships. That day, he had gone down into one bearing Jewish slaves from the destruction of Jerusalem, bound for the mines of Egypt. He had tended their wounds and brought the good news to any who would accept it.

On the night of his return, he and your mother were at prayer in the house that is the Church in Gortyna. Among us were your sisters, and the eldest daughter of Theodosia, and one of Mila's sons, the eldest, and also Leandros, who was weak with a fever and had come for prayers and anointing. Cleon was away on a week's journey with the brethren in Iraklion.

After receiving the Body and Blood of the Lord, we were in silence when a man ran in among us, shouting that the house of Theophilos and Paeonia was afire and that there were people trapped inside it. Indeed, four children were sleeping there, the youngest ones of both your sisters, left in the care of an old servant. Theophilos bolted for the door and ran as I had never before seen him run. He outpaced all, and when we arrived at the house, we saw him plunging through flames at the open doorway. Some of us ran for buckets to gather water from the fountain. We prayed as we worked to quench the fire, but it was too far gone. And then he came out of the flames carrying one child wrapped in a blanket, though his own clothing was wreathed in sparks and smoke. Back into the fire he went for another. Four he brought out of the flames, and none were seriously harmed save for small burns and smoke in the lungs, from which all are now recovering, thanks be to God.

But there was a fifth inside, and neighbors who had crowded into the yard called out that the old woman was not worth the risk and surely was dead, for thick smoke and darts of hot flame were roaring in all windows. His great library was being consumed, and none could bear the heat of it. Even so, Theophilos ran back into the fire once more, and it looked to us that he would not come out again.

When all hope seemed lost, his form appeared suddenly amidst the blaze, bearing in his arms a body wrapped in blankets. He staggered out, his clothing entirely in flames. The others took the old woman, Calliope, from him, and then he fell to the ground. We beat out the flames of his garments, but his flesh was badly burned, all hair singed from his head, and his skin sloughing off as we touched it. The heat was now fierce against us, so we lifted him and the rescued ones and went out into the street.

Loukas, I tell you this, which you must remember always that it might be your consolation and peace:

I laid him naked on the pavement, fearing to cover him with my cloak, for the least touch caused him agony. His whole body had been burned, and his eyes melted too, for he looked up sightless into the heavens. Then he lifted his arms, though it must have cost him everything. His face was a mask of ruined flesh, yet he spoke. I put my ear to his lips in order to hear.

"Who can foresee", he whispered. "Who can foresee?"

Then he said the name of our Savior, and the breath went out of him.

We laid his body into a casket, and now many from all regions of the island are converging to assist at the holy *Eucharist*, which will be offered for his soul tomorrow. The *episcopos* will offer it, with all his priests and deacons. The casket will be laid in a tomb carved into the hillside above the brook north of the city, a place that your father loved for its many birds. Those martyred under Nero are interred nearby.

There is joy among us, much joy. In the space of these two days, there have been healings of the sick who pray beside the body. More significantly, numerous unexpected persons have come to the Church asking for instruction in the faith. It is inexplicable in human terms, for a man rescuing people from fire is not unknown, and while others may be moved by it, an act of heroism soon fades in people's memories. It does not shift the balance of the world. Yet the balance of some mysterious weight has been shifted.

Loukas, your mother sends you her greetings with a kiss, and her assurance that while she grieves, she rejoices. Our dearest friend died in suffering, and in this way he defeated his old enemy. He has come to peace at last and the answering of all his questions.

The beloved here send you their greetings, the elders and children of Crete to the elders and children of salvation in Syria. As do I—

> Your son, the smallest in Christ,
> Gaius Stephanos Varus.

Author's Note

I am indebted to a number of historical sources, notably the writings of Eusebius and Josephus and Philo of Alexandria (from whose life I have borrowed some details for the character of Philetos). My thanks also to Dr. Edoardo Rialti for his valuable help with classical literary references, and Will Pemberton for his extensive help with Greek and Latin linguistics and for his numerous technical corrections and creative suggestions.

This novel is an imaginative reflection on an obscure aspect of the Gospel and is in no way an attempt to present its characters and scenes as visions of what actually occurred. The events described in the New Testament are communicated to us through divinely inspired written accounts of direct experience and through divinely inspired reflections by others, such as Saint Paul and Saint Luke, who did not see the events of Christ's life with their own eyes. Even so, they personally witnessed astounding things done in the name of Jesus. Indeed, they knew that they stood upon the very axis of salvation history.

Human imagination of a later age can reflect on much that was not written down, and our internal visualizations of dialogues, events, and scenes will remain by their very nature speculative and incomplete, and even at times off the mark. It is my hope that this fictional representation of the Great Story that happened, the story that overturned the world and launched a new world, is not too far off the mark.

Two pertinent scripture passages come to mind:

There are still many other things Jesus did, yet if they were written about in detail, I doubt there would be room in the entire world to hold the books to record them.

—John 21:25

Be forewarned, my son: Of the making of many books there is no end.

—Ecclesiastes 12:12

And so the making of this book has come to an end. The stylus ceases to move; the scroll is rolled up. It is my earnest hope that the reader will return to the luminous living word of sacred scripture with refreshed eyes and that he will thirst for the One who is the eternal Word. In Him may what we have considered old and familiar be revealed to us as ever new.

Michael D. O'Brien